James Ernest Nesmith

The Life and Work of Frederic Thomas Greenhalge

Governor of Massachusetts

James Ernest Nesmith

The Life and Work of Frederic Thomas Greenhalge
Governor of Massachusetts

ISBN/EAN: 9783337397371

Printed in Europe, USA, Canada, Australia, Japan

Cover: Foto ©Raphael Reischuk / pixelio.de

More available books at **www.hansebooks.com**

THE

LIFE AND WORK

OF

FREDERIC THOMAS GREENHALGE

Governor of Massachusetts

BY

JAMES ERNEST NESMITH

QUI LEGIT REGIT

BOSTON
ROBERTS BROTHERS
1897

TO

𝕿𝖍𝖊 𝕽𝖊𝖕𝖚𝖇𝖑𝖎𝖈𝖆𝖓 𝕻𝖆𝖗𝖙𝖞 𝖔𝖋 𝕸𝖆𝖘𝖘𝖆𝖈𝖍𝖚𝖘𝖊𝖙𝖙𝖘,

TO WHOSE GENEROUS AND ENTHUSIASTIC SUPPORT GOVERNOR GREENHALGE
OWED THE EXALTED POSITION HE OCCUPIED WHEN HE DIED, AND
ALL THE POLITICAL HONORS THAT CAME TO HIM IN LIFE,

THIS BOOK IS DEDICATED BY THE AUTHOR,

JAMES ERNEST NESMITH.

PREFACE.

THE author has been influenced in the preparation of this book by a belief that the story of the life and work of the late Governor Greenhalge would prove valuable and interesting to a wide circle of readers, by the expressed desire for such a work on the part of many of Governor Greenhalge's political and personal friends and admirers, and by the not unnatural wish of his family that such a record of his life should exist.

The character and career of Governor Greenhalge are indeed worthy to be made the subject of a biography. They were equal to each other, and deserved the admiration and interest which they excited during his life, and the respect which followed him to the grave.

There seeming to be no other person prepared to undertake the work, the author, though with little confidence in himself, felt it to be a duty incumbent on him to perform.

The demands upon the author in its preparation have not, however, been large; and the book is chiefly the work of Governor Greenhalge himself, who through its pages speaks, though dead, to the people, as he was wont to address them in life.

The letters written by Governor Greenhalge are unfortunately few in number, but the few that exist are noble and characteristic expressions of the man; those of the number suitable for publication are contained in this volume. His speeches and addresses, on the contrary, are very numerous; and, on account of their general excellence, it is somewhat difficult to make a selection. Those included in the book are of his best, however, and afford a good idea of the range and power of his oratory.

The life of Governor Greenhalge was a suggestive life, and therein lies its peculiar significance; it could not be written with great amplitude of personal detail. His private life was the ordinary life common to us all, and presents no striking incidents and vicissitudes. The life of a public man to-day is also commonly devoid of exciting contrasts, and is in a measure one of routine.

The story of the life of Governor Greenhalge is necessarily for the most part political. His life, however, was broader in its interests than is common with politicians and states-men, and touched more closely the sphere of literature and culture, which gives it an added interest and variety.

In the preparation of this book the author has enjoyed the co-operation and invaluable assistance of Mrs. Greenhalge. He desires as well to extend here his thanks to Rev. Ithamar W. Beard, Rector of St. Thomas Church, Dover, New Hampshire, who has also assisted materially in its composition; and to those other friends of Governor Greenhalge who have contributed to the book and whose names appear within the volume.

JAMES E. NESMITH.

Febrtary 8, 1897.

CONTENTS.

———

PART FIRST.

THE LIFE AND WORK

OF

FREDERIC THOMAS GREENHALGE.

CHAPTER I.

EARLY LIFE IN ENGLAND.

THE flight of time in this age seems more hurried than ever before. Events that would once have been memorable are quickly forgotten. Things that once would have stood long in the memories of men like an "altar stone or ensigned citadel" soon pass from their recollection. The eyes of all are turned toward the future with expectation, and their thoughts are engrossed with the vast activities of the present.

Life has become like a battle-field where the living still press on, recalled from their pity of the fallen by the stern necessities of war. There is a greater need than ever, therefore, that the memories of vanished greatness should be kept alive among us by sculptured bust or published memoirs, that so what has perished from the earth may still be honored there and the good that men do live after them.

Frederic Thomas Greenhalge, the subject of the succeeding biographical sketch, is not numbered with those who have died in the ripeness of their age, who have reached the full height of their reputation after the exhaustion of all their powers and the accomplishment of all their purposes; nor is he included with those who, though cut off while yet young, have seemed to leave no broken promises behind them, whose lives seem yet complete by the attainment of their ambition and the fulness of their works.

The life of Greenhalge was a broken life in so far as the great things he accomplished were full of promise of yet greater things that he might have done in the future. The reputation so honorably won in the last years of his life would have brought him a larger sphere of action, and in the nation's council he would have found again the opportunity of distinction and raised himself still higher in the realm of national politics.

But his life was complete in so much as the man himself stood at the height of his power and genius; he had reached his full intellectual stature and the maturity of his mind. His equipment would never have been better for action in the arena of public life; his mental grasp would never have been firmer, nor his taste in literature more sound. But the silver cord is loosed, and the golden bowl is broken. He went to the grave in his prime, leaving his high office vacant, lamented by thousands who knew him only in the full vigor of his manhood. There is no shadow on his memory, no stain on his official life, no hint of decay in the vision of intellectual force which he has left behind him. His was the sun of Austerlitz even in its setting, and he fell like a warrior snatched from the car of victory.

This were an enviable fate could we but still our deep regret for the unaccomplished good, the broken promises, the high ambitions unfulfilled, and the sad breaking of our hopes involved in such a sudden and unlooked-for death.

It does not matter so much where a man is born; it is of more importance where he is trained in youth and grows up to manhood, — where his character is formed and the national habits fixed. "As the sapling is bent, so will it grow." Our education shapes us, and the associations of our youth are of more importance than our hereditary bias. Greenhalge grew up a true American; no truer ever lived. The national character was evident in all he ever did and thought. He was a perfect embodiment of American ideas, of American vigor and liberalism; a thorough democrat by instinct and education, a natural republican; a leader of men where men are most advanced, most enfranchised, and most progressive.

Greenhalge was born, however, in Clitheroe, Lancashire, England, on the 19th of July, 1843, the son of William Greenhalgh, who removed with his family to America when the subject of this memoir was twelve years of age, and settled in Lowell, Massachusetts, where the family have since lived. We call him fortunate in being transplanted to these shores, this land of liberalism, opportunity, and unlimited resource. Fortunate, too, is the country which attracts such emigrants, whose opportunities are so great that intrepid spirits everywhere are drawn to it as by a magnet, and become its pioneers and workers; where liberty is so bright and shining a light that the untrammeled spirits of men everywhere hail it with delight and seek it from afar. This nation, which is the bearer of good tidings to the powers and principalities of the earth, reaps a precious harvest of men from the old world, though there is much chaff mixed with the grain,— many feeble helpers joined with the active workers.

The ocean that has brought us some drones has robbed Europe of many glorious spirits since Hampden and Cromwell so nearly turned their backs on England and their faces toward this new world. England has been ransacked to supply the new world with warriors and statesmen. She used to rifle our ships for sailors, but the golden stream of emigration has robbed her of her choicest sons. Our tribute has been heavy upon her, and our debt to her untold. Exiles by choice, and not, like Themistocles, driven forth by edicts and laws, the proud spirits of England flocked to these shores, inspired by ambition and love of liberty, neither influenced by fear nor compelled by want. No new land was ever settled by more haughty emigrants than the Pilgrim Fathers, — the equals in pride in a good sense of Cortez and Pizarro, their proud English spirit intensified by religious fervor and exclusiveness.

England still contributes some of the best of our citizens, and to this class belonged the Greenhalgh family. Clitheroe, their old home, is in Lancashire, which has become the great industrial county of England, and has suffered more than any other that partial eclipse of beauty and purity which has

excited the eloquent philippics of Ruskin.   Yet the loveliness
of England, even of Lancashire, cannot be destroyed.   We like
to link the hero of this book, even in infancy and remotely,
with these old forms of beauty, with rural England.   There
was a natural delicacy and a vein of poetic feeling in his character that would seem to have rightly sprung from such influences; his love for nature was always strong and real, a grand
basis for character, and the ornament of the most distinguished
minds, — especially strong and true in the case of men who
once were boys in the country.   Many of the world's great
men have sprung from the farm.   This was not a fact in the
life of Greenhalge; he never dwelt upon a farm, yet his associations with nature were always intimate, and his home was
never far removed from her confines.

To the writer of these lines Greenhalge always seemed a
great man, perhaps greater than he was; fitted by nature to be
a leader of great masses of men along the paths of peace, — men
civilized, indeed, the men of New England and the citizens of
free America.   I shall freely point out, therefore, what to me
appeared the grand character of his heart and brain, without
the fear of contradiction, without fear that my language should
be called too glowing, or the praise be termed too high.

The sons of great men are seldom distinguished themselves,
but the characters of eminent persons are almost invariably
traced in their ancestors.   Great men are found usually to
have had good mothers.   Greenhalge was fortunate in both
his parents.   The name is that of an old Lancashire family.
The ruins of Greenhalgh Castle still stand in that shire,
raised by the first Earl of Derby, and destroyed after a siege
in consequence of an Act of Parliament in the civil wars
in 1644.   The name is peculiar and somewhat difficult, and
the last letter was changed from *h* to *e*, to simplify it, by Mr.
Greenhalge.   It is not a common name in America, and few
apparently who have borne it have settled here.   There is a
family who bear it located in Maine.   A certain Captain
Greenhalgh is mentioned in one of Parkman's histories, of
which personage the author has learned nothing more.   He
seems, however, to have been a man of some note in our early
colonial times.   In Lancashire the name is well known.

Perhaps the most prominent person who has borne it was Captain John Greenhalgh, son and heir of Thomas Greenhalgh, Esq., of Brandlesome Hall. This worthy was Governor of the Isle of Man from 1640 to 1651, appointed to that post by the great Earl of Derby, who perished on the scaffold at Bolton, in 1651. Captain Greenhalgh, a bold and daring soldier, was present with the brave Earl at the battles of Wigan and Worcester; he died from wounds received in an encounter when Major Edge made the Earl a prisoner in 1651. Governor Greenhalgh had a son Thomas. This son was qualified to be a knight of the Royal Oak, and served as High Sheriff of Lancashire. The tombs of this family are in the chancel of the Parish Church, Bury, or were in 1872, before its renovation.

Governor Greenhalgh was a cavalier and royalist; and among the reasons given for the choice of him by the Earl of Derby was, " that he was of good estate, and a gentleman, well born, and scorned a base action. Next he was a Deputy Lieutenant and Justice of the Peace for his own county; he governed his own affairs well, and therefore was the more likely to do mine so. He had been approved prudent and valiant, and as such fitted to be trusted, and he is that; I thank God for him, and charge you to love him as a friend." These words spoken of one Governor Greenhalgh might have been truly said of that other Governor Greenhalge whom we knew as the Governor of Massachusetts; separated as they were by two centuries, and distinguished in different lands and under such changed circumstances. " Prudent and valiant, and fitted to be trusted," — as such Governor Greenhalge was known to all Massachusetts, and as such he too will be remembered.

It would be fitting indeed if the chain of descent should be found to join these two Governors together by consanguinity and family ties. Such has always been the tradition in the Greenhalgh family. It may be true, and is even exceedingly probable, though the links have not all been traced which would confirm it completely. Greenhalge himself took small interest in questions of this kind, and never concerned himself seriously about his ancestry.

In America we like our public men to spring from the cabin and the farm; we never inquire into their ancestry. America is not by any means a " penniless lass, " nor has she a " long pedigree. " Her favorites spring from the people, and their escutcheons are the axe and the plough. Greenhalge raised himself to his high position, his station of trust and authority in the Commonwealth. He occupied that station by right of his talents, and his place in the hearts of the people, — because he was one of themselves in the common circumstances of life and in his instinctive feelings. He was singularly free from prejudice, and even the natural pride of intellect was foreign to his nature. He was not hale fellow well met with all men; he possessed a native reserve of character, on the contrary, and was the least self-assertive of men. Yet he was loved by the common people always, and well understood by them. All could approach him on equal terms as friends and comrades. He was one of the most sympathetic of men, and could share in the griefs and joys of others naturally and without pretence. Pretension of all kinds was absolutely unknown to him; he loved honor and made himself worthy of it by not coveting it when it was possessed by others, and, as it were, holding himself above it and never seeking to gain it except by the most honorable means. Take him all in all, he seemed born to be a great tribune of the people. His active sympathies were all with them; and to such a man to have sprung from honest though humble ancestors would have been honor enough.

Yet it is human nature to take an interest in coincidence of name, even if it were nothing more, and he showed that common interest which we all have in tracing out our ancestral line.

In the last weeks of his life he was greatly interested in a story published in an English magazine, and introducing as its chief characters the Greenhalghs of Brandlesome. He claimed, however, that beside that branch of Greenhalghs whose members were cavaliers and royalists, there was another branch, the members of which were Puritans and Roundheads; this idea suited his own preferences and habits of thought, which were far from being with the cavaliers.

Whatever interest or lack of interest Greenhalge may have felt in his ancestry, for his father he had the greatest respect and admiration. Some who knew both have said that in intellectual qualities the father was hardly surpassed by the son. He certainly had remarkable characteristics. Some of his talents his son shared but slightly. Greenhalgh senior possessed, for instance, a remarkable aptitude for the art of painting. His water-colors, though by an amateur, are good examples of the English school. The author possesses a note-book in which Greenhalgh has written down many observations regarding the mixture of colors for landscape painting, which show how much he had reflected upon this subject, and how close had been his study of nature. He was also always deeply interested in literature and books, and possessed a truly cultivated mind. His taste for literature, however, and his talent in this direction descended to his son with increased knowledge and appreciation of the best and greatest achievements of the human mind which the world of literature affords. This ornament to his father's character was indeed splendidly worn by the son with increased lustre.

It will not be necessary to refer to all the ancestors of Greenhalge of whom anything is known. The family can be traced for six or seven generations. The link which should unite the family with that of Brandlesome seems to be lost in the person of one Richard Assheton Greenhalge, who disappeared and cannot be traced. The grandfather of Greenhalge was Thomas Greenhalgh, who was born in Burnley, Lancashire, and was married there to Anne Dodson, of Knaseboro, Yorkshire, at the age of twenty-one. Of the seventeen children of this union ten lived to mature age, four sons and six daughters; only two of the sons married. William Greenhalgh, the father of the Governor, was born at Clitheroe in 1810, and there married a Miss Jane Slater in 1840. They left a large family, of which Governor Greenhalge was the only son; and he came to be the sole male representative of his family, his uncle's children having died without heirs.

William Greenhalgh, while at Clitheroe, had charge of the Primrose Print Works. Frederic Thomas Greenhalge was born at Clitheroe, July 19, 1842. Two years after the birth

of his son, William Greenhalgh moved to Eshton, where he
lived until the future Governor of Massachusetts was five years
of age. William Greenhalgh moved again, in 1847, to
Edenfield, an ideal English village, the memory of which
always lingered in the mind of Greenhalge. There the most
of his English life was passed, there his school days began;
and loving recollections of his early home were cherished
by him all his life. He always liked to refer to them; and
the simple, old-fashioned village of Edenfield remained with
him in memory as a charming example of English rural
life and scenery.

England is indeed a charming home; nowhere else is
country life invested with a greater charm. The race of
Englishmen can never forget the beauties of their old home,
whatever land they colonize. The educated American still
remembers the richly cultivated vales and ancient hamlets of
England as the ideal of rural beauty.

At Edenfield Greenhalgh senior and his brother Thomas
became the proprietors of an engraving establishment. His
literary tastes led him to form a society with other gentlemen
of kindred minds for mutual enjoyment and the study of
literature. It contained a number of valued friends. The
Rev. Nathan Nelson, the rector of the parish, was one, — an
intimate and always constant friend. Mr. John Aiken, a
wealthy manufacturer, living on an estate called Iswell Vale,
was another; also Mr. Hewitts, of Horncliff, another mill-
owner; and a Mr. Austin. These gentlemen were accustomed
to meet at one another's firesides for mutual intercourse.

In the meantime the future Governor of Massachusetts
attended a private school located there, and kept by a gentleman named John Ashworth. It was a large day and boarding
school, and even at that early age the young scholar always
stood at the head of his class. But the time came when the
family were to move from their pleasant home and the village,
which is still remembered with fondness. This time Greenhalgh senior and his brother removed to Manchester, where the
business prospects seemed better. Yet to go from this ideal
congenial life at Edenfield to the city life of Manchester was
very distasteful to the father, and caused him many regrets.

While at Manchester, William Greenhalgh received a call from America to take charge of the printing department of the Merrimack Manufacturing Company of Lowell, Mass., as successor to James Prince, who had died in England. This call he accepted, and with his family sailed from England, May 16, 1855.

Here ends a brief record of Greenhalge's English ancestry and of his early life in that country. He left there at the age of twelve years, too young to have been much influenced by his surroundings. It remained for America to form his character, to mould his habits of thought, and to develop the powers of his intellect, affording him at the same time a magnificent field for their encouragement and display. He became a true American in thought and in ambition. The faint recollections of his childhood were of no effect upon his character. Henceforth he became an American among Americans. He knew no other country save the great Republic. An American boy, he grew up in her public schools, and differed in no way from any other American boy. He was as true an American as Napoleon was a Frenchman, who stands in history almost as a personification of France.

It is interesting, as bringing into comparison the two countries, to consider the varying fortunes that might have been his had his life been passed in England rather than in America. The opportunities that England offers to young men of brilliant gifts and political ambition, yet without influence and the advantages of birth and wealth, are comparatively small. The education that America freely gives is not so certain of attainment there, and in its higher branches becomes still more difficult to acquire. Such a career as Greenhalge's would seem almost impossible in any other land save ours. His talents might have remained undeveloped, his ambition might have been quenched or never aroused. The very atmosphere of England is less stimulating than ours, although perhaps affording a stronger support to continued effort. He would not have been surrounded with such stirring political activities. He would have been deprived of the continual object-lessons which here are before the eyes of ambition, where success is always in evidence and seems so easy, — as it were, spread like a lure before us all, like a golden and glittering spoil. Yet, supposing Greenhalge to have enjoyed the advantages that would have enabled him to enter public life with easy access in England, he possessed the talents that Englishmen admire, that take the foremost place in Parliament and are a power in the land. He possessed the genius of a great debater, and might have reached a high position in England's Parliament. It seems so to the writer. Yet his opportunities were higher. It was his destiny to join the great stream of emigration that ceaselessly sets toward the giant of the western star; he became one of a conquering race, the splendor of whose power is doomed to overshadow that of England, as the spirit of Antony was shadowed by Cæsar, —

" Weave o 'er the world your weft, yea ! weave yourselves,
  Imperial races, weave the warp thereof.
  Swift like your shuttles speed your ships, and scoff
  At wind and wave, and, as a miner delves
  For hidden treasure bedded deep in stone,
  Go seek ye and find the treasure patriotism
  In land remote and dipped with alien chrism,
  And make those new lands heart dear and your own."

CHAPTER II.

AFTER a voyage of five weeks, William Greenhalgh and his family landed in Boston, June 22, 1855, and immediately went to Lowell, his future home.

He settled with his family on Dutton Street, in a house belonging to the Merrimack Manufacturing Company, and immediately entered upon the duties of his position in the engraving department of that corporation. His family consisted of his wife, his son Frederic, and six daughters. Mrs. Greenhalgh was a woman of broad mind and strong character, and possessed many remarkable qualities that fitted her to be the mother of a distinguished man, and such as are most commonly found in mothers whose sons have become eminent.

The city of Lowell, which now became and remained throughout his life the home of Greenhalge and his father's family, is the largest manufacturing city in America devoted to the production of cotton cloth. The mills employ thirty or forty thousand operatives. The wisdom of its founders has been justified by the unexampled prosperity which has attended the city which owes its birth to them. The character of its operatives was singularly high in the early years of its growth, and aroused the admiration of Dickens, and other strangers who visited it in the past. The people who were employed in its corporations at their start came from the neighboring villages and farms, — the sons and daughters of New England parents. Many of them possessed literary tastes. Emigration and the changes of times have altered the character of its inhabitants and operatives; but its reputation has always continued high for thrift and industry. Strikes have been rare in Lowell; and the city has increased in size, until it now numbers eighty or ninety thousand inhabitants, being at present the fourth city in the Commonwealth. Its situation is most beautiful, at the confluence of the Merrimac and Concord rivers, both of them naturally charming streams, and still retaining much of the wildness of nature. The suburb of Belvidere, where the residence of Greenhalge is situated, is perhaps the most beautiful portion of the city, — placed upon the high bluffs along the Merrimac River, which it overlooks, and with a distant view to the west of the New Hampshire uplands, " Monadnock, and the Peterboro hills." At the time when Greenhalge came as a boy to the city, its population numbered about forty thousand.

Soon after his arrival, young Greenhalge entered as a pupil the old North Grammar School, of which Mr. Fiske was the principal. He remained there one year, and then entered the High School with the highest rank attained by any of the pupils entering with him. He remained in the High School three years, and left it to begin his college course at Harvard University. Like most men of brilliant talents, Greenhalge, as a youth, was precocious, and his remarkable characteristics soon became evident. Mr. Chase, the principal of the High School while he was a scholar there, has declared his conviction that he was the most brilliant pupil that ever came under his instruction. Many of his fellow scholars still retain the recollection of the vivid impression which he made upon their minds, and have told of the pleasure with which they looked forward to hearing his youthful eloquence upon declamation day. He belonged to the order of men of which Sir William Jones was a prominent type, of whom it has been recorded by one who knew him, himself a distinguished man, that had he been left naked and friendless upon a desert heath, he would have still found means to advance himself to a high position, — to that order of men to which William Pitt belonged, of whom his father, Lord Chatham, declared that it was not in the control of fate to retard the political advancement of that youth.

He belonged to that class of men because his talents were so striking, so ready, so much in evidence all the time, that they could not have been overlooked or neglected. In fact, they were fully appreciated by those who knew him in school or college. This readiness and early display of talent may not always be characteristic of the most profound minds; but it is often found associated with the genius of successful men, of men of action, whose fitting sphere is the world of politics and party.

There was also in the character of Greenhalge, in youth as in manhood, a vein of poetic sensibility and a slight tinge of melancholy. We can trace the source of this in both his parents. His mother was a woman of strong character, courage, and fortitude, and very fond of poetry and music. His father was an artist of no mean talent. His mother was cheerful; but his father was not devoid of a strain of thoughtful melancholy, and he transmitted something of it to his son. This is often true of those who possess an artistic and sensitive temperament. In fact, the future Governor was always an artist at the base of his character, — an artist in disposition, in thought and training; using not the art of painting, nor often that of verse, but the art of speaking, — *par excellence*, a master of vivid, forceful, and eloquent speech.

We shall find this talent of his very evident as we follow his school career; it is a talent he shared in common with many American youths, though few in after life have developed it as he did until he became an accomplished orator at the bar, in Congress, and on the platform.

I have already referred to the intellectual quality of his father's mind; it would seem that he inherited from him in some measure even his oratorical talent. His father was a good speaker. His brother, Joseph Greenhalgh, writing of his talent in this direction, says, in a book concerning the Greenhalgh family published by him in England for private circulation: " He was a good spokesman, and at most of the election contests at Clitheroe, from 1832 onward, he was chairman, secretary, or otherwise, where both writing, auditing, and speech-making were required. I remember, in 1841, when Cardwell contested the borough in the Tory interest, that he addressed the electors from the Swann window in Whalley, and William spoke to them in opposition, it was said that at that period the latter was much the better orator. "

The following letters written by Greenhalge's father to his friends in England after his arrival in America are interesting, and show clearly that he was no common man. That he was a student of literature and possessed a cultivated mind, is evident. They show also that he observed closely, and his remarks about England and America are just and philosophical. He was, of course, an Englishman, and looked naturally at things from that standpoint.

In a letter of Nov. 9, 1855, written to James Greenhalgh he says : —

" Look at the bridge, crossing the river. The river is the Merrimack, and the bridge is called Dracut bridge. Over that bridge I have passed many a time visiting friends who live on the Dracut side of the river. The bridge is a wooden one, covered in to keep the snow off it during the winter season; there are openings in the side, the size of windows, but no glass.

" The view from one of these openings upon a moonlight night is beautiful; the moonlight reaches brilliancy far exceeding ours, though ours is not to be treated slightingly; this extra brilliancy arises from the greater clearness of the atmosphere. Well, upon such a night I did not stand 'within the Coliseum walls, midst the chief relics of Almighty Rome,' but within Dracut bridge, Lowell, Massachusetts, America, some three thousand miles from Fatherland.

" I enjoyed the scene, and it brought to my mind many similar scenes, now gone to the past, as well as some of our old friends who then lived to enjoy those scenes with us. Starkie idolized a moonlight night. Poor Starkie, Porter, and loving ' Old Jos'! We have spent with these and others many a fine moonlight night in Clitheroe; another I think we shall never spend there. ' So mote it be;' we cannot help it; but I have great pleasure in recalling scenes like these, and every moonlight night does its work in this way. We had some gorgeous moonlights on the broad Atlantic, being made sublime by the expanse of waters. I did not forget the Clitheroe moonlights then, nor those kind friends associated with them.

"The only classicality connected with river moonlight scenes or forest moonlight here is that North American

Indians have paddled one in their canoes, and made their trail through the other. The Indians are also added to the past so far as this region is concerned. The only thing remaining of them is the name of the river Merrimack, and a few other Indian names, such as Pawtucket Falls, and Pawtucket town. "

Another time he writes : —

" I am going through a course of reading which I call classic English, such as De Quincey, Sydney Smith, Macaulay, Jeffreys, etc., all the Edinburgh and Blackwood Reviewers in the ' olden time,' when we were boys, and thought everybody a god who could contribute a page or two to those celebrated Reviews. I have been much amused by the memoirs of the Rev. Sydney Smith, written by his daughter, the wife of Sir Henry Holland, the celebrated physician.

" If you can get the reading of it, do it at once ; it will repay the perusal. The Americans have produced some clever authors, both as poets and philosophers ; but still they are mainly dependent on British talent for their literary luxuries, either ephemeral or immortal. Deprive them of Dickens, Thackeray, etc., the vacuum would be insupportable ; not that I am a great admirer of these evanescent writers, yet they are prodigiously admired here.

" James, I have a great favor to ask here. I will ask it, if I am denied, and that is, to send by M. B. the portrait in oil of yourself ; I think I have the greatest and most legitimate claim to it, and it would be so much valued by us. Fred is the only one likely to carry the name down to posterity, and I think he ought to possess the likeness of the head of the family, lineally considered, of our particular branch of the genealogical tree. If the removal of it is not heartily acquiesced in, let it stop, and be lost in the mobs of other names, and valued only for its canvas and colors.

" I like old Boston ; it is such a comfortable place, so English-like ; and it is a great publishing-place. There is the noble (I say noble, and I have reasons for it) Ticknor & Fields, princes of publishers ; Phillips, Samson & Co., Gould, Lincoln & Co., Whittemore, Niles & Hall, and a host of others, all honorable men, not wishing to use English brain

2

without paying for it. We should have an international copyright law if it depended on the Boston publishers.

"Boston is the Athens of the United States, therefore I like Boston; and when I go there, I run through the stores of these eminent publishers and purchase an old book or two, by way of encouraging them; in fact, I patronize them. Last time but one I called at Ticknor & Fields', and bought 'Shirley,' a novel by Miss Brontë, and the 'Tenant of Wildfell Hall,' by her sister Anne. 'Jane Eyre' I had read previously. The last time I was in Boston I called to patronize Little, Brown & Co., and bought Bulwer's dramas, containing 'Richelieu,' 'Lady of Lyons,' and other poems. I gave fifty-six cents for it, a beautiful pocket edition in blue and gold, the popular and fashionable style of external adornment at present in the States."

In a letter of July 19, 1858, he says: —

"Fred is a young man, very tall and healthy. He never gives over eating; as soon as he comes into the house he walks straight to the cupboard, seeking what he may devour. He is very studious and steady. To-day he is sixteen years of age, and is now preparing for the High School examination. He has already distinguished himself, and is considered, not by me, *a boy of mark*. If nothing blasts my prospects, I intend, when he has finished at the High School, to send him to college, and afterwards make a lawyer of him; he must make a barrister of himself."

Oct. 22, 1859, he writes: —

"Fred finished his studies at the High School with all honors, gaining a diploma and a silver medal; he is said to be the best scholar sent out by the school. He passed his college examination, and was admitted Sept. 1, 1859. It is Harvard College, the Oxford and Cambridge of the United States. It will cost me about one hundred pounds per annum during his stay there. I shall keep him there as long as I can afford, four years college education, and two years at the law school.

"Our chief interest is to hear what is taking place in

Europe, and in Europe what is taking place in England, the centre of Europe, the eye of the world, the civilizer of the world, the hope of all men, the little spot of earth that dares all the world, because she is mighty in the justice of her efforts as well as in the wisdom that directs those efforts. America is the great echo of those efforts, or, in practical words, she carries out the principles that are created there; to wit, the principles upon which her present liberties are founded came from England, the means for sustaining those principles came from England up to the present time, and she looks to England for sustenance as the infant looks to its mother for its milk. If England were by some natural convulsion swept from the face of the earth, no country would suffer more from such a calamity than the great United States of North America. "

Another time he writes as follows, referring to a Masonic meeting which he had attended : —

" I made my first speech a fortnight ago, and spoke of the true brotherly feeling entertained in England, having in my eye, as I spoke, the thorough-going Masons I met in Boston a few years ago.

" Tell them there is encouragement enough on this side of the Atlantic to support them in their good and glorious work of benevolence and social reformation. "

The last letter I shall quote was written during the Rebellion. He says : —

" This country for my prosperous interest is done ; everything is high, and, from the taxes for the war in operation, will be still higher ; therefore England, with my large family, will be much better for me, and as soon as I am in a condition to bring me and mine to Fatherland, I shall do so. For months we saw nothing in this city but the training of troops for the war, the drums beating, but the looms silent. To reduce the subject of the war into a small compass, it is this, — a war of free men against a slave oligarchy. "

While at the old North Grammar School, Greenhalge joined a small debating-society, consisting of three members, — small indeed,— and called the Kansas Aid Debating Club, the object of which was to discuss the Kansas question, at that time agitating the country.

In his diary, written during the winter and summer after his arrival in this country, he writes of his boyish experiences. His diary is interesting and characteristic, and I have made the following extracts from it. Written by a youth of thirteen, they show a good deal of spirit in their execution, and contain some vigorous youthful heroics, — snow-fights, boyish encounters on the river with the Mickies, and frequent mention of being locked out of school.

DIARY.

Wednesday, Dec. 25. — Christmas Day! But not the good old English Christmas. The Americans (at least most of them) keep it very poorly indeed. It snows very hard, — more like hail than snow.

Monday, Dec. 31. — The last day of the year. Got locked out morning and afternoon.

Tuesday, Dec. 32. — I mean the 1st of January, 1856; but it was a natural mistake, and I will not erase it. Got locked out in the morning, but went in the afternoon.

Thursday, Jan. 10, 1856. — Went to school all day. We have some fine practical problems in applications of Square Root.

Wednesday, Jan. 16. — Got locked out again. I don't know what Mr. Fiske will say about my getting locked out. I am in a bad fix about it. In the afternoon I learned that Mr. Fiske had threatened to write to my father, which sadly frightened me. In the afternoon we had a snow fort and had some fun.

Thursday, Jan. 17. — Went to school with my excuse, and made an excuse for my absence; but I knew it was not the true one; however, it did pretty well, only I feel sorry for having to tell an indirect falsehood. We set about building a regular castle of good forts. We expect to finish them by Saturday.

Friday, Jan. 18. — Went to school all day. At night

Wallace Hinckley, having vexed A. B. and me, we went at night and knocked both forts down, — a very mean act.

Monday, Jan. 21. — To-day is a memorable day in my life, as I got one of the soundest floggings I ever had in my life, from my mother. I got locked out. In the afternoon I did not go, and Mr. Fiske was told by Wallace Hinckley (I instructed him) that I was sick. This day is well worthy of being called the " Day of Misfortunes."

Monday, Jan. 28.— Went to school in the morning, but got locked out (oh, dear!) in the afternoon. It was a very snowy day, and a great many were absent. Wallace Hinckley was to tea at our house.

Tuesday, Jan. 29. — At night got some books to print names in for the scholars, and also I was asked to do some letters on some pictures by a drawing-school mistress, and I am going to do them when they are ready. Went over to W. H.'s, but soon came back. I am now writing my journal for the last week in my bedroom, all being in bed but me ; so good-night.

Wednesday, Jan. 30. — Went to school in the morning. In the afternoon went over to Hinckley's, and we passed the afternoon pleasantly, as usual, snow-balling. Wallace Hinckley and I were on one side, and F. Wilson and Henry on the other. We had to storm their fort, which was rather a difficult thing, considering what a stout fellow Wilson was, and what an inefficient Wallace was compared with him. I don't say anything about myself, only this : that if it had not been for me, Wilson would have made short work of Wallace snow-balling.

Monday, March 3. — Went to school all day. At night I went to a promenade concert held at Huntington Hall for the benefit of the poor. It was very crowded, and I did not go home till eleven o'clock. During the eve Miss Adelaide Phillips, a songstress of some renown, sang, and we were entertained by the Mendelssohn Quintette Club with some middling poor music.

Friday, March 7.— Went to school all day. At night I went over to Hinckley's ; but I hadn't been there above two or three minutes when Herbert came in and told me A. B. wanted to see me. I must say I felt very angry at his coming to another

person's house for me; however, I went to the door and found
that he wanted me to go with him to the Hospital to take
some crutches to their servant. I scarcely knew what to do,
and I was so mortified at A. for coming for me, that I almost
would have refused on that account; but Hinckley, making
some remarks that did n't please me exactly, such as " You may
go whether you please or not, I shall never invite you to our
house again," decided me, and, almost bursting with anger as
I was, I concluded to go with A. I believe our friendship
— Wallace's and mine — is over; for my part, I don't think it
would exactly correspond with my dignity to go to their house
after what has taken place, without some explanation.

The friendship evidently was not " over," as he feared, for
we find recorded : —

Monday, March 21. — Went over to Hinckley's at night and
had some good play, though there was a bit of a storm.

Saturday, June 16. — Went to school in the morning. In
the afternoon, went over to Hinckley's, and then W. F. W., W.
H. W., and I took a boat and went up the river to Long Island
to bathe. When about opposite the island, we were met by a
boat coming down full of " Mickies. " They began asking us
questions, such as " Where did ye hook that boat ? " that
meant, " Where did you steal that boat ? " We made no reply.
Then one of them said to the rest, " Let 's chase 'em and take
their boat off 'em. " So they turned round and began to row
like fury. I was rowing at the time; and, our boat having
only one pair of oars and those extremely heavy, I knew we
could not escape even if we tried. Ours was a very large boat,
indeed large enough for a sail-boat, while theirs was pulled by
four or five oars, and was a very light, flat-bottomed one, ours
being one of the few keel-bottomed ones on the river. We no
sooner saw them coming after us than Wallace exclaimed,
" Put her up faster ! " I paid no attention to him, and thinking if we could gain the shore we could lick the whole of
them, for Frank and W. H. W. are two stout fellows; but they
gained on us so rapidly that we could not, without rowing
faster, which I did not want to do, as it would seem to imply
fear of them. Well, they caught up with us, and splashed us
with water and the like; but, owing to the fear of some of the

younger fry in the boat, they did not proceed to extremities. We spoke scarcely a word, and at length one of them, happening to know Wallace, told the others to let us go; some of them, however, still held on, and I, having got my oar under their boat, could not row, but I kept pushing theirs farther off. He rowed off after I got my oar loose, which I did pretty quickly, and in bringing it over their boat to get it into the water again, I hit one of the gang a knock on the head; he let this pass as an accident. We had our bath and tried to swim a little, but could n't manage it yet. I mean Wallace and I, as the two Wilsons can swim now.

Thursday, June 21. — Nearly well. Got up *just after* school-time. Wrote up my journal. I will write down a verse I made when I was sick in bed.

THE PATRIOT.

The patriot's sands are well-nigh run,
  And the blood from the deep wound gushes;
For his country's good his deeds were done,
  And e'en in death his pale cheek flushes.

Beside him stands his faithful steed,
  With downcast head and drooping eyes.
Nevermore thy faithful help he 'll need,
  Never from that low bed again arise.

We bought a lot of fireworks.

Monday, June 23. — Went to school all day. Went over to H. 's in evening, and he and I went to a political meeting on the Philadelphia nomination which voted John C. Fremont for President. Mr. Homer Bartlett, an old man, and one of the delegates, spoke, and very well too. The Lowell Brass Band was in attendance.

Tuesday, June 24. — I went to the Library at night. I was rather long in looking over the catalogue, as I usually am, and the librarian asked me if there was any particular book I wanted. I said, " No, " and in a short time he said, " Why don't you begin at the beginning of the book and go through ? " I was vexed, and said I had done. " Well, then, " said he, " you 'd better send word next time you come, and we 'll have the books ready for you." I felt my cheeks burn at this, and also a strong disposition to throw the book at the old fool's head, but I did n't want to be impudent and kept quiet. I asked for five or six books, and he said they were out; at last I asked for one called "Kansas and Nebraska." Yes, that was in. I said very quietly, "It 's a wonder." When I went downstairs, I muttered, though very audibly on purpose, " Old saphead!" I think he heard me, or I hope so. I 'm determined to pay the testy old snob off yet.

Thursday, June 26. — Went to school all day. Wallace and I are going to get up a debating-club.

Friday, June 27. — W. H. and I got a box to make a platform for the speakers in our Debating Club. Went to school all day. The soldiers are going to have a grand review or parade to-day. A great many persons were summoned to Concord to give information of all rum-sellers, etc. ; they got paid a dollar and a half a day; they came back in carriages, and went through the city with a band, brandishing bottles, etc.

Saturday, June 28. — Went to school in the morning. In the afternoon we went into Wallace's room and held our meeting. We have only three members, including ourselves and J. C. W. We made a few short speeches on the State of Kansas (which is the object of our Club, and from which it is named Kansas Aid Debating Club), and elected a President for next meeting. We expected another boy, but he did not come.

Sunday, June 29. — Got out of Sunday-school library a book called the "Mission," by Captain Marryat, a very amusing and instructive book.

Wednesday, July 1. — The boys are making great preparations for 4th of July.

Thursday, July 3rd. — Went to school all day. Marshall, who was absent, brought me half a pound of powder which I had ordered.

The record of 4th of July is missing.

Saturday, 5th. — Did not get up till eleven o'clock. Went over to Hinckley's, and we went to the Doctor's and he had the powder in his face picked out.

We may infer that he and his friends celebrated his first Fourth of July in America in an enthusiastic and patriotic manner.

When a child in England, young Greenhalge was examined by a phrenologist. It may be a matter of interest to some to read the report which was prepared on that occasion. The subsequent career of the subject of it gives it the appearance of prophecy in some particulars at least.

Frederic Thomas Greenhalge, examined when fourteen months old, Sept. 23, 1843.

The head of this young gentleman is at his age large, and the major part of the cerebral organs are, all things considered, well marked. The temperament being almost purely that of the sanguineous, it follows, as a necessary consequence, that the various mental powers will be very active and vivacious, and easily excited by external stimuli; so that it may be asserted that he will evince great energy of mind, as well as considerable force of character. He will not be easily overcome, even although he might be environed on either side by opposing or retarding circumstances; for, having fully developed the organs of Firmness, Combativeness, and Destructiveness, he will be able to contend against difficulties, and will possess both the inclination and the power to strive with and also to overcome them. In consequence of the volume of the brain being large, and the temperament lively, he will have a tendency to be occasionally rather irascible, and not infrequently rather precipitous; but as the mind becomes matured from age, and is cultivated by study and reflection, in the same ratio will that tendency be modified. The functions of those organs ought not to be obtunded, because they greatly contribute, when properly directed, to the prosperity of their possessor; that being the case, great care ought to be taken by his guardians in endeavoring to bring those under the guidance and control of the superior sentiments and intellect. For the realizing of which desideratum, benign treatment and moral suasion will be found eminently useful; as will also the directing of the observing and reflective faculties. The organ of Concentrativeness being comparatively small, he may, at his initiation in learning, experience some difficulty in the employing of his several mental powers; but so soon as he perceives the utility of education, this slight defect will be obviated, for his Firmness is great.

He has a talent for philology, for designing, for history generally, and for geometry. In the study of the latter he will not arrive at any degree of proficiency until the several mental powers shall have been energized by education. His reasoning powers being considerable, he will excel in the abstract sciences.

A. D. SCOTT.

At the High School Greenhalge was always one of the leaders. He was one of the editors of the weekly " Voice, " published every Saturday for the scholars of the school. In one of the numbers still in existence, there is a poem of his called " Huntington Hall. " In this number of the paper the subject of debate for the next meeting of the debating-society to which he belonged was announced as " Resolved : That secret organizations are dangerous to American institutions. "

While in the High School, he wrote short stories for the " Vox Populi, " a Lowell paper. Two of these stories were called " A Skeleton's Soliloquy " and " The Dependant's Story. "

His father objected to these literary exercises as taking too much of his time from his studies; but he persevered.

All this is very suggestive. How similar the record is to that of many other bright boys who were afterwards heard of in the world as brilliant men! These literary ambitions spring up the first of all, and are most often doomed to perish with the youth that inspired them. It shows the generous nature of youth before it has hardened with age, that it should be tempted by literature in the first flights of its ambition. " Youth, " said Napoleon on the " Bellerophon, " pointing to the young English naval officers who still seemed to reverence his fallen greatness and stood with doffed hats, — " youth is always enthusiastic. " It is so, and is generous enough to shame the worldliness by which it is too often succeeded.

These youthful debating-clubs also, — what a nursery they

have been for future orators and statesmen! Read the records of any of their lives, and you will find the debating-club at the root of their ambition; it contains the germ of senates and legislatures. If Waterloo was won upon the foot-ball fields of Rugby and Eton, the great conflicts of Parliament and Congress have their genesis in these debating-societies. They are the source from which the mighty stream of oratory flows.

Greenhalge entered Harvard College in 1859, after completing his course at the High School in three years, taking the studies that usually occupy four years. He received the first Carney Medal given at his graduation, and at the public exercises declaimed Curran's " Universal Emancipation." While in the High School, he was a member of the cricket club.

As a boy, he was not especially devoted to athletic sports; but he was always fond of boating and walking. In after years he was seldom known to ride; he always preferred to walk, which suited his energetic character.

At Harvard, during his sophomore year, he rose to distinction in the Institute of 1770. He was one of the principal participants in a memorable debate on Warren Hastings; Gorham Philip Stevens, who died afterward of wounds received at Williamsburg, being his opponent.

He was appointed orator, and Stevens the poet, of the Institute at the close of the sophomore year; and he also became editor of the " Old Harvard Magazine." Among his classmates were Prof. John Fiske, ex-Secretary Fairchild, and Frank Higginson the banker, Mr. John Brown the publisher, Jeremiah Curtin, Judge Sheldon, and Captain Nathan Appleton. Perhaps the most intimate friend he had during this period of his life, and after he left college, as a young man in Lowell, was the Rev. I. W. Beard, now of Dover, New Hampshire, Rector of St. Thomas Church. Mr. Beard remained indeed an intimate friend throughout his life.

Greenhalge's brilliant career at college was cut short, and at the expiration of his third year he was obliged to leave Harvard and return to Lowell. His College, however, showed afterwards its appreciation of his merits, and in 1870 he received his degree.

The following is an account taken from other sources of the famous barn oration which he delivered in his sophomore year, and ruined thereby his chance of gaining a scholarship. Greenhalge afterward naturally characterized this school-boy rebellion as a foolish attempt to brave the Faculty.

Toward the end of the first term there was a hazing war between sophomores and freshmen, which the Faculty got wind of. Eight sophomores were expelled. The class considered this an outrage, and all loyal '63 men were ablaze with indignation. A class meeting was called in a barn on the " Appian Way," and many studious men of the class, who, like Greenhalge, had nothing to do with the hazing, left their books to attend. Greenhalge, together with J. Collins Warren, afterwards Dr. Warren of Boston, and J. F. Van Bokkelin of North Carolina, were appointed a committee to draft resolutions upon the outrage of the tyrannical Faculty. The committee also prepared a petition to the Faculty demanding that the eight expelled men should be restored to the College. The three committeemen drew lots to see whose name should head the list, and the choice fell upon Greenhalge. Nearly all the class signed the petition. In presenting the resolutions and petition to the assembled class in the barn, the studious Greenhalge, jealous for the honor of the class, stood forth in the rôle of a bold conspirator, and ended a fiery speech with the soul-stirring counsel : " Resistance to tyrants is obedience to God." Greenhalge's barn oration is still remembered by many Harvard, '63, men. The next morning the whole white front of University Hall displayed the legend in two-foot black letters : " Resistance to tyrants is obedience to God." The fiery young orator was appalled. The Faculty regarded him as ringleader in the whole affair, and he thought that his fate was sealed. He went home to Lowell, and in a few days came a letter from President Felton to his father, stating that the Faculty had always taken an interest in his son, but that now his connection with the College had better be severed. But the matter was finally settled, and Greenhalge went back to college.

Another interesting episode of his college career was the burial of the foot-ball. The following is the account of the funeral in the papers of the day : —

BURIAL OF THE FOOT-BALL. MELANCHOLY PROCEEDINGS
AT CAMBRIDGE.

Yesterday, just at dusk, the Sophomore Class of 1863 assembled with proper decorum to perform the funeral obsequies of the foot-ball.

It will be remembered that the Faculty, by a vote of July 2, 1860, prohibited the usual foot-ball match between the newly made Sophomores and Freshmen.

This time-honored institution has heretofore been celebrated on the first Monday in September, and has been witnessed by hundreds of spectators, ladies and gentlemen assembled from Boston and vicinity, comprising all the friends of the collegians.

The procession consisted of a grand marshal with huge bearskin cap and baton, assistants with craped staves and torches; a coffin six feet long, inscribed "Foot-ball, 1860," borne by four pall-bearers; the Chaplain, with a very large craped hat and huge eyeglasses; the class invalid bearers, inscribed '63, and having crape tied on the right leg. Behind the coffin were the gravestones, made of wood painted black, with the following inscription in white letters: —

(HEAD-STONE.)	(FOOT-STONE.)
Hic jacet	Foot-Ball, 1860.
Foot-Ball	In Memoriam.
Fightum.	(Over a Winged Skull.)
Aet. LX. Yrs.	
Obiit July 2, '60.	
Resurgat.	

The procession marched to the music of two muffled bass-drums to the Delta, where the foot-ball game is usually played, and formed a circle surrounded by a large crowd of students and others. The sextons dug the grave while the chaplain delivered the funeral oration, of which we are able to give a verbatim report: —

FUNERAL ORATION. ALBERT KINTZING POST.

DEARLY BELOVED, — We have met together on this mournful occasion to perform the sad offices over one whose long and honored life was put an end to in a sudden and violent manner.

Last year, at this very time, in this very place, our poor
friend's round jovial appearance (slightly swollen, perhaps),
and the elasticity of his movements gave promise of many
years more to be added to a long life, which even then eclipsed
the oldest graduate's, when he arose exultant in the air, pro-
pelled by the toe of the valiant Ropes, looking like the war-
angel sounding the onset and hovering over the mingling fray, we
little thought then that to-day he would lie so low, surrounded
by weeping "Sophs." Exult, ye Freshmen, and clap your
hands! The wise men who make big laws around a little table
have stretched out their arms to encircle you, and, for this year
at least, your eyes and noses are protected. You are shielded
behind by the ægis of Minerva. But for us there is naught
but sorrow, the sweet associations and tender memories of eyes
bunged up, of noses wonderfully distended, of battered shins,
the many chance blows, anteriorly and posteriorly received and
delivered, the rush, the struggle, the victory! They call forth
our deep regret and unaffected tears. The enthusiastic cheers,
the singing of "Auld Lang Syne," each student grasping a
brother's hand, all, all have passed away, and soon will be
buried with the foot-ball beneath the sod, to live hereafter only
as a dream in our memories and in the college annals.

Brothers, pardon my emotion; and if I have kept you too
long, pardon me this also. On such an occasion as this but
few words can be spoken, for they are the outbursts of grieved
spirits and sad hearts. What remains for me to say is short,
and in the words of a well-known poem: —

> But one drum we had with its funeral note,
>   As the coffin we hitherward hurried;
> And in crape we are decked, for proudly we dote
>   On the foot-ball that is soon to be buried.
>
> We'll bury him sadly at dim twilight,
>   As the day into night is just turning;
> With a solemn dirge by the dismal light
>   Of the torches dimly burning.
>
> With pall and bier that's borne by the crew,
>   And the headstone carried behind them;
> His corpse shall ride with becoming pride,
>   With martial music before him.

'Gainst the Faculty let not a word be said,
  Though we cannot but speak our sorrow ;
We 'll steadfastly gaze on the face of the dead
  And bitterly think of the morrow.

We think, as we hollow the narrow bed,
  And fasten the humble foot-board,
That to-morrow at chapel we 'll see no black eyes,
  Or noses that show they 've been hit hard.

The Faculty talk of the spirit that 's gone,
  And o'er his cold ashes upbraid him ;
But little we 'll care, if they let him sleep on
  In the grave where a Sophomore laid him.

'T is time that our heavy task was done,
  And I would advise our retiring,
Or we 'll hear the voice of some savage one
  For the ringleader gruffly inquiring.

The coffin was then lowered into the grave, and while the
sextons filled it up, the class united in singing the following
dirge to the tune of "Auld Lang Syne" : —

THE DIRGE.

Ah ! woe betide the luckless time
  When manly sports decay,
And foot-ball, stigmatized as wine,
  Must sadly pass away !

(*Chorus*) Shall Sixty-Three submit to see
      Such cruel murder done,
      And not proclaim the deed of shame ?
      No, let's unite as one.

O hapless ball, you little knew
  When last upon the air
You lightly o'er the Delta flew,
  Your grave was measured there.

(*Chorus*) But Sixty-Three will never see
      Your noble spirit fly,
      And not unite in funeral rite
      And swell your dirge's cry.

> Beneath this sod we lay you down,
>   This scene of glorious fights,
> With dismal groans and yells we 'll drown
>   Your mournful burial rites.

> (*Chorus*)   For Sixty-Three will never see
>   Such cruel murder done,
>   And not proclaim the deed of shame :
>   No, let 's unite as one.

Cheers were then given for the senior and junior classes, and groans for the Faculty, after which the procession marched home singing their old college songs, and the crowd, which had gathered, dispersed. (Greenhalge was in this procession, and I am not sure he did not write the dirge.)

Then foot-ball fights were literally fights. · It was not the modern game of foot-ball. No skill was required or displayed. It was a general scrimmage between freshmen and sophomores. Hard blows were struck, shirts were torn from men's backs, eyes were closed, noses broken, and blood flowed freely ; it took a lot of pluck to go into them. (Greenhalge was in the fight against the sophomores when he was a freshman.)

In writing of Greenhalge's college life, I am fortunate in obtaining the assistance of some who were with him in Harvard. Judge Sheldon, a friend and classmate, writes as follows : —

"Governor Greenhalge, in his college life, was one of the marked men of his time. Then, as in his future career, his nature was upright and downright, frank and outspoken, richly endowed with ready wit and keen sarcasm, quick and honest, without any parade or pretence, but genial and full of good companionship. He was a close student ; but he already knew how to give his closest attention to those special objects of study which he most affected, and in which he regarded success as most valuable. Perhaps his main distinction was as a writer and debater. He was a powerful speaker, strong and earnest then as he afterwards was in public life, with a vigorous energy which seemed to beat down all opposition, a force of sarcasm which would have scorched and withered but for the kindness of heart which seemed to underlie his most trenchant invectives. But, after all, the most noticeable trait of his character in college was his frank and unassuming geniality. Simple and unaffected, readily approachable and kindly-natured, his lovable qualities were the more attractive because he was wont to cover them, or perhaps to hold them in half-concealed ambush behind a shelter of sarcasm, because he was inclined to express a tender sentiment in biting words, and because he never cared to guard against any misjudgment of his own motives or any misinterpretation of his real meaning. Absolutely independent alike in what he did, what he said, and what he thought, his integrity and self-reliance made it impossible for him to cater to the good opinions of others. And yet he was then, as he always remained, devoted to his friends. But because he loved them he trusted them utterly, and never could have believed it to be necessary to put on any disguise or any shadow of pretence to gain or to hold their affection; they would not have become his friends if he could have conceived that their affection was thus to be gained or to be held. And it is perhaps because he joined this sturdy independence, which scorned to abase itself for the merely apparent honor of others, to a complete and self-neglecting persistence of affection which was ready to give all without any doubt or sense of hesitancy for the real advantage of his friends, that many of his classmates have felt his loss as a personal affliction, as a bereavement which comes close to their hearts, and makes them slow to speak their grief, because it seems too sacred to be put into words."

The dark days of 1861 brought trouble into the homes of rich and poor. Business was interrupted at the Merrimack Mills. January, 1862, the corporation suspended operations. Business remained at a standstill for several months. William Greenhalgh's loss of work was followed by a long illness, which resulted fatally in October, 1862. Frederic Greenhalge had already been at home for several months caring for his father and tutoring a young man for Harvard, continuing his studies as chance afforded; but he now bravely bade good-bye to college hopes and associations, and turned resolutely to the care of his mother and sisters. He obtained the appointment as schoolteacher in District No. 2 of Chelmsford, in the winter of 1862 and 1863. The old No. 2 District had the regular school equipment of those days, — a little red schoolhouse, with green-wood fires and lots of tough boys. But he soon proved himself a competent master. The first boy he flogged was the son of a committeeman, who, instead of taking offence, as the young teacher somewhat expected, treated the affair with great approbation. At this period he was somewhat sensitive to criticism and comment, and was thrown into great dismay one afternoon by the hurried arrival of a friend who announced that two young ladies of their acquaintance had set forth to visit his school, and were anticipating much fun from his embarrassment. He instantly dismissed the scholars, locked the door, and fled. In after life he used to refer with much amusement to the haughty manner in which he was treated by these young ladies on the occasion of their next meeting.

The year 1863 was the darkest period of the war between the States, and it is not surprising to find that, like thousands of other young men, Greenhalge was drawn into the great conflict, and to some extent shared in its vicissitudes. Without military ambition, and inspired alone by the sense of duty and patriotism, the youth of the nation flocked to her standards through all the bloody years of the war, and suffered unimaginable hardships and wounds and death itself in the cause they held sacred. It might have been said, in the language of Pericles after a similar patriotic struggle in ancient Greece, — that the nation had seen its youth perish as the spring fades from the year. Greenhalge never shared in the actual fighting, nor was he long absent from home and at the seat of war. As will be seen, he failed to obtain the commission that he hoped for and expected, and the dreadful scourge of malaria soon rendered him unfit for service. Yet he is to be numbered with that host of distinguished and patriotic young men whom the nation remembers with undying gratitude for the services they rendered, or fearlessly tried to render, even if they failed, in her hour of trial and her fiery ordeal. In October, 1863, he tried to enlist in the army, but he was refused by the examining surgeon, on the ground of ill health. He, however, went to New Berne, N. C., then garrisoned by Illinois troops, and was

assigned to the commissary department. During the attack on
the city in February, 1864, he offered his services in defence of
the city, and was put in charge of the stores and detailed men
of the Twenty-third Massachusetts Regiment, having command
of a force of colored men.

Failing to obtain a commission, and being seized by malaria,
he was obliged to leave the South, and returned home in April,
1864.

The following extracts from his letters from the South give
a vivid picture of his journey to New Berne, and show well the
power of friendship he possessed, the faculty of making friends
with all kinds of men. The letters were written to his friend,
Ithamar W. Beard. The first is dated Nov. 21, 1863 : —

"Do you want to learn patience, do you desire to learn
what an unprofitable sign of nothing you really are, would
you know the mysterious and intricate convolutions of red tape,
get an appointment in the Commissary Department and apply
for transportation from New York to New Berne. I love New
York now, — but why ? Because it's the first point I steer
to when I take my homeward route, — when I set out for
home (if ever I do set out) for dear old Lowell. The fact is, I
had endless trouble in getting transportation from New York.
When I finally got passage on board the —— I had a most
miserable experience at first, — unknown, seasick, sullen,
homesick. . . . The accommodations of the soldiers on these
transports are shameful. Mine were very good, inasmuch as I
was a first-cabin passenger along with a young lieutenant in
the First N. C. Heavy Artillery. I had, during the latter part
of the passage, a very pleasant voyage. Moonlight on Pamlico
Sound is what you want to see, my child. I became acquainted
with two or three good, stout Massachusetts men ; and as all
the poor devils on board were out of rations, I won their good-
will by furnishing them food as long as my money lasted, —
that was not much, to be sure, but they were pleased to think
a great deal of it."

Another letter is dated Jan. 18, 1864 : —

"Since I last wrote, I have had several days of sickness, and
feared much I was about to have an attack of fever. My mind

was filled with the gloomiest apprehensions, and the thought of my mother's and sisters' grief, should the worst happen, was agony itself. As I lay half dozing on the bed, I had visions of home in which I heard my mother's dear familiar voice asking me, as of old, "How do you feel now, Fred?" and could almost feel her hand on my forehead. Had I not improved considerably yesterday, the next steamer for the dear old North (you don't know how one gets to love the sterile old region) would have borne my body, alive or dead, back to my home and my friends."

CHAPTER III.

AFTER his return from New Berne, Greenhalge resumed his study of law in the office of Brown & Alger. His life in Lowell was uninterrupted from this time until he was elected to Congress and went to Washington to fill his term. Steadily through all these years he raised himself in reputation as a man of unstained integrity and brilliant talent, first among his friends and fellow-townsmen, then in the wider circles of State and national politics. It is especially interesting to trace the beginnings of such a career, and to follow its development through the years.

We do not give credit enough to young men. We forget Chatham's lament that he was charged with the unpardonable crime of being a young man. In times of public disturbance and war, youth comes to the front; its energy is resistless. The Republican armies of France were led by young men. In quiet times of peace, however, the progress of youthful talent is slow, like promotion in the army. This gives rise to a storm and stress period in the minds of young and brilliant men; they feel that they are greater than they know, that others do not give them credit enough; their field of action is confined, and their talents do not have room for display. This leads to a passing mood of cynicism; and one of his early friends has told me that Greenhalge was not without a trace of this cynicism in his youth. Real cynicism was foreign to his nature; not an atom of it existed in his character. He was never, however, without a light spirit of mocking banter in private and social intercourse. This sometimes was misunderstood, and appeared to wound when nothing of the sort was intended. He had the reputation, with some people, of possessing a sharp tongue;

yet his speech was ever kindly in its purport, and known to be such by his friends. He had the kindest heart imaginable; a spirit almost feminine in its delicacy. He was, it is true, a master of sarcasm; and sarcasm in public debate is a perfectly legitimate weapon, employed by the great masters of eloquence, and by none with more force and polish than by the subject of this memoir. The keen wit of Greenhalge was bright and sparkling, and seemed sometimes to be in a state of perpetual effervescence; yet, though Greenhalge possessed high natural spirits, the deep undercurrent of his mind was always serious, and he could instantly be recalled to serious thoughts by any pitiful tale or matter of grave import; indeed, his sparkling wit seemed only like the light and brilliant waves that play over the profound depths of ocean. It could be instantly stilled, and he was never carried away by it.

As a social companion he was delightful, and his company was much sought. Since his death much has been said about his being a remarkable example of the results of our high-school and college education. Truth to say, nature gave him great talents; he acquired knowledge with ease and rapidity; he needed less teaching than most boys. Schools and colleges cannot of themselves produce such men.

Greenhalge took the leadership of men because he was gifted with great powers. Genius is born, not made. It shows itself early, and reveals itself without effort; its movements are as natural almost as those of the arm or hand. It borrows from every quarter, and repays the debt abundantly as the moon gathers light.

The personal character of Greenhalge was such as to endear him to all who knew him, such as to win the respect and confidence of all with whom he came in contact. His comrades were bound to him by hooks of steel. "Many are the friends of the silver tongue," and the eloquence and ability of Greenhalge gained him a host of friends; but by those who knew him well he was beloved more for himself than for his gifts and talents. He was the soul of generosity and honor. He was absolutely unprejudiced, and judged men solely by what they were, without regard for the accidents of fortune. He

loved honor, and was truly with "divine ambition puffed."
He lived upon a high level of thought and action habitually; he loved the common elements of human nature, and
knew the virtues of the people; he loved humor, and looked
kindly upon the amusing foibles of men; he liked those persons best who appreciated humor, and felt more at home with
them.

The conversation of Greenhalge was remarkably fluent and
interesting. In whatever company he found himself he easily
took the lead. Ordinarily his talk was light and brilliant.
In his conversation he seemed to be seeking relaxation and to
entertain the mind, and he never wearied his hearers; he was
always a very busy man, and he seemed glad to throw off the
fetters of business and politics, and in his social intercourse
he rarely talked of either subject unless it was introduced by
others. He was not fond of large social gatherings, and did
not enter much into general society.

A brother humorist of kindred spirit has written as follows
of his flashing wit and brilliant repartee, his love for fun, and
the entertainment he got out of the little weaknesses of his
friends : —

"Greenhalge was a man of infinite wit and humor. He
possessed the power of entertaining a room-full of people. He
had the tact to seize upon the weak points in a man's character,
— his little vanities, his personal peculiarities of gesture, dress,
or speech. His wit was audacious and atrocious, although
always kindly. His best friends were his most frequent victims. He was not a story-teller; I cannot remember one story
that he ever told. He was not a punster; I don't think he
cared for punning, esteeming it rather a low order of wit. But
for banter, quiet sarcasm, brilliant raillery, ready repartee, I
never met his equal. He was always graceful in his movements and gestures. His face was one of rapidly varying
expression; his voice exactly fitted the thought he wished
to express. All these instrumentalities were brought into play
as he set before you any humorous thought. Tell him some
slight circumstance in your own experience of a humorous
nature, give him but the slightest hint, he would seize upon it,
magnify it, turn it over, inside and outside, until it became

replete with fun. I recall one such experience of my own. It was at the time when I was President of the Lowell Y. M. C. A. There was in Lowell at that time a self-constituted missionary, more than a fanatic in his zeal. At the same time there was a woman evangelist holding services in one of the churches. The missionary, whom we will call Jones, asked me to go and hear this evangelist. I went, stayed a short time, and came away disgusted. Jones met me a few days after, and asked how I liked the preaching. I stammered out something in the way of apology, not wishing to offend. Jones became very angry, and said, 'You are no Christian, you have never been converted, you stand in the way of the cause; I shall pray the Lord to take you out of the world.' The whole experience amused me, and in an evil moment I told Greenhalge about it. In his hands it grew and grew; to each new audience he gave it with an added item. He told how Jones met me, how at his threat my cheek blanched and my knees began to fail me, how at last I broke away, made such haste as I could to the rooms of the Y. M. C. A., got a special praying-band together, and that, as Jones was praying for my removal, the band prayed that I might be spared, until at last they conquered. It does not sound much of a story to tell, but, as I have said, to hear him run on, it was delicious. At another time he gave me a narrative of how he and a delegation of Freemasons attended the funeral of a brother Mason in a neighboring town, and, being dissatisfied with the ministrations of the officiating minister, took possession of the church and the proceedings, and, calling on their own chaplain, held supplemental services. I never quite knew how much of truth and how much of romance there was in this story; I do remember all the graphic detail and delicate touches and keen appreciation of the situation that he put into his narrative. His wit and humor were the keenest and most delightful when he had a listening audience and plenty of time to work up his matter. Sometimes, when in the midst of an elaborate narrative, he would notice that his audience were not attending or talking among themselves, in an irresistibly funny way he would shrug his shoulders, throw up his hands, and say, 'There, I see I have lost my audience.' Besides these long narrations, now and again there would flash from him in his talk a witty remark. I remember once a man saying to him, 'Fred, how bald your head is!' 'Yes,' he replied; 'I was born so.' Once again, in speaking of a man who was an indifferent lawyer but a very fine singer, he said, '—— is one of the best read and most successful lawyers at the bar, but he cannot sing at all.' The expression came from him in such a serious and judicial way that I was taken by surprise, and was obliged to think a moment before I detected the fallacy."

Greenhalge had all the elements of a successful actor in him; these humorous sallies were of the nature of a dramatic exhibition.

The countenance of Greenhalge was striking, and full of intellectual power; its features revealed the vigor of his character. It was moulded upon antique lines, and showed strength of will and brain power; these revealed themselves more plainly as he grew older; as in the case of other leaders of men, the habits of control and the increased experience and force which he had gathered during a lifetime of effort appeared clearly in his face. His figure was erect and energetic, and he walked with an elastic and rapid step. Until the last year of his life he was strong and active, and enjoyed the most excellent health.

A common love of nature and delight in walking led him and a few other friends to join together in a sort of informal club, and they were accustomed for many years to make excursions into the surrounding country. Their usual place of rendezvous was at Willow Dale, by a lovely little lake in Tyngsborough, about five miles from Lowell, and kept as a place of entertainment by Jonathan Bowers. His life-long friends, Dr. Nickerson, Frederick Buttrick, and Judge Lawton, with others, were his usual companions on these trips. The storms of winter could not daunt them, nor the sun of July. In some of the heaviest snow-storms they have been known to make the journey on foot, tramping over the fields and through the woods. The following song, written by Greenhalge, commemorates in a joyous strain one of these excursions : —

WILLOW DALE — A SONG.

AIR : *Cockles and Mussels.*

I.

Oh, good Johnnie Bowers, how jocund the hours
    That rang their sweet chime o'er thy glimmering lake;
In June or December 't is sweet to remember
    Thy crispy potatoes and juicy beefsteak.

(*Chorus*)   Oh, John of the Dale! Oh, John of the Dale,
        We'll praise thy good suppers, oh, John of the Dale.

II.

Thy face apostolic (yet just a bit frolic)
    Has brightened our banquets for many a year;
And now thy deep laughter would ring to the rafter,
    And wake all the echoes on mountain and mere.

Chorus)   Oh, John of the Dale, etc.

III.

As Life becomes drearer, our song shall rise clearer
    Among the still woodlands of sweet Willow Dale:
We'll banish all sorrow from morrow to morrow,
    And pray that Mascuppick's bright founts never fail!

(*Chorus*)   Oh, John of the Dale, etc.

IV.

Then soft be thy pillow beneath the green willow,
    And never may sorrow thy rosy cheek pale ;
And we will remember, in June or December,
    To praise thy good suppers, oh, John of the Dale!

(*Chorus*)   Oh, John of the Dale, etc.

In a more serious mood he records in his diary the memory of another journey on foot to the same place : —

"*Saturday, Jan.* 2, 1886. — Yesterday Dr. Nickerson and I walked to Tyng's Pond, starting at one o'clock P. M. 'What is rarer than a day in June'? Why, such a day as this second of January was. The deep, clear blue of the sky, the gleaming trunks of every tree, the distinct outline of mountain in the northwest, Monadnock rising 'in silent majesty' — this is the Doctor's phrase — over all, like a noble nature above the crowd without any proclamations of superiority, except its own grand lines, conscious of truth, justice, and eternity; the stillness which suggested Saturday afternoon, or was suggested by it, the blue ice of the pond, the deep green of the pines, the ineffable glories of the sunset, flooding lake, hill, woods, and sky with wonderful lights and wonderful influences, making us anxious to grasp the fleeting beauty of the day and keep it with us forever. And to come to more concrete things, the fresh, splendid pickerel, the wood-fire, and Johnnie's good humor made a day that ought never to have become 'the prey of setting sun,' and it never will."

The following imaginary conversation, also taken from his diary, and written in a half-playful, half-serious style, refers also to the same friends and scenes:—

B. I am tired and worn. I have been holding a long and troublesome conference with disagreeable people.

G. Leave your office and come into the country with me; you shall hold a conference with Nature.

B. It would cost too much. Nature's fees are higher than a lawyer's.

G. "A thousand pound, Hal, a million: thy love is worth a million." Give Nature your love, and you more than pay her bill.

B. Do you want me to pack my valise and start for the White Mountains?

G. (by an impatient gesture waiving the White Mountains out of the question). No; neither valise nor White Mountains meet the case to-day. Yes; the *re*creation I offer to you — and observe that I dwell upon the first syllable with a Pogram-like accent, to show that I mean not sport or pleasure merely, but new life and strength — is at your door, or, as the real-estate brokers say, within easy reach of the post-office. Listen. About six miles from here is a pond, — not a lake or a lakelet, mind, — two miles long and three quarters of a mile wide; its waters are remarkably deep and clear; it is encircled by hills thickly wooded; its shores are rocky and wild, and the country about it is picturesque and lonely. The nearest railroad is at least five miles away. In the summer this retired

spot is the favorite resort of the sleek, well-fed citizen and
his invariably amiable and accomplished wife and daughters.
Sunday-school picnics and innumerable Orders of good this and
that invade the crystal solitude of the mere, and the tall pines
hold their heads higher than ever to avoid seeing the fragments
of crockery and eggshells and the scraps of newspapers which
strew the ground.   Swings and flying-horses add their delights
and peculiar effect to the abomination of desolation which
summer brings to this lovely bit of wilderness.   But —

B. I thank you for that " but."

G. But when October comes, she drives these money-
changers out of this temple of Nature. The hateful smell of
crowds is dispersed by a scornful puff or two, and Nature has
her own again.   Then we call the pond by its sweet Indian
name, Mascuppick, a name never breathed while the summer
vandals are prowling about.   In the journey I propose we
have no chance of meeting those myths we read about in the
newspapers, — the courteous baggage-master, the gentlemanly
conductor, the obliging landlord, the efficient and popular
steamboat clerk, and all the rest of the gang.   Instead of these,
we shall have as *compagnons du voyage* the northwest wind,
the countless sweet odors of "fresh woods and pastures new,"
bevies of fleecy clouds frolicking over our heads, and the music
of birds and trees and streams.   We shall walk.

B. Walk! — and how about dinner?   I can give up the
conductor, the baggage-master, and so forth; but I make a
stand for the obliging landlord.

G. You shall have the finest host in Christendom, — a
Boniface fit for the place I have described : florid as October,
jocund as the day, with a wit as clear as the waters of Mascuppick, and a disposition as genial as the sky is to-day.

B. Is he the summer landlord too?

G. Yes; but under compulsion.   His poverty and not his
will consents to furnish entertainment for man and beast, —
with a decided preference for the beast over the man of summer.   In the season he is a drudge working for his daily bread;
and, unlike most of his brethren, he thanks Heaven that the
season is short; and from September to May he is a man of
humor, of taste, of thought.   When he posts up his notice

"Closed for the season," his soul walks abroad in its own majesty, and he stands redeemed, regenerated, and disenthralled. Such work as comes to him in the autumn and winter he does *con amore*, for only choice spirits ever brave chilly winds and deep snow-drifts.

B. Pardon me if I still harp upon the dinner, — a walk of six miles makes it a matter "hung round with honors and importance." What can your Sir Launcelot of the lake or pond give us?

G. John of the Dale we call him. What can he give us for dinner? Chickens whose necks are wrung in your sight. You don't want to see the process? Well, you will profit by it. Hornpouts that, after baking, give occasion for discussions of the humanity of vivisection; a wood-duck, in the line of possibilities; and of a surety a juicy beefsteak smothered in onions.

B. "The sober certainty of waking bliss."

G. With sincere mince-pie, and the choicest vintage of the apple and the grape. Cigars of one brand only, but delicate, rich, and true.

B. Your description would create an appetite under the ribs of death. I am hungry now. Must we walk? When do we start?

G. Ah, ah! "Now you are flames, I'll teach you how to burn." We will march in ten minutes. Are you equal to twelve miles over hill and dale?

B. I have marched twenty miles a day for a week with knapsack and gun in Tennessee. I fancy I can travel to this Mascuppick.

G. Very well; won't Dr. Nixon go? He knows the place, and his profession lately has required long vigils of him.

B. The more the merrier. Perhaps Buxton, the banker, would join us, and we should have a perfect hollow square or quadrangle.

G. Telephone both of them, and ask them to report here instanter. They will be taken by surprise, and before they can calculate what their respective families and the great public will think about their escapade, we will have them out on the Mammoth Road by Ledge Hill chasing the flying leaves like two swains of Arcady.

Greenhalge was much interested at an early period of his life in private theatricals, and assumed various parts. He was by nature a good mimic, and had some of the talents of an actor. The parts he assumed were well executed. Nov. 21, 1867, at the residence of General Butler he took the part of Colonel Ferrier in "The Barrack Room," and Aminadab Sleek in "The Serious Family." April 22, 1869, in Lowell Music Hall, at the entertainment of the Lowell Boat Club's theatricals, he was cast for the character of Sidney Maynard in "The House-breaker." At the meeting to form the Channing Fraternity Dramatic Club, held April 27, 1873, he was one of the most active organizers, and, Feb. 21, 1877, volunteered for the entertainment given in aid of the relief fund of Post 42, G. A. R., and played a part in "The Romance of a Poor Young Man."

Greenhalge had few business affiliations; he was, however, for many years president of the City Institution for Savings. He was a member of several social organizations. He belonged to the Central Club, and afterwards to the Highland and Yorick Clubs. He was one of the originators and the first president of the Martin Luthers, which was an association formed to promote out-of-door sports among its members. Its outings were held for many years at Tyng's Island, in the Merrimac River, where base-ball was played in a muffin sort of way, as he described it, and other exercises were enjoyed. He was also until his death president of the People's Club, which was founded for the amusement and instruction of the working men and women of Lowell. He was president of the Humane Society for three years, and of the Unitarian Club. He was a trustee of Rogers Hall School for Girls, the Westford Academy, and the Lowell General Hospital.

His home is surrounded by grounds in which are many fine old trees that he admired, and he took an interest in studying the various kinds. In summer he enjoyed working at times in the garden, and has sometimes planted and raised a crop of vegetables in a small plot of his own. He said one could derive benefit from digging in the fresh earth when depressed or out of health.

In summer Greenhalge removed with his family to his cottage at Kennebunkport. When first married, he spent his summers at Scarborough, Maine. Greenhalge enjoyed Scarborough. Its magnificent beach was to him a delight. In sunshine and in storm he walked there and enjoyed the wild prospect, the grand waves, or the blue expanse of peaceful waters. Among the guests of the hotel he had many warm friends. At Kennebunkport his cottage stands upon a hill overlooking the river and across it to the beach, and over the ocean to York and Mount Agamenticus. His piazza commands a magnificent view, which he never wearied of watching. He enjoyed bathing and boating on the river, and, most of all, sailing or fishing in the bay.

Greenhalge was a man of simple tastes, and the social side of the life at summer seaside resorts did not appeal to him. With the native population and villagers he was on good terms, and spoke in the town on several public occasions. He was liked by them, as he was by the people everywhere. He always returned from the summer holidays with his face bronzed and burned by the sun and with increased vigor. In the last summer of his life he enlarged his house at Kennebunkport, which, alas! he was never destined to occupy again. All his life he was fond of the ocean, and preferred to pass his summers beside it.

He loved too the mountains; and the memory of a walk which the writer enjoyed in his company over the rugged crest of Monadnock is very vivid. His delight in the grand rocks of that stern peak was intense, and he quoted this verse of Tennyson more than once, —

> "From scarpèd cliff and quarried stone
> She cries, 'A thousand types are gone :
> I care for nothing, all shall go.'"

In 1872 Greenhalge was married to Isabel Nesmith, daughter of John and Harriet Rebecca Nesmith. The father of Mrs. Greenhalge was a prosperous business man, and distinguished by many high intellectual qualities. He enjoyed the friendship of many eminent men, among them Charles Sumner and Wendell Phillips. He was elected Lieutenant-Governor of Massachusetts in the same year when Governor Andrew was elected. Mrs. Nesmith, the mother of Mrs. Greenhalge, was a very remarkable woman; and her daughter, Mrs. Greenhalge, inherited many of her characteristics. Mr. and Mrs. Greenhalge had four children, three sons and one daughter. The eldest, Nesmith Greenhalge, died in infancy; the next was Frederic Brandlesome; the third child was a daughter, Harriet. Richard Greenhalge, their youngest son, most resembles his father, and was his adored and petted child. He is well known as "Dick" to a very wide circle of friends of all ages.

The home of Greenhalge is at the corner of Wyman Street and Nesmith Street. It was built by him in 1878; the land on which it stands was formerly a part of the estate of Mrs. Greenhalge's father, and the house is near the homestead where she was born. It has always been the centre of a home life remarkable for the strong ties of affection and the community of spirit that bound all the members of the family together. Greenhalge was a most indulgent father, and was almost worshipped by his children. He was never known to speak a harsh word; he loved his home, and was always best contented among his books and while sharing in the mutual enjoyment of home life. He was so busy a man, however, that much of his time was necessarily passed away from it, especially in later life. The petty vexations of life never seemed to disturb him. From its littleness he was singularly free. He possessed a mind above small things, and they never either depressed or elated him.

Mrs. Greenhalge, his beloved wife, he reverenced as a perfect woman, and the felicity of their married life was without a passing cloud. She devoted herself to him, and, without ambition herself, watched his public career with admiration and loyalty to all his best interests. To her counsels he listened, and he depended much upon her sterling common-sense and high ideals. She was a devoted wife, and, like the wife of Disraeli, was a constant support to her distinguished husband. Her chief interest centred in the home circle; but where her husband's interests were concerned she was always willing to sacrifice her own preferences, and, while never going much abroad, always gave to public questions that concerned him her undivided interest and attention.

Greenhalge, though ordinarily the most gentle of men in his

disposition, was not incapable of that "noble rage" of which the poet speaks. He was a good hater. He hated meanness and littleness, falseness and arrogance. Occasions that rightly called for such display could always raise the fire of indignation in his eyes and voice. His tongue was a sharp sword, and did not spare an unworthy victim.

Yet, after all, the best thing that can be said of him was said also of Lord Macaulay by Sydney Smith : " I believe him to be incorruptible ; stars, garters, ribbons, titles, and wealth might be laid at his feet and he would not be tempted ; he sincerely loved his country, and could not be bribed to forsake her true interests."

That verse of "In Memoriam" which he liked to quote seems very applicable to him now, cut off in his prime as he was, when we reflect upon all that he might have accomplished, all that he was, and would have continued to be had he lived, —

> A life in civic action warm ;
> A soul on highest mission sent,
> A potent voice of Parliament,
> A pillar steadfast in the storm.

It is wellnigh impossible to give an idea of the animated conversation of Greenhalge ; of his wit and humor, light and sparkling as champagne, and as impossible to recall as to give a form and being to the "foam of fairylands forlorn." His wit is hard to remember because it was so airy, so light, so effervescent, so nimble. His audience was kept perpetually smiling ; in the social hour he was inimitable, full of high spirits and good fellowship. Alas, how difficult it is to give an idea of his unique personality, that gave a zest to all he said !

To one who did not know him in his youth, his prime of gayety and high spirits, for "the days of our youth are the days of our glory," it is fortunate that he can avail himself of the experience of one who did know him then, who was his friend and comrade, the Rev. I. W. Beard, of Dover, who has contributed to these pages the following reminiscences : —

"As nearly as I can remember, my acquaintance with Governor Greenhalge began in 1859, the year he entered college. I was a member of the class of 1862, he of the class of 1863.

He was two years younger than myself. In those days the
classes were comparatively small, a class of one hundred members being a large class; consequently we became acquainted
not only with our own class, but with most of the members
of the other classes. Greenhalge and myself soon formed
that intimate friendship which endured, without a break or one
single breath to mar it, till the end of his life. Being both
Lowell boys, we were mutually drawn together; our tastes
were congenial; but although I was his senior in years, it was
I who sat at his feet and not he at mine. Some things stand
out in my mind as the characteristics of the youth Greenhalge;
one thing particularly, — he was a man of a manifest destiny.
Robert Browning in his last poem, written in his last illness,
said of himself, —

> 'One who never turned his back but
> Marched breast forward.
> Never doubted clouds would break,
> Never dreamed, though right were
> Worsted, wrong would triumph,
> Held we fall to rise, are baffled to fight better,
> Sleep to wake.'

Of this verse Browning said to his daughter-in-law and sister,
'It almost looks like bragging to say this, and as if I ought
to cancel it; but it is the simple truth, and as it's true it shall
stand.'

"It comes to some men — and they are generally great men
— to see themselves clearly. Lord Beaconsfield, when a youth,
told Lord Melbourne that some day he intended to be Prime
Minister of England. Abraham Lincoln in the days of his
squalid poverty affirmed that he meant to be the President of
the United States. Such a prevision of a great destiny young
Greenhalge always had. I can remember well how in those
early days he confidently asserted it; to some such assurance
might have seemed like self-conceit, and in many it would
have been so. In Greenhalge it was only a just estimate of
himself, and the end has justified that estimate. There was
much of impatience with his surroundings which hampered
and hindered him in his early youth. There was a touch of
cynicism in his early view of things which entirely passed

away in manhood. It was the mere chaffing on the bit of
the race-horse that is over-eager to take his place. I think
his college days were far from being his happiest. He was
not the man to have borne patiently the thwarting of his
just and lawful ambitions. He grew, throve, and mellowed
in the attainment of his desires. I cannot think, I have often
trembled as I tried to think, what would have resulted had he
not attained them. Real worth and unusual ability do not find
so quick a recognition when clad in the habiliments of poverty
and obscurity. Young Greenhalge did not succeed in taking
the place in college as a leader in his class that legitimately
belonged to him. He was *facile princeps* among them all;
but in that microcosm, a college class, family position and
wealth have the same undue weight that they have in the
larger world. Such men as Greenhalge must wait to be
crowned; but the crown, when it is won, is all the more glorious. Yet there were happy days and hours for him in college.
There were rare symposia in 'the resorts' we most frequented
when such men as Greenhalge, John Fiske, Oliver Wendell
Holmes, Jr., Jack Dennett, Edward Dorr McCarthy, and many
other brilliant men got together, as they frequently did, and
exchanged their views on literature and poetry. At one time
he had an opportunity of showing out the independence of
character and the fire of eloquence that was in him when his
class reached a crisis which almost amounted to a rebellion
against the college authorities.

"My intimacy and friendship with Greenhalge began after
we had both left college and settled down to the study of the
law, — he in the office of A. R. Brown & E. A. Alger, I in
the office of D. S. & G. F. Richardson. We were in the
same building, only separated by the width of a hallway. It
was our duty to come down to our offices early to sweep the
floors and put things in readiness for the business of the day.
It was here, broom and dust-pan in hand, that we used to
exchange our common confidences, tell our stories, and make
our jokes. How vividly can I reproduce in my mind those
days! What long talks we used to have! How easily we laid
aside our Blackstones or our Chittys to pass over to each
other and while away the time that we ought each to have

been spending upon our books! I do not think that either of us in those days cared over-much for mere drudgery. It was the last social event we had participated in; it was some bit of college news; it was some funny thing that somebody had said, or a bit of quiet humor over the eccentricity or ignorance of some client or acquaintance. Greenhalge was rare good company; nobody could be dull with him. If you had one spark of intellect or wit or humor in you, a half-hour's conversation with Greenhalge would bring it out. He was the very best of talkers, because he would let you have your say; he was as interested in your story as in his own. About this time we both felt the imperative need of earning money; so we each took a country school, — I at Middlesex, he at Chelmsford, about two miles farther on. We walked every day to and from our schools over Westford Street in the bitter storms and the biting cold of a severe winter. It did not seem much to do then. I can well remember visits I made to his school, the conscientious work he put into his teaching, the originality of his methods. I remember particularly that he invented a 'system of mnemonics' by means of which he very materially facilitated the task of learning. I do not remember what that system was. I can only recall it as an original and useful scheme. Later on he engaged himself to work in a bolt-shop. It was an irksome and utterly uncongenial employment. His duties were those of a common laborer. This fact shows his willingness to lend a helping hand in the great family exigency of the hour. It could not be expected that he should long continue in such employment. It was in these walks to and from school that we formed the determination of starting a literary society. When our school-teaching days were over, ' The Club' — it never had any other title — was fairly launched on its long and prosperous voyage of usefulness and discovery. Its original members as I recall them were F. T. Greenhalge, Joseph H. McDaniels, James O. Scripture, who died young, John Davis, Albert Moore, Solon W. Stevens, and myself. The first three in this list were as brilliant, bright, witty, and well-furnished men as ever were the members of such a club. As time passed on, some dropped out and others took their places. Among the new members were C. E. Grinnell, then

the Unitarian Minister in Lowell, Dr. Nickerson, and Alfred
Lamson. Our work was real work; our fun was of the
purest and rarest. Our range of reading was wide; we began
with the dramatists before Shakespeare, Ben Jonson, Chap-
man, Massinger, Beaumont and Fletcher, and the rest. Our
method was for each member to take one play, read it through
by himself, and come into the Club and give a synopsis of
his play and read extended passages; and so with all the
books we took up. We read, besides this, Spenser's Faerie
Queene and other poems, Buckle's History of Civilization,
Dante, Tennyson, and I know not what else, for the Club
was long-lived and did conscientious work. It is hardly necessary to say that Greenhalge was the very life of the Club.
It was the privilege of a lifetime to listen to his reading; he
was a born elocutionist. Of all professional readers, I never
heard any who could read as well as he.

"He was unspoiled by any 'lessons in elocution.' He had
a naturally musical voice, easily modulated to the expression
he wished to convey; his ready literary tact enabled him to
seize upon any striking and dramatic incident; his intimate
sympathy with his author enabled him at once to render the
passage correctly and make it stand out a living thing in the
presence of his audience. His reading was utterly free from
the tricks of the professional; the effect was produced by his
own intimate sympathy with the thought. To listen to him as
he read was like listening to a prima donna singing. What a
discipline and education the Club was to us, the lesser wits!
The criticism was always friendly; we were all of us on the
most brotherly terms of intimacy, but woe be to the luckless
wight of us who was guilty of a false quantity or a false
literary allusion. It was never forgotten; it stuck to the man
like a burr. I remember one such when we were on the subject of 'Ben Jonson.' One unfortunate member in good faith
said he thought Jonson was happier in his dramas than he
had been in his dictionary. This was never forgotten; it grew
into colossal proportions under Greenhalge's masterly manipu-
lation. I am sure that member learned a lesson at that time
that has been of use to him his life long. The Club met
one evening in every two weeks; there was good, honest work,

but it was not all work. There was no end of fun, and such
fun! There never was anything like it. It was akin to the
'Noctes Ambrosianæ' of Kit North. First, those suppers!
We always had a supper, and such suppers! I had at that
time a good mother, the Lord rest her! who took the liveliest
interest in the Club; she might have been its matron; it
was her delight to exhaust her rare skill in catering for our
hungry stomachs. While others vied with her, she easily led
them all in the culinary art. Her pressed veal and grouse
and cream-pies became the peculiar property of the Club.
As Greenhalge easily led us in other things, he was not
behind as a knight of our round supper-table. There was
nothing of the gourmand about him, but the same refinement
that marked him in everything was his characteristic at the
table. He had inherited the taste for good living which is
peculiarly English; and that which we all keenly enjoyed he
enjoyed with the keenest, but in his own way, and that the
best way.

"This allusion is not out of keeping with my subject, since the
suppers were so distinctive a feature of our Club and so much
a part of our fun, and he himself enjoyed them so thoroughly
that the picture would be incomplete without it. What capped
the climax of our hilarity was our annual picnics. One day
was set apart in the summer to be spent out of doors, — sometimes at Willow Dale, sometimes at Tyng's Island, sometimes
on the banks of the Merrimac River, below Belvidere. On
these occasions there was no innocent wild hilarity we didn't
indulge in; there was nothing that any gentleman might do
that any one of us would not do to add to the wild jollity of
the occasion. I remember once, for the delectation of the
Club, one of our tallest members bestrode a wandering cow
that then frequented Tyng's Island, and rode about, a veritable
Don Quixote on an original Rosinante. We had a Club song
which was composed by Greenhalge. It originated in this
way: When a boy in England, Greenhalge's mother used to
sing to him an old English ballad, the first two lines of
which only I remember. It went thus: —

'Queen Dido sat at her garden gate
A-darning of her stocking, Oh!'

" Then a rollicking chorus came in as follows : —

'Ri fa la la la, ri fa la la la,
Ri fa la la, la la ly, Oh !'

"Greenhalge retained the tune in his memory, and wrote our Club song to fit our own circumstances. A copy of this song, in his own handwriting, is now before me. I give it as follows:

SONG OF THE LITERARY QUINTETTE.

Sweet Attic nights,
Your pure delights,
When fled, will haunt us ever, Oh !
By joy and wit
Young souls are lit ;
Care dims the bright hours never, Oh !
Ri fa la la la, etc.

Here sit unseen
Great shades serene,
From Tartarus, land of fable, Oh !
Free for a time,
These guests sublime
Shout gayly at our table, Oh !
Ri fa la la la, etc.

If from our lips
A wise word slips,
T is Plato or Bacon that 's croaking, Oh !
When the laugh rings free,
Don't frown on me ;
It 's that wicked Dean Jonathan joking, Oh !
Ri fa la la la, etc.

Then glasses clink,
And merrily drink,
Good luck to the dead and living, Oh !
Still may we find
Dame Fortune kind,
More nights of jollity giving, Oh !
Ri fa la la la, ri fa la la la,
Ri fa la la, la la ly, Oh !

"Our hilarity was not dependent upon our stimulating drinks, but upon our effervescing youth; our Club drinks never exceeding coffee, pop beer, or possibly cider or claret.

"As I have said, where Greenhalge was fun must come out of a man if there was any fun in him. I have wished to make it understood that Greenhalge was not only the originator of the Club, but that all through its history he was the very inspiration and life of it.

"The events that I have recorded cover the time between 1859 and 1873. Changes had been gradually coming to us both. In 1869 I was married; in 1872 he was married. We were passing from the light-hearted freedom of boys and youth to the responsibilities of manhood and family life. Up to the time of my changing my profession in 1873, we had been in almost daily personal communion; now all this was to be changed. Our communication was to be limited to very occasional letters and still less frequent visits. We both found the responsibilities and cares of life thickening upon us; though separated in body, in heart and spirit we were as much one as ever. It was never necessary to appeal to him for sympathy in time of need or affliction; before the appeal could be made, his own word of courage, aid, or sympathy had come to hand. His heart was always a fountain of love and brotherhood, which never failed. The events that I remember most vividly in all these years of separation were his occasional visits to my home. Alas that they were so 'short and far between'!

"Just here let me interpolate an illustration of Greenhalge's literary acumen and acquirements. Many years ago he called my attention to the use of this expression 'short and far between,' telling me that it was borrowed by Campbell in his 'Pleasures of Hope' from a much older poem, 'The Grave,' by Robert Blair, and that in borrowing it Campbell had misquoted and spoiled it; that Campbell quoted it, 'few and far between,' which was tautological; that in Blair it reads, 'short and far between,' which was right. Then he went on to say that Blair's poem was very fine and very little known or read; that he had known it since he was a boy; that it had been a great favorite with his father, and that he had often heard his father read it. To return to my subject. Greenhalge's visits to me were 'short and far between;' but if they were short, they were sweet. Those at Dover I remember the best. Twice he came to read and lecture to a little audience

of my parishioners and friends; on one of these occasions he
delivered a subtly satirical paper on Tennyson's Locksley Hall.
I recall it clearly. It was a delicious bit of satire, so delicate
and subtle that most of his audience took it in good faith. It
was very original in its conception, as everything was that
came from him. He took the side of Amy; he represented
the hero of the poem as a cynical misanthrope, utterly im-
practicable; he set forth Amy's husband and Amy's home life
in the glowing colors of domestic blessedness. I remember
well his reading of the poem, and his own enjoyment of the be-
wilderment of his audience. I remember afterwards one of our
Dover young men, who was a reader of poetry, saying to me,
'That was a fine paper of Greenhalge's, but I don't agree with
him in his view of the poem.' But the best visits we had
together were those when he got away from the town and the
people, and went for a drive or a walk into the country. Two
of them I shall never forget. The first was August 24,
1888; it was a trip to Mount Agamenticus. The mountain
was a prominent feature in the landscape from his summer
home in Kennebunkport. He had said that he wished to visit
it, and he came on the day appointed. Our way lay through
South Berwick, one of the pleasantest of our New England
villages. Nothing in the landscape missed his eye or his
appreciative admiration as we drove along. At the foot of
the mountain, two miles in from the main road, lived a
veritable specimen of the old-time Yankee farmer (John
Norman), with his wife and his son (Silas). No man had a
keener or more kindly appreciation of such folk as this than
had Greenhalge. His intercourse with these hardy sons of toil
was no small part of his enjoyment of the day. It was an easy
matter to reach the summit of this little mountain. The view
is one that is unparalleled, in New England at least. The whole
vast reach of seacoast, from Cape Ann to Cape Elizabeth, is
spread out before the vision of the beholder. We easily identi-
fied Kennebunkport. We had sufficient time fully to grasp the
scene. When we came away, the full extent of the pleasure
he had enjoyed and which had not found expression in gush-
ing words, he packed into one touching and characteristic act,
of which nobody but a poet, and nobody but Greenhalge, would

have thought. Standing erect and viewing it, he silently and
most gracefully threw a kiss as a lover might kiss his hand to
his sweetheart. This may seem very sentimental to some
minds. To me it was most beautifully, most gracefully and
appropriately done. Those who really knew Greenhalge will
understand and appreciate the act. It was the silent and
expressive act of his poet's soul. Two years after this trip he
alluded to it, saying: 'It was on August 24th, two years ago,
that we ascended Agamenticus; that was a day always to be
remembered.' One more experience of this kind I must tell.
November 22, 1890, he visited me in the same way for the
same purpose; this time we planned a walk of four miles into
the country. In our way we passed through our richest
farming region on Dover Neck, thence up Huckleberry Hill,
whence we got a view of a very broad sweep of water, a wide
river on either side of us and Great Bay stretching out far to
the southwest. In walking we met, here and there, the
farmers in their fields doing up the last of their fall work.
Our tramp terminated at one of these farmer's houses, 'Uncle
John's.' We met and accosted 'Farmer Austin' and 'Farmer
Tuttle,' a sterling man of the Quaker persuasion. It was a
cloudy, lowery day, threatening rain. Such days had a special
charm for Greenhalge which I could never understand. Everything in this tramp was viewed by him from the poet's point
of view. There was not one feature of it that he did not
idealize. 'Farmer Austin's' prediction of a shower which did
not come was replete with amusement for him. 'Farmer
Tuttle's' honest, hearty greeting touched his heart. 'Uncle
John' reminded him of Bismarck. I chuckled in my sleeve
as we went along at this beautiful web of ideality that he wove
and threw over everything and every man that he saw. It was
not for me to brush it away ruthlessly (even if years of intimacy
had reduced the men and the scene to the commonplace in my
own eyes). Greenhalge's 'Dover days,' as he always called them,
were bright spots in his weary life of care and responsibility.

"My reminiscences are assuming inordinate proportions. I
will make some extracts from letters illustrative of the thoughts
I have suggested, and conclude.

"The following is from a letter dated 'July 18th, 1874,' and gives a brief description of one of the Club picnics which I was not able to attend. He begins, 'My dear old Parson;' then, after some grateful allusions to some birthday gifts he had received, he goes on to say:—

"After we had given up the idea of a Club picnic for Friday, comes a telegram from Grinnell saying he would be up in the 9 A. M. train ready for the fray. I got it about 9.30 P. M. the day before; the next day I went round to get the Club together. Joe was away, Albert not approachable; but Davis and Nickerson I gobbled, met the lengthy man of God, procured a carryall with two flaring horses, also four bottles of California claret, six cigars, and bowled away to Tyng's Pond. The river was flooded, the current awful; we had made no preparation for food, and so we didn't go to the Island. At the pond we had to wait long for dinner, but, with that drawback, had a splendid day. We bathed, talked philosophy and poetry, ate and drank and smoked; then drove up over the new bridge at Tyngsboro', and went back on the other side of the river through North Chelmsford, stopping at the tavern at the invitation of C. D. Palmer of '68, who runs a mill up there, and talked Harvard, drank cider, and smoked; then we came home, Grinnell stopping with me. . . . We shall repeat this jollity before the summer is over. We missed you greatly. Accept my thanks for your kind [birthday] wishes. Don't talk about giving me anything. I am thoroughly ashamed of myself for my forgetfulness of duties towards you,—actual duties, you know,—and if it were not for my sublime confidence in what will be brought out by 'one of these days,' I should hide my head in shame.

"Yours ever,   F. T. GREENHALGE.

"Here follows a letter which illustrates his poet's habit of idealizing things and persons that he loved, and gives us a glimpse of a strong undercurrrent of pathetic longing for rest and peace from the world's rush and turmoil:—

"MY DEAR ITHAMAR,—Yours received. It came like a breath of pure fresh air on my heated, troublous life. I sometimes envy the good Rector of Groveland down in his quiet little village 'walking worthy of the vocation wherewith he is called,' performing the labor he loves, and doing good to himself and all around him. I should like much to be with you now in these golden October days, — were there ever such before since the world began? Roaming about the yellowing woods and "leaping the rainbows of the brooks," taking the winds into our pulses, and enjoying life as it should be enjoyed. But I have a wife, — a most excellent one, — whom I cannot leave now, and we cannot come together. . . . —— has been nominated; the sordid base elements as usual were in the majority, but I most devoutly trust an honest Democrat will save us from the disgrace of this base man's election. . . .

"Love to all.

"Yours ever,   F. T. GREENHALGE.

"Again he writes : —

"MY DEAR ITHAMAR, — I cannot tell you how surprised and pleased I was in reading your sermon on 'Total Abstinence,' etc. [Here follows a review of the sermon in flattering phrase. Then he goes on to say:] This is really a candid opinion, and in giving it I prove myself, as Punch says, a fool. But you won't get 'cocky' about it, I know, and begin to dress like Phillips Brooks and Dean Stanley, — both stout men, I believe, or they ought to be for the sake of the joke.

"I intrusted certain moneys as to Christmas presents to a woman, which is tantamount to saying they were not executed. Tell your mother so, and at the same time thank her for her splendid remembrance (there is a phrase for you!) of me. I was fortunate in my gifts, very. Grote, Aristotle, The Science of Law, Mass. Reports (5 vols.), Macaulay's Lays, Khedive's Egypt, Evelina — ye gods! could bounty go farther? If it did it would fare worse. My love to you and yours, all of 'em.

"Ever yours,   F. T. GREENHALGE."

Mr. Beard here concludes his interesting reminiscences.

Greenhalge was a man of deep religious feelings and convictions. His father's family were brought up in the Church of England, and on their arrival in America joined the Episcopal Church; afterwards Greenhalge united with the Unitarians, and until his death he was a frequent attendant at the Unitarian Church in Lowell. That belief was suited to his broad views and the nature of his mind. He was not accustomed to talk much on religious subjects, but it is evident that he was supported by a strong faith. Some of his letters and diaries reveal the serious nature of his thoughts. He believed in the goodness of God, and loved righteousness. To do good was his desire, and "to be known to desire to do good." He was unselfish, self-sacrificing on the thousand small occasions that occur in all men's lives when they can sacrifice their own feeling for others, and most often fail to do so.

He was ambitious, but in a wholly laudable way. He was much mistaken and misrepresented. This is the lot of most active workers and leaders. The world does not give credit for greatness and goodness until they are proved and tried. It takes time to overcome men's prejudices and preconceptions. The strong man will overcome them if the opportunity and time are given him. Greenhalge won at last the confidence of all who knew him, and their respect for his integrity and worthiness.

The following letters and notes show the real worth of the man : —

LOWELL, Sept. 27, 1886.

The day is warm and sunny; an ideal day for the mountains, whither my heart follows you. This has been so far a busy day with me, and on such a day there should be no business but with the woods, the mountains, the ocean, and the sky. But I know that among the mountains and close to the sky I shall have a faithful agent for the transaction of the high business to be done there, and that the richest profits will come down to us from the airy heights where you are now.

I may go to Boston to-morrow on business; small politics, relating to county offices, are buzzing round my head, and I detest any attempt to get me into them.

This next letter was written to Mr. Beard at a time when he was undergoing the fire of a sharp criticism for a course of independent action in opposition to the prevailing public opinion.

My DEAR ITHAMAR, — "Be strong," and let the clamor of fools go unregarded; the crowd have no right to interfere with thoughts and purposes they cannot comprehend. I have had many a heartache because I could not "suffer fools gladly," and I am not quite ready to do so yet; but I cannot be bullied, nor can you, as those ignorant people up there with you will learn.

I shall try to run up soon and get a quiet Dover day like that peaceful and cheering 7th of December last year.

I was elected by a large majority. We are all comfortable. Love to all with you.

Yours,   F. T. GREENHALGE.

The following letter addressed to the same friend gives us a glimpse of his tender sympathy and religious principles: —

My DEAR ITHAMAR, — I write just a line to express my deep sympathy with you in your present family trouble and danger. Since your mother's letter was read I have counted the hours, and cannot help feeling a sense of relief as they go by and bring no message of sharper grief. I know something of that affliction which seems to cloud the face of a good God, — to rob Him of Omnipotence, — and to fill the soul and the mind with black darkness; but I hope the Deliverer may come in all his strength and drive this affliction from you. Though I may doubt, I will pray. Hope on and fight on.

I am yours in hope and trust,

F. T. GREENHALGE.

These notes and aphorisms are selected from his diary. At odd times he jotted down his thoughts in it, but it was not kept consecutively. More often the items were written when he was feeling blue and depressed.

Wednesday, Nov. 14, 1877. — Saw old Mr. ———. He is a fanatic, and I think an opium-eater. He wanted me and all my friends to sign the pledge and profess religion! We had a sharp discussion, — rather amusing when it is considered that my mission was peace and charity and for his benefit. Yet he assailed me impertinently and discourteously, in a mild

Christian way, of course, but rudely just the same. He chewed tobacco fiercely all the while. I told him I did n't "profess" religion, I tried to *live* it; that I did not believe in having more religion on hand than I could use in my daily life; and that the hypocrites and humbugs who paraded their virtues at Sabbath-school but nowhere else and then went off and robbed their masters on week days, I detested and despised. He seemed dazed, and made no reply; but began to talk on the business in hand. He took milder ground on that matter too.

March 11, 1883. — There are times when one's body in perfect rest seems to be a positive pleasure to oneself. Health makes itself felt, and is a joy of itself, independent of action or thought.

We speak of the human mind as finite. This is an assumption. The mind is, in its powers, its resources, its capacities, its possibilities, infinite as the spaces of the sky. As in those spaces we are ever discovering some new star, some new solar system; so ever and again we see some new thought, some new power, shine out star-like in the infinite spaces of the mind.

Alluding to some one unknown, he writes: "He has a value which impractical men are apt to overlook; he is an interpreter between the highest order of minds and the lowest.

You cannot play with your opportunity; you must take it "for better for worse," cleaving only to it.

When two persons meet as friends, as enemies, or what not, there is only one question of importance to settle, — which shall profit, get the most out of the other? In whose favor shall the balance be struck? You open an account as it were with your new acquaintance.

Men fail nowadays from a want of courage. They mean to do right, but consequences loom up before their terrified vision in a magnified form like the spectres on the Hartz mountains. This or that interest may be injured, this or that friend offended, this or that prospect endangered; but if the right course has been found and decided on, if the forces of truth and justice are marshalled, the true man cannot be stopped by a flag of truce from the stronghold of iniquity, he will not stop to parley.

Saturday, Nov. 17, 1883. — For myself, I have been much dispirited of late. I see no future before me; an aimless life is death. If ambition is strong, but endurance and courage small, ambition is a curse. Mine is not a very selfish ambition, though. To do good and to be known as doing and wishing good, are what I seek; and the latter half is the damned nonsense that breaks up the whole scheme. I don't know which is worse, — to do evil and be thought to do good, or to do good and be thought to do evil. The moral babbler will say the former is by far the worse. I have tried both; the suffering is about the same. I feel that the world ought to know good when it sees it, even if the world does n't know evil always. Evil seeks disguise, good does not; yet the stupid world makes mistakes as often one way as the other, and this fact crucifies the good man.

A glorious November afternoon ! Such rich, soft, refined (there is no other word for it) light suffusing everything ! The beautiful naked trees, symmetrical and grand, with their columns, trunks, and their tapering airy pencil-drawn lines of sprays with this soft radiance over and in them as it were — are more beautiful to me than when robed in their June leafage.

> " Induitur, formosissima est ;
>   Exuitur, ipsa forma est."

The half-brown, half-green grass, too, catches wondrous tints from the afternoon sky; our soft, mellow winter afternoons have never been recognized by a blind people. Oh for a Ruskin to preach the gospel of this phase of our winter loveliness !

CHAPTER IV.

GREENHALGE possessed a versatile mind; he had much of the dramatic element in his character. He was a born orator, and had cultivated his talent to a high degree of finished excellence and polish. It is not strange, therefore, that we should find that he was always a close student of the best in literature, — for literary study is the basis of all oratory of the highest class. If action and thrice action is the secret of oratory, it is the study of literature that gives it ornament and style, and the imagination that exalts it is full of the inspiration of poetry.

There is an oratory that speaks from the heart in simple and homely words, — like Lincoln's Gettysburg address, — and transcends in power the greatest efforts of genius. But the occasions and feelings that give rise to it are rare. The orator must depend upon his art without the aid of such sublime circumstances. The secret of that art resides in the classics of the English language.

The love of literature is, indeed, native to the most exalted minds; it reveals itself in the most unexpected places, wherever real intellectual ability exists. It animated the lofty mind of Cæsar; it accompanied Frederick the Great to the camp, and graced the character of Pitt and Fox.

Among the public men of America, however, it is not so commonly found as to make it pass without remark. Americans lack the leisure to cultivate a love of letters; we are engrossed in business, and our statesmen are practical men, — this is our excuse, but a poor one. If literature were one of the ideals of American life, we should find it instilled in the young, and putting forth shoots. It is not inconsistent with a busy life, and is the road to excellence in public speaking,

5

—which is one of our principal means of government, and the main path of ambition.

New England has sometimes been called the brain of our country; and its authors have produced the best of our literature. Their names are emblazoned on the walls of our legislative hall, and held in honor by America. England has enrolled them in the catalogue of her authors, and it is fitting that a Chief Magistrate of Massachusetts should have been inspired by their works, and a lover of letters for their own sake.

Napoleon, when it was remarked that he took pleasure in wearing the uniform of the French Academy, replied that every drummer boy in his armies would think better of him for being something more than a mere soldier. We think the more of our statesmen if they are cultivated men as well as firm and just magistrates.

Greenhalge by nature was inclined to literary studies. He knew the imperial step in literature, which I have heard him say was not understood in these days of the commonplace. His taste was severe and chaste, and formed upon the grand models of our classic English. He loved his Shakespeare, and its volumes formed the most cherished part of his library. Their pithy sentences and marvellous bursts of poetry are everywhere underscored by his hand, with perfect precision pointing out the supreme passages of beauty and wisdom. These marked volumes of Shakespeare reveal his mind in a literary sense, a mind capable of appreciating the best. Shakespeare indeed is well fitted to be the statesman's book and amulet. There, if anywhere, shall he find the nature of man revealed; and if he aspire to lead mankind, let him learn their virtues and their foibles in the great book. Knowledge of men is his necessity. Greenhalge, when a young man, belonged to a literary club, and there he laid the foundation of his knowledge of that supreme writer.

Among modern poets, he held Tennyson to be the greatest; and the wonderful art of that writer aroused his admiration. He liked to read his poems aloud. He was especially fond of reciting " Œnone," and delivered several times a lecture which he had somewhat humorously prepared upon " Locksley Hall. "

" In Memoriam" he often quoted. He also read aloud frequently Swinburne's " Queen Mary," with great skill and
appreciation. " Atalanta in Calydon " he was among the first
to welcome. For Lowell he always claimed the chief place
among American poets, and he was intimately acquainted with
his poems. " Columbus" he read much aloud, and ranked
it with Tennyson's " Ulysses. " One of the new poets of the
day he held in high esteem, — William Watson, — and was
especially pleased with that poem of his entitled " The things
that are more excellent. "

Among prose writers he valued much the quaint works of Sir
Thomas Browne, full of wisdom and truth. He was not
unfamiliar with the grand characters of Plutarch ; and he
might have been fitly called " one of Plutarch's men, " in the
simplicity and truth of his nature.

He was naturally interested in political history and biography, and possessed many works of that class.

Greenhalge was not a student ; but his scholarship, as far
as it went, was exact. He was aided in this by his strong
memory ; and he did not forget his Latin, as many college
graduates do. His classical quotations were always accurate.

He liked novels, and read them frequently. He had in his
library, and enjoyed reading, Balzac's works. His English
favorites were Walter Scott and Thackeray.

History, particularly American history, he had always
studied, and was a well-read man in every sense of the term.
Parkman was, I think, in his opinion, the best American historian, as he is in fact the most imaginative and interesting.

Greenhalge loved his library, but he did not haunt the book-
stalls. He seldom, in later life, purchased books himself ;
yet he sometimes returned home bearing a prize in triumph.
The shelves of his library contain about a thousand well-
selected volumes.

He was more than a lover of literature ; he was a poet himself. We have seen that the earliest stirrings of his ambition
were in the direction of letters. As a man of letters, he might
have achieved distinction. He possessed many of the necessary qualifications : he had the fine taste, and much of the
imagination of a poet. In the variety of his intellectual

powers he possessed the arsenal of a man of letters. His ambition, perhaps, would have been satisfied in the republic of letters; he liked seclusion and retirement, in spite of his active life. Yet he chose the proper sphere for his activities; he was a natural orator, and his eloquence was a power in the world.

Authors and orators have often many characteristic qualities in common; they enjoy a common reward in the love and admiration of men. Cicero, a supreme type, from certain weaknesses in his character, cuts a somewhat sorry figure among the grand forms of Pompey and Cæsar, Antony and Octavius; yet he in a larger degree possesses our love. His weakness, after all, was rather that of his situation. The sword cut the Gordian knot that his rhetoric could not solve. Yet the greatest figure in history to many of us is the inspiring author or orator devoting his talent to the enlightenment of the human mind and the advancement of the race.

Greenhalge was not a literary craftsman, he did not give up his mind to poetry as a fine art; yet it is wonderful how beautiful some of his poems are. Their publication needs no apology, and is certain to give pleasure to all who were interested in him, and to lovers of poetry for its own sake, — a fact rare in political biography.

The sonnets which he wrote are remarkable. A sonnet offers great difficulties in its composition. The poetic feeling is apt to disappear, the original motive to be obscured, overcome by the intricacies of its construction; the result seems labored even if it is a work of art and beauty. Greenhalge's sonnets, on the contrary, are simple and natural, feeling and full of tenderness. The emotion is easily expressed, and the art is never too obvious.

The poems are not the work of a literary artist, pure and simple; they are free, and not labored; they read easily, like the verses of a writer unwilling to be trammelled, and well express a spirit too earnest to spend its energy in elaborating decorated diction and an ornate style. They are not to be judged by the standard of a purely literary art. Written by so busy a man, they are surprising enough. The language is without a flaw; true and simple, without the least striving for effect. There is nothing but what is excellent, and in point of style natural and true. The poem that follows — one of the best he ever wrote — is like a flowing rivulet of harmony, gentle and melodious, a sweet inundation of sound expressing in the sad metre of " Evangeline " its burden of sorrow and melancholy regret. It seems not to be a work of art, except it be that art which nature makes. Like a soft and complaining stream in the green meadows, it gives its song spontaneously to the listening ear. It commemorates the death of Harriet Nesmith Coburn, untimely like his own, in the bloom of womanhood.

This poem speaks for itself; the voice of criticism is stilled in reading its verses. It is a beautiful performance, and is worthy of the name of the most distinguished author. He gave it no title, and it needs none.

Still for a moment, O River, the song of thy murmuring wavelets,
Glad as thou art with the fulness the Spring pours into thy bosom;
Here do we anxiously wait for the first low cry of an infant,
Eager to see and to share in the joy of the beautiful mother.

  .   .   .   .

Stillness and gloom on the hill, — deep stillness and gloom in the valley!
Heart-chilling silence when joy should have chanted a jubilant pæan, —
Darkness and death where life should have flashed with a multiplied splendor!
This is the end of our plans, — of the hopes and the fears we had harbored;
Here is the castle we built laid low with a terrible ruin,
Whelming in one great doom the beloved it should have protected!
Innocent joys we had pictured are blighted and withered to ashes;
All our fond preparations, — the toys and the love-woven raiment;
Lay them aside, all wet with our tears, — sweet emblems of sorrow, —
Tender memorials now, to be cherished and wept o'er forever.
Could not the radiant hopes that circled like cherubs around her,
Plead with the white-faced Death, and turn him aside from his purpose?
Why should the fond, deep love of a mother be all unavailing?
Was there no pity, O Lord, for the woe of a desolate fireside,
Reft of a wife and child and plunged into uttermost darkness?
Poor is the comfort we offer, and weak are our words of compassion, —
Would that their hearts could feel that 't is God who has given and — taken!
Purest of flowers, shed fragrance around the sweet babe and its mother;
Softness and beauty of Spring, whose softness and beauty she loved so,
Be with us now, as we bear her away to her rest on the hillside;
Softly, O River, glide on, soft and low as the voice of a mourner, —
Long as thy current shall flow by the home her sweet presence illumined,
Requiems chant for her, for she loved thy crystalline waters.

Oft did the voice of her gladness unite with thy musical murmurs,
When in the sweet summer days she was borne on thy glistening surface,
Circled with friends, while rang happy laughter and music around her.

Father of Mercies! we pray thee, console the fond hearts thou hast wounded;
Soothe them with loving compassion, and tell them, in whispers angelic,
Safely their loved ones rest in Thine arms forever enfolded.

The three sonnets that follow are remarkable examples of the ease with which he wrote. They are regular in form, and the rhymes are not forced. The division between octave and sestet is observed, and they should be included in any anthology of American sonnets. "A sonnet is a moment's monument." "'T is the pearly shell that murmurs of the far-off murmuring sea." Much has been written about it as a form of verse. The writer has not much sympathy with the modern view that would limit it to one unvarying form, — the Petrarcan, — arranging the thoughts and structure like the ebb and flow of a wave. Rossetti used a great variety of forms, and Shakespeare a form of his own. Greenhalge's, as it happens, are very nearly regular, and cannot be criticised on this score. The thought, too, is translucent, and never obscure. Rarely has true feeling been expressed more clearly in the sonnet than in this example; it is like a rose exhaling its own fragrance without effort or self-consciousness. It was addressed to his wife on her birthday, on presenting her with a picture of their dead child.

Oh, sweet, grave face ! No weight of years could bring
  The wisdom sitting on that smooth white brow.
  Less than a year those deep eyes shone ; and now
To this faint image comfort bids us cling.
Yet what rich memories from the brief life spring
  And twine round all things! — flower, and bud, and bough,
  And indoor sights and sounds, all show us how
In his *our* lives were daily brightening.

Dear spirit of our child ! shine through these eyes
  And smile on us with warmer love this day
    That marks thy mother's wedding and her birth;
Let thy loved accents thrill with sweet surprise
  Her stricken heart that pines for thee alway,
    And make for her *again* a Heaven of Earth.

The sonnet upon Lake George is a word painting full of quiet beauty, and a charming picture of natural scenery; and the one commencing " I love the busy haunts of busy men " in another way is equally good.　Greenhalge loved nature, and felt its absence as a deprivation, especially during the summer that he was obliged to pass in Washington.

LAKE GEORGE.

Like silent giants stand the mountains round,
Guarding thy sleeping form with anxious care,
Lest some grim storm lurking in cloudy lair
Should, with its threatening roar, open the bound.
Now all is still, save where with silvery sound
A hidden rill steals on thee unaware,
Whose sweet and artless song was such a snare
That silence listened — and so sweet death found.

Each changing cloud, dark hill, and leafy isle,
Seen in thy depths are clothed with softer grace, —
Faint images, sweet as the dawning smile
That happy dreams bring to a sleeper's face.
Sweet Horicon!　May naught that 's base or rude
Ever disturb thy crystal solitude!

THE CITY AND MY COUNTRY HOME.

I love the busy haunts of busy men :
The strife of courts, the bustle of the marts,
The gathered life of all these earnest hearts
Might fire Prometheus' fainting soul again!
Here first is heard the voice of Science when
Her lonely votary's secret she imparts;
Here freshest bloom clothes Learning and the Arts,
And thoughts flash newest from the sage's pen.
But more I love my home on this green hill,
Where to my window comes the evening breeze,
Faint songs of birds, the river's muffled sweep.
Within, my wife sings lullaby; yet still
Our sleepy boy will not be lulled to sleep,
But winks and babbles at the waving trees.

The poem entitled " Blessed are They that Mourn, " is worthy of any pen; and I insert it without comment, as surely it will speak for itself, and is certain to win the heart of all lovers of poetry.　It commemorates a loss common, alas! and touch-

ing to all humanity, — the death of a child, his infant son,
Nesmith Greenhalge, who died July 25, 1874.

BLESSED ARE THEY THAT MOURN.

Oh, when does sorrow for our lost ones leave us,
    And vanished sweetness cease to claim a tear ?
When does the heart, freed from its burden grievous,
    Beat as of old, as though Death were not near ?

Why, sorrow 's but the shade of the departed,
    Gentle and loving as the loved in life ;
She calleth ever to the faithful-hearted
    To turn their hopes from earthly toil and strife.

Some souls there are that sorrow will not enter, —
    They have not room for such a stately guest, —
In the base earth their shallow thoughts all centre ;
    They live unpurified, and die unblest.

But they who cherish her, although she chastens,
    Find her a friend, and not a spectre stern ;
And ever as their brief life onward hastens,
    From her prophetic lips sweet truths they learn.

Oh, heart of fire ! What brought thee to such meekness ?
    And, sordid soul, what maketh thee so pure ?
Could not proud strength withstand a sick child's weakness,
    Nor selfish greed a wife's last kiss endure ?

Ah ! pass not this mild spirit by unheeding, —
    She is the link that binds us to the dead ;
Their voices and dear eyes are for her pleading,
    So we will keep her with us in their stead.

She leadeth us away from fading pleasures,
    Where joy's loud trumpet sounds his own quick doom ;
And from lone heights she pointeth to the treasures
    That shine in the far land beyond the gloom.

She does not fill us with a vain repining,
    But nerves us rather to heroic deeds ;
For in her eyes a better hope is shining,
    As on from height to height she swiftly leads.

Then wait, dear mourner, for that blessed morrow,
    Which, taking naught of thy fond love away,
Will bring the sweet, deep peace that 's born of sorrow,
    And fit thee for the realms of endless day.

The following poems are also among his best, and with them
I will conclude my extracts from his poetical writings : —

HYMN

WRITTEN FOR THE UNITARIAN CELEBRATION OF THE LAST SUNDAY OF THE
FIRST CENTURY OF THE REPUBLIC.

Hail to the Sabbath sweet, — the last
    Of all a century's Sabbath days !
Float, blessed day, into the past,
    Rich with a nation's prayer and praise.

Thy power, O God, shines through these years,
    That bound the nation's splendid morn ;
Thy hand each needed bulwark rears,
    Thy voice 'gainst secret foe doth warn.

Still keep, dear Lord, yon flag unfurled
    O'er Freedom's chosen citadel, —
Cheering anew the slavish world,
    And lighting up each captive's cell.

That faith in man teach to mankind,
    That 's born of purest faith in Thee ;
Then tyrant can no longer bind,
    And right will rule from sea to sea.

FALLEN LEAVES.

I know a streamlet, deep and still,
    That through wild woods seeks out a way, —
I saw it when the blasts were chill,
    And o'er it Autumn brooding lay.

But soon the wind flung on its wave
    A gorgeous mantle of bright leaves, —
Scarlet and gold and green ; they gave
    A glory man's art never weaves.

And as those fallen leaves lent grace
    Unto the streamlet's darkening flow,
And, falling, found as high a place
    As when they bloomed in Summer's glow ;

So, though our labors seem to fail
    And low our blooming hopes are hurled,
Like fallen leaves, they still avail
    To beautify a dreary world.

SUNDAY, NOVEMBER 30, 1884.

How still and calm the day ! How still and calm
   My heart, that lately throbbed with wrath or pain !
The week's wild tumult now is as a psalm
   Borne faintly to us from some distant fane.

And from the glory of this silent hour
   Confusion flies, like Satan and the night, —
Strong truth stands forth, clothed with seraphic power,
   While cowering baseness seeks to share the light.

See noble Purpose, clouded until now,
   Shine with the flame of Bethlehem's great star;
And Prophets, smiling, point us to the brow
   Whose whiteness wreaths and glories cannot mar.

From the still height of this serenest day,
   I trace Life's motion with a clearer eye;
Men's deeds and lives are only God's highway
   Which leads unto His glory by and by.

Before concluding these remarks upon Greenhalge's literary characteristics, it will, perhaps, be interesting to consider in detail some poem held by him in high esteem and admiration, that it may be seen how sure was his taste, how correct his judgment, and with what sincere appreciation he read the masterpiece of a great poet.

It may thus be learned also upon what intellectual food his mind was nourished. The poem of "Columbus" by Lowell was always one of his favorites. This poem he made his own by his appreciation of its sublimities, as we all may do; not ours the genius to conceive the words, but ours may be the feeling and susceptibility to receive the message and assimilate the thoughts. He has marked passages of this poem in brackets, which I quote: —

     " The trial still is the strength's complement,
      And the uncertain dizzy path that scales
      The sheer heights of supremest purposes
      Is steeper to the angel than the child.
      Chances have laws as fixed as planets have,
      And disappointment's dry and bitter root,
      Envy's harsh berries, and the choking pool

Of the world's scorn, are the right mother-milk
To the tough hearts that pioneer their kind,
And break a pathway to those unknown realms
That in the earth's broad shadow lie enthralled ;
Endurance is the crowning quality,
And patience all the passion of great hearts :
These are their stay, and when the leaden world
Sets its hard face against their fateful thought,
And brute strength, like a scornful conqueror,
Clangs his huge glaive down in the other scale,
The inspired soul but flings his patience in,
And slowly that outweighs the ponderous globe, —
One faith against a whole earth's unbelief,
One soul against the flesh of all mankind.

" It is God's day; it is Columbus's.
A lavish day ! One day, with life and heart,
Is more than time enough to find a world."

This poem he often read aloud; it affords a good test of
poetic sensibility ; it is grand and severe. It would naturally
appeal to one who had suffered some of the slings and arrows
of fortune, who had endured the dulness of fools, who had
fought the good fight and won at last, after toil and defeat.
He never learned, as he said, to suffer fools gladly. Only
once does he presume to criticise, — the passage beginning
" Let not this one frail bark," he notes as diffuse and weak.
This was the man who was called a hustler and place-hunter
by some who knew him not. He sought, it is true, and found
at last, a place in the hearts of men; it was their service he
sought, not his own advancement. He was in public what he
was in private, what his intimate friends knew him to be.
Such poems as " Columbus " are not the usual mental food of
selfish politicians and office-seekers.

Our political leaders wage an eager party strife, which
seems bitter at times and fierce. It is not, however, like the
ignoble struggle of Pompey and Cæsar, ignoble in spite of its
grandeur.

Our statesmen can never be more than the servants of the
people. Purely personal and selfish ambition of a high order
is not possible to-day; small ambitions alone can be selfishly
gratified. Men of a high order of intellect, if not inspired by

patriotic motives, would not be drawn into political life. What glistening spoil can lure them? They cannot hope to gain wealth or personal power; they may desire fame, but the love of fame is not ignoble, it is " that last infirmity of noble mind. "

In the heat of party strife our feelings may blind us; but once our political leaders are lifted out of the arena of party into the sphere of the nation, when they become by election our magistrates and legislators, it is true patriotism to give them the credit they deserve, for the, as a rule, unselfish character of their efforts and the purity of their motives.

Lincoln and Grant, thank God, are of no party. In a narrower sphere Greenhalge has come also to be of no party.

CHAPTER V.

GREENHALGE was admitted to the Bar in 1865. For the practice of this profession his talents were fitted in the highest degree, and he soon began to make his mark. The law was his chosen sphere of action; all his life it held an exalted place in his esteem and admiration. The great system of jurisprudence, built up slowly through many centuries of growth by the toiling intellects of the most eminent men, holding as in garnered sheaves and mighty granaries the combined experiences of millions of men and the wisdom of ages, excited his imagination and aroused his enthusiasm. He loved his profession, and took pride in belonging to it. He was content to practise as a lawyer, though his career at the Bar was early interrupted by political calls and duties. He always returned to it with ardor and satisfaction. It was the means by which he gained a livelihood. It brought him the money he needed, and he held it in honor, as all men should hold the profession by which they subsist. The honors it brings would have satisfied him, as they well might gratify the honorable ambition of any man.

The sublime figure of Justice with her equal scales is reverenced by all true lawyers: standing like an eternal mediator and peacemaker between men, it is her image that they behold and remember, and not the law's delay, the tedious litigation and the faults inseparable from any system.

The great lawyers of England are said not often to have gained a high reputation as Parliamentary orators; excellent speakers at the Bar have failed when called from their profession to a seat in Parliament. It is not so here. Our

great orators in Congress have almost without exception been
brought up to the practice of law.

The oratory of Greenhalge was successful at the Bar, in Congress, and upon many public platforms. It never failed to
elicit applause. It appealed to both the mind and the imagination of his hearers. It was never dull and formal. It was
often unpremeditated, yet it never lacked brilliancy and force.
His facility was remarkable, and stamped him as an orator
by right of birth.

Ruskin has taught us that what is done well is done easily;
that if our work comes hard to us, if we perform it with difficulty and labor, the result will not be the perfect work of
genius. Genius does its appointed task with ease, just as it
is evident that Shakespeare wrote and Raphael painted. "The
victories of Timoleon are the best victories, — which flowed
like Homer's verses, Plutarch said."

Ease and grace of delivery, an unlaborious style, were
always distinguishing qualities of Greenhalge's oratory. Many
instances of his remarkable readiness in debate and on the
stump are well known. He was never at fault for lack of time
and preparation. He was also an inspiring speaker; he
aroused enthusiasm and excited interest. There were energy
and fire in his words. He possessed the secret of action to
animate his words, his gestures, and his face. The audience
never sat unmoved, as they often have in the presence of
many wise and weighty orators. There was a nervous force in
him that became apparent as he spoke, and passed insensibly
into the minds of his listeners. There was also a glamour
about his oratory, — the glamour of poetry and imagination.
This cast a glow over his words. His speeches were enriched
with imagery, and he borrowed phrases and passages from
the poets. He never lacked an apt allusion or quotation to
illustrate what he said. "Ridet domus argento," — "The
house laughs with silver," — how fine a suggestion to fling
into a tedious debate on the Silver Bill in Congress was this
verse of Horace! It might have come from the lips of Burke
or Fox. It gave lustre to his speech, and raised it at once
above the tiresome routine of debate.

Greenhalge was an impractical speaker, if to be practical

means weight and wisdom with tediousness and without illumination. He could speak, and speak well, upon the spur of the moment, without preparation. He could trust to himself to respond to a sudden call, and perhaps he placed too much reliance on his readiness of speech. He spoke latterly much too often, and upon too many comparatively trivial occasions, to be able to do full credit to himself. The people have come to make such innumerable demands upon the time and strength of the Governor of the State in the character of a public speaker, that if he is to fulfil his engagements it must be often in a perfunctory manner. The fire and energy of an orator are not inexhaustible. Whenever time and opportunity were afforded him, Greenhalge thought a great deal about his speeches; they occupied his mind a long time in their preparation. He was accustomed to make many notes. His best orations were always so prepared.

But it was his alertness and readiness of speech that singled him out among his compeers, and distinguished him as a born debater. Congress would have been his fitting sphere. Had not defeat withdrawn him from that arena, he would have risen high. He possessed courage also, and could not have been daunted, — that courage which draws to itself the suffrages of all men, which more than all other qualities makes men admired and followed. He had the highest form of courage, — moral courage, the courage of his convictions. This made his eloquence valuable to the world, a power for good. He needed no time to think and prepare his words when once he heard in Congress the fame of Massachusetts impugned and insulted. He had come into the hall suddenly in time to hear the close of an invidious and insulting speech, whose mark was the reputation and honor of the State he revered as his own; his tongue did not fail him then, neither did his heart. He replied with force and effect, and his defence was instantaneous. He was never caught without his arms, — his sword and shield. In his reply he said: —

"Mr. Chairman, I am sorry that a discussion of an important appropriation bill has called forth so much acrimony in this House. As a colleague of mine has reminded me, with an Indian outbreak upon our hands — with 'Hannibal at the gates '— it is singular that so much virulent opposition should be manifested to the bill now before the House. I came into the hall a few moments ago, and heard a few of the closing sentences of the gentleman from Missouri [Mr. Stone]. I cannot understand the motive or the animus of his opposition to the bill before the House. I do not comprehend the reason of the severe denunciation which even the Commonwealth of Massachusetts has received at his hands.

"I only know, Mr. Chairman, that whenever any man 'runs amuck,' whenever he is demoralized, and ceases to be master of whatever mind he may have, there is an attack made upon the Commonwealth which for a month or two to come I have the honor — a sort of obituary honor — to represent in part. Now I desired to ask the gentleman from Missouri (but, content with his triumph, he has retired suddenly from the House) one momentous question, and that was, whether his attack upon Massachusetts was prepared before the 4th of November or subsequently. His answer might have had an important effect upon my manner of treating that attack. I should admit that if his remarks were composed after the 4th of November, there was much truth in what he said. If they were composed before the 4th of November, then I should resent with all my power, with all my force, little as it may be, any attack upon the old Commonwealth.

"But how these gentlemen when they want to get a breath of life in this Congress have to go back to 1812! You would expect from them, Mr. Chairman, words of eulogy for the Hartford Convention. Yet we hear none. We hear only the very principles which they pretend have been successful at the last election condemned — why? They tell us that those principles were wrong in 1812, but they are right in 1890. I say that the same principles held up by that convention are what will animate the majority that will sit in that wonderful angle described by the gentleman from Illinois (Mr. Springer) the other day — an angle of 45° — in the next House. Ah, gentlemen, you may think that we Republican representatives from Massachusetts have not amounted to much as you have looked upon us in this House; but wait till you see our successors!

"Mr. Chairman, I appreciate fully the complaint which is growing louder and louder upon that side of the House; and as 'the subsequent proceedings are interesting me no more,' I take some pleasure in seeing the real, sincere manifestations of feeling upon the other side. You have a right, my friends on the other side (and I leave you this as a sort of farewell address) — you have a right to complain of the treatment of your Northern brothers. They do not give you fair representation upon their tickets, they do not carry out the logic of their convictions. My friend from Ohio tauntingly asks — no, I am not sure about its being his taunt; he made a taunt of some sort or other — we have been tauntingly asked about our friend from Virginia [Mr. Langston]. Why do you complain about our action in regard to that gentleman? You were more disgusted, you were more irritated by the action of this side of the House upon the question of seating that gentleman than upon anything else which has been done on this side of the House or under its auspices.

"Mr. Enloe. Will the gentleman allow me a moment?

"Mr. Greenhalge. Certainly.

"Mr. Enloe. I made the suggestion to which you refer; and I want to say that I was speaking of a matter over which your side had jurisdiction. You elected him to this House after the people had repudiated him. I say, when you have the right to elect at the polls, why do you not put such men on your presidential tickets?

"Mr. Greenhalge. Is that the gentleman's idea of a question? [Laughter.] Well, let it go at that!

"Now, I say that while we certainly have done our part by any man who marched under the banner of the Republican party, you have the right, my friends, in the next House to demand your full rights. You have the right to demand the repeal of the Fifteenth Amendment to the Constitution; you have the right to declare for the last three amendments to the Constitution; you have the right to require that the ablest man upon your side shall be elected Speaker, in spite of his record as a Confederate soldier. I say to you, act out the courage of your convictions. Be true to yourselves. The great trouble between political parties is that they do not state the

6

true issues. We have had men skulking and hiding under this side and under the other side. Now, then, come out fairly and boldly, and the people of the country will have at least the privilege of getting the question before them stated fairly and honestly. Stand up, then, my friends, in the next House. This is my parting benediction.

"Ah, you talk to us kindly — and I want to express my gratitude for the kindness of the other side of the House in my supposed unfortunate condition — you talk to us about the 'lost cause.' If it were a lost cause, we should have more sympathy, active and vital, from the other side of the House than we have. It is simply because it is not a lost cause that you still have a rankling and ill feeling left.

"Now, my friends, I consider it a matter of magnanimity, perhaps, on my part, to stand forward in these last moments to defend the old Commonwealth; but in spite of her errors — and I stand here as one of the errors, and I know it will suit gentlemen on that side in one aspect, and will suit gentlemen on this side in another — I still say that these attacks upon the first Commonwealth of the Union are unworthy of the men who make them, and the posthumous arguments upon the federal elections bill, the little miserable attacks and personalities, unworthy, shameful, and cowardly attacks upon the person of any member of this House, his father, his mother, his ancestors in any degree, or upon members in the coordinate branch, are not worthy of any man of chivalry or honor or self-respect.

"These things come too late. You project upon us an attack upon a bill which has gone from this House. We are ready to meet that attack in any proper time. We are ready to meet it when it is before the House or at any other time, and still appeal to the chivalry and decency of the House to condemn this resuscitation of arguments projected months and months ago and then brought forward in their sepulchral shrouds, I hope to the contempt of the House."

Much eloquence of a high order is buried in the law courts. The ability displayed by advocates in the practice of their profession does not bring them, as a rule, wide and enduring fame.

Yet great nations are now ruled mostly by lawyers. Carlyle has railed at the race of talkers who rule England; yet the men of the sword have not always guided nations wisely and well. The world has not always advanced under their sway in the past. Briefless barristers are said to govern France; in America the seats of the mighty are filled by lawyers. We honor them as a class, and elect them to high office. The laws of our country are their life-long study, and we believe that they are able to frame them wisely, that they make good magistrates, that their education fits them to execute the laws with justice and moderation. Greenhalge came into contact with men at many points. His legal career is a worthy object of emulation and imitation to his brothers of the Bar.

The foundations of his success were laid in the practice of law. He was, first of all things, a good lawyer, a brilliant advocate, and a wise legal counsellor. He was singularly free from pedantry. He could brighten a dry argument with flashes of wit. He understood human nature, and could reach and influence a jury; he studied them individually, and was a good reader of character. He understood his cases, and knew the salient points of attack and defence. He was logical, cogent, and urgent in his arguments. He had a clear insight into the great underlying principles of law; consequently he understood quickly the bearings of each individual case, its relation to those principles and the great body of legal precedents. He had no interest in the trivialities of law, its curiosities and phrases, its quiddits and its quillets. Above all, he was always a gentleman, a courteous advocate, gracious to friend and foe. He was never unmannerly or rude on any provocation.

Perhaps the highest compliment he ever received as a lawyer, and the most gratifying, was paid to him and the opposing counsel in court by Judge Aldrich. The compliment itself, and the words that express it, are worthy of a great judge. It was honorable alike to the Judge and to both the counsel whose conduct of the case called it forth. The following is an account, taken from one of the papers at the time : —

" Messrs. Greenhalge and Lilley [now Judge Lilley] were trying a case before Judge Aldrich. When it was closed and his Honor took it up, he turned to the jury and said: ' Gentlemen, I can congratulate myself and you upon the manner in which this case has been tried by the two able counsel in it. The law has been presented ably and decidedly; there has been an utter absence of wrangling between attorneys, and of browbeating of witnesses, and it has been a rare pleasure to hear it. Seldom in the course of my judicial experience have I heard a case that has been conducted with so much legal ability and proper spirit; and for these two days it has seemed as if the sweet spirit of lofty jurisprudence had filled this court-room. I congratulate the gentlemen in the case; I congratulate the jurymen who have had this rare privilege, and I congratulate myself upon having the opportunity to sit and hear it.' "

Coming from Judge Aldrich at the close of a trying and irritating week, this expression of approval meant a great deal. Coming from any Judge, it would have been praise as high as it was rare.

A high authority, as will be seen, has joined the name of Greenhalge with those of Everett and Choate and Webster; if no direct comparison was intended, the compliment was great and well deserved. The fame of Greenhalge as an orator was a growing fame. The laurels that he planted would have attained a luxuriant growth with years. As it was, he had few equals in life; he possessed the wide and varied powers of great speakers, — the wit, the pathos, the imagination and ardor, the reading, and gift of expression that have distinguished them.

The following letters, written by Senator Hoar and addressed to him, are unique, and, coming from such a source, as great a compliment as could have been paid him. They were a great pleasure to him, and their kind and laudatory expressions were highly valued. The first was written after a speech he delivered in Worcester during the political campaign of 1891; the second, after his election as Governor in 1893.

WORCESTER, MASS., Sept. 29, 1891.

HON. FREDERIC T. GREENHALGE, Lowell, Mass.

MY DEAR MR. GREENHALGE, — I desire to say to you a little more fully than I said it last night how much I was delighted and stirred by your admirable speech. It seems to me nearly, if not quite, the best political speech I ever heard, and I have heard a great many. You stated the point on several questions about which the people are in doubt, and where good men are apt to be confused, with wonderful clearness and vigor.

I think you and your friends were entirely right not to present your name for the office of Governor this year. I suppose your constituents will return you next year to the House of Representatives, which is your proper and best field of service. If you had been elected Governor at the end of two or three years, when the time for your retirement came, your district would very likely have another Representative, and it is impossible to say what opportunity for public service would then present itself. Besides, the House of Representatives is now a much better and larger place, especially for a man who is a skilful debater, than the office of Governor of Massachusetts, honorable and dignified as the latter may be. I have no doubt that if your health lasts you will have a great place in our national service.

I am, with kindliest regard,

Faithfully yours, GEO. F. HOAR.

WORCESTER, MASS., Nov. 7, 1894.

MY DEAR GOVERNOR GREENHALGE, — Amid all this " din and tempest" of delight and exultation, I think I ought to put upon record my opinion of the very great debt which the Republicans of Massachusetts owe to you for their triumph in this campaign. It is the only instance I think of in our political history where a State campaign has been made, and the opposition has no fault whatever to find with the State administration. This is peculiarly gratifying, because our Democratic friends would have been very glad indeed of an issue which should divert attention from national questions. This credit is yours. It is very unlikely indeed that the same thing will ever be said of any successor.

I trust there will be no indelicacy in my saying to you what I have said very often to other people : I do not believe you are yourself aware of the great qualities which you possess for becoming a consummate orator.　I do not know another person living in this country who seems to me to possess them to so large a degree.　You have a beautiful, racy, fresh, and original style of great purity, and adapted to convey your thought, without diminution of its clearness or force, into the minds of your auditors.　You have the gift of pathos, of wit, and of stirring lofty emotion.　I do not think the public, although they listen, as you must yourself know, with great delight to your public utterances, are as yet aware of the extent to which you possess this capacity.　I hope you will not content yourself with answering satisfactorily the ordinary demands which come to you by virtue of your public station, but that you will do what our other great orators did, — what Edward Everett, and Choate, and Sumner, and what Webster in his earlier years did, — take such opportunities as may come to you for the preparation of careful and elaborate addresses on great themes which will take a permanent place in literature, and which will contain the very best you can do with full and thorough study.　What any of us has to say, however well it may be said in ordinary political discourses, is not remembered long.　But it is to be hoped that while you are answering to these ordinary calls better than anybody else we have now upon the stage, you will find it in your power to do something which may live longer.

I trust you will excuse this somewhat grandfatherly tone from an old fellow who has got only two years left to him of the seventy which the law allows, and finds it much easier to give good advice to youngsters than to follow good advice himself.

I am, with highest regard,

Faithfully yours,　　　Geo. F. Hoar.

The letter that succeeds was written to Greenhalge by Judge Abbott after hearing him argue a case in court, and shows how high an opinion that eminent lawyer had formed of his ability. Greenhalge had been intimate with his sons and written a poem commemorating the death in battle of one of them, Captain Henry Livermore Abbott, who was killed in the battle of the Wilderness.

MY DEAR MR. GREENHALGE, — I thank you for your kind note; but I am the obliged party. I have desired to make your acquaintance for a long time. I first knew of you by some kind things said by you of my sons, who I think were in the same school with you; and I have watched your progress professionally and politically since with much interest. I never happened, however, to be fortunate enough to hear you in court until the other day, when I was delighted with the manner in which you argued a case that did not look at first very promising.

I trust your great success in politics may not tempt you away from the profession, for that would be a misfortune to you and the law.

Permit me to say, I trust that I may have the pleasure of continuing the acquaintance so pleasantly begun.

I have not been so long away from the city in which I spent the best and happiest part of my life, that I have forgotten to feel a warm interest in Lowell and Lowell men.

Faithfully yours,   J. G. ABBOTT.

317 COMMONWEALTH AVE., 28th of Feb. 1889.

There is a very interesting note in the diary of Greenhalge, written May 15, Sunday, 1881, which illustrates his manner of preparing his speeches. The oration he speaks of was delivered at Concord on Decoration Day in that year. The fragment is as follows: " At home working on oration at Concord. I cannot write orations, — I have to speak them, and then try to remember them as the best results of the trial speaking, for the grand occasion. A written style for speaking is damnable. " This is significant; he could not compose and polish his orations as if they were literary essays. This seems like the dictum of a true orator. He wanted the enthusiasm of large assemblies, the electric thrill which moves the audience and speaker alike; he missed the emotions born of the occasion that stir the heart to utterance, that unseal the lips and wing the orator's words with flame. To be sure, what he had to say he thought out and remembered as far as he could; but the shape it took in his mind was not rigid and unchangeable. It flowed easily into new forms to receive the sugges-

tions of the moment. It is impossible to give an idea of the
delight and fascination with which Greenhalge's orations were
heard when he was in his prime, when his health was at its
best, and his spirits most high and buoyant. Only those who
listened to him in such a happy and fortunate moment can have
a conception of it, and they are not so numerous as may be
supposed. He spoke too often in many political campaigns,
and was often tired. The calls upon him as Governor were
innumerable; in the last years of his life his health could not
have been perfect. Greenhalge's oratory at its best was inimitable; it was wise and witty at will; it was full of poetry and
pathos; it overflowed with high spirit; it was decorative; it
was delicious and rich with humor; it was a lavish repast
spread for the mind's delight. He possessed the temperament
of an orator; though subject to fits of depression and discouragement, it was naturally ebullient, rich in animal spirits
and cheerfulness.

Greenhalge did not live to reap what he had sown; he left
his growing fame to the people. It should not be allowed to
wither prematurely; they should see that it still continues to
survive and flourish.

It is as an orator, perhaps, that his memory will remain
with them longest; he made his highest mark as such, and in
spite of the incompleteness of his life and work his name will
be honored with those of Sumner and Phillips. He belongs
to the glorious galaxy of Massachusetts orators, and is certain
of a niche in her temple of Fame.

To some people it may have seemed that the peculiar qualities of Greenhalge's mind were not such as go to the making
of a great lawyer; that his extreme versatility of talent, his
brilliancy and sensibility and poetic nature, unfitted him, in a
measure, for the serious study of the law, for the drudgery that
it entails, the exactness and concentration that it demands.
Such was not the opinion of his brothers of the Bar, who knew
him best.

He was, as a lawyer, acute, intuitive, and profound, fully
armed and equipped for the fray, — resourceful and in the possession of ample learning. In some measure he may have
earned the reputation of being averse to tedious labors, from the

fact that he acquired knowledge with such ease and quickness that he did not seem to labor when most immersed in toil.

He had a large practice, and might have had a larger if he had held aloof from politics. It was the sense of duty that withdrew him from the law. He did not desire or seek public office; there was always a public demand for his services, and he could not help but hear and respond to it. It will be seen in this chapter that he was engaged in important causes, and in their conduct displayed all the powers of a good advocate.

Judge Sheldon has written for this book the following character sketch of Greenhalge as a lawyer. It shows well in what esteem he was held by the members of his profession : —

"As a lawyer, it was well said by one of our most able judges that he never found it necessary to give up candor and manners in order to fight hard and prevail. So another eminent judge, now deceased, spoke, after presiding in a case which was prosecuted by Greenhalge and defended by one of the most skilful lawyers, of the pleasure he had felt in hearing a case fought hard and closely by men who were both able lawyers and upright gentlemen. He did not fail to bring out the whole strength of his client's position, and he was never reluctant to meet the hardest onset or the most obstinate defence that could be made by his opponent. His powers of oratory and discussion were unfailing; but he never sought by these powers to mask any unfairness of argument or any distortion of truth and justice. Utterly loyal to his client, he was unfailing in his loyalty to the court. He was eager to obtain victory for his client, and he could toil terribly for this end; but he could not fight his forensic battles otherwise than fairly and honorably. He was a sincere man; he could not deceive himself, and he would not deceive others. He was a lover of justice, and he realized the fact, so often overlooked by sciolists, that under our system of administering the law justice can best be practically obtained when the opposing interests are each zealously supported and vindicated with the greatest acumen and professional ardor, with an impartial tribunal finally to hold the balance between them. So he sincerely and with an earnest zeal, but fairly and courteously, supported the claims of his client, and expected and welcomed the same conduct from his opponent. If any unfair means were used against him, he was capable of an honest indignation that could trample upon such means and bring them to naught. He loved the truth; and his bearing, his demeanor, the tones of his voice, the very features of his countenance, his heart and mind manifesting themselves in all that he said and did, showed this love of truth so plainly that none could fail to see and appreciate it.

"He was successful as a lawyer. Early in his professional career, he found that he had obtained a good practice, which was increasing yearly. There is no room for doubt that had he continued in the active practice of his profession he would have attained both wealth and that measure of fame which is within the reach of the practising lawyer. He turned his attention to public affairs, and his renown is the greater. But he was the same man as a lawyer that he was in other walks of life. His practice was a varied one; and he did all his work well; it was ever his habit to rise at least to the level of each occasion, and to discharge successfully whatever duty came to his hand. 'The brave make danger opportunity;' and each new difficulty was for him a stepping-stone to new success.

"I have said that he would doubtless have gained wealth had not his attention been turned from the law to politics. But he never practised law in the commercial spirit; he was not inclined to magnify the pecuniary value of his services, or to consider his own emolument so much the object to be striven for as the welfare of his client. He desired professional success; he was ambitious to attain it; the contests of the Bar suited his eager nature. His arguments to juries were strong and effective, just as in political affairs his speeches were influential and persuasive. He knew what to say, and how to say it; and while his wit and sarcasm and force of denunciation made his arguments and speeches attractive and fascinating, the unflinching manliness and integrity that constituted the basis of his nature shone forth in all that he said, and gave the weight and strength that carried conviction to the minds of those whom he addressed. He had the qualities of the sound lawyer; he was —

'Strong to keep upright the old,
   And wise to buttress with the new,
Prudent as ever are the bold,
   Clear-eyed as only are the true.'"

Such was Greenhalge as a lawyer, in the opinion of Judge
Sheldon, a high authority. As an orator his fame was of course
far greater. He spoke upon a vast variety of occasions,—
anniversaries, dedications, receptions, and funerals,— all the
multiplicity of calls that come to a distinguished speaker he
responded to willingly, and with never-failing eloquence, if
not always with equal brilliancy. Even before he was elected
to Congress, his reputation was wide-spread.

The first speech I shall mention was delivered in the Old
South Church, Boston, in 1877; he spoke then in company with
many distinguished men to demand the preservation of that
historic building which the spirit of patriotism has saved for
the people, that it may remain an enduring monument of the
great deeds of their ancestors. He appealed eloquently to
public sentiment, and introduced a striking passage from the
history of almighty Rome.

He delivered the Fourth of July oration in Lowell in
1878. His speech on this occasion I have inserted entire. It
is a good example of his style; it is fervid and glowing, and
full of patriotic fire.

"MR. MAYOR, LADIES AND GENTLEMEN,— In this assembly
there are, I presume, men of various nationalities, — men differ-
ing from one another in religious creed, in the complexion of
their skin, and in their condition in life. But on this day we
are specially reminded that all who compose this promiscuous
throng — foreign and native born, Protestant and Catholic,
Christian and Infidel, black man and white, rich man and poor,
— stand upon a common level; for every man before me is the
equal of his fellow, because he is, or may be, clothed with the
dignity of American citizenship. If I should wish to obtain an
audience of the rulers of other lands, I should have to walk
through lines of bayonets, through ranks of courtiers, and to
conform in all particulars to an inexorable law of ceremony
which is there the divine law. Here things are different. I

know, as I look upon this assembly, made up of all classes and conditions of men, — of capitalists, tradesmen, laborers, — I know that I am standing face to face with the rulers of America; there is nothing of ceremony required here, no empty forms to be complied with, no useless splendor, no royal pomp, — there is nothing royal here but the royal spirit of equality!

"Now, what is this equality I speak of? We hear much about equality, but what does it mean as we find it here? They had a kind of equality in France during the Revolution. If a man appeared superior to his fellows, if he had a clearer brain, a nobler heart, if he had more money or more virtue than they, the headsman's axe soon put a stop to his dangerous career. The old robber, Procrustes, had a craving for equality among mankind. When he captured a prisoner, he put him upon an iron bed; if the victim was too short, he stretched him upon a rack until he attained the requisite length; if too long for the bed, he shortened him by the simple process of amputation. This sort of equality is equality in chains. The equality we mean is not of this stamp. The spirit of equality which prevails here is the spirit which gives the greatest opportunity to every man for the highest development; which frees every man from the shackles of caste; which insures to honest industry the reward of its labors; which visits condemnation upon the base, the idle, and the vicious in whatever sphere of life they may be found; which takes this man or that man from whatsoever source he has sprung, and, as a fitting crown to a life of industry, honesty, and heroic self-denial, makes him a ruler of the people. We read that during the transfiguration of the Saviour of mankind upon the mountain, the fashion of his countenance was altered and his raiment became white and glistening; and thus, speaking with all reverence, if a man in our land, however humble his station, should be transfigured by the divinity of genius, this garb of equality, like the raiment of Christ, will take on new glory and shape itself to adorn the exaltation of its wearer.

"I look over and beyond these faces, and I seem to see a figure seated upon the hills. It is the genius of Freedom; and why is it that this fair and majestic shape sits upon *our* hills and gladdens our land with her beautiful smile? Did she come unsolicited? Was she easily won? No. She was chained like Andromeda to a rock, with the monster of Despotism keeping guard over her, when the young nation of the west came, like Perseus, to slay the monster and set the beauteous captive free. Every right which gives sweetness and dignity to your daily life was paid for in the ruddy drops that flowed from heroic hearts, — the men who made this republic did indeed coin their hearts' blood into drachmæ, and in that precious coin bought for themselves and for you liberty. Look at the nation's history. Upon that history three great wars stand out in lines of fire. When the smoke of the first war rolled away, the world saw for the first time a nation of freemen; and a voice was heard, the voice of Thomas Jefferson, proclaiming that 'all men are born free and equal.' This thought was not original with Jefferson. Fifty years before the Declaration of Independence was written, a Frenchman had uttered the same thought; and a thousand years or more before Jefferson was born, the Roman lawyers had written in their books, 'Omnes homines sunt natura æquales.' But the Roman and the Frenchman saw merely a radiant vision. Jefferson declared a living truth; and though men in all ages had babbled about liberty and equality, it was in America that these names first became realities. And the music of those melodious words of Jefferson's was heard far and wide. It floated across the Atlantic; the French peasant lifted his wan face from his slavish toil, and as he caught the strange music that issued from the wide portals of the west, a new light came into his sad eyes and a new hope thrilled his heart. The Irish cottager heard it, and exulted as he shouldered his pike and strode once more swiftly forward to the midnight rendezvous on the lonely heath. The weary and heavy-laden of every clime were cheered by the voice of Freedom. Liberty in America illuminated not only the west; its rays penetrated to the darkness of Siberia.

"The second great war confirmed and enlarged the rights of the young republic. A navy sprang into being which gave lustre and power to a flag hitherto almost unknown. The declaration of human rights made by Jefferson was repeated, this time by the broadsides of a fleet. Men who had been torn

from their homes by press-gangs heard that declaration of
rights with joy; and when Paul Jones lighted up the English
Channel with the flashes of his victorious guns, all Europe fell
to seriously considering this strange doctrine of freedom and
equality, which made men fight so well.

"And the third great war, — why, its drum-beats, its death-
shots, are ringing in your ears to-day. Most of you remember
the opening scenes of that war. You remember the terrible
April days of 1861; you remember the great fear that fell upon
all men, how the keepers of the house trembled, and strong
men bowed themselves. Your own Sixth Regiment had gone
through Baltimore then, — the two men whose bones lie under
that column had been shot or stoned to death in that city. A
pale and anxious people turned to Abraham Lincoln asking
what could be done, what was constitutional and what was
possible, could the nation be saved; and in an agony of suspense awaited his answer. And Abraham Lincoln said calmly:
'This is my answer. Listen!' And in the silence and fear of
that terrible hour the answer came; it was the measured tread
of seventy-five thousand men marching *unconstitutionally* to
save the Constitution and the country! You remember, too,
as the contest went on, how Bull Run went like a blot into
our history; how Fredericksburg and Chancellorsville fell like
heavy blows on the nation's breast.

"You remember how one day we heard here in our streets
nothing but the roll of muffled drums and the strains of the
Dead March, as we carried our dead to the grave; how another
day, as fresh regiments filed through the city on their way to
battle, these streets rang with the thundering chorus, 'We are
coming, Father Abraham, three hundred thousand more!'
You remember, too, how Vicksburg and Gettysburg lighted up
that memorable Fourth of July fifteen years ago, and how, at
last, Grant's army, issuing from the hell of the Wilderness, like
a 'thing of blood' pinned Lee to the walls of Richmond, while
Sherman's bayonets, glancing like lightning from the mountains
to the sea, completed that circle of flame in which rebellion at
length met its death! Now, my friends, have I told you a
tale of little meaning, —

'A tale of little meaning, though the words are strong'?

"No. It is because true-hearted men made tracks of blood on the snow at Valley Forge, it is because Lawrence gave up his heroic life in Boston Bay, it is because thousands of the flower of our youth are to-day lying in nameless graves in Southern lands, that we are able to gather here now and thank the God of Battles for the blessings of Freedom and of Peace.

"My friends, the Genius of Freedom is a spirit fair, but inexorable. Other guardian deities are content with meaner sacrifices, — with the flesh of bullocks and the blood of lambs. But Freedom turns away from such offerings. She comes and asks the mother for the blood of her first-born; she says, 'I must have the tears of the widow and the orphan; I must see the anguish of strong men, — the eternal sorrow of pure hearts. Nothing less will content me or purify and save the nation.' And you who have given these precious offerings, you who have built up this majestic temple where the Spirit of Freedom dwells with Law at her right hand and Equality upon her left, —will you allow a roving tramp, a communistic loafer, to raise his hand and harm a single stone of it? No. Plunder and violence — socialism — or whatever it is called, has no place here. The skies of Europe may be reddened by rebellious fires, assassination may try to cut off an old man from the few days of life left him; for Despotism begets Disaffection and Rebellion, — one implies and creates the other. But there need be no fear from such danger here. You have heard the boast that

'Britannia needs no bulwarks,
No towers along the steep.'

That may all be true. The danger nowadays is not from foreign enemies, but from internal discontent and dissension. But I say that this Republic has already erected bulwarks against this danger. As I stand here, I can see a chain of impregnable fortresses. In front I see a school-house; just beyond stands a poor man's cottage, reared by the labor of years, and every timber in it, every blade of grass that grows around it, is as dear to the spirit of our equal laws as the palace of the millionaire; there, behind those trees, I know that the tower of the Court House rises, and there I see the gleaming cross of a Christian church. Here we have a quadrilateral of mighty forces, — education, industry crowned with plenty, even-handed justice, and religion teaching the beauty of holiness. Here, too, we find no undue accumulation of property in the hands of one man; we have done away with the law of primogeniture, which allowed one man to live in extravagant luxury while ten men starved at his gate; we have freedom of bequest, indeed, but the law of entail is opposed to the genius of the people. In a small city like Lowell our owners of real estate are numbered by thousands; and our laboring-classes have to-day some twelve millions of dollars standing to their credit in our savings-banks; and even the poorer laborers find their real interest in the well-being of society. There is another class, too, — a class of trained and intelligent men, who are not rich, who do not hold riches to be the choicest prize that earth can offer; their minds are stored with the lore of the ages; they keep before their eyes the noblest ideals, their ears are quick to catch the cry of suffering men; they take broad and philosophical views of all social questions; they are the champions of the poor and the down-trodden, the heralds of science, the very flower of the forces of progress. Here, then, is our standing army; and with such fortresses and such an army we may emphatically say that the republic is safe.

"But there is a danger which is to be guarded against, — a danger of a more insidious nature, which may gradually and slowly but surely corrupt and canker the wreath of blessings which encircles the radiant brows of Freedom. Jefferson dreaded this danger and warned the people against it, and Macaulay has described the terrible shape with the gloomy fervor of a Jeremiah. Political power swayed by ignorance and selfishness can do more harm than cannon and bayonets, than all the banded armies of the world. Consider that danger a moment. Here kingly power is put into the hands of the humblest citizen; and as you hate and despise the tyranny of kings, see to it that our republican kings do not become tyrants. Ignorance is the parent of oppression. Let each man, then, strive to cast out ignorance. Knowledge and wisdom are hostile to tyranny, for 'oppression maketh a wise man mad.' If you do not want tyranny in another man, get wisdom, get knowledge, and when you have got them you will have more power but less disposition yourselves to tyrannize over your fellow-man.

"The American Revolution was achieved by a people full of knowledge and understanding. Every man had intelligence enough to know what his rights were and courage to defend them. The drummer-boy who was shot dead at Concord Bridge had studied the relations of the colony and the mother country as closely as Thomas Jefferson or John Adams; and it was this equal education which made at once the truest and purest equality the world has ever seen, and the strongest nation. Kings, lords, and commons have passed out of sight; distinctions of rank are abolished; an aristocracy of wealth can never foist itself upon this country, — the only aristocracy fit to exist here is the aristocracy of virtue and intelligence, and that is an order of nobility to which, under our just and equal laws, every man can and ought to belong. If there must be classes of society, let the barrier be such that the cunning workman, the man of intellect, of skill, the man of pure life, the man who loves his fellow-man, may pass unchallenged wherever he desires to go, and find a hearty welcome. Let the laborer love his employer, and let his employer give him cause to love him. Let the poor man cultivate the virtues of sobriety and industry, and *get rich;* and let the rich man see to it that the sleep of the laboring-man is sweet.

"In some organizations, before a man is allowed to vote upon a question he is called upon to remember the sacred obligations of the order, and to consider well the effect of his action. And when we, fellow-citizens, are called upon to exercise the highest privilege of freemen, to give our opinion upon some complex and vital question of government, it would be well to pause a little and recall our obligations to the republic, to our families, and to our Maker. Weigh well the character of our public men, seek for men of honesty and ability; but let them be, at all events, *honest* men. Honor God by honoring his noblest work. The old song says, 'It is good to be merry and wise,' but it is better to be 'honest and true.' All men are selfish; but there are different kinds of selfishness. One man wants power and greatness, and to attain his end tramples on the

rights of his fellow-men and on every principle of honor and
decency; another man wants power, but wants it to make his
fellow-men happy. His highest ambition is

> ' To scatter blessings o'er a smiling land,
> And read his history in a nation's eyes.'

"Give your interest, then, into the keeping of righteous and
strong men, who find in your happiness *their* happiness, and
who believe the true glory of their country to be *their* glory.
And when you find a man clutching at riches while he 'fools
the crowd with glorious lies,' deceiving and betraying a people
whom he has sworn to protect and support, defiling a nation's
honor for the passing applause of a mob, swindling a government and carrying off the swindle with a joke, — when you find
such a man, blast him with that chosen curse which God holds
in store for the wretch who 'owes his greatness to his country's
ruin !'

"My friends, we talk about national corruption. It is only
the aggregate of individual corruption. There can be no
national or public virtue without private virtue. You cannot
reform the country until you have reformed yourselves. Let
the work of reformation begin to-day. Raise your own standard
of conduct. Your public men will be compelled to conform to
it. In this way, and only in this way, may the second century
of the republic continue and heighten the glories of the first.
In this way only may we be sure that in this favored land
'there be no decay, no leading into captivity, and no complaining in our streets.'"

The reader has already seen the note in his diary which
tells of his manner of preparing his speeches. The address he
was then at work upon was given on Memorial Day at Concord, Mass., May 31, 1881, and is as follows : —

"FRIENDS AND FELLOW-CITIZENS, — Twenty years ago this
country of ours drew a full breath, and found itself a nation.
It was amid the tumult of drum, of cannon, and the quick
tread of marching hosts that this impulse of real national life
was first felt. The effort made to divide the republic proved
it to be indivisible. For four years the smoke and flame of

civil war hid the republic from the world, and Despotism, sitting on his well-guarded but ever-threatened throne, pointing Westward, said, 'Behold! those flames are writing the doom of popular government and human rights.' But a wind from Heaven blew, the cloud of smoke and flame was lifted, and the young Titan of the West was seen standing flushed and breathless, covered with dust and blood, but erect and radiant as Hyperion, his foot upon the neck of Rebellion, his face smiling as he listened to the song of thanksgiving chanted by ransomed slaves and by a redeemed republic.

"And so once a year — at least once a year — you assemble to speak and to think of the precious dead who upon the field of blood, in hospital or prison, have

> 'sunk to rest,
> By all their country's wishes blest;'

and for this purpose you have set apart and consecrated one of these days of the latter spring, — a flowery boundary, as it were, between spring and summer, when the youthful year, smiling farewell to gladsome May, reaches forward to take the roses which June is bringing, — and all over the country, from the sleepless founts of your Merrimac — and *my* Merrimac — to the farthest sweep of the Mississippi, year by year the narrowing ranks of the Grand Army of the republic stand over the graves of their dead, and deck them with these garlands of the opening year. As your bugles and drum-beats are heard, Commerce droops her flag to half-mast; Industry, with finger on her lips, ordains silence in workshop and factory; and the day is filled with the lamentation of a great people. Lamentation, did I say? Not entirely so, — no! There is hope and joy and inspiration in a day like this; and as the files of the dead are marshalled, and move by in solemn review to the music of a grateful nation's blessings and praise, and we look again into eyes now shining with heavenly light that we know were closed at Antietam, Vicksburg, Port Hudson, these bugles of the Grand Army, ringing from one end of the continent to the other, seem like the nation's challenge to Corruption and Mortality, demanding, 'O Death, where is thy sting? O Grave, where is thy victory?'

"But it may be asked, why this same memorial ceremony year after year? Do these banners fly merely 'in monumental mockery'? Why this annual commingling of flags, drums, trumpets, flowers, graves, and the weak words of lamentation and praise? It comes, you may say, with dreary sameness, — there is about it a 'damnable iteration.' No! there is no sameness here. We dwell in no sleeping palace. The river flows by your city to-day as it did last year, and for countless years before, bearing to you the music of its tributary rills and the coolness and freshness of mountain heights. But every drop of water in its current is a new creation; every wavelet, eddy, and ripple is a new combination of matter. There is nothing new under the sun, we are told. The elements are from the beginning; they change not, they are the same; and yet they are *not* the same. Their existence is in the mind of man; they change as the mind of man changes, and that changes with the moment. You are not what you were last year. You differ from your former selves by the countless experiences of a year. Photograph the world at two different moments and you have two different pictures, and to the clear-seeing eye the difference is infinite and incalculable.

"Look at the 'World's large spaces.' On one hand you see a vast empire stunned by the assassination of its ruler; here, an oppressed people struggling at last into the light of freedom; there, the destiny of Christendom, the movements of armies and fleets, diverted into new courses by the last breath issuing from the lips of a dying statesman; and, in the realm of thought, some long-buried truth, suddenly throwing off the cerements of the grave, appearing before the astonished eyes of men, like a risen Saviour; and all these things have happened within less time than is required for the earth to complete its flaming circle round the sun!

"And so we stand here this year, new beings, with new hopes and fears and thoughts, under new conditions and in new circumstances. Let me ask you if it is well to stand year by year over these graves, to listen to the voices which come from them, to take counsel of the dead. Do these voices tell us anything which makes it well for a great people, pressing onward in the rush of life and business, to pause, to listen, and to heed? The men who speak to us from their urns to-day are worthy of our respect. They loved their country, — they were 'faithful unto death.'

"And what says this Voice that we hear above these muffled drums? It says, 'Keep in safety and honor and as a sacred trust the country which we redeemed with our blood.' What is it they ask of us? Duty to our country, — patriotism. It is the least they can ask; it is the most!

"Duty to country? Patriotism? What is this spirit of patriotism, and how is it revealed? Is it a spirit that appears only with the roll of drums, amid sounds of trampling hosts and tragic thunders, illumined by the blaze of serried columns, guiding like an angry God the storm of shot and shell, and at last folding in bloody shrouds the dead who died for their country? This is one of its manifestations, but not its best, or noblest, or most heroic. Thanks to the God of battles, that manifestation of this majestic spirit has passed; the lustrum from 1860 to 1865 was filled by that terrible presence, and the republic lives in safety and peace.

"How does the spirit of patriotism manifest itself to-day? What are the essential elements of the true patriotic character? It seems to me that in this age, in this country, considering the work required to be done for the safety and glory of the country, the prime essential in the character of a patriotic man, the very foundation of such a character, is culture. By culture I do not mean the erudition which makes the mind a chaos of unmeaning facts. I do not mean a hurricane of information in which judgment goes by the board, and the whole character drifts about like a dismantled wreck. Nor do I mean that dilettante spirit which has of late been pirouetting and posing before the world under the name of culture; nor do I mean that thin veneer of æstheticism which expresses itself so lavishly, and yet so feebly, in the painting of tiles, the decoration of china, the construction and arrangement of furniture and apparel. No; these things are not wholly to be decried. They have a value; they are blind gropings after the spirit of beauty, the first feeble movements of a new-born faculty, the 'infant crying in the night,' —

'And with no language but a cry.'

But culture is something broader and deeper and higher than all this. Culture is the equal and harmonious development of the physical, the intellectual, and the spiritual nature of man.

"To the individual, culture means self-control, — a nicely balanced and rounded character, — the faculty to make the faculties of body and mind work together with the least possible friction and to the greatest possible advantage. It means a body strong, graceful, and compact, fit to be the temple of the living God; a soul pure, aspiring, trustful, fit to be the vice-gerent of God, sent to occupy and rule that temple. It means to the nation power, majesty, victory. Tried by the touchstone of a mercenary age, it is most desirable. There is money in it, wealth, prosperity, greatness. History shines with splendid instances of the truth which I state. Germany sat in the school-room for more than forty years; and Sadowa, Sedan, Paris, were the circlet of jewels that Fate awarded to her faithful labors.

"When Asiatic barbarians were thundering at the gates of Europe, it was a nation of scholars that confronted the invaders as the wardens of the continent. If we wonder when we read that a handful of Greeks swept a mighty host of Persians into the sea, we cease to wonder when we learn that the flashing intellect of Themistocles controlled one division of the Greeks, the seraphic purity of Aristides inspired another, and, better still, Æschylus, fresh from communion with the gods and with god-like Prometheus, fought with his brother in the ranks as a private soldier. And it was the philosophy of Franklin, the rich learning of Adams, Otis, Jefferson, and Lee, and the ripe experience of Washington that compelled men to write over the wide portals of the West, 'Consecrate to freedom forever.' And physical culture is of paramount, supreme importance; it is the basis of all other culture; without it nothing else is possible. The philosophic Greek knew this, and he made the wreath of the Olympic victor more precious than the laurels of poet, soldier, or statesman.

"But culture cannot be general, effective, national, without loyalty to duty in all classes and conditions of men, in all walks of life, in humble as well as high stations. We cannot have virtue in our great men until we have virtue in the commonalty.

The stern spirit of Duty leads us all at times into silent, lonely, and obscure places. But nowadays men think too much of public acclaim; the trumpet must be blown before them; they must have salutations in the market-place; their good deeds must bring them glory of men. And true-hearted, honest men do their work in a spiritless and hopeless fashion, because it seems obscure and unimportant in the eyes of God and man. But I tell you there is no position in life, no station, no condition, so humble, so obscure, so unimportant, that it cannot be made into a shrine where the saintly spirit of Duty may be enthroned and worshipped. That sentinel at his post holds the fate of an army in his hands; upon the pickaxe of that laborer working in the street depend the health, the comfort, and welfare of a great city; every stroke of that mechanic's hammer is telling the story of the wreck or the salvation of some great steamship. Lately, you have seen a world doing homage to that iron Captain whose genius led your bayonets in the path of Victory; you have heard the name of another great soldier uttered by thousands of freemen as the symbol of their political faith; and a third you have seen elevated to as high a station as any man can reach in a country where all men are 'born free and equal.' But I tell you that high above the name of every captain, not upon any particular page of history, but upon every page and in every line, in every word, and in the people's heart of hearts, is written the record of that nameless legion who, in the ranks, in the trenches, in every place and post assigned them, did their work in a manly, honest, thorough way, and to whose simple lives, loyalty, fidelity, obedience gave a 'daily beauty' which has now blossomed and brightened into immortal glory. Yes, it is the individual that must do the work of the world. We talk about the government, the party, the church, the association. These are abstractions, and abstractions never did any real work. It is the individuals who compose them that must do the work; it is you and I and all of us. The man who keeps his own house in order, who educates and maintains himself and family to the best of his ability, is doing patriotic work; the man who, to use a common phrase, plays his game for all it is worth, is a true hero, — as much of a hero as the Greek who struck at

Marathon, or the soldier who made part of the living rampart
of loyalty at Gettysburg.

" But another force is needed to set culture in full operation,
to give it its full effect, — courage. Men fail nowadays in their
good works from lack of courage. They see the path of duty,
— they mean to follow it, but they faint and fall by the way-
side. A great opportunity comes, a great deed is to be done,
voice, hand, heart, are ready, a pæan of joyful thanksgiving
already trembles on the lips of angels and men, but consequences
loom up before us like the giant spectres of the Hartz mountains; we shrink back appalled, and Opportunity, sad as a
rejected angel, departs from us forever. We need the calm,
patient courage that ' looks on tempests, yet is never shaken ;'
that heeds not, though vituperation howls itself hoarse; that
falters not, though old associations are sundered, old friendships
broken forever; that keeps on its course in spite of the condemnation of good men, not yet able to see the shining goal at
which we aim; that flinches not from the pale face of Failure ;
that moves on steadily and irresistibly, step by step, rising from
height to height, until from the clear upper air we hear a voice
of triumph saying, ' Mine is the deed that duty dictates ; the
consequences are for God.'

" And if to-day or at any time we hear the discordant voices
of baseness and selfishness filling the country ; if we see Falsehood, Fraud, and Cunning enthroned in our halls of Justice ;
if we hear in the high places of the nation the tinkling bells
upon the head of the fool ; if we see ambitious men standing
on stilts and fancying themselves on pedestals ; if they,

> ' like angry apes,
> Play such fantastic tricks before high Heaven
> As make the angels weep,'

then will rise up to Heaven from the lips of every honest man
a prayer for that heart of courage, that body of health and
strength and grace, — that soul mighty and beautiful with true
education and culture, —

> ' That still, strong man in a blatant land —
> Whatever they call him, what care I ?
> Aristocrat, Democrat, Autocrat, one
> Who can rule and dare not lie.'

" Thus have I attempted, in a feeble way, to interpret to you
the voice of the Dead which speaks to us to-day. As I stand
here, I wonder if ever in succeeding years you will shrink from
the faces of the immortal host? — if ever, conscious of having
been recreant to your duty, false to the great trust they have
committed to you, you will tremble before the indignant
majesty of these dead soldiers when they come and ask you to
render an account of this sacred trust? God forbid! Let us
hope that in the years to come, when the last bugle of the
Grand Army is silenced, — when all that is left on earth of the
Grand Army itself is but dust and ashes, — that our children
and their posterity to the latest generation may stand by the
graves which hold these precious ashes, and, looking up at the
radiant arch of the republic, glittering at one extremity with
the spray of the Pacific, and at the other bright with the first
smile of Morning as she ' rides shoreward on Atlantic waves,'
and seeing under that vast expanse only the chosen dwelling-
place of Liberty and Justice, Peace and Prosperity, they may
feel and understand the goodness of the God who has given
them ' beauty for ashes, the oil of joy for mourning ; the gar-
ment of praise for the spirit of heaviness.' "

At the Semi-Centennial of Lowell, April 1, 1886, Greenhalge was selected for the orator of the day, and delivered
his address in Huntington Hall. He spoke beautifully on
that occasion, inspired by sentiments of loyalty to his native
town.

" MR. MAYOR, FRIENDS AND FELLOW-CITIZENS, — As I enter
upon the honorable duty assigned me by your courtesy and
partiality, I am impressed by a profound sense of how much
of whatever tends to give comfort and inspiration to life I
owe to the city of Lowell, its institutions and its influences,
and I rejoice that this occasion affords me an opportunity of
offering humbly and reverently a tribute of earnest gratitude
to the city of my affections, my memories, and my hopes. As
I have said, the duty I am to perform is an honorable one ; it
is to me something more, — it is a duty welcome, agreeable,
and full of interest, because it requires me to review — curso-
rily, it is true — a cycle of municipal history marked by a

development and a prosperity little short of marvellous. A wise physician, who was still in the freshness of manhood, but who had learned how uncertain human life was and what perils and vicissitudes it must encounter and through what wonderful experiences it must pass every moment, stated his age in these words: 'For my life, it is a miracle of thirty years.' How much greater a miracle we are called upon to contemplate to-day, — a half-century of the life of a great community, comprehending thousands and tens of thousands of individual lives with all their countless experiences! And at the outset, how strange and mysterious seems the transition by which in little more than fifty years a rude Indian fishing-village, maintaining a precarious existence by the scanty means possessed by a barbarous people, has given place to a community considerable in numbers, progressive, thriving, and intelligent, controlled by morality, inspired by religion, and rejoicing in all the 'glorious gains' of learning and art! The wigwam of the savage, the type of one epoch, has vanished; the type of another epoch rises before us in all the beauty of proportion, combining strength, symmetry, and airy grace, — the great Merrimac chimney, illustrating no bloody contest, no freak of art, but, as it towers above and yet aids constantly the toiling city at its base, proclaiming by day and night, to the morning and the evening, a truth charged with more of blessing to humanity, to you and to me, than the Tower of Pisa or the Column of Trajan. And what mighty force or what gracious power brought about this wonderful change? It was industry, yes, industry, throned at the confluence of our shining rivers, that, with Christ-like touch, transmuted the water of barbaric life into the wine of civilization and progress.

"And the community whose history we are contemplating was one of no ordinary character, and at the beginning it entered upon a daring experiment. The building of the first factory in Lowell was an event of more than local importance. That event was a revelation to America, a revelation to the world. It was a declaration of industrial independence scarcely less momentous in its results than the declaration of political independence in 1776. I know that the preliminary draft of this declaration was made at Waltham, but it was here in

Lowell that the principles of the declaration were adopted, put in action, and published to the world. And in the glimmering dawn of Lowell's history could be seen the promise of a prosperity which would soon diffuse its warmth and radiance over the whole country; in the founding of Lowell was involved the founding of many other manufacturing communities based upon the intelligent and philosophic plan adopted here, and even in our earliest day it needed no prophet's eye to look into the future and to see the airy circlet jewelled with prosperous cities which would soon crown the stern forehead of New England.

"As we look at the great fact which we call Lowell and mark the influences radiating from it, the results, direct and indirect, of its establishment, we are impelled to trace back the stream of events to its source, to analyze this progress and prosperity and discover its original elements, to find the faraway solitary springs of thought and action, the results of which are spread before us now. I am told that among all the treasures of art and beauty in Florence, the works of sculptor and painter, the marvels of palace and church, the images of statesman, captain, and saint, there is one grand figure in the sacristy of San Lorenzo which more than all else awes and impresses the beholder. It is the work of Michael Angelo, and perpetuates not so much the life or memory of any mortal man as the ideal character born of the kingly genius of the sculptor. It is known as "The Thinker," and by its attitude and expression seems to be the material representation of profound repose, but in that profound repose we know there glows the undying flame of thought; we know and feel that, as from the quiet depths of the lake the sword of Arthur suddenly flashed, so from the quiet depths of this repose action may at any moment flash to smite or to deliver the world. It is to this silent figure that the reflective mind refers all the greatness, all the power, and all the achievements of Florence. You remember that some years ago the philosopher Buckle startled the world by declaring that the number of marriages was regulated, not by affection, not by sentiment, but by the price of flour; and a long array of statistics seemed to prove the truth of the assertion. But it must be remembered, on the other hand, that nothing happens in the world of thought which does not, sooner or later, affect the price of flour; that is to say, a new reaping-machine, a new song, a new political theory, are forces which soon make themselves felt in the ordinary every-day life of every one of us. And so, for the beginning of Lowell, for the original creative force, we must look to the solitary chamber of the thinker, wherein we see him seated in the very attitude of the sculptor's thinker, absorbed in studying the complicated machinery of the power-loom, and the comfort and development of the more complicated machinery of humanity.

"If it was wise to stock a factory with the best inanimate machinery, Francis Cabot Lowell thought it wise to obtain the best human machinery too. The welfare of the operative, mental, moral, and physical, was as important in any wise man's scheme of a factory as the ten thousand horse-power of the river. The factory system as then established in this country and in England was execrable. This was twenty years before Shaftesbury had led public opinion in England to the coal-pit and the factory, and showed how stunted and deformed, how feeble and hopeless, how ignorant and depraved, men, women, and children had become under the cruel system followed by selfish employers. The factory system was looked on as accursed; and if the daughters of New England were to run the looms in the new enterprise, a very different system must be adopted. And so the great plan was formulated; the neat, well-kept boarding-house, with pleasant, homelike habits and restrictions, was established; the church, the library, and the lecture-room followed; and religion, culture, and refinement lent their sweet influences to the life of toil. A new doctrine was proclaimed, — the welfare of the employed was a necessary factor to the success of the employer, just as the welfare of the employer was necessary to the success of the employed. They were one in interest, one in the loss and in the gain, one in prosperity and in adversity. Milton tells us of a music so divine that it 'would create a soul under the ribs of death.' Lowell discovered and applied a principle that created a soul under the ribs of political economy.

"The life of this man counted by years was short; by

results, an eternity. His foot never trod the streets of our
city, yet the men whose hearts caught fire from his thought
decided that the Manchester of America should be his monument. But it is not so much a monument to the illustrious
dead as it is the active and living creation of the living
thought which warmed the soul of the founder. His life, I
say, might seem to reach to eternity; for from that seemingly
brief life, as from the fabled statue of Memnon, every sun that
rises evokes a melody which cheers and lightens the daily
toil of thousands.

"But the glowing thought was yet to be taken and beaten
and fashioned into action, and there were apt, skilful, and
heroic workers ready for this important task. Here comes
into play the mighty and indefatigable force of Patrick Tracy
Jackson, a man who seems to have had infinite resources,
indomitable courage, and exhaustless patience; whose genius,
restless and tireless, never hesitated and never allowed itself
to be baffled; a man great indeed for prosperity, but in adversity rising to colossal proportions. His powerful and original
mind has stamped itself indelibly upon the economy of our
industrial life. Not content with the herculean task of building this city of ours, he surveyed and controlled the building
of others. His eagle eye looked across the Atlantic, kept
keen watch on the experiment of George Stephenson; and
no sooner had the success of the railroad between Manchester
and Liverpool been assured than Jackson had a charter in
his hand and was at work building the railroad from Lowell
to Boston.

"Close behind Jackson appears another figure, — the commanding figure of Kirk Boott, — the incarnation of executive
ability. As this man dashes through the early history of
Lowell, there is a rush as of charging squadrons, the clank of
sabre, the jingle of spurs, and over all the tumult rings the
sharp word of command, 'Forward!' Lowell heard the word
and obeyed, and that glorious command has been ringing in our
ears ever since this great captain of industry uttered it to his
peaceful battalions. I trust the command has been obeyed
even in this last half-century.

"Lowell, Jackson, Boott, — these are the colossal figures of our history belonging to our heroic age, as Theseus, Hercules, and Jason belonged to the heroic age of Greece.

"And what a remarkable group of workers those were who first stood by the looms of Lowell! Never before in the history of mankind was such dignity, such grace, given to labor. True manhood and true womanhood then and there accepted, not merely with resignation, but with courage, cheerfulness, and hope, the burden and the destiny of the human race. These true men and true women have passed away; a new order of things has been established; but the glory which their lives gave to the morning of Lowell will, through every change, through doubt and adversity, through darkness and fear, still console and encourage their descendants and successors to the 'last syllable of recorded time.'

"With such thinkers, with such controlling minds, and with such workers, it is not surprising that marvellous results were accomplished. Has the quality of the work been kept up to the standard? Let us see. We are to deal especially with the half-century beginning in 1836 and ending at the moment of time when you are gathered together here to examine the record. There can be no question that even in that space of time there has been a great increase in material prosperity. The development has been thorough, harmonious, healthy, and symmetrical. When Industry erected a factory, Religion and Education planted a school-house and a church. Let us glance at a few figures. There is a beauty even in figures, an æsthetic aspect to statistics, as there is to everything else under the sun. When, on the thirtieth day of March, 1836, Mr. Justice Rockwell, the Speaker of the Massachusetts House of Representatives — spared to us now to grace this commemoration with the dignity of his years and the long record of an honorable and useful life, — subscribed his name to the legislative act which gave us municipal life, there were in the limits of the new city 17,633 people; to-day, in a period of great business depression, we have in our city, at the lowest estimate, 65,000 souls. The taxable property of Lowell in 1836 was $5,248,723; it is now $51,308,335. Then 40,000,000 yards of cloth were made here annually; now there are upwards of 250,000,000 yards. There are 4,776 owners of taxable real estate, so that about one to fourteen, including men, women, and children,—and we must not forget that we have 11,000 school children,—is the ratio of distribution of real estate in our city. It is true that sixty-five corporations are among these holders of real estate, but it is also true that every stock-holder in a corporation may, in a certain sense, be considered a proprietor of real estate. In our savings-banks we have $12,311,000, owned by 36,520 depositors; an average of $340 to each depositor.

"We have upwards of 50,000 volumes, good, bad, and in-different, in our libraries; and as for our societies organized to promote learning, charity, art, social culture and enjoy-ment, and every good thing under the sun, their name is Legion.

"Now, when Lowell began, the population may be described as homogeneous,—they belonged to one race, with the same mode of living, the same habits of thought, the same religion, and the same patriotic past and future. This state of things, it is perhaps unnecessary to say, has been changed. Exiles from many lands have sought here a larger liberty, and a wider opportunity for securing life, liberty, and the pursuit of happi-ness. Now, as my illustrious predecessor, who stood here ten years ago, pointed out, there were great fears about the flood of immigration which poured in upon Lowell; those fears have proved groundless. You have seen that wonderful work of engineering, that cyclopean wall of Francis,—separating the river and the canal, which most of us know familiarly as the 'Canal Walk,'—a curve of beauty and strength, repressing on one side the wild torrents of the Merrimac and on the other guarding and distributing, as industry requires, the orderly, placid, and effective elements of strength drawn from the same rushing river. In the same way the wise policy of the makers of Lowell, not discouraging but controlling the tide of immigration, drew from it the elements of strength, order, and progress, and made those elements a part of the people, and gave to that part a share of the common prosperity.

"Of course our population became cosmopolitan; it repre-sented many races,—every part of the British Isles, of Cana-dian France, and the British Provinces, unified Germany, free

Sweden, and free Italy, and even more remote countries, — all were and are represented among our people.

"There were gloomy prophets who foresaw the extinction of the ancient and original type. The New England race was to die out or be lost sight of in the whelming tide of new-comers. To what a thin line had it been reduced already! Yes; but remember that it was the thin line of an unconquer-able army, — which might narrow but could never recoil, — of which history must write, 'It never dies and it never surrenders!' Look through two centuries and a half and observe the little band appointed to reclaim a continent and give new beauty to freedom. Foremost is Miles Standish, the standard-bearer of an indomitable race, planted upon the rock of Plymouth and facing with unquailing eye the wilderness, the storm, and the future. There is the standard! The count-less voices of those who have found protection, liberty, and justice under its folds assure us that there is no blemish, no stain, upon the standard yet. And I say to all, to those born beneath it and to those who have come from afar to seek its shelter, There is the standard! Make it more glorious if you can, but never suffer it by any deed or word or thought of yours to be tarnished. Bring to the land where it flies the best your nationality has. To one, I say, Give us a ray from the wis-dom of Grattan, a flash from the patriotic fire of Emmet. To another, Come to us glowing with the devotion of La Salle, speak to us as if you had communed with the soul of Montcalm. Let the spirit of Garibaldi inspire your every action. Let your loyalty and honor be as stainless as the sword of the great Marquis, your purpose high as the heart of Hampden; and if you loiter, the trumpet voice of Gustavus shall impel you to the front. In this way these different elements can be har-moniously blended with the ancient and abiding type to form a splendid composite character made up of every nation's best.

"But new Lowell, as we term it, has actually been put to the test, with a result which would gladden the soul of Cap-tain Standish.

"Midway in our half-century, almost precisely twenty-five years ago, a great national crisis arose. Men's minds were at white heat. The irrepressible conflict was to be settled by wager of battle. North and South had been moving on to the decisive point. Then, for a moment, suspense fell upon the country. There was a lull, a stillness, that was not peace. The people of Lowell pursued their quiet industry apparently as usual, the bells rang, the looms hummed, and the rush of Pawtucket over its rocky bed was heard in the quiet night. But a deep anxiety prevailed in Lowell, as everywhere else; some great event seemed to be brooding in the air. And Lowell must be on the alert; she had a reputation to make. Concord and Lexington might dream in the shadow of their monuments, and if any ominous sound was heard, they might fancy it was but the midnight march of Pitcairn echoing through their dreams. But the quick ear of Lowell at length caught a sound faint and far off, but appalling. Above the sound of bell and loom and the rush of Pawtucket was heard the footstep of Rebellion! — Rebellion, rising to stupendous proportions — vast and dark and terrible, as Milton's fiend. In this very hall where you are gathered now, the men of Lowell assembled to bid farewell to kindred and friends before rushing into the wild and bloody tumult which awaited them. That hurried march of theirs proved that the loyal men of America were ready for the conflict; and when the sun set that day on Baltimore, the drum-beats of the gathering North were heard on every side. From Baltimore to Appomattox the honor of Lowell was upheld, not only by the great leader, whose daring and resolute genius first declared to a hesitating nation the inflexible principles on which alone the War of the Rebellion could be brought to a successful issue, and who convinced the world that, whatever else it might mean, the name of Butler never stood for half-way measures or a dubious policy, — not only by him, I say, but by thousands of brave and true men who, following the colors of one regiment or another, represented Lowell in almost every conflict from Gettysburg to the Gulf; and old Lowell and new Lowell clasped hands in the hour of national peril.

"I do not pretend to present here any detailed history of Lowell, to narrate events in their order, or to give biographical sketches of men prominent in our municipal life. This work

8

was done so fully and so clearly by the distinguished man who stood ten years ago where I stand now, that I could only follow in his footsteps, as to a great extent I must do now, without the advantage of that personal knowledge which gave authority and character to his testimony. It only remains for me to comment on a few of the great events of our history, to note as far as possible the permanent features and the chief characteristics of our community.

"We have had a strong progressive element, eager-eyed, fresh-hearted, watching for a new idea as men watch for the sunrise, making progress themselves, and profiting by the progress of others, ever among the foremost who delight in

'the march of mind,
In the steamship, in the railway, in the thoughts that shake mankind.'

"One bold spirit projected and built a railroad; another constructed a canal, seized in his strong grasp a careless, idle river, and made it the servant of industry; and another, after converting a barren hillside into a garden blossoming with graceful households, with one hand assisted in planting the city of Lawrence, with the other helped to subdue and draw down for our service the free waters of Winnipiseogee. And there were a host of others who in every line of human action were always to be found in the advance column; and the names of Nesmith, Livingston, and Whipple were written on the later era of Lowell, as the names of Lowell, Jackson, and Boott upon the former era.

"And we have had, too, a notable conservative element here, — cautious, sagacious men, who loved the past and eyed the future with suspicion, looking upon all change as dangerous. This element is not without value to a community. It regulates, though it cannot prevent, progress. The system of public schools, the construction of sewers, the introduction of city water, the fire-alarm telegraph, military drill in the High School, all provoked the violent opposition of this element. It would provoke a smile if I should read to you now the arguments against some of these beneficial measures. The introduction of city water, it was said, was simply arranging for a deluge before we had built an ark; as for the fire-alarm telegraph, it was regarded simply as an infernal machine which might lay the city in ruin and ashes at any moment. A witty friend of mine has a list of the remonstrants against these various improvements; but I doubt whether, if I should read over the names, I should contribute to the harmony of this occasion. But it is so with all improvements, and an improvement which does not provoke opposition cannot be of much value. Even wise men must live and learn. Remember the great English statesman who declared that he would swallow the boiler of the first steamship that crossed the Atlantic! I need not say the promise yet remains unfulfilled. But let us have charity for those who were slow to perceive merit in the great projects I have named.

"Many shining names are written in the necrology of Lowell for the past few years, — names that stood for honest worth, for benevolence, for lasting services to their fellow-men, — names that gave lustre and character to our various departments of business, — to the mill, the bank, the school, — and that seemed in some cases to add even sanctity to the Church. Your own hearts must fill the catalogue. But what a glorious company I might call around me of those who shed the sunlight of their cheerful and worthy lives upon our civic history, — the reverend men of God, the scholars, the jurists, the wits, the thinkers, and the workers!

" It was in our forum that Butler and Sweetser and Abbott awoke the admiration and apprehension of Choate; Bonney and Richardson alone are left with us to attest the reality of what seems a legendary age. It was from the pulpits of Lowell that Edson, Miles, Blanchard, and Miner preached. Banks, the bobbin-boy, began here a public career, useful and splendid, seldom vouchsafed to men. The man destined to wake the American people to the thought of liberty for others as well as for themselves, Wendell Phillips, a careless law student, dwelt among us once, playing the pranks with which even great men beguile their youth, — now satirizing society, and now climbing Dracut heights to watch the lighting of the mills, describing the resplendent spectacle in language more resplendent still. The learning and influence of John P. Robinson made him the worthy mark of the first of living satirists, the kinsman of our founder, James Russell Lowell, who ought to stand where I stand to-day, making our history shine in the light of his genius.

"And what wits and humorists, what minstrels and story-tellers, have filled our half-century with wisdom, hope, and recreation under the guise of frolic and humor! The rubicund face of Perez Fuller rises before us now; 'Governor' Brownell, the stateliest of wits, comes with the lofty port of the 'buried majesty of Denmark;' Warland, Schouler, Ball, and Goodwin join the circle, and the voice of McEvoy rings above the chimes at midnight; Lucy Larcom and Mary Eastman have been there with poem and speech: but devotees of propriety left at ten o'clock, the good old regulation hour.

"And there was always a certain gravity, a peculiar sombreness, in the humor and wit of Lowell. One or two examples will suffice. In the first contest for the mayoralty, feeling ran high; a grand type of man must be chosen to set the standard for all time (and some of us will stoutly maintain that the standard has never been lowered). Bartlett was elected, and a banquet was given to celebrate the victory. Hilarity rose to a great height, the viands were superb, and the 'foaming grape of eastern France' lent its sparkle to the hour. A pious, steady-going citizen who among other wares occasionally dealt in pictures and Bibles, had participated in the festivity. When the collector, a wag, called for the assessment, our worthy friend had grave scruples about paying money for such a cause. But a happy thought occurred to the collector, — 'Pay your share in Bibles!' And although history is silent, malice declares that the compromise was effected.

"At a meeting called to take action as to a school system, the imperious Kirk Boott was opposed to the measure, and declared that it was folly to incur any expense in its behalf. Lowell was but an experiment, and a traveller visiting the place in a few years might find only a heap of ruins. Theodore Edson replied, that if the traveller examining those ruins found among them no trace of a school-house, he would have no difficulty in assigning the cause of the downfall of Lowell. There is logic and wit enough in that retort to have made the reputation of an English prime minister!

" Now, I do not pretend to say that this community of ours is perfect. I am not here to flatter; it is not perfect. It is deficient in many respects; it lacks in public spirit. The close, fierce struggle for existence has not been so favorable as might be to broad and liberal projects in the interests of education, charity, philanthropy. Public benefactions have been comparatively few and small. All honor to those who fill that narrow circle of our benefactors in which Tyler and Thomas Nesmith are most prominent! But we have no library, hospital, art gallery, or academy to signalize the wise liberality of any living man or to commemorate the patient forethought of the dead. We have, it is true, a prospective park, planned with judgment and persistence by two devoted women, who wished the memory of their father to be linked forever with the comfort and enjoyment of a toiling people.

" Again, the community lacks in local pride and ambition. Our independent local life needs to be developed. This responsibility falls upon all of us, — upon the tradesman, the clerk, the mechanic, the journalist, the professions. Compared with other places, is our work in every line above or below the standard? Can we stand up, — mechanic, trader, teacher, lawyer, — and challenge the world to a comparison? Is there as much purity among our politicians, as much zeal and intelligence among our clergy, as in other places? I fervently trust so. As the clock strikes the closing hour of our first half-century, these questions wait for an answer. I know that the future upon which we are about to enter is dark and lowering. I do not pretend to ignore or underrate the perils gathering round us. I see the social and economic forces thrown into confusion, arraying themselves under this or that banner, and shouting strange war-cries; but I have faith to believe that courage, patience, and intelligence will soon evolve order out of this chaos; that the rights of man and the rights of property will still be safe under the standard of Miles Standish; and that under the providence of Almighty God, this city of ours, founded upon the noble thought of Francis Cabot Lowell, will stand against every storm, the example and the admiration of all coming time. "

In August, 1888, at the dedication of the Unitarian Head-quarters at The Weirs, Greenhalge delivered the principal address as follows : —

"This voice of summer is surely the voice of God, calling, as it does, from the North and the South, the East and the West, these various religious organizations to assemble here, and, under the open sky, to commune for a few short hours with the Maker of heaven and earth, the Father of us all.

"We often read of grand military demonstrations, of impos-ing naval pageants, where man's destructive forces are gathered together to show what carnage and havoc they could work, if Hell gave the word. Here we have a demonstration of a dif-ferent kind; here we see man's noblest forces arrayed to study and contrive the best way to elevate, ennoble, and to save man-kind, when Heaven gives the word. And as we glance along the shining lines marshalled here to-day, should we not be justified if we felt a thrill of pride to find that this organization of ours was in the van, and was indeed 'the Hesperus that led the starry host'? Ought we not to be the pioneers, the makers of roads and bridges, for the great army moving along the pathway of spiritual thought? Should we not hasten for-ward to occupy every height, to storm every advanced post of the enemy, so as to make the painful steps of our brethren easier, safer, and clearer? This post is, I know, one of danger, but one of glory; of struggle, but of triumph; of labor, but of rest. Let us take it, and deserve it, if we can.

"This array of intelligent faces, kindling with the warmth of the great thoughts suggested by this hour, convinces me that the Unitarian faith is a prosperous and growing fact. Wher-ever we look, we observe signs of prosperity, — we are, in fact, so prosperous that there is danger of our indulging in luxuries. Now, I suppose that as nobody realizes that he owns a house until he puts a mortgage on it, no church realizes its prosperity until it has a schism. I do not believe, however, that a schism is ever, in any sense, a witticism. If this denomination can be said to have factions within it at all, I should say there are two leading factions, and they are both small. One of these believes that we don't believe enough ; the other believes that we believe too much. There is a good deal of make-believe, you see, on the one hand ; and on the other hand, the champions of unbelief have got a creed of what they don't believe longer than any the world ever saw, composed not of thirty-nine articles, but thirty-nine hundred, and the list is increasing every day.

" There is, my friends, a beautiful and peculiar propriety in meeting here by these still waters and green pastures, under the shadow of these great hills, to confer together on the high purposes I have referred to, — purposes as clear as these sparkling waters, as heaven-reaching as the hills ; a peculiar propriety, I say, because we must remember that Jesus of Nazareth made the blue waters of Gennesaret his pulpit ; and the glory of nature, shining as to-day, the song of the birds of the air, the fragrance of the flowers of the field, the changing loveliness of sky and hill and lake, all lent their grace and grandeur to the earliest declarations of Christian truth. And if the ears of living men were deaf to that truth, the mountains heard it and the sea. And if the lips of living men are not ready to declare that truth here to-day, I doubt not that Chocorua and Winnipiseogee will repeat to us the words of life spoken to Lebanon and Jordan. Nature is an open book in which he who will may read the word of the Lord.

" Many of you, doubtless, have seen the great cathedrals of the Old World. You have looked on the multitudinous pinnacles of Milan, on the grand front of St. Peter's, — you have stood and observed Strasburg and Cologne ' kneeling in their robes of stone,' great images of devotion ; but tell me if the hand of man ever reared a cathedral as grand as this in which we now meet ?

" We have here a great lesson, a great truth, one of the distinctive truths of the Unitarian faith, — the simplicity of the truth, and the necessity of using simplicity in worship, in creed, and in all things spiritual. One of the objections urged against us is that we lack beautiful ceremonies, impressive rites and forms ; and it has been suggested that we run out and borrow of our spiritual neighbors a candlestick here, a rubric there, a rite or ceremony elsewhere, or an article of religion ; and, as they have thirty-nine articles, some of which are not in active daily use, we could easily get what we wanted, and then we

could furnish our house in the latest and most approved fashion.
I say no.   You cannot put any real life into your church
by adding the excrescences of others; you cannot widen or
strengthen its foundations by adding a spire here or a pinnacle
there.   In what guise do you want religion to come ?   Shall
she

> ‘ like gorgeous tragedy,
> With sceptred pall come sweeping by ? ’

or do you prefer that other picture of the great Puritan poet, —
shall religion appear

> ‘ devout and pure,
> Sober, steadfast, and demure,
> Her looks commercing with the skies,
> Her rapt soul sitting in her eyes ’ ?

"Some people seem to prefer religion caparisoned and appointed, like the fine lady of Banbury Cross, who

> ‘ With rings on her fingers and bells on her toes,
> Carries fine music wherever she goes.’

" Which will you choose, — the feverish and fretful magnifi-
cence of the Turkish mosque or the simple and serene majesty
of the Parthenon ?   Will you take the road to Banbury Cross
or the road to Damascus ?

"But they tell us we have no antiquity, no traditions; we
are not archæological; we are very modern, very young; we
feel like young Copperfield in presence of the old waiter who
seemed to reproach him constantly with his excessive youth.
Now, I say, this notion is entirely false.   We draw our inspiration, our life, from the very fountain-head; we go back to the
very beginning.   Our spiritual neighbors invite us to step
down the ‘ corridor of time,’ and go and see the ancient sources
of their wisdom and power.   Well, we accept the invitation.
Our friends start off at a weary pace, and we follow.   By and
by they pause.   They stop at Strasburg, at St. Peter's; they
repeat the words of Augustine, of Paul, — we cannot get them
beyond the second or the third century.   We go forward still;
we do not pause until we have passed these other shrines and
sacred places, until we have come to the very shores of Galilee;

until we listen to the words of that wondrous Son of man and of God, whose voice for nineteen centuries has been the harmony of the universe; the light of whose countenance is the civilization of the kingdoms of the earth to-day, the refuge and the hope of humanity forever. And we mean to keep the faith, not covered by the dust of ages, not tricked out by fashion or folly beyond recognition, not as the result of incorrect transmission and ignorant interpretation; but the faith in all its original simplicity, in all its original beauty and majesty. We mean to keep that faith as it was set forth when the 'goodly fellowship of the prophets' made the ages ring with their foretellings of it, as it was when 'the glorious company of the apostles' welcomed it with heart and soul, as it was when 'the noble army of martyrs' died for it to live forevermore. Keep the faith ' as it was in the beginning, is now, and ever shall be.' "

The following speech was delivered by Greenhalge at the celebration of the one hundred and fifteenth anniversary of the battle of Lexington, before the Sons of the American Revolution : —

" LADIES AND GENTLEMEN, — When I heard the President mention my name in a somewhat irregular fashion, — I forget what he called it, — I consoled myself with the reflection that ' A rose by any other name would smell as sweet,' and also by the familiar adage that you may call me by any name, provided you do not call me late to dinner.

" I regret, however, that under whatever name we are called to-day you and I will be late to dinner. I do not like to stand between a hungry audience and the meal for which they are so well prepared. It is generally my luck to lead the retreat, to be the Marshal Ney of an occasion like this. I am accustomed to that sort of disaster.

" One or two things said by General Porter excited my admiration. I respect the intelligent patriotism of that gallant son of New Hampshire who offered up so many hogsheads of rum in the cause of freedom. We can appreciate that sort of sacrifice. I am a little inclined to view with suspicion the watchword which was given by that gallant son of New Hampshire who said, 'Meet me at Medford.' That remark, permit me to say, seems to be very much in the same spirit — or after the same spirit. There was a good deal of rum consumed in the Revolution upon one side and the other, and I am very glad if it rendered any service. It does not often render any.

"I am glad, my friends, to be permitted to stand in this place to-day, and I have hastened hither because I had a desire that before this day should fade into the past, I might at least have the opportunity of paying my humble but earnest and fervent tribute to those men of Middlesex who 'fired the shot heard round the world;' and, while I must say with my friend General Swift, and with the many other friends perhaps present here to-day, that, under the conditions of your Society, I cannot be enrolled as a member, still I have a right to stand here and to speak to you, because no living man has been permitted to share more generously in the blessings springing like flowers from the bloody dews which moistened the fields of Concord and this village green of Lexington, a century and more ago. And the large-minded character of those men is shown in this, that their last will and testament was that even the stranger and the exile might be co-heirs with their own flesh and blood, their own lineal descendants, and true heirs of that priceless heritage.

"My friends, you heard those words, which always seem to be so powerful, spoken by my friend Judge Deming, — Marathon and Thermopylæ. There are certain words in history — Leuctra, Marathon, Thermopylæ — which always fall upon the ears of men like music. It is not the music of the simple euphony, of a mere silvery ode to courage; it is a music which always rises from a grand achievement, filling the world age after age with sounds that echo now. Yes, and we remember some other words which may parallel in their music the words of the ancient history, — Concord, Acton, Lexington, are invested with the same divine music for the ears of all mankind.

"You remember the impassioned exclamation, the despairing prayer of that poet and freeman who died at Missolonghi to make Greece free; you remember how, looking at the descendants of Miltiades and Pericles, he cried, 'Of the three hundred, give me three to make a new Thermopylæ!' There was no response. Yet, my friends, here, within sight of us now, the freemen of Middlesex made a new Thermopylæ without waking a single Spartan from his stony sleep.

"Give us, in the sweet spirit of this Americanism which you have combined to keep alive upon the altar, — give us illustrations not two thousand years old, when we have them here at our own doors, in our own houses, and on our own village green. Let us begin with consecrating and preserving the memorials of the heroic deeds which have been done most recently, and have been done with most effect for you and yours, your children and yourselves.

"I was struck most forcibly by the train of thought followed by my friend from Connecticut when he mentioned Runnymede and Bunker Hill; and, if I may be permitted, I desire to show briefly that there is an intimate and indissoluble connection between these memorable places. There was a vast meaning in the beacon fire kindled on the plain of Runnymede, and the world and mankind everywhere understood that meaning; and then another beacon fire was kindled a few centuries later on Marston Moor, and that beacon fire had a tremendous meaning; and then again, while the world was wondering and trying to understand the significance of Runnymede and Marston Moor, there was an answering beacon fire blazing on Bunker Hill, with a meaning which even the darkness of tyranny comprehended. And when that shot of Middlesex was fired, it announced a most important departure; it announced that another great step had been taken, and that another mighty epoch in the history of English freedom had begun, and the most advanced condition of freedom in the world. There are these sequences, there are these connections; the same spirit is there, and the world sees the progress that has been made. Why, those shots fired at Lexington are reverberating now in Brazil, and ringing even to dark Siberia; and while men have hearts and a desire for freedom, which is innate and ineradicable from the minds of men, those echoes will always fall upon the ears of men everywhere.

"Sons of the American Revolution, do you pine for the brave old days? Do you sigh for opportunities such as your fathers had? Do you not find to-day room and opportunity for heroic action? Ah! there is a call for heroic souls to-day, if there ever was in the history of the world. In our complex life, with all the difficulties of thought, with all the new order of things, with the changed conditions which have taken the place of the old order, there is a call for men like Barrett and Buttrick and Davis. You cannot prove yourselves to be the lineal descendants of those men without showing deeds worthy of them. Our good mothers taught us what seemed an easy lesson: Always do right, always shun evil. But there comes in the great trouble of our lives to-day. If our good mothers had told us what was right and what was wrong, we should see fewer failures and have fewer heart-aches than we have to-day; we should have been furnished with that spear which, being pointed, at once detected the false and knew the true. We have not that to-day. That was an angel's weapon. But we can to-day stand in the spirit of the men who made this green a Thermopylæ one hundred and fourteen years ago. It would be so pleasant if, as in an opera, the good man was always the tenor, and the villain was always the basso; but we cannot have that convenient arrangement in our hurried and troubled life; yet there is as much call for heroic action in determining what is right as in going forth to do what is right.

"Ah, Mr. President and friends, would it not be convenient if some Paul Revere would come galloping through the night knocking at our doors and saying with a voice in which you must put trust, 'The enemy are there; go north, south, east, and west, and meet him!' But no such dictation comes to us. We fight to-day, not with battalions, but with opinions; and any opinion that goes forth from the brain or heart of man and hopes to succeed must be clad in proof armor, with sword and buckler and shield. It is for you to prove by action that you are the same flesh and blood of those men who worked for the foundation of this republic. And then, with such institutions as yours grasping the standard and standing close by you ready to support in case of need, the iron ranks and the bronzed faces of the Grand Army of the Republic and kindred organizations, I say that, come what may of weal or woe, of enemy or corruption, battle or pestilence, if you demean yourselves in the spirit of Lexington and Concord and Boston, I say then we may be sure that the power and glory of the United States of America will not be dimmed or lessened, and no true brave heart will ever have occasion to despair of the republic.

Nov. 6, 1890, before the Unitarian Club of Lowell, Greenhalge spoke upon the subject of Practical Christianity. In a sentence of his speech he said: " We have need for no more religion than we can use in our daily life. I object to no creed which lifts men up from the mud and mire; for it is not what you believe that helps, but what you carry into action." There is a whole sermon in this fragment.

I have given so many of his addresses entire because they should be preserved; enough is lost as it is. The glory of the orator is to a great extent ephemeral; what remains in printed books is but the pale reflection of the living presence of the orator, the cold shadow of the words that sprang from his lips like flame. The energy is gone that made them live. If the orator's efforts are to survive, they must live as literature, be judged by the severe tests of time. Yet, judged even by the standard of literary art, the speeches of Greenhalge are worthy of study and admiration. In many cases they were badly reported, and the report is often the only form in which they remain; but they were so glowing, so full of energy and thought and poetry, that the essence of their beauty has been preserved.

We are sometimes inclined to think the orator's career a rather ornamental one, — as if it were not a part of the serious life-work of the world. Yet, in the case of this one man, what a vast body of inspiring material his speeches make! He constantly sought to raise his hearers to a higher level of thought and action. His orbit is always among the stars of poetry and patriotism and moral and political purity. This is indeed " labor that is crowned with laurel and has the wings of the eagle." Much labor that is called practical, and honored

as such, instigated by cupidity and selfishness, is " labor which
is crowned with fire and has the wings of the bat. "

He was called once in a public print the " frivolous Greenhalge ; " he was the deeply serious Greenhalge. He has been
called " sarcastic ; " he was, in fact, appreciative and kind.
The surface may have been disturbed, but the depths of his
character were always the same.

In 1893 he was invited by the city of Boston to deliver the
oration at. the memorial service in honor of General Butler.
He gave an admirable address. The characters of these two
remarkable men were totally unlike ; yet some of the things
that Greenhalge said in his oration of General Butler are
strikingly applicable to himself : —

" There are some public men who never seem to reach the
heart of the people. Their services are great, their purpose is
high, their lives are pure and stately ; but the people, while
recognizing their merit, and feeling a certain moderate, well-
regulated gratitude, always maintain toward them a cold and
dispassionate attitude.

" Then there is another type of public men. You can count
the numbers of these on your fingers, in any age, in any
nation. The name of any one of them, uttered in a vast
assembly, will electrify thousands as the soul of one man,
and thrill and kindle heart, eye, and lip ; the name is a flash
of lightning followed — accompanied — by the thunder of
popular acclaim. There is electric communication between
this type and the soul of the people. The difference between
these two types cannot logically be explained ; it is clear only
to that finer, subtler, that almost divine intuition which we
attribute to woman. In these matters the logic of men can be
fathomed and answered ; the logic of women and of nations,
never. . . .

" Benjamin Franklin Butler was not born among ancestral
laurels or luxury ; and if a single wreath adorned his 'dream-
less head ' that winter day as he lay in his coffin, it was all his
own. He was the son of a widow. Not infrequently poverty
walked by his side in his early youth, and taught him its
severe but salutary lessons. No boy in America ever marched
to do battle with the world with less *impedimenta*, with less

artificial aids and advantages. But he carried in himself, in his own natural forces, supplies sufficient for every exigency of life's journey.

" In these days of form, rule, and routine, when life so often runs in a rut, it is good to see a man who lived and moved in his own right and not in the right of an ancestor, a family, or a class; whose powers were not limited or confined by environment, condition, or precedent, not tied and trammelled and labelled, not weighted down by ancestral possessions or ancestral ideas, but a man clothed in the royalty of his own individuality. . . .

" It seems difficult to believe that all this intense, this marvellous activity could suddenly cease; that all this rich glow of life should be extinguished at a breath; that so many 'enterprises of great pith and moment' should in an instant all 'their currents turn awry, and lose the name of action.' Yet, 'after life's fitful fever, he sleeps well,' — he of the sleepless brain, of the inextinguishable fire, of the dauntless spirit, of the irresistible and tireless force. "

In 1887 Greenhalge delivered the closing argument for the defence in the case of the Commonwealth *versus* George F. and Mary J. Baker, charged with murder. His argument occupied three and one-half hours in its delivery. It was afterwards printed by him in pamphlet form, with the title of " The Groton Murder Case. " It was a brilliant effort, and gained him considerable reputation as a criminal lawyer. The closing sentences and a passage touching circumstantial evidence were as follows : —

" I say that again and again, in the history of jurisprudence, circumstantial evidence which seemed overwhelming, and which did overwhelm the minds of jurors, was found to be as rotten and unstable as if a band of perjurers had marched before the jury and fired their falsehoods by platoons; yet every fact was truly stated. The veracity, the capacity, were there; but the conclusion was wrong, because some great and vital fact had been left out of the inquiry.

" Now I say, gentlemen, in conclusion, for one brief moment to you are committed the functions of the Almighty. You hold in your hands the issues of life and death. The only possible course lies between these alternatives; it is either liberty, and the doors of the jail open, or it is death upon the gallows, in a most shameful form. I beg you — and I have no doubt you have a full sense of the importance of the duty with which you are charged — to make no mistake. The old maxim is: 'It were better that ten guilty men should escape than one innocent man be convicted.'"

The voice of Greenhalge was always lifted in the cause of humanity. As an orator, the highest interests of the race engaged his constant attention; he sought to raise the moral standards of the community. In this respect he was the equal of any of our public speakers; his aims were as high, his tone as elevated. His was the most persistent voice heard in New England in our day in the cause of the highest culture, morality, and political purity, — the cause of Phillips and Sumner and Everett.

In times of depression he has been heard to say of life, "It is all a grim tragedy." Yet it never was to him a tragedy. Our lives may be composed in some measure much as we may compose a tragedy or comedy; it rests with us to mould them at our will.

To the resolute soul of Cæsar life was not a tragedy; to the active and ardent spirit in any age it is not a tragedy. The serene mind accompanies the active spirit all the world over.

Let us glance at the many speeches of Greenhalge, the speeches which are called occasional. Note the variety of subjects, all taken from the higher range of thought: —

Nov. 30, 1887, he lectured on literature before the St. Peter's Total Abstinence Society of Lowell.

January, 1888, on Self-Government, before the Matthews Temperance Institute, Lowell.

On Literature, Nov. 25, 1886, to the students at Amherst.

On Stonewall Jackson, April, 1886, before the History Club, Lowell.

He preached in Fifth Street Church, December, 1888, on the Lessons of the Hour.

He spoke in Watertown, January, 1889, on the Dangerous Tendencies of the Times, before the Unitarian Club.

In Lowell, April, 1889, on Ireland's cause.

In Plymouth, August, 1889, at the Dedication of the National Monument.

In September, to the Spalding Light Cavalry, on Our Country.

October 12, to the Paint and Oil Club, on New England Supremacy.

December 29, before the Pennsylvania Club, on Labor and Capital.

The list might be extended to cover all his life; for he spoke and continued to speak with ever-increasing multiplicity of place and topic. His oratory was a lamp which shone brightly over a small circle at first, yet gradually shed its beams over all Massachusetts.

In 1886 Greenhalge was engaged as counsel in the Bell Telephone cases. I have copied the following brief sentences from his argument. They are characteristic : —

" It is not all demagogy when we speak of monopoly. There is such a thing as a monopoly, and it is to prevent a monopoly that I think the Legislature is bound to act. "

" I have always taken this ground, — it is Jeffersonian, and to that extent I am a thorough Democrat, — that the people in every case where they understand the question are infallible. "

" Gentlemen, there is a principle involved here. The character of Massachusetts legislation must be kept clean and pure, pointing ever as the needle to the pole to the welfare and comfort of the people. "

Greenhalge delivered the eulogy at the unveiling of the statue of William Lloyd Garrison at Newburyport, Mass. It was widely quoted and praised for its eloquence, and is one of his best-known orations. He spoke as follows : —

" FELLOW-CITIZENS OF NEWBURYPORT, — On the 10th day of December (though your town records say the 12th), A. D. 1805, William Lloyd Garrison was born in this town of Newbury-

port in a frame house still standing on School Street, between
the First Presbyterian Church, in which Whitefield's remains
are interred, and the house in which the great preacher died.
Nearly eighty-eight years afterward a public-spirited citizen
of Newburyport, Mr. Swasey, commemorates by the statue to
be unveiled to-day your immortal fellow-townsman.

"Such a recognition of such a man, in this age of silver
and gold, of iron and steel, of manufactures and commerce,
is a fact of more than ordinary significance. It proves that
liberty and equality are still words of power and meaning,
that they have not yet become as 'sounding brass or tinkling
cymbals;' it proves that old Newport and young Newburyport have not forgotten the strongest and bravest of the
thousands of strong and brave men who have sprung from
her loins.

"And, further, I may say that Newburyport owes this day's
reparation to Garrison. In her pride and strength and prosperity, she atones to-day for the injustice done to her own
son in former days. Not always did Garrison find his native
town a loving mother. She turned too often a deaf ear to his
burning words.

"Then, too, it was a son of Newburyport who was assisting
in the domestic slave-trade of the country, and who, when re-
proached by Garrison, flung the liberator into prison in a far-off
city.

"But half a century has passed away, — you can read the
Declaration of Independence to-day and feel that every word is
true and just. You can take up the Constitution now, and
know that it is not a 'league with death,' but in every line and
word a book of life. And in the noble shape of this grand
statue now unveiled to the light of heaven, Newburyport
welcomes back her mighty son, laurelled with the enfranchise-
ment of millions and the purification of the republic. This,
then, is more than a day of celebration, it is a day of reparation.

"And, my fellow-citizens, what better day than this could
you have chosen for this great ceremony, — the day consecrated
to liberty and independence, a day yet ringing with the trumpet
blast of 1776, proclaiming the birth of a new principle and a
new nation? What better or more appropriate place than

Newburyport, the town which witnessed not only his birth, but his earliest struggles, trials, defeats, and victories?

> ' Here about the beach wandered moodily a youth sublime,
>   With the fairy tales of science and the long result of time.'

"The strong-hearted, kindly people of Newburyport know how the more than fatherless boy stood by his more than widowed mother in her distress. They know how he walked with poverty as a friend, how he clasped hands with labor as a brother, how he sat at the cobbler's bench, how he rose to the printer's case in the old 'Herald' office in Newbury-port, and how his own teeming brain originated the very articles he set up in type with his own hand.

"And what grander example of a high-souled, heroic man can you celebrate on such a day, in such a place, than William Lloyd Garrison, the ever-faithful priest of liberty! Permit me, then, to congratulate you that you are able, here and now, to celebrate that rare trinity, — the time, the place, and the man. On this auspicious day, in the most fitting place, then contemplate with me briefly and swiftly the life-work of William Lloyd Garrison.

"It would be hard to find anywhere a life of humbler beginning, and it is inspiring to trace that life from its early obscurity to see how, day by day, it was lighted up by the clear flame of high moral purpose and indomitable patience and courage, till at the close it shone and blazed with a splendor of achievement such as seldom crowns the efforts of man. Look at the condition of the country as Garrison came to manhood.

"The sounds of the last great war had died away; the evils of that war and of the embargo had been severe; but peace had brought about a new state of affairs. Cotton was growing in the South, and was manufactured in the North. Industry, trade, commerce, business, began to flourish. The Missouri Compromise had been effected. An 'era of good feeling' had arrived. There was a lull, a truce, in the irrepressible conflict between freedom and slavery.

"The people were devoted to material considerations and interests. They planted, they watered, and they harvested;

they toiled and they spun; they married and gave in marriage. The law gave its sanction to the existing conditions of things; the clergy added their benediction and 'all went merry as a marriage bell.'

"But the triumphal march of their prosperity was not altogether pleasing to one strong soul, — the soul of William Lloyd Garrison. In 1828, July 4, sixty-five years ago, the man who will give a warmer glow to our hearts to-day stood here in Newburyport, as I stand now, and read to your fathers, — perhaps to some boy who stands before me now a gray-haired sire — the Declaration of Independence. He also wrote a fervent ode for that occasion, which seems to have been conducted under the auspices of the artillery company of Newburyport.

> ' For the reign of free thoughts and free acts has begun,
>   And joy to the people whose hearts are but one.'

These were the words which finished one stanza of his ode. His soul was filled with great thoughts on that great day, and his beloved country and the reign of freedom and equality were foremost ideas in his mind.

"As he contemplated, under the influence of these feelings, the conditions of his country, as he read again and again the glowing words of the great Declaration, he saw a gloomy figure, the figure of slavery, sitting at the fireside of the South and casting an appalling shadow beyond the household over all the country and over the world. He was startled and dismayed.

"His sense of justice led him to desire the destruction of slavery; but his clear judgment showed him also the peril of his country, and led him to desire the salvation of his country from that peril. He knew, with Homer, that ' he who enslaves a fellow-man takes half that man's worth away,' but he knew also that the enslaver loses more than half his own worth. The captor is the captive, the master is the slave.

"He knew that all the iron ranks of Lacedæmon were but as straw and chaff while a single Helot remained to desire his right in his revenge; he knew that all the conquests

of Rome were empty dreams while a single bondsman pined
for freedom; and he realized that all the crescent power and
glory of his own beloved land were but dust and ashes
while three millions of his fellow-creatures, living under the
Constitution and the flag, were subject to the auction-block,
to chains, to the lash, to slavery and all its dark incidents.

"The pomp of prosperity, therefore, did not dazzle him, and
over the hum of industry, above the somnolent drone of the
pupil, the soothing tones of the 'clerical appeal,' the cold
measured accents of the bench, — he heard, like muffled
thunder, growing louder day by day, the voice of God saying, 'Let my people go, that they may serve me.' And he
felt a personal responsibility.

"The command came to him to remove at once the danger
which threatened white man and black. He knew the truth
of Whittier's words; he knew

> ' That laws of changeless justice bind
> Oppressor with oppressed;
> And close as sin and suffering joined
> We march to fate abreast.'

The march of the nation was brought to a halt. It was the
type-setter of Newburyport that gave the command. He says:
'The clergy were against me, the nation was against me; but
God and his truth, and the rights of man' were with him.
In the cooler temperature of to-day we can see how the uncom-
promising spirit of Garrison awoke the wrath and the dread of
the communities infected with slavery; and how to many he
appeared, not as a philanthropist, a Christian, a man of peace,
but as a reckless agitator menacing life and property, —

> ' A maniac scattering dust,
> A fury slinging flame.'

"But great causes cannot be compromised. Garrison believed that every day the guilty country was piling up the
wrath of Heaven. The necessity for action was pressing, not
only to give liberty to the African, but safety to the white
man. The body politic was tainted with leprosy; the Constitution was a 'league with death and a covenant with hell.'

He was willing to suffer himself. He had the blood of the martyr in him. He felt it coursing hotly through his veins. He was willing to shed it and seal his faith with the ruddiest drops of his heart. He took up the cause of the captive, — his opponents said it was vanity. It was a vanity for which he was willing to pay in stripes; for which he suffered imprisonment, poverty, obloquy, loss of friends, and loss of comfort.

"There was no great cause which he espoused for which he was not willing to suffer. Temperance, the equal rights of women, all found in him a whole-souled advocate and supporter.

"The present is not an age of martyrs; the great age of antislavery agitation was. Garrison declared and wrought for his convictions. He received stripes, blows, obloquy, — he languished in jail; he suffered the penalties of the law, the bitterness of poverty. These evils he took upon himself in a Christ-like spirit. His personal sufferings meant the rescue of millions from worse sufferings.

"In our practical day the agitator receives, not martyrdom for his labors, but a salary and a place. It is our duty to respect the martyr of the old days, if we have no desire to imitate him.

"Fellow-citizens, it is fitting that the statue of this brave, loyal, resolute son of Newburyport should stand here, an image, eloquent though silent, of an inflexible purpose of a soul faithful unto death, of a mind capacious enough to hold vast conceptions of constitutional freedom, of the rights of man, capacious enough to include all classes and conditions of men.

"Garrison is the first in the great line of protagonists in the cause of human freedom. Look at that splendid line: Garrison, Phillips, Sumner, Andrew, Lincoln !

"Let every bold, free spirit of the universe be present here, hovering around this figure. Let the wind and the rain and the sunlight rejoice in this kindred spirit of freedom regulated by divine law alone. Let the northeast blast, exulting in its liberty, dash from the font of the free Atlantic ever and again baptismal spray over this child of the God whose service is perfect freedom.

"Let every boy and girl of Newburyport, of Massachusetts,

of America, learn the lesson of Garrison's life and philosophy, — that you cannot deprive another man of his right without losing your own ; that the safety and happiness of men and of nations can only be found in the path of justice and truth ; that slavery of any sort, physical, moral, social, or political, debases the master as well as the servant or slave, and that the law of nations as well as the law of States can have full force and effect only when in meaning and purpose they are in harmony with the law of God."

Greenhalge spoke in March, 1893, before the Press Club of Lowell, on Journalism. Those who heard him on that occasion say that he then appeared at his best; his spirits were bright, his manner fresh, and his speech full of wit and wisdom.

"I am to speak of 'Journalism and its Opportunities.' Journalism is an art, it is also a science; and it has much to do with all arts and sciences. In fact, it is the mirror of all arts and sciences. It is the panorama of all the progress of all the world. Its agents and servants are steam, electricity, mechanics, and every branch of human knowledge and invention ; and every forward step made in any art or science, in knowledge or invention, every improvement in steam, electricity, mechanics, — each and all are reflected and repeated in journalism. The tutelary deity of journalism is Hermes or Mercury, the god of intelligence, of news, flying over the earth with wings on hat and heels, bearing his staff (caduceus), which may have been a pencil, the herald of the Immortals, the Journalist of the universe.

"What wonderful progress has been made in this art of journalism within fifty years ! Some of you can remember when a newspaper was a rarity, a luxury more talked of than seen ; borrowed or stolen quite as often as bought, treasured like a family Bible, and sometimes nearly as old ! An editor sat in a niche like a saint, and a reporter was spoken of with bated breath ! But steam presses, telegraphs, telephones, countless improvements in types and forms, in systems and methods have made great changes. The daily newspaper is as daily bread to the people ; it is no longer a luxury, but a necessity of life, like fuel or light; a necessity in every family, and a power in every nation, — guiding, checking, and inspiring the thought and action of millions, in business, politics, art, education, and morals. Here, then, is a stupendous power, and upon the whole a power wielded with intelligence and beneficence.

"Journalism is the bright living record of the day's doings in action and thought, — catching glimpses of the 'Cynthia of the minute,' — making a permanent picture of ephemeral and evanescent things, reproducing like an instantaneous photograph the ever-varying forms of human existence in actual motion. Journalism is the first flash of the daylight of truth, of fact or opinion. It stands at the gateway of the day, and, leaping into the chariot of the sun, completes the circuit of the world from east to west. It presents to the eyes of men the life of day, and

'Every moment, lightly shaken,
Runs itself in golden sands.'

"To establish and maintain a great journal is a noble and a difficult task. Money, talent, skill, patience, industry, experience, all are needed. To please the public taste without pandering to bad taste; to be constant in principle without getting 'out of touch' with the people; to maintain a high standard, a pure tone, and not become prosy and didactic; to give the news and yet not deprave by the manner of giving it; to stand out against the open or covert bribery of powerful interests and yet not offend stockholders; to refuse to sell editorial indorsements and yet pay dividends, — these are some of the difficulties of journalism.

"The advertising department, too, is a source of danger or evil to good journalism. The 'pot-boiling' business is allowed to encroach too much upon the legitimate ground of the newspaper. The public gets very tired of reading thrilling episodes terminating in glowing eulogies of a superior vermifuge or a panacea for pulmonary diseases. Nor do the people gaze with unmixed admiration on the genial countenances of the fortunate or unfortunate beings whose solitary distinction consists in having been cured of some terrible complaint. And the long gallery of benefactors of humanity, like Lydia Pinkham, ceases to charm. Even the interesting physiognomy of Mr. Douglas, the three-dollar shoe-manufacturer, is no longer regarded 'a thing of beauty and a joy forever.'

"It not infrequently happens that a quarter-page portrait confronts us as we take up our daily paper. We know that it is a time of crisis; that Europe is standing on a volcano; that a new star has been discovered in the constellation Auriga; that the stars and stripes have been run up on a great Inman liner; that Gladstone has spoken or Bismarck is silent. Who, then, is the hero of the critical hour? Simple John Smith, who is alleged to have been brought back to life by somebody's indescribable compound of inexpressible ingredients. We heave a sigh, and thank Heaven it is no worse.

"The great requisites of good journalism are character, individuality, enterprise, and originality, and, above all, sincerity. The great journals of the United States rise like the White Mountain peaks, each distinct, easily recognized by tone and spirit; and they reflect the light of public opinion as the great mountains reflect the light of the morning sun. But the lesser peaks, the little hills of journalism, have quite an important part to play. Here and there a 'country paper,' so called, rises by its special features or situation to a considerable prominence as a metropolitan journal; it is the journalistic Monadnock or Agamenticus of the neighborhood. Such a paper speaks with authority, and is quoted with respect. Such a paper stands like a Highland laird, or a great nobleman in his Northern fortress in 'the brave days of old.'

"Sincerity, I say, is the great desideratum in the editor, in the reporter, in the business agent, in the advertising department; and neither department must encroach on the other. They must be kept apart as sacredly as the Constitution keeps apart the executive, the legislative, and the judicial departments of the government. Venality is the great danger of the day in journalism as well as in everything else. Newspapers must be the mouthpieces of principle, not of the highest bidder; the spirit of truth, and not of subsidy.

"The opportunities of journalism are vast. Journalists are the uncrowned sovereigns of republics; their power is as absolute as that of justice and honor. Their edicts are obeyed, if truly their own edicts, and not those of impostors. The journalist is accepted by the people, except when he plays the lobbyist, the speculator, or the quack. If he is ever dethroned, it is by his own act, his own abdication.

" And what a striking figure of this bright age of ours is the journalist ! If we regard the newsboy as the journalist in the chrysalis, it is not a disparagement of this responsible profession. The eager little messenger is learning promptness, tact, dexterity, patience. He is bearing news ; he is learning, and at a very early age, that

'The proper study of mankind is man,'

and the boy is father to the man. All doors are open to him. He stands before the rich and powerful, and is undismayed. He listens to the cry of the poor, and is filled with pity. He must look upon crime and virtue. All learning and knowledge comes within his ken. He cannot catch and keep all of it, but he cannot help absorbing education.

" The true journalist is a man of high and inflexible purpose ; no more than the gladiator can he yield to debauchery or folly. Every muscle, nerve, and fibre is on duty at every hour. Take Macaulay's fine description of the members of the Society of Jesus, and apply it to the journalist : 'They glided from one country to another under innumerable disguises, — as gay cavaliers, as simple rustics, and Puritan preachers. They wandered to countries which neither mercantile avidity nor liberal curiosity had ever impelled any stranger to explore. None of them had chosen his vocation or his dwelling-place for himself. If he was wanted at Lima, he was on the Atlantic in the next fleet ; if he was wanted at Bagdad, he was toiling through the desert with the next caravan.'

" In peace and in war he goes at a word, a sign, into scenes of darkness and danger. He is on the track of the murderer swifter than the detective ; he explores the depths of African forests with Stanley ; he is in the front of battle with Archibald Forbes and Charles Carleton Coffin ; and he is buried, like Barker, pencil in hand, under the blazing ruins of a great conflagration.

" Journalism has a mighty influence to guide public opinion in the way of public good ; and in its mission of enlightenment and progress the press of Lowell has a golden opportunity. We lack here that quality called public spirit. We know all about cotton-mills; our enterprises, corporate and individual, are stupendous, the admiration of the country; but in the enterprise which beautifies, elevates, and gives pleasure to the community, we are sadly deficient. And it is not because we have nothing in ourselves to arouse our pride. We have our mills, and we have had men illustrious. We buried a great man the other day, General Butler, — the most unique, the most individual man, if I may say so, the nation has ever known. We have but recently laid away one of the greatest hydraulic engineers in the world, James B. Francis. We have had musicians and painters born among us, — a David Neal in Vienna, a James Whistler in London, and a Chadwick in Boston. These are men whose genius redounds to the credit of Lowell. When you seek a modern hero, you go to the Pacific isles where Father Damien died. In Lowell, when the small-pox raged, a physician, trained in the schools of Paris and Vienna, rich and delicately nurtured, immured himself at the pest-house, and there conducted the treatment of the disease upon such a scientific and practical plan that it was speedily stamped out. And the fame of his self-sacrifice spread abroad, and from other cities smitten with the plague came requests that the successful methods of Dr. Abner Wheeler Buttrick might be imparted to them.

"We have much to glory in, but we do not glorify as we should. We have a limited admiration for art, paintings, sculpture, music, and oratory when the weather is fine, but we do little to encourage these accomplishments. We have crude notions of beauty in color, form, or sound. When Pericles seized the treasure of Delos, the people cried out in protest. Pericles said to them : 'You know much of war and of commerce, but you know nothing of art. You men of Attica must rise above your grosser selves ; you must learn of art;' and he spent the treasure in rearing those beautiful forms that refined a people and survived all their other institutions.

"The newspapers of Lowell should unite to lead Lowell from its indifference, from its narrow plodding in the service of the exacting dollar, into the higher and less selfish influence of a

public ambition that is not subservient to commercial or industrial considerations.

"Let journalism, then, be true to itself, worthy of the vast
confidence reposed in it by the people. And let the journalist
know and realize that the trust he holds is sacred, and large
enough to call forth all the ability and all the training which
he can possibly bring into its service."

At the dedication of the Milford library in Milford, Massachusetts, speaking of Lincoln, Greenhalge said : " There was
the great nature of the man to begin with ; but it was only the
rude marble in the quarry, the ore in the cavernous mine.
It was the sweet power of the library — of books — that brought
forth the rich colors of that marble and fashioned the rude ore
into polished steel. It was the close and diligent study of the
Bible, of Shakespeare and Milton, his constant companions,
that enabled Lincoln to compose that wonderful funeral oration
which will rank with the masterpieces of the Attic Genius,
with the orations of Lysias or Pericles, delivered on similar
occasions. "

I have said much in praise of Greenhalge's oratory, and
have not attempted to give a critical estimate of his talent.
His style was not without its defects, its exaggerations.
Fire and intensity it had in abundance. He shared in the
common defects of modern times. He employed, perhaps, too
much rhetorical embellishment, and a certain amplitude of
style. The conciseness and simple earnest strength that are
said to have distinguished Demosthenes are not distinctive of
modern oratory. Burke says, in reference to Hyder Ali :
" Compounding all the materials of fury, havoc, desolation,
into one black cloud, he hung for a while on the declivity of
the mountains ; while the authors of all these evils were idly
and stupidly gazing on this marching meteor which darkened
all their horizon, it suddenly burst, and poured down the whole
of its contents on the plains of the Carnatic. " Demosthenes
says more simply, referring to Philip: " The people gave their
voice, and the danger that hung upon our borders went by
like a cloud. " Modern taste might prefer the former quotation with its wealth of detail.

Greenhalge did not often strive for the sublime and grand in his speeches. He belongs, rather, to the order of graceful and brightly imaginative orators, with Everett and Phillips. He was interesting; he could never have been called that " tocsin of the soul, the dinner-bell, " as Burke came to be described. Greenhalge always sought to inspire, to elevate; he did not often invoke figures of terror and sublimity.

Some of his set orations may have contained too many quotations, though they were always apt and just. The style he employed, however, was admirably suited to the occasion of his discourse, which sometimes demanded ornament and rhetoric. His political speeches are direct, logical and simple in manner, and present the issues clearly and forcibly. They were admirable instruments in political warfare and contention. His other speeches possess symmetry, poetry, elegance, felicity, variety, and ardor. They drew their inspiration from the sentiments of patriotism, poetry, and political and moral purity. They are worthy of the man, and he of them.

POLITICAL LIFE.

CHAPTER VI.

MAYOR OF LOWELL.

THE author has now come to the more serious task of attempting to write the history of the political career of Greenhalge, — a career full of instruction and interest to patriotic men, to all who desire the regeneration of the political world, who desire to see a higher tone prevail in the contests of freemen, and a higher level of thought and action maintained by their political leaders.

The career of Greenhalge shows with peculiar force the value of the scholar in politics. That phrase which, on the lips of politicians, means weakness and inefficiency in party struggles, as illustrated by his career, means virility, a high code of honor, morality, and perfect fitness, — nay, even genius, for the exercise of political duties and the warfare of party.

It is a peculiar and demoralizing feature of our democratic American life that the politics of the country, and even its sports and pastimes, are in constant danger of falling into the control of a class of unscrupulous and low-minded men, who enter political life solely for the spoils to be earned in a nefarious trade in offices, who mingle in the games of the people in the basest spirit of professionalism for the sake of money. These men are uneducated, immoral, avaricious, mean-spirited. Their natural intelligence is often of a high order, however; but it is perverted and prostituted. In political

10

contests they are no mean antagonists, and are frequently left in sole and victorious possession of the field.

To rescue the great city of New York from their control, even for a brief interval, is considered a great achievement, accomplished only by the united efforts of several parties. These men indeed have long held, in some measure, an almost undisputed sway. Young men of means, leisure, and education are withheld from the public service by a not unnatural disinclination to be brought into contact with the sordid elements that must be encountered by all who embrace a political career. Other young men of ability and action, who might become the leaders of the people, are attracted by, and drawn into, the great world of business; the opportunities of which are so splendid, and the prizes so alluring.

The American people, pure and enlightened as any in the world, have nevertheless sometimes allowed their municipalities to become the spoil of men politically almost as corrupt as Clodius and Milo. They devote themselves to the business interests of their country, but its political affairs are left, to a large extent, to a class of men who have come to be known as " Ward heelers " and " Bosses. "

The civil service of the country requires leaders certainly of as high a character as its military service demands. The people should turn the bosses out of their undeserved positions of trust as quickly and as thoroughly as Cromwell turned out the " tapsters " and " serving men " whom he found commanding as officers the Parliamentary armies. The need is as great that they should be replaced by men of principle, of conscience, and of intellect. There is immense reserve force in the virtue and intelligence of the American people and nation. Our people are, in all respects, worthy to be the citizens of a great republic. Evils cannot make great inroads upon the nation while its citizens remain what they are, — industrious and virtuous.

The political bosses, however, have one stronghold in the ignorance that prevails to some extent in the millions of immigrants unprepared for the duties of citizenship that await them here. To remedy this evil has become the task of the American people. They need the help of the most enlightened classes;

they need leaders of the highest character, of ability, and
education.

There is a pressure exerted for evil upon the State, both from
below and above, — the pressure of the lowest stratum and
the highest, of poverty and wealth. Between these two forces
stands the nation, armed with immense power. In itself it
embraces almost all that is valuable in human life, all that
it is necessary to maintain and defend.

" You cannot deceive all the people all the time." So
spoke the wisest of Americans. The people have indeed often
been deceived and betrayed by both politicians and parties;
but their eyes have always been opened at last, and their
wisdom vindicated. It has been said by a keen observer that
the judgment of Parliament is always more to be trusted than
that of the wisest of its members. The collective wisdom of
the people is also greater than that of the wisest man. Great,
however, as is the intelligence of the nation, it is not quick;
its judgment is often delayed, its convictions slowly formed,
its penalties long put off, its faith and trust not easily disturbed. The mind of the nation is slow, trustful, incorruptible, and infallible.

The political boss does not believe in the virtue of the
people. He is not dismayed in the least, though on the one
side stand trickery, bribery, chicanery, falsehood, the lowest
partisanship, and public dishonor; on the other, the immense
power of the people, the majesty of the law, statesmanship, and
public credit, — on the one side Themis, on the other Caliban.

The cry of the people in all their immense conflicts is for
leaders, — leaders worthy of their high position. It is because
Greenhalge was a worthy leader, endowed with conscience,
courage, and loyalty, that his life should not be left without
a record. He was not linked by fortune with great events.
His career was, however, exemplary and suggestive, full of
lessons which ought to be learned and remembered.

Government by party is a necessity of democracy. It is a
means of government; with all its imperfections we must
accept it. It is the marvel of democracy that what we see is,
below, the incessant and bitter strife of factions and parties;
above, the constitution, stable government, the firm magistrate

and just judge.   Out of the discordant elements of party issue firmness, moderation, national credit, and stability.   Party government justifies itself.

By instinct, inclination, and education Greenhalge was not a partisan.   The necessity of party government he accepted, as all men must in a free country.   In political warfare he became a partisan chief.   All his life he belonged to the Republican party; all his efforts were directed to achieve its success.   The honors that came to him were the gift of that party.   His services were long-continued and great, and with indefatigable energy he gave himself to the cause.

We do not, however, expect that the forensic efforts of the advocate will represent truly in all things his own private convictions.   We need not think that all that Greenhalge found it necessary to say in the interests of his party represented always his own private belief.   He owed no divided allegiance, however; he was never separated from the Republican party by any divergence of opinion in matters of deep importance.   Yet he was not the man to give up to party what was meant for mankind, though he willingly sacrificed his private opinions when conscience allowed.

He never was a fanatical partisan, and he never could have been.   The grand work accomplished by the Republican party in the past, its great history in war and peace, the heroic names emblazoned on its standards, aroused his admiration.   Its great principles of government represented his own profound convictions.   Its great impetus he believed to be far from exhausted, and capable still of carrying it over all obstacles triumphantly.   The intelligence of the country to him seemed mainly to stand on that side.   The base and sordid elements that exist in every party he never denied or palliated; his opposition to them in his own could always be counted on. He was never, in fact, a mere politician; he said so himself, as will be seen in his letters.

Political life was, in many respects, distasteful to him; he was disgusted by its baser side; he had learned to know men. Like all political leaders, he had seen much of the worst side of mankind.   He knew well the selfish office-seeker and place-hunter; he had experienced the plague of men eager for self-advancement; he had seen their self-abasement and disregard of personal honor.

His sense of duty called him into politics. I do not say that he was not ambitious, but it was the sense of duty that bound him to political servitude. Apollo had to serve Admetus. Greenhalge never shrank from the duties of the hour. He fought a man's fight, he took a man's part in the conflicts of men, and he died in harness. His ambitions in life, his characteristic aims and purposes, his own character, in short, are well explained in the following pages, contributed by his old and intimate friend Judge Lawton, of Lowell : —

"It is probable that Greenhalge's youthful ambition was not for distinction in the public service. He had a love of oratory; he cultivated it; he excelled in it. He did not do it that he might shine in Congress. If he dreamed of glory, it was of a literary kind. His father's classical tastes and love of literature may have shaped the boy's mind and his ambition. The difference between him and the bright American boys around him was in their purposes. The end they aimed at was an election to something, — anything to begin with, and the highest elective office in the world to end with. They all wished to learn to make speeches to help them to get and to keep votes. He desired perfection in the lines of oratory and of literary accomplishment as an end in itself. He thought of the prepared and finished oration rather than of the political speech. He had the taste and temperament of the artist rather than that of the politician. He yearned to do work in these lines that should be artistic. He has been quoted as saying with mingled seriousness and playfulness, ' I have had but one ambition, and that was to write a successful novel.' He did not mean that this statement should be accepted literally. He certainly had ambitions in other directions. He did love to prepare, to criticise, and to deliver public addresses. He had a playful, imaginative, philosophical, didactic spirit, which, without doubt, did draw him toward the entertaining and instructive work of the highest fiction. He could not paint on canvas nor carve on marble, but wherever he could paint or carve perfect forms, he loved to do so.

"Such was the man, and his ambitions were such as such

men have. He was so different from most successful statesmen
that most of them failed to comprehend him. His mental
constitution was so different from that of the ordinary politician that it remained an impenetrable mystery to very many,
even to the day of his death. He was precocious. He matured
early. He was considerably cultivated at an age when most
boys of his time were raw and crude. His passion for symmetry, his comprehension of it, his attainment of it; his imagination, at once powerful and disciplined; the quality and
finish of all the results he reached, — were marvellous to his
immature associates. They looked upon his genius with as
much awe as such boys were capable of feeling for anything.
It was this impression, never effaced from the minds of his
schoolmates, which led them, on his return to Lowell from
college, to urge him for ‘ political honors.’ Such a wonderful
fellow as Greenhalge ought to be ‘ elected ’ to something at
once! This tribute to his excellent parts by those who knew
him best was sweet to him. He was not a cynic. The power
to please carried with it the desire for appreciation. He deserved applause; he liked it.

“Lowell was then, as it is now, in many ways a ‘ very
democratic place.’ In all parts of the great democracy of
America, the continued counting of votes and the frequent
announcement that ‘ Blank appears to have the majority,’ tends,
doubtless, to perfect equality. The king is not made by birth,
but by votes. Still there is not a hamlet in the world where
there is not a ‘ ruling class.’ That class may maintain itself
by majorities of all the votes cast, or by military might, but
it will maintain itself until the millennium. Lowell was
founded by a few strong men. They built huge mills controlled by a dozen incorporated companies. These ‘ corporations ’ were united closely in order to control the water power,
and doubtless for other good purposes. Their capital stock
was held and owned everywhere except in Lowell. In the
early days of Lowell the managers of these mills managed the
people who worked for them. They managed them prudently,
wisely, and for those days benevolently. They managed the
schools, they managed the churches, they managed Lowell.
The resident ‘ agents ’ were the chief officers in control,

who were visible to the people. Under them, and supposed to act by their direction, were the master workmen, —
' overseers,' — who served as captains, not only in the industries, but in the government of the community. In the early
days these men were men of character and capacity; their
government was far from intolerable. In course of time they
were gradually supplanted by men whose management was
stupid, while the mill management had been intelligent, —
exclusively selfish, while the selfishness of the mill satraps had
been joined with a regard for the best interests of the city.
Greenhalge's first candidacy for office was when the old order
of things was passing away and the new was coming in. The
only reason for mentioning the old is to account for one characteristic of both the old and the new. The new inherited a
dictatorial authority and power from the old. The men who
composed the new came into power one by one, humbly;
they crept in. In turn, they required that everybody else
should creep in, and should come in by their permission.
Some of them were still employed in the mills. But they
appeared more to act in their individual capacities than as
subordinates of their employers. No political bosses of the
present day, even with the corrupt use of money, maintain
their authority more undisputed than these Lowell bosses,
without money, without ability, without public spirit, maintained theirs for years. In fact, it is only recently that they
appear to have been unseated and overthrown by still newer
men, perhaps more reckless and audacious than they; but
possibly no more selfish nor more indifferent to the public
welfare.

" The first public office Greenhalge ever held was that of
a member of the municipal council of Lowell. Whatever
ideals he had, he never despised what is meant everywhere in
America when the word ' politics ' is used. Although it has
been said that he was an artist by nature, he always had a
wholesome regard for every useful thing. In all his life, in all
the offices which he held, he saw little difference of grade.
The constant struggle of a free people to legislate well for
themselves, to govern themselves, whether in the Lowell
Common Council or in the National Congress, was always to

him an effort of dignity and honor.   The principle that was
operating, and not the field of its operation, was to him
sublime.

"At this time the hostility to him of the Lowell management became apparent.   If it ever ceased, it did not cease for a
quarter of a century.   Admitted to be the most brilliant young
man in Lowell, it was at least twenty years before he was
permitted to represent a larger constituency than that of Lowell.
The captains of tens in the ward in which he lived long opposed
his selection as a representative to the General Court of Massachusetts.   Had he desired a political career, had he pushed
himself forward, and had he fought for political place, he would
have become distinguished much earlier.   That he was a man
of extraordinary genius was readily admitted even by the managers of affairs in Lowell; but the long line of those regularly
initiated into the ruling order never shortened.   Greenhalge
they all 'admired,' but they feared he was not 'practical.'
The real objection was that he was absolutely independent of
everybody's control, and they wished nobody to be in any
position of power whom they could not command and be
sure that he would obey.   Men of his stature rather dwarfed
the smaller men who were to be promoted regularly and
judiciously."

So writes Judge Lawton of the opposition Greenhalge encountered in some quarters.

Greenhalge only once voted out of the Republican party.
He was thoroughly consistent in his allegiance to the principles of that party, even in this divergence from its outward
course.   In the presidential election of 1878 he voted for Horace
Greeley.   General Grant was the nominee of the Republicans.
That great American, the greatest captain of his age, possessed
in military affairs an all-embracing mind.   He had the especial
talent common to all great commanders, — that which serves
them best, the talent that enables them to choose the best subordinates, to discover the value of men for special services.
Such men invariably surround themselves with able lieuten-
ants, men capable of forwarding their far-reaching plans.
They seem to know by instinct the characters of the officers

they employ. Such was Grant, — in war the most discriminating of men. As President, his judgment was not so infallible. The men whom he trusted were not always worthy of esteem. In civil life he seemed often wrongly to conceive the character of men. He was deceived in many cases. Scandals were not unknown in his administration; in consequence the conscience of the country was affected, and discontent with the administration arose in many quarters. General Grant also had too much of the absolute in his nature to fit him entirely for the management of civil affairs. Like Wellington, in a similar position, he was somewhat autocratic; he did not like to be crossed in his plans even by public sentiment. In the case of San Domingo, it even looked as if he wished to force his ideas upon the country.

Dissatisfaction grew during his administration, and led to a split in the party, and the nomination of Greeley for President. Greenhalge shared in the common feeling, and voted for Greeley. I believe he afterward came to think it a mistake, and perhaps he regretted it. He never after showed any disposition to revolt from the party; even in later years, when the great Mugwump exodus occurred, when men of high character and education deserted the party of their sires and forgot its great deeds and traditions, he stood by his colors. He might have sympathized, to some extent, with their dissatisfaction with the course of events; his personal ideas might have differed in some things from those that governed the Republican party, but he never, after the Greeley campaign, swerved from open allegiance to its great principles.

Judge Lawton, who appreciated at the time the feeling under the influences of which Mr. Greenhalge acted, though he did not share it, writes as follows of the position of affairs, the reasons that operated in Mr. Greenhalge's mind, and the political circumstances that led to his bolt from the Republican party : —

" The year 1872 marks an epoch in Greenhalge's political career. It may be nearer the truth to say that it marks the beginning of it. He was thirty years old.

" General Grant had been renominated to the Presidency by the Republican party. He had quarrelled with Charles Sum-

ner, or Charles Sumner had quarrelled with him. Sumner
was the idol of Massachusetts. In the great moral conflict—
in that great national debate which preceded the appeal to arms
— Sumner, in the eyes of Massachusetts, had attained heroic
stature. In fact, he was at once a hero and a martyr. In the
assault on slavery he early took the lead, and behind him,
nearly unanimous, stood the people of Massachusetts. Brooks,
of South Carolina, answered his 'Crime against Kansas' with
blows, and left him for dead upon the floor of the Senate
Chamber at Washington. When the flag was fired upon at
Sumter, the entire North was aroused by a passion that was
fervent and patriotic; but no such wave of wrath and indignation swept through the old Commonwealth as when her Senator
was beaten down by Brooks. The war, emancipation, and
reconstruction were Sumner's triumph and vindication. The
best of his life had been sublimely devoted to the 'cause.'
Such men as he have opinions and wills of their own. He
came into conflict with the gentle, inflexible, indomitable
Grant. The men of camp were still around Grant. Perhaps
some of them he trusted too much, — trusted as he always
trusted his friends, even to his financial ruin in New York.
Those of them who were unworthy of the great captain could
not prevent his great, substantial success, either in the Cabinet
or in the field, and they can never dim his fame.

"Sumner, first hurt, then indignant at his own treatment by
a soldier president, and then shocked by what seemed to him
to be 'nepotism and corruption,' 'bolted' the second nomination of Grant. With him went Horace Greeley and scores of
the leaders of the Republican party, followed by thousands
of patriotic civil-service reformers, young and old, all over the
country. Nowhere was the revolt proportionately so great as
in Massachusetts. There was a rush to the side of Sumner.
Very many of the best and truest of those who were leaders
then, or have become leaders since, trusted implicitly to
the judgment of their spotless Senator. Greenhalge was
borne along in that generous tide of 'civil-service reform.'
To the day of his death he was a 'civil-service reformer,'
although he did not agree with all who used or misused that
name. He believed in a constant reform looking always

towards fitter men for all departments of the public service.
He never took part in any political trick; he never counte-
nanced any. Under the flag of reform he followed Sumner
into the Democratic party. The management of Lowell was
not so potent then in the Democratic as in the Republican
party. The reason was that the Democratic party was then in
the minority, and the management dealt only with majorities.
Greenhalge was nominated as candidate for State Senator on
the Democratic ticket. He was nominated because he was brilliant and talented, and because the young men who did the
nominating had no desire to keep him in obscurity. Lowell
was a Republican stronghold, and he was defeated. The great
number of votes he received much disturbed those who regarded
him as a constant menace to their stupid and selfish control of
local affairs. They rejoiced, however, that he was at last out
of the party that was in power. To their dismay he did not
stay out. Only four years later he was again in good standing
in the Republican party. Many good Republicans would
doubt that he ever had good reason to leave it. Many good
Democrats could see no good reason after he was once well out
of it for him to go back again to it. He was so frank, so logical in his own treatment of this change and rechange of parties, that he was seldom accused of fickleness. The bosses of
the party to which he finally returned had more to say about
it than those whom he finally abandoned. In 1872 he
thought that, with Greeley elected President, with Sumner the
power behind the throne, and a host of old antislavery heroes
in places of power, whether the administration were to be
called Democratic or not, the old Republican principles would
never suffer injury. He had a broad and catholic confidence
in the common people, which was truly Lincolnian. He never
believed that the Democratic party was composed of rascals.
It was seven years after Appomattox; he thought that the time
had come to drive out of the public service the rascals of both
parties. Nobody saw better than he that great political parties
are necessary in a free democracy. He understood that no
such party, with its millions of thinking men, can be an
absolute unit in opinion. He knew that to decide great questions each party must act as a unit. On the other hand, he

believed in the 'divine right to bolt.' It was weak to bolt
continually. It was a matter of conscience with every voter
to decide when the emergency was so great as to justify him
in deserting his standard. He stayed with the party with
which he could agree in 'essentials,' and claimed the right to
disagree as to 'non-essentials.' In 1872 he thought he differed
in essentials, and he bolted. In 1876 the two chief planks in
the Republican platform were 'Hard Money and Civil Service
Reform.' It seemed to him that the question of honest payment of the national obligations, as against the 'greenback
heresy,' had become an 'essential.' He was for resumption,
as against what seemed to him to be repudiation. It seemed
to him, also, whether he looked at the platforms or the candidates, that if either party was for civil-service reform, it was
the Republican party. For that cause he had left that party,
and for that cause, and to maintain the nation's currency and
the nation's honor, to that party he thought he might well
return.

"Perhaps it was not until 1872 that his brilliant work upon
the political stump fairly began. He was heard outside of
Lowell, and from that time forth the demand upon him for
political speeches and other public addresses and orations
rapidly increased. If he ever had a secondary ambition for
political office as subordinate to the objects of his supreme
ambition, it is practically certain that at this time he had
given it all up. He did not expect office; he did not wish
for it. He had found delight in work upon the public platform. In politics his ideals were high. He raised his standard; he followed it, not caring into which political camp it
led. His artistic temper had found a new delight in certain
kinds of political work. He was freer from anxiety than
many, because at that time he cared for no political reward.
His subsequent elections to public office came to him literally
unsought. Being once elected, no man in America, either living or dead, ever did the work he was called to do with a more
disinterested, spotless, patriotic, public purpose than did he."

Greenhalge had few more intimate friends than Judge Lawton, and the above sketch explains much in his career.

Greenhalge, as a young man, seemed destined at once to enter into the political life of the country. He belonged to that class of young men who by their talents immediately attract attention, to that profession which insensibly leads its votaries into the field of politics. He was marked for political preferment from the outset of his career; his oratorical talent was recognized at once; his ambition stirred within him, and he felt himself destined to share in the conflicts of party. He wished for action and excitement, induced by his energetic nature, and he early turned to politics. He had felt the emotions of literary ambition; his taste revolted from the sordid elements of political life, but his active spirit led him on.

We are active beings, and our larger sympathies are always with an active career. We long to influence directly our fellow-men, to realize the results of our endeavors without the long delay that chills the fruitions of literary toil, to see our influence expand and our powers develop in the actual world, cheered by the sense of immediate recognition. It is impossible that a young man should feel all the sense of duty that comes with years and experience. Duty became the prime motive of Greenhalge's career; but it was ambition, no doubt, that first moved his spirit to effort, — the generous ambition of young and fiery spirits, of Fortinbras and Henry V. By a cold and calculating spirit of ambition he was never moved. A record of the career of young men in our Republic who enter upon the public service reads somewhat like that of a young noble of the Claudian or Julian families in the ancient Republic of Rome, rising by regular stages from ædile and prætor to the consulship. Our offices are not so splendid, and their titles have become commonplace to us; but the order of progress is the same.

Greenhalge was admitted to the Bar in 1865; in 1868–69 he was elected to the Common Council of the city of Lowell; in 1872–73 he was a member of the School Board; in 1879 he was elected Mayor of Lowell; and so on to Congress and the Governorship.

If for a long time he seemed to linger in the obscurity of local politics, it was due to the circumstances of his position.

The talents of Greenhalge were nevertheless ripe at an early age; his youthful efforts were brilliant. His first political speech is still remembered in Lowell; it happened while he was a law student, when with great *éclat* he addressed a crowd that had assembled in the street.

A rather amusing instance of the influence of his youthful eloquence occurred when he was a member of the Municipal Council. During that time the necessity arose for a new grammar-school building. At the meeting of the committee which was to decide the matter, young Greenhalge was late, and before he arrived, the question had been discussed and a vote passed, appropriating a far from liberal sum for the erection of the building. When the late comer learned the result of the discussion, the amount voted appeared to him entirely inadequate; and he protested most eloquently against what he considered such false economy, lack of public spirit and civic pride.

The members of the committee were moved, — voted to reconsider; and the result of their reconsideration is the present Green School building, which, whatever may be thought of its architecture in these days, was then considered a fine structure, and which was the first of the many handsome school buildings that now beautify our city. It was Greenhalge too who insisted that the Common Council might adjourn at will, and not await the pleasure of the Board of Aldermen, — which action made a precedent for all time.

From the time that he became a lawyer he spoke in all succeeding political campaigns with increasing frequency until he became one of the most active speakers on the stump. In all these contests he gained the reputation of a fair and consistent adversary. His power of sarcasm and invective made him a dangerous opponent; but his character was respected by the opposite party, and he made few enemies. The Democratic citizens of his native city admired his brilliant talents, and always manifested a liking for him personally. They knew that in private his tastes and habits were Democratic, that he himself cherished no enmity.

When Disraeli addressed the electors of High Wycombe at the hustings from the porch of the Red Lion Tavern, a keen observer might have been able to prophesy with confidence all the future successes of the youthful orator on the grand stage of Parliament. So one who heard the young Greenhalge speak to the electors of Lowell could have foretold his after career with full assurance.

His talents, indeed, were incontestable when he stood at the threshold of his career; he was a bright boy, a brilliant youth, a man of indefatigable intellect. It would be interesting to trace his political life from the beginning and in detail. The record, however, of those early years is difficult to recover, even though so few years have intervened. Prior to his election as Mayor of Lowell, comparatively few of his speeches have been preserved.

His reputation was, however, already high in his own city. He was known as an able lawyer and eloquent speaker; he had served in the Common Council and School Board. His character was much respected, and it was natural that he should be selected as a candidate for the office of Mayor of the city. In the convention, Dec. 3, 1879, he was nominated by the Republicans for that position by a majority of forty votes, and was elected, December 9, by a majority of 856 votes.

In American history the office of mayor has often been the first step in the ladder of high political preferment. Executive ability displayed in that field of effort has always been highly prized by the American people. The government of our cities is indeed one of the crucial questions of the time; presenting a dilemma which the people are called upon to solve. It is the rift in the armor of Britomart, — a flaw which endangers the safety and honor of Republican institutions.

As Mayor of Lowell, Greenhalge won a large increase of popularity. His administration gave satisfaction to both political parties; on all the occasions when he was called upon to represent the city, he acquitted himself well. People felt that he was able to act as their representative with credit. His eloquence, often called into request outside of the city, flattered their civic pride. His character was respected, and his ability and firmness became better known. On Dec. 11, 1880, he was renominated by acclamation. At this election he received the unusual honor of being nominated also by the

Democratic party, — a rare distinction in political annals. It was an honor that came to him justly, and shows the personal popularity that he enjoyed among all classes of the community, the general appreciation of his unusual ability, and the respect that his character evoked.

He was re-elected by a majority of 3,675 votes over his only opponent, put in nomination by the Anti-License party.

At his inauguration, Jan. 3, 1881, Mayor Greenhalge in his address advocated the erection of a new High School, of a new City Hall, and the introduction of free text-books into the public schools; all of which ideas have since been carried into execution. During his term of office, also, military drill was introduced into the High School.

The City Government of Lowell has not heretofore been in the same predicament with some others in the country. It has been comparatively pure and free from political scandals and rings. In its early history a very high tone prevailed in the politics of the city. The character of the officials was singularly estimable. It has changed since for the worse, yet Mayor Greenhalge found no great evils to reform, no very dark corners to clean. He could not distinguish himself very much in such ways; but he enhanced his reputation in others, and when he left office, the chance of further political preferment was greater than ever before. As to his career as mayor, a friend of his said: —

"In 1879, without his own desire, and in spite of the persistent opposition of the local managers, with a very popular and capable opposing candidate, he was nominated, and by a large majority elected, Mayor of Lowell. He served two years. It can hardly be said that there was an organized opposition to his second election. In this service, when he was thirty-seven and thirty-eight years of age, he showed, beyond all question, that he was 'practical.' It surprised some of the little burgesses that a 'literary feller' could comprehend the mystery of the city debt of two or three millions and the sinking funds to pay it off. Through his enterprise and persistency, and to their amazement, the city borrowed money at a lower rate than ever before. Some of them were frank enough to own up to their surprise. Others still clung to the view that a man could not excel in so many directions; it seemed safer to intrust business to men who were a little dull."

The inaugural addresses which he delivered as Mayor are models of concise statement, and contain the evidence of much foresight, and a wise consideration of public affairs. The following are quotations from his speeches upon his first and second inaugurations : —

" Efficiency and character are the only tests to be applied to appointments, and a fearless fidelity to the highest interest of the whole city the only principle by which your official conduct should be tried. That man among you who shall square his conduct, not by these principles, but by some theory of future political preferment, betrays the trust reposed in him by his fellow-citizens, and violates the solemn obligation he has first taken."

" As with everything else, a good government commands a good price, and the best is the cheapest. But before making any expenditure, you must be satisfied that the public good really requires it, and then be sure that for every dollar of the public money there shall be a proportionate return of public benefit."

" The instruction of our youth gives us a security and peace beyond anything that law or police can give. These are the external armor of the body politic. Education is the very breath of life."

" The education of the people, then, must be the first object of public concern; herein lies the very safety of the Commonwealth. ' Salus civitatis est suprema lex.' "

" Our coming here does not mean the proscription of any class of our fellow-citizens. If we may not win enthusiastic praise, at least let it be said of us that, during our administration, no man was abridged of his rights, and no harm came to the city which we might have averted."

Dec. 30, 1881, he delivered a closing address before the Board of Aldermen. In regard to harmony, he said he would not give a straw for a man who, having any convictions, is afraid to stand up for them. He believed in differences, and

11

did not think there was a man in either board with which he had served with whom he had not had differences.

It was during his mayoralty that the death of President Garfield occurred. This event called forth the following letter to the pupils of the public schools, a copy of which was presented to every child : —

MAYOR'S OFFICE, LOWELL, MASS., Sept. 21, 1881.

To the Pupils of the Schools of Lowell :

James Abram Garfield, President of the United States of America, departed this life on Monday, the nineteenth day of September, 1881. At the time of his death he held the highest office in the republic, — the most honored position in the world. He was gifted with powers and graces seldom bestowed upon the sons of men; and his brief but brilliant life was illustrated by his truth, his intelligent strength, and his love for mankind. To the heart of youth and early manhood the story of the life just brought to an untimely close must forever be an example and an inspiration. In whatever station of life it pleased God to place him, he walked clothed with the majesty of a true man.

Courage and honor brightened the dark ways of poverty; modesty and simplicity gave a new grace to prosperity and greatness.

In the humblest paths trodden in the days of his toilsome youth, in the heroic struggle for the worthy and ennobling prizes of life, and in the full splendor of achievement, he leaned upon the Almighty Arm. Yes, in the valley of the shadow of death, he walked with God.

Scholars, in James Abram Garfield you have a product of our institutions, of our education, our civilization, — a perfect type of the citizen of the American Republic.

In the hall of statues built in the people's heart, Garfield stands a fit compeer with Lincoln, Sumner, and Andrew.

I have said these brief words to you, because it seemed very fitting that the memory of so grand and childlike a man should be enshrined in the loving hearts of youth and childhood.

May he rest in peace!

Sincerely,   FREDERIC T. GREENHALGE, *Mayor.*

The following speech I insert entire; it was spoken on Decoration Day before the Grand Army of the Republic during his mayoralty : —

" MR. COMMANDER, SOLDIERS OF POST 42, LADIES AND GENTLEMEN, — The rude tablet erected on the graves of the Spartans who fell at Thermopylæ bore this inscription : ' Stranger, tell the Lacedæmonians that we lie here in obedience to their command.' Simple, stern, yet pathetic words! The Spartan knew the cold, relentless nature of his countrymen, and felt that the testimony of some cold and impartial stranger was needed to wake their gratitude. But our heroic dead, whom we commemorate to-day, need not appeal to any *stranger* to remind us of their patriotic deeds. The memory of their services, like the flowers strewn over their graves, blooms with added freshness year by year ; and faithful comrades, preserved through the storm of battle, loving children, and grateful fellow-citizens, make this annual pilgrimage to deck with flowers of May the consecrated earth where

> ' Sleep the brave who sink to rest,
> By all their country's wishes blest.'

" To-day, in pursuance of time-honored custom, the city of the dead has been made to shine with a glory that the summer cannot give ; for over every soldier's grave, rising above the flowers scattered by loving hands, we have seen what we may regard as the richest of flowers, nourished and strengthened as it is by patriotic blood, — the banner of our redeemed republic. And we know, my friends, that were it not for these graves and the deeds of the dead who lie there, that banner would not, as it does to-day, ' shine like a meteor streaming to the wind,' telling in every land and upon every sea a story of the freedom, the equality, and the brotherhood of man.

" But there are other graves than those you have honored and wept over to-day. It is something to the stricken mourner — to the mother, the widow, the orphan — that their beloved ones are resting here, — here, where our two bright rivers, our Merrimac and Concord, unite their murmurs in a requiem to these sleeping warriors, — here, where love and gratitude may offer their frequent tribute. Let us not forget to-day the true-hearted men who gave up their lives for their country to lie down in nameless and unknown graves.

" Is this a day of festival or a day of mourning? Does it not partake of the nature of each? We lament the husband, the father, the brother on the field; but the angel of love and patriotism blows a blast of resurrection, heard all over the broad land, and our lost warriors rise from their graves to mingle with us and to receive the wreaths of honor prepared for them by a grateful country.

" A soldier broken in body, mind, and fortune, applied for aid. ' What is your disability? ' He rolled up his sleeve and showed a terrible scar upon an arm shrunk and twisted out of shape. ' Chancellorsville,' he said simply. He displayed a great wound upon the breast, saying, ' Mechanicsville.' Each wound was an indelible record, — he carried about with him his history in a form shorter and clearer than any book.

" It is pleasing to think that the humblest soldier, with the history of his battles written upon his body in scars and wounds, can lie down to his eternal sleep and know that with every recurring anniversary of this day the muffled drum will beat above him, and grateful hands will make his last resting-place beautiful with flowers and with the flag for which he fought. "

Mayor Greenhalge spoke, March 3, 1881, at the Y. M. C. A. Trade Reception. The following fragment is taken from his speech on that occasion : " If religion should tell anywhere, it should tell in the every-day life of the individual; and as it is good to have the spirit of religion in business, so it is good to have the method, the scientific arrangement, the character and judgment of business in matters of religion. "

One thing that Greenhalge always insisted upon in his speeches as the chief part of the statesman's duty was the necessity of maintaining the character of the people in its integrity and strength. Few statesmen have seemingly seen and insisted on this truth. It has been overlooked and put aside by many. To some politicians the people are but figures to be manipulated, pawns upon the political chessboard to be manœuvred, means by which victory can be organized and party success assured. Material prosperity is in their eyes the chief factor in civilization, — to be maintained at any cost. This question strikes at the root of our economic theories and ideas of government.

There is an interesting passage in Froude's Life of Lord Beaconsfield, in which he speaks of the necessity of maintaining the character of the English people. Disraeli he claims was the only statesman of his time whose constant aim it was to uphold and develop it; and he quotes a curious remark of Aristotle, that while aristocracies have always fostered the national character, it has been neglected by democracies, the latter seeming to think that character will grow by itself. Many statesmen and politicans seem incapable of grasping any save abstract ideas.

Cheapness is not the chief desideratum. It is first necessary that the work done should be good; not scrimped and scanted, but performed under the sense of responsibility and conscientiously. This is a primary and elemental truth; yet it is often forgotten. Success is to be won, but never by unfair methods. National prosperity should be the just reward of the people, and advance hand in hand with the character of the people. Whatever tends to undermine that character is not to be endured or tolerated, even though wealth flows in its train, and power and dominion. The politician may neglect this quantity, but the statesman cannot. Greenhalge always appreciated and upheld the necessity of character; it was a basic principle with him, — the foundation of all good government, the source of strength, the nucleus round which all the attributes of power cluster.

Napoleon understood the volatile nature of the French, and undermined their character still more to suit his own selfish ends. By his victories he overcame the conscience of his subjects, until he rendered them incapable of self-government. He made them the tools of his ambition, and the mighty fabric he reared fell into the dust. The character of the British people, on the contrary, during all their immense struggle with the Imperial Corsican, continued to develop and strengthen. It emerged from the conflict with glorious pride and power.

Greenhalge said, in a quotation already given, that the

standard of public men should be raised to correspond with
the higher standards of the people. He himself will always
be found supporting the men of highest character as he understood them. If other men than those whose claims he advocated prevailed in the political conventions of his party, he
bowed to the popular will, — and it is right to do so, except
in extreme cases, for it will often be found that the decision
of the people vindicates itself, and the course of events justifies their action; even if the choice of the people or party is
not the best that it would have been possible to make, a middle
course must often be taken in public affairs.

Greenhalge, however, was of the opinion that civilization,
good government, and the true grandeur of nations were not
merely questions of statistics and numbers, nor of political
tactics and strategy, nor even of cheap production, national
expansion, and party triumph, but matters chiefly of bone,
sinew, and brains, of blood and iron in the human character,
and the light of a free intelligence shining in the spirit of
man.

He always joined himself with the best element of his party;
their candidate was primarily his candidate. In 1876 he
supported Benjamin Bristow as candidate for President, and
formed a Bristow Club in Lowell. At a meeting in Lowell
held for the formation of the club, he said : " We want men
in position and as party representatives who will give their
highest and best thoughts alike for the interest of country and
of party. Bristow commands the respect of all for his honesty,
ability, dauntlessness, and incorruptibility. "

In 1884 he was an Edmunds delegate at the Chicago convention when Blaine was nominated on the fourth ballot.
Blaine, the popular candidate, carried all before him at the
convention; but the election of Cleveland justified the opposition of those who held that success could not be achieved under
the standard of Blaine, — that, notwithstanding his great
ability, he would not carry the people with him. Blaine's
political escutcheon was tarnished in the opinion of many;
suspicion was attached to his name, and his defeat was assured.
Nothing of this appeared, however, at the convention, and the
utmost enthusiasm prevailed for the plumed knight of Maine.

Greenhalge's private feelings during the time the meetings were being held are apparent from the following letters written home to his family. They express the dislike he felt for some of the conditions of political life, for its noisy and vulgar side.

CHICAGO, June 4, 1884.

I got through the first day of the convention tolerably. I don't like the business at all. A pandemonium without the least necessity, — all for show and humbug. We carried our vote, defeating Clayton for temporary chairman. The Blaine men were surprised. I shall take no part — that is, public part — in the convention; it is not in my line. If I were directed to present somebody, I could do it; but Governor Long and Senator Hoar are to do that sort of thing. I yearn for my dear ones, — we never fully value our home when there. I am not made for a politician; I don't fancy Chicago, and don't see how anybody can — except the people who like to go to sleep to brass bands.

CHICAGO, June 6, 1884.

I hope and trust I shall not be under the necessity of communicating by letter more than once again. We are going in the morning to begin balloting. I went to bed this morning at about three, the convention holding till about two A. M. The speeches were made last night, Long making an incomparable speech for Edmunds, and Curtis a fine one, but not equal to Long's. The people about here were silenced and charmed by the Edmunds oratory, and are compelled to respect our position. But of all ridiculous performances the " demonstrations " for Blaine and Arthur were entitled to the palm. Grown-up men acting like lunatics, carrying about a helmet, a " floral tribute," to Blaine, — and men, women, and boys screeching in a maniacal manner during the progress. And these are the kind of people who are to name the Chief Magistrate! God save the republic! I offered A——, one of the Blaine men of our delegation, $2 to put on the helmet and march round the hall, but he declined. Well, well! I am anxious to finish and get home.

A friend of Greenhalge's relates the following incident, which occurred in the early days of his political career.

Show and pretence were always odious to him; he was no moral babbler, but of incorruptible integrity. The story shows, moreover, that his power of oratory and sarcasm made him feared at an early date by political makeshifts, and that he was already a person to be conciliated.

"A trait in Greenhalge's character which has fixed itself in my mind was an almost morbid dread of seeming to be better than he was. He had no religion, no goodness, to speak of. His ideal of what a good man ought to be was so very high, his consciousness that he was far below his ideal was so very keen, that his attainments seemed to him not worth the mentioning; he felt he had nothing to boast of; that he had an honest and sincere love of goodness, and an earnest desire to be a good man shows itself in his whole life, is written into every line of poetry and into almost every letter he ever wrote. Such a spirit as he had was the spirit of true Christian humility. It was the same which led St. Paul to class himself among the chief of sinners. It is the feeling that has been at the foundation of the character of every sincere and honest man the world over; this trait of character is well illustrated by an incident that I have retained in my memory since the days when we were both practising law in the old Mansur Block. A certain prominent citizen of Lowell was before the public as a candidate for a high office. He was an unscrupulous man, and through his agents was subsidizing votes right and left. Greenhalge opposed his candidacy, and issued a pamphlet which was in the richest vein of that satire and sarcasm which no one knew better how to use than Greenhalge did when occasion presented. This pamphlet did much harm to the cause of our candidate. It became necessary to silence this battery. Greenhalge was approached, and the bribe was offered. In telling me the circumstances afterwards, I said to him, 'Well, what did you say to him? Did you not kick him out of your office?' 'Oh, no,' he said; 'I told him his bribe was not big enough.' 'Why,' I replied indignantly, 'did you say that? You know perfectly well that no bribe could buy you.' 'Yes,' he said, 'I know that, but that answer was the only one that man could understand.' This was always his way; he was no man for moral heroics. He did the right thing. He stood on the highest platform of righteousness, but he did not care to cry aloud to the populace, ' Look, see me here ! ' He was no man to pose. "

In 1884 Greenhalge was elected to the Massachusetts House of Representatives. He distinguished himself there as much as he afterwards did in Congress, though in a narrower sphere. He soon acquired the reputation of being the best debater in the House, and gained the respect and consideration of its members by his judgment and the sterling nature of his mind. He supported the bill in favor of Biennial Election, introduced in that session of the Legislature, Feb. 18, 1885 ; in a speech in support of the bill, he said : " I am sorry to see gentlemen here who have fallen under the ban of the antiquarian feelings, who cherish and cling to anything old, and can't bear to give it up because it is old. The traditions of Massachusetts are sacred, but they do not apply to the future ; that calls for progress, and in progress in this direction Massachusetts is far behind the rest of the States. "

He also opposed the granting of pensions to the judges of the Supreme Court. In his speech in opposition to the bill, he said that he opposed the amendment and the bill itself as contrary to the principles of our government, that it would be better to pay them larger salaries while in office, and that he believed the bill was hostile to the spirit of our institutions.

He also, while in the Legislature, favored the abolition of the poll-tax prerequisite for suffrage. He would retain, he said, all the safeguards necessary for the protection of the ballot-box, the educational qualifications should be insisted on ; he would trust the people, and believed that as a measure of justice and expediency the resolve should pass.

A committee to investigate the finances of the House being appointed, Greenhalge was made chairman of it, because " he is a strong, able man, and has the confidence of the House. " He was also chairman of the committee on mercantile affairs.

Upon a discussion by the House of the bill to reduce the rentals of telephones, Greenhalge spoke and characterized the bill as careless and reckless. He considered it was more dangerous to the right of self-government than any other bill of the session.   The House afterwards rejected the bill by a large majority.

A bill to exempt sailors and soldiers from the operation of the civil-service laws was defeated in the Legislature during this session.

The Legislature remained in session one hundred and sixty-two days, at that time the longest term with one exception since 1874.   Though a new member, Greenhalge rapidly came to the front.   In many points the resemblance is striking to his term in Congress.   In both cases it was remarkable that a new member should acquire such influence and renown.   In both cases defeat came to cut short a brilliant career, — defeat most unmerited and most unexpected.   The reason was in both nearly the same.   Greenhalge did not make selfish and personal efforts to gain his re-election.   He did not seek the office, and the office which should have sought him fell to other hands. In a letter to the " Lowell Mail," dated Oct. 31, 1885, Greenhalge said, in response to an item in the local column: " You say Greenhalge refuses to lift a finger for himself.   In a certain sense this is true.   A free, spontaneous election by the people is the noblest tribute a man can receive.   An election obtained by purchase, by bargaining, by log-rolling, is not worth having.   I desire an election by the people, fairly obtained, and not otherwise. "

After his defeat the " Boston Advertiser " said: " Greenhalge's course was very dignified; he showed little interest in his election, having been in Boston nearly all day and not making any efforts to get votes. "

In Greenhalge's ward there was a tie vote; but upon a recount Mr. Shaw proved to be elected by one vote.   As usual, Greenhalge bore his defeat with equanimity; he was no politician, and could not feel as one.   The disappointment was general, however.

The " Boston Herald " said at the time: " It is not an encouraging symptom when so good a legislator as Greenhalge is defeated because he declined to work for his own re-election. Greenhalge made an admirable record in the last House.   He was a man of sound judgment, gave close attention to his duties, was active in aiding good legislation, and was the best debater in that body. These qualities should have secured him a support that would have been an honor to the people he represented. Conscious that he had done his duty, he relied upon his constituency to do him justice by showing their appreciation of his services. There are people who believe that the office should seek the man rather than the man the office. They are old-fashioned people in our days."

The " Lowell Courier " said : " The result is to be regretted. Mr. Greenhalge would have been a leading man on the floor of the House. His remarkable talents and his experience would have been invaluable, both to his local constituency and to the Commonwealth."

The " Fall River News " said : " Honest, considerate, and fearless, he won the respect of both parties, and acquired an influence second to none in that body. To set aside such men for others of no particular qualifications reflects little credit on the intelligence and good judgment of any constituency. The State will suffer rather than Mr. Greenhalge ; he has a future, and will be heard from."

These opinions the people and the press everywhere seconded. A prophet is sometimes without honor in his own country, and at this time small justice was done to Greenhalge by the voters of Lowell.

The following lines formed part of a poem read before the House by a member, on the closing day of the session, June 19, 1885, which was printed by request of the House : —

> "When Greenhalge mingles in debate
>   Which others oft prolong,
> His logic, like a mighty stream,
>   Flows calm and deep and strong.
> To listening ears his eloquence
>   Gives ever fresh delight,
> While keenest wit illumes his theme
>   As lightning's flash the night.
>
> " O statesman, blest with rarest powers
>   To move the listening throng,
> Be thine the work to aid the right,
>   And aye condemn the wrong.
> Defend the weak, the fallen raise,
>   The bold oppressor smite ;
> And e'er contend, like knights of old,
>   For justice, truth, and right."

These verses were an exceptional tribute to Greenhalge, and well express the position to which he had risen in the estimation of the House.

After his defeat, it was said that his friends would seek revenge, and that the party might suffer. This rumor called forth the following letter from Greenhalge: —

SATURDAY, Dec. 5, 1885.

EDITOR OF THE " MAIL," — I do not believe that any friend of mine will oppose, or in any way abate, his efforts for the Republican party, from any feeling of bitterness on my account. The coming election I consider of the most vital importance to the people of Lowell, and the continuance of the present government in office is of the greatest importance to every lover of honest and economical administration. I write this on account of a paragraph in the " Boston Advertiser " of to-day, referring to the possible action of my friends, which I think without foundation. I certainly have not the slightest sympathy with such sentiments, nor have any of my friends that I know of.

Feb. 8, 1886, Greenhalge spoke at the Middlesex Club in Boston upon the question, " Shall the poll-tax be a condition of suffrage ? " He said: " The theory of our government rests upon the equality of man. Each man, by virtue of his manhood, is to contribute to the maintenance of the government, and to receive his just share of its benefits. The property qualification is an incongruity. . . . Let us have the courage to put in practice the theory of popular government in every way and under all circumstances. The theory has been tried by the fire of rebellion, by the most appalling political crises, and it stands to-day more beautiful than ever. Let us erase from our book of laws a principle which is unjust, unwise, unstatesmanlike, and unrepublican. "

After the speech there was much talk of Greenhalge as a candidate for the office of Lieutenant-Governor of Massachusetts. It was a premonition of what was to be later. The talk called forth many expressions of approval. The " Lowell Weekly Sun," a Democratic paper, said: " Mr. Greenhalge would be a good man for the Republicans to have on their ticket, and a bad opponent for the Democratic nominee. The democratic and honorable doings of Mr. Greenhalge while Mayor of Lowell, and also while in the State Legislature, have been gratefully remembered by Democrats all over the State, and many of them would be glad to vote for him for any office to which he might aspire." Many Democrats afterwards did vote for him for the higher office of Governor of the State. There was always a predilection for Greenhalge in the Democratic party.

Urged to be a candidate at this time in opposition to Congressman Allen, Greenhalge replied: "I decline to entertain the idea for two reasons: the first, that I should be disloyal to my party and to the principle of fairness if I entered the field against Mr. Allen; and the second, for considerations of a purely personal nature. I say now, what I said two years ago, that I am not prepared, no matter what my ambition may be, to abandon entirely my profession for a political life."

Oct. 20, 1886, Greenhalge wrote to the chairman of the Republican City Committee the following letter, after receiving some votes in the Middlesex County Senatorial Convention:

DEAR SIR, — I supposed that I had made it clear that I could not, under any circumstances, become a candidate for any political office at this time. I owe a duty to those who have confided their interests to me, and that duty has too long been subordinated to public duties. . . .

I consider Mr. —— entitled to hearty support in his candidature for the Senate, and I trust that his election will be a further proof that the Republican party in Lowell is once more a unit, and that while

> " Their ranks may be thousands,
> Their hearts are as one."

Speaking, April 28, 1887, before the Catholic Union on " Government by the People," Greenhalge said: "You can have no national virtue without individual virtue. It matters little if the Legislature is bribed, or the City Council corrupted, if the masses of the people remain true to virtue, honesty, and religion."

Sept. 28, 1887, at the Republican State Convention, Mr. Greenhalge was pushed by his friends as a candidate for Attorney-General. The "Lowell Citizen" said, next day: "That Mr. Greenhalge should receive one hundred and thirty-two votes on the informal ballot, and mainly due to the esteem of many personal and political friends, is an outcome of the short Lowell campaign for the Attorney-Generalship that should be appreciated at its full worth; and the reception accorded Greenhalge at the Tremont House during forenoon hours preceding the session of the convention was specially significant, as it bears upon the future."

This vote was almost purely a personal compliment. The work done by his friends was little, and covered a brief interval. The movement was not in the nature of a machine boom, and the result was very gratifying. Greenhalge considered it a mark of personal esteem. He had not sought the position himself, as indeed all through his career it is clear that he did not seek political preferment. His popularity, however, was steadily growing, and his friends were many and irrepressible.

His name was prominently mentioned at this time also for Overseer of Harvard College, and as the successor of Judge Bacon on the Bench.

Oct. 8, 1887, he delivered an address at Melrose under the auspices of the Melrose Republican Club. Speaking of the party, he said: "We may say further, it is a progressive party. But the spirit of progress is tempered and controlled by a warm conservatism. Conservatism is the foundation; progress is the superstructure. We do not want a building to be all foundation, we do not want it to be all superstructure; we require a just proportion of each."

There had long been an earnest desire on the part of the Republicans of the Eighth Massachusetts District, in which the city of Lowell is comprised, to send Greenhalge to Congress. His candidature had been sought in former elections, but, as we have seen, he had refused to allow his name to be used as a candidate. Colonel Allen, who had served two terms in Congress, declined at this time to enter the campaign for re-election. The Republican party at once turned to Greenhalge, and the pressure brought to bear upon him was very great. He had always been indifferent to public office, and foreboded the change in the habits of his life that would come should he be elected to Congress.

The following letter well illustrates the state of his mind at this time in regard to his candidature : —

LOWELL, Sept. 3, 1888.

I send you a paper to show the "movements" in political fields. I hardly know what to say or to do. I drift, as it were. Yet, upon the whole, I am inclined to think it may be an opportunity. It has danced before my eyes for four years, and has found me adamant. It comes again; must I reject it the third time? You know how much I care for you and the darlings, but must I show lack of courage, of hope, of ambition? It is a trial to me. I know what it means, — the hardships, the cares, the worries; but for Heaven's sake what are we made of, and what are we made for?

This time, however, there was to be no refusal. The demand for his services was too great to be resisted. The following petition was circulated throughout the district, and obtained the signatures of a very large number of voters, representing many of the most prominent citizens and politicians :

LOWELL, Sept. 1, 1888.

Hon. F. T. GREENHALGE.

DEAR SIR, — A declination by the Hon. Charles H. Allen, Congressman from this district, to longer remain in public life after the completion of his present term, leaves a vacancy in our Congressional seat for the Fifty-first Congress, which the interests of this industrial constituency demand shall be filled by a successor who will maintain the high reputation of its representation in past years, and who can render such services as the importance of so large a manufacturing community must of necessity require in the halls of national legislation.

While conceding to Congressman Allen a measure of success which is not surpassed by his predecessors, we are mindful of the fact that the district is constantly growing, its varied **enterprises are constantly multiplying, and the duties and** responsibilities of the office of its representative at Washington are likewise increasing in the same ratio, calling for a higher degree of effort on the part of its incumbent, and necessitating closer attention to all the innumerable details that comprise the round of a Congressman's vocation. In this emergency the undersigned, Republicans of the district, respectfully ask that you will permit the use of your name for the succession to Colonel Allen in the approaching convention, assuring you of our hearty and unremitting support in the canvass, and of a complete and gratifying success at the polls.

Greenhalge replied to the letter as follows : —

GENTLEMEN, — I am not regarded as an eager or inveterate seeker of public office. I am told that it is folly, in these busy, practical times, to expect the office to seek the man. Yet my purpose is, and has been for many years, to wait until the voice of the people calls me to public duty; if that voice is not raised in my behalf, I am, and always shall be, content. I have plenty of opportunity for labor in many fields, and I have never been out of employment. Still maintaining these opinions, I am required to answer your request. I cannot be insensible to the honor which you do me. A nomination, an office, tendered in such a manner, is the true gold of political life. Coming, my friends, from the heart, I shall accept your kindness from and with the heart. If the Republicans of the Eighth Congressional District desire me to take up (as well as I may) the brilliant record of Allen (too suddenly interrupted), they shall have my name, my hand, my voice, my heart. I rejoice at the prospect of defending our State, our district, our industrial system, our people, before the country. If I am nominated, gentlemen, the cause and the campaign of Harrison and Morton, protection and prosperity, shall have an earnest laborer in myself.

I am, gentlemen, your faithful servant,

FREDERIC T. GREENHALGE.

LOWELL, Sept. 7, 1888.

The satisfaction his acceptance gave was general, and many expressions of approval appeared in the daily press. The following is from the " Lowell Mail " : " His personal character and his splendid abilities will make him at once an influence in the Massachusetts delegation, and his election will therefore not only maintain the reputation at Washington of the Eighth District, but it will also serve to perpetuate the influence in Congress of the Massachusetts delegation."

To a letter inquiring his view on the tariff, he replied : " I stand firmly upon the Republican platform on each and every issue before the country to-day."

The Republican State Convention was held that year in Tremont Temple, Boston, on September 12. Greenhalge presented the name of William F. Draper, of Hopedale, as a candidate for Governor. In his speech before the convention he said, in regard to the qualifications which the Republican party demand should be possessed by their candidate for Governor : " They require that, in the first place, he should be a typical Republican. They desire, in the second place, that he should be a man of high, clear, moral purity, for Massachusetts demands high moral character in her public men. They desire, also, that he should be of scholarly tastes, with nothing of the schoolroom or the pedant about him. They desire, furthermore, that he should have a worthy political record."

The Eighth District Republican Congressional Convention was held in Jackson Hall, Lowell, Sept. 26, 1888. Greenhalge was nominated by acclamation. He began his speech of acceptance as follows : " I thank the people of my own city of Lowell for their cordial, I may say enthusiastic, support. Their approval is a mark of honor beyond the glittering distinctions of office. May I live and die in such a way that I may keep their regard."

During the ensuing campaign Greenhalge devoted his energies entirely to the interest of the party and the duties of his position. He spoke nearly every night with good effect.

In an address before the Boys in Blue in Lowell, he said : " We prefer to sell our goods to our own people, and we should strive to perfect our own local industries, so that, were it required, we could build a locomotive or rig an 80-ton gun and not have to send away anywhere for any of the appliances. We should strive to forward and help our own people and industries, so that in time we could in every respect challenge the world. "

In a speech at Lowell, October 4, he said: " We have what may be called, and what seems to us, an unexampled prosperity. As we hear the song of the mills, the sound of the engine, the ringing of the anvils, it seems that we have the right to believe, and I believe it right to believe, that Lowell is one of the richest jewels in that diadem of prosperous cities with which the genius of our industrial system has crowned the brow of America. "

The result of the canvass was the election of Greenhalge by a plurality of three thousand. A Republican jubilee meeting was held in Lowell, at which Greenhalge spoke; he referred to his prediction, at the first meeting to ratify the nomination of Harrison and Morton, that the country would make a President of " Ben Harrison. " The prediction had been verified. He returned thanks not for a personal victory, but for a Republican triumph all over the country.

CHAPTER VII.

DURING the months that intervened between the election of Greenhalge and his taking his seat in Congress, he delivered several speeches of note.

November 22 a joint debate took place at Harvard College between Greenhalge and Col. T. W. Higginson, the subject of which was " Lessons of the Campaign."

November 27, at the Republican City Convention to nominate a candidate for Mayor, he spoke at length. He said: " The great national contest which has just ended, and the glorious and shining results spread before us, is of no consequence to us unless our local self-government is attended to. The government of your own fireside, your own home, and your own city is of as much importance as the government of your State and nation; for it is here you are to build up the nation."

Feb. 15, 1889, Greenhalge spoke at the annual meeting of the Garfield Club at Pawtucket, Rhode Island. His subject was, " The Position of the Political Parties." In his speech he said: " You remember it was the little mound and rail fence built upon Bunker Hill by Prescott and Putnam that enabled them to protect their freedom and liberties against the attacks of the British. So it is this little rail of protection that enables you to guard your industrial freedom against the attacks of the world."

June 28 he was made chairman of a meeting in Boston the purpose of which was to advance the interests of Lieutenant-Governor Brackett in regard to the Governorship. Mr. Brackett was finally nominated by the Republicans; and in the ensuing campaign Greenhalge, as usual, took a very prominent part.

October 15 he spoke at a ratification meeting in Music Hall. In the course of his speech he said : " The Republican party is a party of practical purposes.   It is not a party of chimera or of theories ; it is a party of action, of achievement.   Never in peace or war, in adversity or prosperity, in defeat or victory, never under any circumstances did that party despair of the republic. . . .   That same invincible courage and spirit, that same practical purpose, will still guide us on to grander triumphs than we ever won in the past. "

October 24, at Fall River, he said: " Scientific school men tell us we are not philanthropists, but I say that we have taught the world, from our men in Fall River and Lowell, what the true standard of living is.   Every workingman in Germany, France, Belgium, and Great Britain is watching the American workingman, and the result is that every steamer coming to our shores brings hundreds of working-people who come to us and ask for a share of the blessings to be had under the Stars and Stripes. "

Demosthenes used to compare eloquence to a weapon.   It is necessary to possess also the skill to use it.   The partisan speeches of Greenhalge show with what art he employed it. They always told ; they never failed to produce the effect intended.   Greenhalge did not belong to a class of orators of which " Single-Speech Hamilton " is a type.   The stream of his oratory was abundant.   Bolingbroke has said : " Eloquence has charms to lead mankind, and gives nobler superiority than power, that every dunce may use, or fraud, that every knave may employ.   But eloquence must flow like a stream that is fed from an abundant spring, and not spout forth like a frothy water on some gaudy day and remain dry the rest of the year. "

The oratory of Greenhalge was indeed a weapon that shone in almost constant use.   He almost carried out the precept of Correggio, — " No day without a line. "   This was especially so in later years.   It became a matter for expostulation and grief on the part of his friends that he should feel himself bound to respond to so many demands upon his strength.   To Greenhalge, on the contrary, the exercise of his talent gave delight.   He enjoyed his work.   In the opinion of the author it never was a labor that he could not have supported easily as

long as his health remained unimpaired by disease. After
all, it is considered shameful in a captain to spare himself in
the prosecution of his tasks. If life is a battle, should the
contest be shirked by any one? Should not all our energies
be used to the utmost, — whether the instrument we use is
tongue, or sword, or pen?

The voice of Greenhalge was now to be heard in the halls
of Congress. He soon acquired a brilliant reputation at the
Capitol.

It is not the intention of the author to write the history of
the Fifty-first Congress. Its record is written in the memory
of the American people. Only a few years have elapsed since
it was in session. Though it has passed from the stage of
public affairs, it is still a powerful factor in the politics of
our country. The full results of its deliberations have not yet
been reached. It is still living and vital in the spirit that
animated it, — the spirit of Republicanism that has survived
defeat and opprobrium, which is dominant and triumphant
to-day, and seems destined to rule the people and government
of our country for years to come.

It was a great Congress, aggressive and determined. Even
its enemies will confess as much. It was also patriotic and
American, and adopted no half measures where the interest and
prosperity of the nation were concerned. It was rewarded by
obloquy and defeat; it was misunderstood, reviled, and for-
saken. The support it should have had from the people was
withdrawn, and it saw itself supplanted by a party eager to
undo the work it had accomplished.

The power and effect of a shibboleth were never before so
plainly disclosed in the political world as they were in the case
of the Fifty-first Congress. The Tariff Bill, not then put to
proof, which events have seemed to justify, became a term of reproach and reproof in the mouths of the people for whose benefit
it was framed. It came to have the sound of a condemnation.
In reality it lost all meaning, and became a mere shibboleth.
It resulted in a stampede, a blind movement of the people in
opposition. A campaign of exaggeration and abuse was inaugurated. The Democratic politicians were skilful, and the result
was a conjurer's trick in which the people played the part of

gulls. Such at least is the stalwart Republican view, in which, no doubt, Greenhalge shared, as his Republicanism needed no brace. In reality these destructive and overwhelming movements of the people are common enough in politics. Public opinion, like a vast pendulum, vibrates between extremes when unstable conditions exist, and settles at last usually in some middle place. The Republican party to-day is reaping the full benefit of the reaction, and it rests with that party to keep the public favor it has recovered.

The Democratic party, like the old classic race of fable, seemed to hasten on its own destruction. It encountered its share of very stormy financial weather, and the disturbance in the business world reacted on the party itself. Yet by its own acts it lost the confidence of the people with unexampled rapidity. The country, sunk in the depths of despondency over the business depression, — a depression unexampled in modern times, — distraught with financial panic and long-continued distress, sought in vain for any help from the Democratic party. In Congress it undid all the work of its predecessor in power, but it built nothing on its own account. It justified to some extent its reputation as the party of destruction, but not of construction. It tore down, but it could not rebuild. It showed incompetency, schism, and heterodoxy in its own councils. It showed that the strange jumble of ignorance and quack nostrums, financial heresies and political juggleries which prevail to some extent in all parties, formed a much larger share of the Democratic organization. These develop with astonishing rapidity in the untutored American mind, fertile and full of devices, inventive as the American mind is ever.

There are labor heresies and silver heresies and political nostrums of all sorts. They spring up in the political world without number, just as creeds do in the world of religion.

America has become the great mother of creeds and forms of worship. So it has of political creeds and propaganda. The large hopefulness of the American character has made it credulous, as if with all these large results of time, with all these accomplished marvels of science and commerce, there was nothing impossible. This credulity is a spirit of mischief continually attacking the established order and ancient methods. " Lath-swords and scissors of destiny, Pickle herring and the three Parcæ alike busy in it."

Human development moves along old and established lines of thought. Its great current continues for ages in the same channel. Such credulous theories are the mere froth upon its surface; being surface aspects, they are very evident, and conceal to some extent the great tides below.

They are not perhaps as serious in their import as they seem to be. They cannot prevail against natural laws, yet they are the source of continual disturbance. The Republican party seems at the present time to be most free from their influence. It is less bewildered by the disturbance in the political magnetic needle which is due to their action. It keeps a steadier course. The American people, it is evident, desire its guidance in the immediate future.

The great leaders of the Fifty-first Congress, Reed and McKinley, are to-day the foremost men in the country. They have heard their names reviled by the people; they have seen their far-reaching plans overturned, and have suffered the spurns of fortune; yet in so short a time the people have come to stand with them and for them in the great conflict of parties. These two men have come to be almost like an embodiment of the Fifty-first Congress. It has passed from the stage of the world, yet it still lives in the minds of the people in the persons of these two men. They are its great representatives as they were its great actors. Round them its memories cluster, and on them, in some measure, its power devolves.

Of these two, Reed seems to possess the most powerful nature, and McKinley the most ingratiating personality. Reed is sturdy and honest, and possesses a virile intellect. He is the favorite son of New England, and his character and intellectual force aroused the admiration of Greenhalge. There was an affinity between them, — the bond of character and force. The strength of Reed expresses itself visibly in his face and form; he is the picture of concentrated force. As Speaker of the House, he exhibited to the world the power of his individuality. He is indomitable, intrepid, and inflexible. To Greenhalge he represented more than any other the Fifty-first

Congress, — that Congress which he admired, and in the conflicts of which he shared.   " All of which he saw, and part of
which he was. "

Greenhalge took his seat in Congress on the second day of
December, 1889.   He occupied a seat in the second row on
the right of the Speaker, and next to the venerable General
Banks.   He was fortunate in being appointed a member of
three influential committees, — the Civil Service Committee,
the Committee on Elections, and the Committee on Revision of
the Laws.

It will not be out of place to sketch slightly and generally
the task that lay before the Congress, and the work accomplished by it.   That body was almost immediately involved in
a bitter conflict over the new code introduced by the Committee
on Rules.   It was designed to carry out the policy of the
Speaker in refusing to entertain dilatory motions, and in
counting a quorum by recording members present but not
voting.

The minority were indignant over the innovations and there
were many disorderly scenes.

The Republicans claimed that the constitutional convention
had clearly in mind the idea that the presence only of a majority was necessary to make a quorum, and quoted as a precedent the English Parliament.

The Democrats retorted by citing the action of Blaine while
Speaker, when solicited to enforce the view contemplated by
this rule for counting a quorum.   February 14 the new rules
were, however, adopted by the House.   Their enforcement
drew down much animadversion upon the Speaker, and he
came to be designated as dictator by the Democrats.   His
calmness and determination made him famous in the Republican party, and he stands to-day in that party as a type of
force.

April 16, 1890, the renowned Tariff Bill was introduced by
William McKinley, of Ohio.   This bill, which came to be
known as the McKinley Bill, made McKinley the best-known
man in the country, — the most denounced person in America
by the Democrats and Mugwumps, and the most honored by
the Republicans.   It became the war-cry of the Democrats, —

a cry which caused the defeat of the Republican party. Perhaps the Republicans themselves would not adopt so strong a measure to-day, yet events have fully justified the principle of protection which it carried into effect; it made McKinley President of the United States. After long debates and conferences with the Senate, many amendments and revisions, the bill was adopted July 12, 1890, and approved by the President July 14. Unreason and misrepresentation did their work in the end, and the revulsion of feeling that followed reversed the action of Congress, and the country reverted to the Democratic party and its policy of free trade. The result was disastrous to the business of the nation. The period of depression that followed was unprecedented. Ultimately the sun of Republicanism, which seemed to be for a time eclipsed or extinguished, shone out with increased brilliancy, and became the guiding star of the nation. There never was before such a swift repentance on the part of the people, — so complete a justification of any party by the stern logic of events.

Two new States were admitted to the Union during this Congress, — Idaho and Wyoming.

A bill was passed controlling Trusts and Combinations. The "Original Package Bill" became a law August 8; the Federal Election Bill was introduced in the first session of Congress, and finally defeated in the second session; this bill rivalled the Tariff Bill in the bitter party strife it evoked. Congress passed the International Copyright Bill December 3, 1890.

One of the most discussed measures was that "to provide against a contraction of the currency," or free-coinage bill. It was brought up in the Senate, December 20, 1890; after being amended in various ways in the Senate, it was finally defeated in the House.

No question before the country to-day is as ominous as the silver question. Selfish considerations and crude and faulty logic are at the bottom of it. It strikes at the root of the financial credit of the country. The mercantile and business world is shaken by its continued discussion. In this question "Pickle herring and the three Parcæ" are indeed busy. These will-o'-the-wisp theories have a strange fascination for the

American people, many of whom seem to be, even in the
nineteenth century, Fifth-Monarchy men and Millennium
seekers, particularly in the West, which has seen so many
marvels that the marvellous passes current with ease.

The epitaph of all these silver bills, as they come up to
meet, let us hope, speedy defeat, should be always the
same.   Cupidity, credulity, and incompetency express all
there is in them.   The one in question was sent down from
the " crazy Senate," as Greenhalge described it.   In the discussion of these bills, Greenhalge took but small part.   He gained
his reputation in Congress during the debates on the election
cases.   His selection as a member of the Committee on Elections was a fortunate choice, both for himself and the Republicans.   It was an important committee, more important than
usual in this Congress; it immediately entered upon a wide
sphere of action.   There was a large number of contested election cases before the House.

In the debates that ensued, Greenhalge drew the attention of
the whole assembly upon himself at a time of intense interest
and in the midst of a fierce party struggle.   It was perhaps
the acme of his career; he proved himself to be the right man
in the right place; could he have continued in Congress for a
few years longer, what might he not have become?   He was
pre-eminently fitted for the place he held.   He had not been
taught politics at his father's knee, as Pitt was said to have
been, but nature had given him the talent of a great debater.
He made, perhaps, as great a success as any new member that
ever sat in Congress.   New members are usually silent.
Congress is a formidable audience for any speaker who is not
accustomed to address it.   To gain its favor is usually a task
of years; by his first speech Greenhalge succeeded in winning
its applause.   His power of sarcasm and keen wit captivated
his hearers; his logic and legal lore gave weight to his words;
his invective made him formidable, and his eloquence found
an appreciative audience in that House, which is frequently
bored with tedious displays of oratory.

His readiness was equal to the swift emergencies of public
debates.   He made himself famous in the Congress, and members flocked to hear him.   His success was no surprise to his

friends. It was exactly what they expected; all who knew him well were certain that he would take a distinguished place in any legislative body to which he might be called. Success came easily to him, and he must have enjoyed it intensely. Yet all through his career in Congress, when congratulations were heard on all sides, in the midst of his success, while Congress sat delighted to listen to him, the slight tinge of melancholy in his character is strangely manifest. He did not feel at home among the eager politicians who surrounded him.

He was overcome at times with his old distaste for a political life, of which the sordid part was often manifested in the struggle that went on around him. His letters show that he was dissatisfied with much of his Washington life. One cannot fancy them the letters of a politician written in the midst of political successes; they breathe a sort of spirit of exile, and a tone of revolt runs through them; yet, in a way, too, he loved his life. He did not desire a life of inglorious ease; he felt the duty that is laid upon men to enter into the battle of life, to give themselves freely and without reserve to the task that lies before them, even though it be to fight with beasts at Ephesus. His letters show the inner consciousness of his mind, the deep undercurrent of his thought that set steadily toward the goal to which he was insensibly drawn; the haven of peace he was to find in so short a time, after a life of singular stress and unselfish consecration to the duty of the hour.

In December, 1889, Greenhalge went to Washington, and was present at the organization of Congress. He returned to Lowell for the Christmas recess, and then removed his family to Washington for the winter. He lived at 825 Vermont Avenue. The family life was quiet and domestic in the midst of the political and social hurly-burly of Washington.

The first session of the Fifty-first Congress continued through the entire summer of 1890, — a period of exile to Greenhalge, who regretted the absence of his family, which had returned to Lowell in the spring, who missed his quiet home life, and sighed for the sea-breezes and out-of-door life he enjoyed at Kennebunkport. The disorderly scenes enacted in Congress filled him with disgust. It was under the influence of these feelings that the letters that follow were composed. The later ones were written during his second winter in Washington, while his family were at home in Lowell. They did not spend the second winter with him at Washington, and their absence made his life there lonely, and in a sense solitary.

WASHINGTON.

I miss the beautiful mornings, noons, and nights of K-port. I miss my life, my calm summer life, fountain of strength and hope. The organ man outside has played "Home, sweet Home," and the prison song from Il Trovatore, and the tears are in my eyes. Good-by. I look at the picture of my cottage; I see you all on the rock at the door, or in the open parlor. Adieu. God bless and keep you all.

WASHINGTON, Sept. 22, 1890.

No, there is no truth in the "Herald" article, though I have not seen it. Of course there are suggestions of rivalry from outsiders; but "I will none of it." I am planning for nothing. I am not a politician, and I know it.

WASHINGTON, Dec. 15.

I want to settle down into a regular way of life. The experience I get here is valuable, and gives me much light on men and affairs; but I do not regard it as my real life. I miss my family, my beloved wife, and the regular order of existence.

WASHINGTON, Jan. 19, 1890.

A cool, bright morning. I did not speak on the Indian Bill because it went along. Professor L—— and I sit at our table and comfort each other as well as we can. We shall have a grand row over the Silver Bill, which came from the crazy Senate yesterday. Our only hope is to stave it off until we can get a reasonable bill. I get sick of all the small and large jealousies of this life, — the competition is so much keener than anywhere else. The most trivial things are seized upon, — to exalt one man, and to lower another; but I think my conscience is clear of envy, hatred, or malice to anybody. I want only justice, and am willing to give justice to everybody else.

WASHINGTON, Dec., 1891.

There are several pleasant people here : Professor —— and wife from Cambridge; he a member of the faculty, and, " mirabile dictu," a Republican. He said he expected to find me hoofed, horned, and tailed. It is better than election to meet such a case. I am counting the days till I can come to you. How I wish my way of life were settled, and I were going on quietly and easily and regularly. But even in the old, quiet days, I remember I was not always quiet. I used to get very blue and dismal, and I thought that action of any sort — good, bad, or indifferent — was better than quiet, and that a man should be fighting, defying, seeking obstacles for the sake of overthrowing them. Upon the whole, I am not dissatisfied with myself. Strange, is it not ? I am only dissatisfied with a base and mean-spirited community, and the odd turn of affairs.

WASHINGTON, Feb. 5, 1891.

My life here seems aimless and listless. I do not feel any interest in anything. I am compelled to go through a deal of routine work, — offices, patronage, influence, favors, documents, information, — and I am told that is the true business of life, and real greatness. As if everybody were grasping, — grasping for himself, and in a mean, sordid way. I am a dreamer, an impractical man, because I do not wallow in the slough of personal gain and " swap " favors with office-seekers. I sometimes wonder if, after all, these folks are not right and I all wrong. The meanness of men has no limit. I find no real pride, no self-respect, but fawning, threatening, lying men, where offices are in question.

WASHINGTON, Jan. 21, 1891.

A rather gray morning and chilly. The hurly-burly still continues, and even grows worse; as you have seen in the papers, there was a disgraceful scene in the House yesterday morning. I had just taken Mr. Bachelor into the gallery; he must have been much edified by Mr. M——'s demonstration. Of course it all indirectly grows out of the election bill, and my view is, that the country is not behind us on this (apparently). The Senate should not have forced it at this time.

The Bill is right — a good many things are; but you can't do them. But the brutality and idiocy of —— are unjustifiable on any ground. The A—— Post Office contest annoys me extremely. I am more and more anxious to close up this business, and I will reform and " be happy forever after. "

WASHINGTON, Jan. 14, 1891.

A bright, cheerful morning. I have just received your Monday's letter. Yes, the W——s are here. I played whist with them last night, with my usual bad luck. Lodge made a reply to the attack on him yesterday, which was really very fine. . . . What ferocious partisans independent and pure-minded people become ! . . . I wish I were at home now. This business is not at all to my liking. It is " fighting with beasts at Ephesus. " Senator —— said to me yesterday : " You will always be before the people; no man can have more opportunities for high public duties than you. Continue to study the great questions of the day. Your voice will always be one of authority. " I replied that I had no " political future," had never had one, or wanted one. I took things as they came, etc. And I mean every word of it. I propose to allow others to share in the glory and in the labor.

It is a contrast to turn from the letters of Greenhalge to his speeches in Congress; the latter reveal the man in action, engaged in actual duties and the earnest struggle of a political life. They are keen-witted in the extreme, virile and forcible. There is an abrupt change from the slightly melancholy tone of his letters. All is vigorous and vivacious; they show the power of action to invigorate the mind and raise it to the heights of cheerfulness.

Greenhalge first addressed the House February 3, at a moment of intense excitement. The House was crowded, and by rising to make his first speech at such a time he challenged the attention of Congress in a manner that assured him either a brilliant success or a disastrous failure. It was his opportunity, and in a masterly way did he avail himself of it. The attention of all was riveted upon him at once. He did not shrink from the ordeal, and his talent carried him triumphantly through it. The attention of the House changed to admiration. His speech was an exhibition of wit and sarcasm, and also showed the higher qualities of logic and legal knowledge. It revealed a power of invective and aroused the enthusiasm of his own party. The Democrats felt that they had encountered a powerful enemy, yet could not help being pleased with his display of oratory. The case upon which he spoke was that of Smith *versus* Jackson. Greenhalge said : —

"Mr. SPEAKER, — After the diatribe of the gentleman from Virginia, every word of which we have heard a thousand times before, it may be well to consider gravely the nature of the question now pending before this House. The question before us to-day, sir, is one of the highest privilege. It is a primal duty on the part of this House to organize itself, and to determine under the Constitution who are the members duly elected to hold seats as members of the House. It is a duty, Mr Speaker, which precedes the adoption of any specific rules or by-laws or regulations designed to govern the conduct of the House in regard to matters of ordinary business which come before it. Given us the Constitution and the parliamentary law, which is the governing principle of every assembly of American freemen, the principles of which are 'familiar in men's mouths as household words,' and we need no other rule of procedure.

"I have heard questions upon the floor of this House time and time again as to what this parliamentary law is, and whither we are going to find it. I say that the body of the parliamentary law is as well defined, as strictly limited, is as easily ascertained, and as readily applied as the common law; and in its history, its origin, development, and application it bears a close analogy to the great body of the law which we know as the common law.

"Gentlemen upon the other side of the House admire perhaps this system of parliamentary law so much that they have come to admire its appurtenances, its incidents, and even its defects, more than the system itself.

"Why, they talk about these forty-seven rules of the last House of Representatives, some of which prescribe the duties of the officers of the House, — one that the Chaplain shall open the session of the House with a prayer each morning, rules which govern the use of the Hall, granting it for certain purposes and denying it for others, rules with regard to the right of admission to the galleries, and so on, — I say they talk of these forty-seven rules in a spirit of adoration, very similar to that which inspired Mrs. Gamp whenever she spoke of the angelic 'Mrs. Harris.' Why, you remember that Mrs. Gamp used to say of Mrs. Harris that she had 'the countenance of an angel — which it would be if it were n't for the pimples.' [Laughter.] I do not like to compare the Democratic party to Mrs. Gamp, though the points of similarity, perhaps, are somewhat obvious.

"A MEMBER. Especially the pimples. [Laughter.]

"Mr. GREENHALGE. Yes. And I do not want the Democratic side of the House to go beyond Mrs. Gamp in admiration of these rules. I do not want them to admire the pimples more than the countenance itself. [Laughter.]

"Mr. Speaker, I like to speak well of the other side whenever I have an opportunity. I desire to say of the minority report that it does great credit to the gentleman from Georgia [Mr. Crisp] who prepared it. I think the language of the report is in admirable tone and in Machiavelian form. [Laughter.] I cannot say it is a good report absolutely, but I will pay it as much of a compliment as I can.

"Ralph Waldo Emerson, who, if he had been so fortunate as to live long enough, would have been a constituent of mine, once received a prize at a horticultural exhibition. He was very much surprised, however; but his surprise turned to disappointment when he found that the first prize was for the very worst specimens of the best varieties on exhibition. I will pay my friend from Georgia the compliment of saying that this minority report is the best report on the worst case that has been presented to this House for fifty years. [Laughter and applause on the Republican side.]

"There is such an air of graceful concession about it [laughter], such an assumption of judicial spirit. The gentleman would not ask for anything that is not backed up by the reading of nine hundred pages of printed testimony. Oh, no; but when you find the actual points and facts in this case, you will see that wisdom and art were shown by my friend from Georgia in his peculiar treatment of this case, and were not shown by the gentleman from Virginia who has just taken his seat.

"Let us look at this question broadly for a few moments. It appears from the discussion already that the subject before the House embraces a great variety of questions. We have questions of law and questions of fact; and these questions take a wide range. Upon the one side we have a question as to the construction of a statute, and upon the other a question as to whether John Diggs and a number of other railroad laborers were residents of Putnam County, West Virginia. We have upon the one hand a question involving the conduct of the chief magistrate of a sovereign commonwealth, and upon the other a question as to whether a payment by the authorities of a bill for a child's coffin brands the father as a pauper, and deprives him of the dearest right of an American freeman. Such are some of the questions presented in this case; but the whole case divides itself naturally into two great branches.

"First, was not the contestant elected duly and fairly, and was he not entitled to the certificate of election; and was he not deprived of his right by the governor of West Virginia by a prostitution of power which would be farcical if it were not shameful? The second branch of the case is the charge of illegal votes alleged to have been cast upon the one side and upon the other.

"I will briefly take up the question of illegal votes first. One hundred and two votes are charged by the contestant to have been illegally cast for the contestee. The contestee alleges that 127 votes were cast illegally for the contestant. Let us see how these illegal votes divide themselves. They divide themselves into four principal groups, — non-residents, minors, paupers, and persons of unsound mind; and mark the numbers of those votes upon each side claimed as illegal. The contestant says (and he is the first person to give the count upon his side, the contestee replying), 'Sixty-eight non-residents voted for you whose votes were illegal.' The contestee replies, 'Sixty-nine non-residents voted for you.' 'Fifteen minors,' says the contestant, 'voted for you.' 'Eighteen minors,' says the contestee, 'voted for you.' 'Eleven persons of unsound mind voted for you,' says the contestant. 'Fifteen persons of unsound mind,' says the contestee, 'voted for you.' 'Five paupers voted for you,' says the contestant. 'Twenty paupers voted for you,' says the contestee. 'One convict voted for the contestee,' says the contestant. 'Two convicts voted for you,' says the contestee, and so on.

"Each time and in each class the contestee, in his innocent and candid way, always goes a little beyond the figures stated by the contestant. Now, when we come to throwing out votes for unsoundness of mind in political matters we are treading upon very delicate ground. [Laughter.] We know what unsoundness of mind is in a man making a testamentary document, or in a matter of criminal responsibility; but I am afraid that the first test made by a political party of unsoundness of mind would be that the man voted the opposite ticket. [Laughter.]

"I am afraid that some gentleman might have thought that unless a man believed that the appointment of tellers in a division of this House was the palladium of American liberty he was a person of unsound mind. [Laughter.] Why, we find in some of these cases to which the gentleman from Virginia has adverted — we find men charged with being of unsound mind who are able, according to the testimony in the matter of Pard Robinson, to discuss constitutional amendments intelligently, perhaps not as eloquently as some of the silver-tongued gentlemen on the other side discuss constitutional amendments; but we do not want too many silver-tongued orators, Mr. Speaker, in the country. I think, after the experience of this session, the House would vote by a large majority against an unlimited coinage of silver-tongued orators. [Laughter and applause.] And I think the gentleman from Missouri [Mr. Bland] would be found voting with the majority upon that point. [Renewed laughter.] But, I say, we have adopted a rule, and we will stand by it; and here is the recorded testimony, that where a man has intelligence enough and energy enough to interest himself about a political question, to stand up and to vote, it does not lie within the mouth of any member of any political party to say that he shall be disfranchised on the ground of unsoundness of mind.

"Take the question of what constitutes a pauper. This question is raised in the case of William Lee. I was surprised to hear again my impulsive and impetuous friend from Virginia go so far beyond that acute and astute gentleman from Georgia, in claiming that the vote of William Lee ought to be rejected on the ground of pauperism. Why, the record shows, on page 741, that William Lee, a man pursued by disaster, had on one or two occasions been obliged to ask for help of the public authorities; and that on a certain occasion, when death had taken a child from his house, he went to a man named Fowler, who happened to be the overseer of the poor, but who was a friend of William Lee, and for whom William Lee had worked, and asked that he furnish him with a coffin for his child; and Lee testifies in the record here that he went to this man Fowler as an individual and as a friend, and not as to an official, expecting to pay the bill himself; and Fowler's testimony shows that if Lee had voted the Democratic ticket the question of pauperism would never have been raised.

"MR. COOPER, of Ohio. He asked him to vote the Democratic ticket.

"MR. GREENHALGE. Yes, sir. I am reminded that this very overseer of the poor asked William Lee to vote the Democratic ticket; and the fact that he did not vote it was made a sufficient reason for this challenge of his vote at the polls.

"Now, my wise and astute friend from Georgia [Mr. Crisp] says — I have no doubt he said this in their private gathering, the caucus of the minority of the committee. I have not the 'Baltimore Sun' or the 'St. Louis Globe-Democrat,' as the gentleman had, to tell me what took place in that caucus, but at least I am allowed to imagine and to infer how this matter was discussed. The gentleman from Georgia probably said, 'It won't do to go before the country on this pauperism matter; we must go slowly; I would not say too much about that child's coffin being paid for; drop it out.' Because he knew, with his political sense, which I imagine is pretty keen and pretty strong, that the political party which should insist for such a reason upon depriving of his franchise a man whom 'disaster follows fast and follows faster' until death stands within his door, taking away a beloved child or a beloved wife, and poverty stands outside denying a decent burial to the dead, will find that child's coffin wide enough and deep enough to bury that political party beyond all chance of resurrection. [Applause on the Republican side.] So, of the twenty paupers he drops out eighteen, and if he had examined the record, as he pretends to have done, he would have had his right hand burned off rather than have left the name of William Lee upon the list of illegal votes to be charged against the contestant.

"Now we come to the question of non-residents. I do not care to discuss what has been so exhaustively and so thoroughly and so ably discussed by the gentleman from Pennsylvania [Mr. Dalzell] and the gentleman from Illinois [Mr. Rowell]. We come now to what I consider the keynote of this whole case, another point where the wisdom and acuteness of my friend from Georgia come in. He does not want much said about that proclamation of the governor of West Virginia. He says, 'Oh, that matter has been practically settled; we make no contest about that.' And here comes in the judicial tone, the air of utter fairness and impartiality. The governor, he says, perhaps was right, upon the record which he had before him; but we, with the light that we have received in the committee, must say that in two or three of his conclusions he was not accurate.

"My chivalrous friend from Virginia [Mr. O'Ferrall], however, takes no warning from the cautious and prudent tone of the minority report. He plunges in recklessly and impulsively to the defence of the chief magistrate of West Virginia. Now, I want to speak in terms of great respect of this remarkable State document, and the only question in my mind at this moment is whether the minority report of our committee or this proclamation of the governor of West Virginia should stand highest in political literature. I ought not to speak in simple words about this proclamation. It is a monument of massive and majestic constitutional learning. [Laughter on the Republican side.] I think it ought to be treated of in sesquipedalian words, and I apologize beforehand if, in speaking of it, I happen to use a word of less than three or four or five syllables.

"Now we come to the remarkable reasoning of the governor of West Virginia upon this 'eight hundred and twe.' I do not think that in this debate sufficient importance has been assigned to that great question. I know that my friend from Georgia [Mr. Crisp] will not give it much importance. He is too wise and too keen for that. Even the gentleman from Virginia [Mr. O'Ferrall] takes a mild, apologetic tone, and what my friend from Ohio [Mr. Outhwaite] will do afterwards about it I do not know, but I venture to say he will go over it in a very tender and gingerly manner. Listen to the magnificent reasoning of the governor. He says, ' J. M. Jackson received eight hundred and twe votes,' and I submit, Mr. Speaker, that the real question in this case is contained in the construction which you will put upon that one sentence, and that all this talk of illegal votes is something superadded and something thrown in as a make-weight to confuse the real issue in the case. Now, what does the governor say about these wonderful hieroglyphics? He says:

"'The words and letters —' mark you, this is a Democratic governor who is talking, and I want proper respect to be paid to his manifesto —'the words and letters are too plain for any mistake. For the reasons heretofore given, there is no authority to go behind the returns. The vote certified must be counted if enough appears to ascertain the meaning. In an action upon a note it was held —' I presume this governor is a lawyer —

"A MEMBER. No.

"MR. GREENHALGE. Well, I mean a member of the bar. The governor says further: —

"'In an action upon a note it was held: "There was no error in admitting the note sued on in evidence, because the amount thereof is written four hund." (Glen *vs.* Porter, 72 Ind., 525.)'

"How convincing it seems, when you make a citation of a law report in that manner! [Laughter.] The governor proceeds: —

"'So it has been held that the abbreviation in a declaration, "damage one thous. dollars," is not an error.'

"MR. NIEDRINGHAUS. Does the gentleman know that 'twe' is the original Anglo-Saxon way of spelling the word 'two'?

"MR. GREENHALGE. Oh, yes; I am familiar with the whole language from its very beginning [laughter]; but I thank my friend for the suggestion, because that corroborates our position.

"Now, I want gentlemen to listen to this Pickwickian reasoning, which certainly is the richest piece of political reasoning that I ever read in my life. I want my friend from Georgia to give us a little more debate upon this point. He has two or three hours left, and I want his best opinion upon this, and none of that suppression of the truth which appears to be the governing policy of our friends on the other side in this case. I read : —

"'If enough appear to make the returns intelligible, it should be made so. This cannot be done without striking out one letter and inserting another, or by supplying the seemingly omitted letters. Acting upon the face of the paper, the latter appears more in consonance with adjudged cases. (1 W. L. J., Mich., 395.)'

"You remember, my brethren of the bar, how glibly that comes from our lips at times, — that beautiful phrase, 'in consonance with adjudged cases.' Why, we roll it under our tongue as a sweet morsel; and the governor has culled that choice phrase from some library in West Virginia.

"'The least number would give to said Jackson 812 votes. It will be so entered.'

"This is a decree of the Medes and Persians, 'It will be so entered.' Yes, he takes credit to himself — a credit probably claimed also by the contestee and the gentlemen supporting him — for extreme moderation, because the same reasoning which would enable them to claim twelve votes on that return would enable them to claim twelve hundred or twelve thousand. I am willing to give them credit for moderation. I am surprised that they stopped at twelve, and did not say that it was more 'in consonance with adjudged cases' to make the number twelve thousand.

"But there is another word, Mr. Speaker, which I think will suit this abbreviation which my friend says is the original Saxon spelling of the word 'two'—about which I have no doubt in the world—a fact which I have always been acquainted with. [Laughter.] I say there is another word;

and reasoning as the governor does by parity of reasoning—gubernatorial reasoning, I mean—I can show that my word has a better right to a place in that return than the governor's substitute. I say the word 'tweedledee' exactly fits the requirements of this case and stamps its spirit upon the whole case. Now, by parity of reasoning, you will observe that the word to be supplied could not be the word 'tweedledum,' because the terminate letter 'm' is not suited to the 'adjudged cases.' [Laughter.] We need a terminate letter 'e.' 'Tweedledee' entirely fills the bill.

> '"Tis strange such difference there should be
> 'Twixt tweedledum and tweedledee.'

"But so it is. I remember a good deal of talk about a gubernatorial proclamation in my State once, where the sarcastic clerk, being required to read a proclamation on Thanksgiving Day, read: 'Blank, blank, governor of Massachusetts; God save the Commonwealth of Massachusetts.' [Laughter.] I say, Mr. Speaker, 'E. M. Wilson, governor of West Virginia; God save the State of West Virginia.' [Laughter and applause.] And I think, Mr. Speaker, God will save the State of West Virginia before long. [Renewed laughter and applause on the Republican side.]

"It would be impossible for me to discuss these individual votes, but I ask the attention of the House, not to a reading of this record, but to a simple statement of the kind of vote which has been given under each one of these four classes.

"I ask you to take the case of William Lee as branding the kind of vote which they ask you to find illegal under the category of paupers. I ask you to take the case of Israel Cullen, page 741 of the record, as stamping the kind of votes they want excluded under the head of non-residence. I ask you to take the case of Pard Robinson and William Britton as the kind of persons they want excluded on the ground of unsoundness of mind. Take those cases and '*ex uno disce omnes.*' You will find that from the beginning they have taken up these individual cases, not for the sake of explaining to the House or to the country their reasons for disputing the seat of this contestant, but simply to cloud the issue and to give them a right to say that we have proceeded unfairly and not in a judicial way.

"My time, Mr. Speaker, is short. I say if ever there was a case where the voice of the people was the voice of God it is the voice of the people of the Fourth Congressional District of West Virginia, speaking to you, to this House, and to the country to-day. I say you are bound to hearken to that voice, to obey it, and to give to the contestant his rightful seat in the House. [Long-continued applause on the Republican side.]"

His next speech was delivered February 26, in the contested election case of Atkinson *versus* Pendleton. Most of these election cases were of the same origin. The Republicans believed that the members seated in the first place obtained their places by means of fraud, and often of intimidation. They thought that a free vote by all the people of their districts had not been permitted, that party manipulations and fraudulent returns had given them their seats. The Federal Elections Bill grew out of this belief of the Republican party. A free ballot, the privilege of freemen, the ground-stone of Republican institutions, was denied to many citizens of the South. This was to violate the Constitution and undo the results of the war. In these cases the Republicans were determined to vindicate the principles which they thought involved, and the Democrats in Congress were equally fixed in purpose to maintain their individual rights. Therefore the contests were bitter and hard-fought.

The following speech was delivered by Greenhalge during the debates over this case of Atkinson *versus* Pendleton : —

"The question before the House has about it, sir, a special and peculiar interest. The election in the First Congressional District of West Virginia in 1888 was a close one, and it was hotly contested. It was known beforehand that the impending contest was likely to be doubtful in its issue, and each party strained every nerve and put forth every effort to attain success. By each party the ranks of the opposing forces were carefully scanned to detect illegal voters, and the vote of every person presented was subjected to a rigid examination. Voters who had deposited their ballots for years and years without question were challenged, and required to prove their right.

"The situation, Mr. Speaker, in West Virginia, and particularly in this first district, was peculiar. The circumstances were most interesting. There seemed to be a new impulse in the political life of the people, which pervaded the whole State. A whisper of the doctrine of protection had floated down across the hills. That whisper had been heard in every coal-mine, in every workshop, in every household, in every farm and family. More than that, there was another influence at work. Labor, springing to his feet, like Samson with the cry of the Philistines in his ears, stood forth, and, bursting his bonds of iron, stood prepared to meet his enemies.

"Then there was another influence. A new political watchword had been given out in that section of the country, 'A free ballot and a fair count;' and there seemed to be a kind of music, a kind of rhythm about that watchword, 'A free ballot and a fair count;' and thousands of men, hitherto totally indifferent in political matters, were stepping to the rhythm of that watchword as men step to the beat of the drum,—'A free ballot and a fair count.' Such were some of the influences which arrayed the forces under the Republican banner; and the old Democracy, confident in a hundred victories, buckled on its armor and prepared to meet the new challenger.

"The contest, I say, was close. It was some days before the result was at all understood, but finally a rumor pervaded the State that somehow, not merely in the contested congressional districts but throughout the whole State, the Republican party had been victorious all along the line, and that in this particular district Atkinson was elected by seven votes. Then it was that the mysteries of the recounting process came into active operation. Then it was that Lee Snodgrass and Judge Earnshaw, whom my friends on the other side defend with so much vigor and enthusiasm, pirouetted down to the front of the stage and said, 'Behold the saviors of the First Congressional District!'

"I think it important, Mr. Speaker, to examine a little into the character and conduct of these alleged saviors. I think, however, that this House ought to pay a tribute to Judge Earnshaw on one account, — on account of his display of conjugal affection, which will carry his name down to the remotest ages. [Laughter.] Perhaps we admire conjugal affection, Mr. Speaker, on account of its exceeding rarity, but I am always willing to do justice to such an exhibition of it as this judge of elections manifested on this particular occasion.

"Oh, they tell us that the beloved Mrs. Earnshaw was not actually ill, although her alleged illness, communicated by telegram, was the cause of postponing the recount in Wetzel County. She was, according to page 415 of the record, at a merry-making; but still I desire the House to pay a proper tribute to Judge Earnshaw on this principle: that if his grief at an unreal sickness of his wife was so great, how extreme would his grief have been at a genuine illness. [Laughter.] Do not let us forget this exquisite proportion. I remember that once an ostentatious showman (and my colleague from Massachusetts, Mr. Morse, would probably assure me that all showmen are ostentatious) exhibited a sword, and said, 'This is the sword that Balaam had.' Then some strict constructionist of Biblical literature said, 'But, my friend, you make a mistake; Balaam had no sword; he only wished for one.' 'Well,' said the ready showman, 'this is the sword he wished for.' [Laughter.]

"Now, I say that if we are inclined to underrate the grief of Judge Earnshaw, if we are inclined to undervalue the tears which saturate page 414 of the record in this case, we must remember that those tears are what he would have shed in case the calamity which was imaginary had been real. [Laughter.] There was a telegram which my ingenuous friend who prepared the minority report speaks of in tender and compassionate terms. He cannot believe that a judge of elections in West Virginia could exhibit any bad faith. Of course not. And the gentleman [Mr. O'Ferrall] has prepared a mild and somewhat apologetic report upon those telegrams, which are confessedly insincere, false, and fraudulent; but perhaps they pass over that as a trivial incident in the Democracy of West Virginia.

"When I compare the tone of this report with the careful and diplomatic tone of the report in the case of Smith against Jackson, I seem to hear in this report the rattle and clang of cavalry and the dash of hoofs, and to see the shaking of plumes and pennons. Now, I spoke very tenderly, and, I hope, kindly, of the first report made by the minority of the committee, because, strange as it may seem, I have quite a liking for the majority of the minority of the committee. [Laughter.] But I want to stigmatize as severely as I can this report of my friend from Virginia.

"I wish I could, in a rapid and hasty generalization, distinguish between this report and the one prepared by the gentleman from Georgia [Mr. Crisp] in the case of Smith against Jackson; and when I considered the topics taken up and defended by the gentleman who prepared this report, it occurred to me that I wanted to say that 'fools rush in where angels fear to tread.' But, I said, there are two objections to making a quotation of that sort: In the first place, the gentleman from Virginia is not in the least like a fool, and, in the next place, the gentleman from Georgia is not in the least like an angel. [Laughter.] So I had to abandon that method of rapid generalization.

"We come now to the testimony as to the behavior of another one of this precious pair, Mr. Lee Snodgrass; and the tender and compassionate treatment given to him by the minority report is worthy the admiration of all philanthropists and the imitation of all eleemosynary institutions. [Laughter.]

"Why, Mr. Speaker, when the record in all its enormity shows forth the character of Mr. Lee Snodgrass, who, it is confessed, dickered and haggled for the sum of $3,000 as a price for making a clean breast of his conduct in this case; when it is perfectly evident, by every word relating to Snodgrass in this report, that he was conniving with Earnshaw and with other conspirators to obtain possession of these ballot-boxes and to tamper with these votes; when we hear the story of these trumped-up telegrams, these false and fraudulent sicknesses, — we find it impossible to understand the mild tone in which the minority speak of this inestimable benefactor of the democracy of West Virginia.

"I read from the minority report: 'From all the testimony it appears that however censurable Snodgrass's proposition may have been, he had the moral courage (God save the mark!) to

resist the strong temptation held out to perjure himself'—
That is, they offered $1,000 and he desired $3,000. [Laughter.]
—'that though inducements of the strongest character were
presented, he came forth from the interviews'—and I can
hear my friend from Virginia as he declaimed that sentence in
his quiet room—'he came forth from the interviews without
perjury on his soul and without ill-gotten gains polluting his
pocket. His perhaps unguarded remark and immature proposition'—Immature proposition! I like that term!—seem
to have reached the ears of men who were as willing to buy as
he was to sell, but they were unwilling to pay unless they got
full value.

"Why, Mr. Speaker, what was their part in the transaction?
The Republican State Committee had offered openly a reward
of $1,000 to discover the villains who had tampered with these
ballots. That was their part in the transaction. And Snodgrass would not sell his guilty knowledge for less than $3,000.
That was his part of the transaction.

"I call Snodgrass and Earnshaw—the House will notice
that I treat Earnshaw with a little more indulgence on account
of his conjugal affection—I call them *par nobile fratrum* in
this great work of ballot reform. They thought they were
saving, not merely the First Congressional District of West Virginia; they thought they were saving the State, and in a peculiar manner,—perhaps peculiar to the party to which they
belonged.

"It has not been denied here that the main facts which have
been represented upon the floor on the part of the majority of
the committee are true. My friend from Missouri [Mr. Wilson]
says: 'Why all this hue and cry about the recount in Wetzel
County? Did they not recount in Ohio County also? And
there Pendleton lost eight votes.'

"Will gentlemen examine the record and see why there was
not a hue and cry upon their side? It will be found that the
net gain of Pendleton, even in that recount, was some twelve
or thirteen votes. Oh, but the opportunity being given to
examine into this dark vault, to go and take possession of these
ballot-boxes, is no evidence that any crime was committed!

"Can anything be more farcical, more amusing, in political

history than that midnight march down into that vault when three men went ostensibly to search for one bottle of beer? Why, sir, they had an opportunity. It was a close election. The three factors were, — an opportunity, a close election, and Snodgrass, the Democrat. And is not the inference inevitable that the ballot-boxes were tampered with, while the beer was undiscovered?

"Let me do justice to some of the Democratic members of that board of election officers. Under the strongest pressure to suppress the truth, Mr. Speaker, those men testified that not a scratch was made upon those ballots when they passed under their observation at the first examination. When we know that eighteen days elapsed between the time the county commissioners began their examination and the time when it closed, when we have these mysterious telegrams from Arnett and Wells and from the mysterious 'McG.,' and when we find that the condition of the ballots was materially changed from their condition as testified to by the commissioners of election, I confess that I am astounded to see my respectable, my intelligent friends of the other side stand forward and claim that those votes in Wetzel County had not been tampered with!

"When we consider, Mr. Speaker, that midnight marauding party, when we know that the election of the present governor of West Virginia, worthy, I should say, from all the reports, to be successor of the 'tweedledee' governor of that State, depended to a great extent upon the vote in this county, and that he was perhaps seated by reason of some of the iniquities occurring in Wetzel County, it seems to me we have the right to say that a great moral question is presented to the Democratic executive of West Virginia, and that great moral question is this: Ought the facilities for obtaining access to beer bottles to be increased, and the facilities for obtaining access to ballot-boxes to be diminished, or *vice versa?* I say that is a great moral question, and nothing would please me better than to see the Democratic party wrestling with a great moral question.

"I have heard, Mr. Speaker, of the proverbial danger of wrestling with a chimney-sweep; but you will observe that with nice delicacy towards my friends on the other side, I do not say which is the chimney-sweep, — the great moral question or the Democracy. [Laughter.] I leave that an open question for the House; and I do not doubt that the Speaker, with that extreme leniency which he always shows to the other side, would preserve to them their constitutional right of demanding the yeas and nays upon the question. [Renewed laughter.]

"It is easy, of course, in all these election cases to file a number of charges of illegal voting; but how empty most of these are — I speak impartially; I speak for one side and for the other — is shown by the promptness with which great numbers of those charges are instantly abandoned upon an examination. Now, the contestant charged there were 223 illegal votes cast for the contestee, and the contestee charged that 174 illegal votes were cast for the contestant.

"I take some pride, Mr. Speaker, in the fact that we are laying down some good law on election cases, in which we have even the concurrence of our friends on the other side; and one of those rules, as this committee has unanimously decided, is that where a voter honestly casts his ballot, and where the only question is some technical question as to the boundaries of the particular district where he ought to vote, votes cast under an honest error of that sort shall be counted; and that ruling of the committee disposes at once of 73 votes charged as illegal in the Wellsburgh district. And, upon the other hand, — for we do not propose to be outdone in magnanimity and fairness by the other side, — we consigned to its proper place the charge that at Braxton Court House 35 votes were cast illegally for the contestee, and that in certain wards of the city of Wheeling 25 votes were cast illegally for the contestee. So that you will find upon examination that by one honest ruling 100 votes are stricken from the number of illegal votes charged by the contestee, and almost an equal number stricken from the number charged by the contestant.

"Mr. O'Ferrall. The gentleman will permit me to ask whether the majority report and minority report do not agree on that point.

"Mr. Greenhalge. I say that we have agreed upon the

rule; and I congratulate the House and the country upon that one point of agreement. [Laughter.]

"MR. O'FERRALL. I very much enjoy listening to the gentleman while he draws upon his memory for his wit and upon his imagination for his facts. [Laughter.]

"MR. GREENHALGE. I have heard that remark before, but I am not so cruel as to say so. [Laughter.]

"Now, Mr. Speaker, it seems to me the whole question, after all, centres around the great fact of the conduct in relation to these ballots in Wetzel County. There cannot be any question, in the eighteen days Earnshaw devoted to his domestic duties and the delay of the count, that at that time in one precinct ten votes were stricken from the ballot in favor of the contestant, and in another case fourteen votes were taken from him, and two votes illegally given to the contestee.

"I say that here centres the whole story of this case. The flight to these questions of illegal votes is simply a flight to the underbrush, an attempt to evade the great central point in the case. And if every member of this House cared to take home this somewhat voluminous record, should take it to their homes and to their beds, if they have double beds [laughter], and familiarize themselves with the details of the testimony contained therein, I say that the careful examination by the majority of the committee of these, as alleged, illegal votes will stand all honest and fair criticism. And I believe this House will conclude, if they are not too closely bound to the other side by party ties, that the contestee has no right to sit in the seat which he occupies; and which I judge, from the argument of my friend from Missouri [Mr. Wilson], is not his seat, but the seat of his ancestors, his sisters, his cousins, and his aunts. [Laughter and applause.]

"I am willing to go any length in eulogizing my friend from West Virginia [Mr. Pendleton]. I am willing to say he is superior to Grover Cleveland, following out the comparison instituted between him and Mr. Cleveland by my friend from Missouri [laughter], for I might safely go that length; and while justice compels me to say that my friend from West Virginia was not duly elected to the seat he occupies, I take pleasure in saying, at least, that not a bit of this record is stained by any improper conduct on his part. And I take a greater pleasure in saying that his conduct while in the House has been that of dignity, of manhood, and of courtesy.

"I say, Mr. Speaker, that it is a great pleasure if the bitterness of political warfare can be ameliorated by finding our enemies, — the men we have to contend against, — to find them of heroic and chivalric mould. Under those circumstances we have a right to love our enemies; and I thank my friend on the other side he has at least permitted me to know

'The stern joy that warriors feel
In foemen worthy of their steel.'

"Why, Mr. Speaker, when the other day under our very eyes we saw a number of gentlemen on the other side undergoing the horrible transformation effected on the unhappy followers of Ulysses by the art of Circe, I am glad to say that one of the noble exceptions from that horrible rout was the gentleman from West Virginia. No billingsgate polluted his lips. He did not writhe in parliamentary or unparliamentary convulsions [laughter]; he did not froth at the mouth and then protest he was making a constitutional argument. [Renewed laughter.] And when you, Mr. Speaker, 'the still, strong man in a blatant crowd,' were controlling this House, and standing like Gulliver among the Liliputians, with shrieks of anger and pain following his every movement, the gentleman from West Virginia was setting an example which many of his colleagues would have done well to follow.

"Therefore, although I must admit that the contingency of my friend's return to this House is somewhat remote, despite the gloomy vaticinations of the gentleman from Missouri, — and I notice the vaticinations from that side always are gloomy [laughter], — I say that at least he goes back to the people of West Virginia with the assurance of one Republican, if it is worth anything, — and I do not know how much it is worth in the First Congressional District of West Virginia, — that he has at least proved to the House and the country that the good old name of 'gentleman,' with the nobility and manhood and refinement that the name implies, has not lost all honor and respect in the first legislative body of the world, — the Congress of the United States of America. [Great applause.]"

March 4, in the case of Featherstone *versus* Cate, the oratory of Greenhalge was again heard in Congress. The occasion of the speech was the declaration of Mr. Breckinridge that no evidence could be found that any negroes had been killed in Arkansas in connection with politics, and that no evidence had been taken by the Committee on Elections to prove that there was any unfairness about the election of congressmen in the first district of Arkansas.

Greenhalge's sense of justice was stirred by the evidence in this case, and in his hatred of any form of oppression and political fraud, he poured forth a flood of denunciation in some passages of his speech. The impression he made upon the House was deep. His reference to the Clayton-Breckinridge contest was dramatic in its tone and effect. I quote the following sentences from his speech : —

" Mr. Speaker, the recorded testimony in this case is, I believe, briefer, of smaller compass than the testimony filed with the Committee on Elections in any other case before that committee; but I venture to say that the question raised in these 281 or 282 pages of testimony will be found to be as important as those raised for your consideration in the most voluminous record which will be presented to you in any case whatever.

" We have here, Mr. Speaker, for the first time, the necessity for opening the door and seeing the skeleton in the closet of our continental republic. We have here, for the first time, at least this session, the stupendous question of the rights of a race, — the question whether one race has the justice to do justice to another race. I said, Mr. Speaker, that this case raises the most important questions to be presented for the consideration of this House. I forgot the notable exception which has just been brought to my mind by the gentleman from Arkansas [Mr. Breckinridge], who has just taken his seat. I should have excepted the case in the adjoining district in the State of Arkansas, I mean the case of Clayton *versus* Breckinridge, where the House will be called upon sooner or later, and not later, if I have anything to do with it, to sit in the somewhat singular position of judge between the living and the dead. . . .

14

" And then this peaceful, intelligent, respectable gathering of gentlemen, armed with their rifles, or whatever name you may choose to give them, proceeded to evict these helpless citizens, whose crime appeared to be the fact that the sun had burned upon them a deeper color than upon the Caucasian race. . . .

" Are we to be met here, Mr. Speaker, when we are trying the right of a people, of a race, the right of a member to his seat in this House, the greatest and most honorable right that a man can have, — are we to be met by tuppenny technicalities, such as I should not dare to use in a police court in Massachusetts ? . . .

" I say that there was no safety, there was no law, there was no fairness in the County of Crittenden and State of Arkansas, and whether we are required to count up a certain number of votes, whether the quibble be made about 73 votes counted here or 224 allowed there, in order to preserve the purity of the ballot, we have a right to require a reasonable interpretation and application of the rigid rule which, if enforced, would make felony and violence rampant and triumphant. We are bound in this high court, not limited by petty technical restrictions, to throw away all petty technicalities, and to say that the general spirit, purpose, and character of this essay [holding up the record of testimony in the case] on political assassination, which is vastly better than De Quincey's essay on ' Murder as a Fine Art,' as found here, shall not be encouraged ; and that be this contestant Democrat or Republican, be he black or white, as he comes here and demands his right, the justice of the American people, which never fails and never sleeps, requires that he should be seated because his right is established. "

April 11 the case of Waddill *versus* Wise was before Congress. Senator Lodge characterizes the speech of Greenhalge on this occasion as his most eloquent effort in Congress. The speech was as follows : —

" MR. SPEAKER, — I have been at a loss to understand the pertinency or relevancy of the remarks of the gentleman from Virginia [Mr. O'Ferrall] upon this case. But a whisper has come to my ears that there has been some mistake in the time of delivering it. There is, I understand, at a not distant day, to be a State convention in Virginia at which the question of a gubernatorial nomination is to come up; and the speech of the gentleman relates not so much to the question of whether the contestee shall retain his seat or the contestant take it as to whether the gentleman from Virginia [Mr. O'Ferrall] shall be nominated for governor of Virginia.

" MR. WISE. Will the gentleman yield for an interruption ?

" MR. GREENHALGE. Well, my time is exceedingly limited.

" MR. WISE. Just a second.

" MR. GREENHALGE. Very well.

" MR. WISE. You do not want to labor under a misapprehension or to make a mistake ?

" MR. GREENHALGE. Certainly not.

" MR. WISE. The gubernatorial convention will not be held in Virginia for four years.

" MR. GREENHALGE. Well, you cannot tell what views as to the future the gentleman from Virginia [Mr. O'Ferrall] may entertain. What are four years in his sight ? They are like a watch in the night. [Laughter.] And the speech is to be taken, Mr. Speaker, *nunc pro tunc.* [Laughter.]

" Now, I am glad to inform the House that in our journey towards some important conclusions arrived at in the report of the committee we have been cheered and sustained by the always welcome company and sympathy of the minority of the committee. The resolution which has been appended at the close of their somewhat illogical remarks seems to imply that whatever else may be true in this case, whatever other questions may arise in this connection, the sitting member, whose position in the case seems to be somewhat in dispute at present from his own standpoint, was not duly elected and is not entitled to the seat, which candor compels me to say, and which I am perfectly willing to say, he has occupied with so much grace and dignity as almost to tempt me to forget occasionally the invalidity of his title thereto. [Applause.]

" You may remember, Mr. Speaker, that at the opening of this session, if such trifles hold place in your recollection, gentlemen upon the other side contended that the liberties of the country depended upon a certain doctrine, to wit, that physical presence in this House was not incompatible with constitutional or constructive absence of members. That opinion was negatived by a majority of the House; but in the interest of good feeling and from a desire to promote the era of good feeling, I desire to present as near an illustration of that doctrine as we shall ever get in this House in the person of the sitting member concerned in this investigation, — physically present, but according to the dictum of the minority and of the majority of this committee, constructively and constitutionally absent.

"MR. LACEY. Perspectively absent.

"MR. GREENHALGE. Certainly. Now, Mr. Speaker, it is pleasant to know that in this vast volume of testimony, the most voluminous record, I think, presented to the Committee on Elections, there will be found very little conflict of facts. Where, according to the excerpts, the choice excerpts, in the minority report, and the extracts presented in the report of the majority upon one great set of facts, it appears clearly that in three precincts of what they call 'Jackson ward,' there was a long line in each of these precincts of colored voters endeavoring to vote; that they remained there, some from the night before, showing some interest in their rights as freemen, some standing there 'from the rising of the sun to the going down thereof,' tendering, as we claim, their votes to the proper election authorities. There seems to be no question made upon this point, upon this great fact, and around that great fact centres the only dispute which is presented in law or in justice to this House to determine now.

"The number of those men who stayed in line, who were examined in the taking of testimony for this record, is sufficient to overcome the majority claimed for the contestee; and the only question is whether this House will say there was a legal tender of votes under those circumstances, or whether, upon some quibble or technicality, those votes shall be cast out and not counted.

"Now, Mr. Speaker, it is contended in the report of the minority, first, that the judges of election were guilty of no wrong-doing; that all they did was strictly in the line of their official duty; second, that the Democratic challengers were not guilty of fraudulently, unlawfully, or unnecessarily hindering or obstructing the voters in casting their ballots; and thirdly (and these are their conclusions solemnly recorded in this report, written by the ablest man upon their side of the House), that while there was some unnecessary delay, some votes were probably lost to the contestant, it was the result of the tardiness of the Republican judge at the first precinct in finding the names of the voters on the registration book and the conduct of the Republican Federal supervisors at the first and second precincts.

"Then mark the concluding passages, and see if you can tell why the minority have come to the conclusion which they record in their resolution : —

"'In the case before us we have before said we do not believe there was any considerable obstruction to the voters in their right to vote, but it appears that, at the time the polls were closed, at three of the precincts of Jackson ward there were a number of voters present at each polling place desiring and intending to vote who were prevented from doing so by no fault of their own, and it is possible that the number of such voters was sufficient to change the result had they all voted for the contestant.

"'As we have shown, under such a state of facts, the courts determine the result by the vote actually cast. The enforcement of that rule in this case would give the seat to the sitting member.'

"Now mark the magnanimity of the minority : —

"'But we are not satisfied of the justice of such rule. While it is true that neither the contestee nor his partisans can justly be held responsible for the failure of any of the voters to exercise their right of suffrage, yet we believe that some were deprived of the opportunity to vote, and that the number might have been sufficient to change the result.

.   .   .   .

"'We therefore submit the following resolution : —

"'*Resolved*, That the seat now held by George D. Wise as the Representative in the Fifty-first Congress from the Third Congressional District of Virginia be, and the same is hereby, declared vacant.'

"I say that this is the most preposterous law upon elections ever laid down in cold blood in this House. Do the gentlemen whose names are signed here mean to put forward the doctrine that if, without any fault of any candidate or party, without any conspiracy, without any fraud, without any act of God or of the public enemy, as by the breaking down of a wagon, by the overthrow of a railroad train, voters are prevented from being registered or from having their votes received — that because it is no fault of the voter these votes are to be counted as lost and a new election ordered? If that is their reasoning, I say their law is abominable. I ask, in God's name, why, if they believe these facts as they recite them, — why have they deserted the sitting member on this occasion? If the facts are as they state them, the betrayal and abandonment of their brother and colleague upon this floor is the most shameful case of desertion that has ever darkened the annals of this House since its foundations were laid by the fathers. [Applause.]

"Why, Mr. Speaker, there is no man whose name is signed to this minority report, from the distinguished name of the gentle man from Georgia [Mr. Crisp] to that of my excellent friend, Judge Moore, of Texas, who if the facts proved to exist would have warranted the belief that neither the contestee nor his partisans, agents, or his party were implicated in the obstruction of these voters or in any of the frauds alleged, would not have said, 'May my tongue cleave to the roof of my mouth, and may my right hand forget its cunning,' before I put my name to any such report as that.

"Mr. Speaker, as a distinguished predecessor of mine from Massachusetts, to whom I think I was compared a few days ago, one Daniel Webster [laughter] — though I am not sure whether I was compared to him or to one Mr. Sullivan, but Massachusetts always produces the best type, whether it is a gladiator or a statesman [laughter and applause] — as that distinguished predecessor of mine said in a murder case when the alleged murderer committed suicide, 'Suicide is confession,' so I say that in this resolution we have the confession of the minority of the committee that the facts are not as they stated them, but are as they are charged in the report of the committee. We can lead the Democratic horse to the waters of truth and life ; we cannot make him drink. [Laughter.] He is not accustomed to that sort of tipple. [Laughter.]

"Now, Mr. Speaker, when the distinguished contestee makes his valedictory remarks here — and I hope the speech will be as good as the valedictory speech of my friend Compton, whom I suppose I have helped to the post of State treasurer of Maryland [laughter] ; when the distinguished contestee makes his valedictory address I trust he will ask for some logical explanation of this report of the minority of the committee. With those voters in line in the 'act of voting,' — for as my friend from Iowa [Mr. Lacey] puts it in his statesmanlike and philosophic report put forward for the majority, the act of voting is a continuous act — it is clear that that long line of colored voters ought to be counted first, last, and throughout.

"What, then, Mr. Speaker, is the remedy ? Is it to declare the seat vacant and say that a new election must be ordered ? Shall the law be ineffectual ? Shall the white majesty of the law stand silent, powerless, inactive as yonder obelisk, or shall that law be clothed with power and strength enough to give to every man in that colored line the same rights that the white millionaire has ? Mr. Speaker, I have heard and read with admiration of that memorable 'thin red line' which repelled the fiery onset of Napoleon at Waterloo, but I say that this 'thin black line,' standing from sunrise to sunset in Jackson ward, means as much for human freedom and civil liberty as the memorable 'thin red line' at Waterloo. [Applause on the Republican side.]

"I go farther, Mr. Speaker : I say that if this House does not do justice to every man in those lines in the first, third, and fourth precincts of Jackson ward in the city of Richmond, and count every vote there legally tendered, then the flaming lines of Gettysburg were nothing more than a vain and empty show, and even the grand words of Lincoln spoken over the graves of Gettysburg become only as 'sounding brass and a tinkling cymbal.' What remedy shall we apply in this House ? Shall we give a half-hearted, half-way remedy ? When the two mothers, or rather the two claimants for the child, came before the wisest of kings, each claiming the maternity of the child, the king said at first : 'Divide the living child in two ; give

half to the one and half to the other.' That is the Democratic
plan as proposed in this report. But when the cry of anguish
broke from the lips of the true mother, the king gave the living
child to her, the true mother. That is the Republican plan in
the majority report of the committee.

"Now, Mr. Speaker, I say do justice. Do not slay justice.
Every principle of law and equity, of justice and right, every
fact in this case, the same frauds, the same double-dealing which
lead the minority to declare this seat vacant must compel this
House to declare that the contestant is entitled to that seat;
and I say, in the name of justice and right, of law and equity,
of logic and common-sense, the seat which is vacated by George
D. Wise must by all these principles, and by the voices of sixteen thousand free men of Virginia, be given to Edmund Waddill, Jr., the contestant. [Prolonged applause on the Republican
side.] "

One of the strongest speeches delivered by Greenhalge in
Congress was on the Federal Elections Bill, June 28, 1890.
He spoke in the midst of an exciting debate. He did not
believe that the country was behind the Republican party on
this question, as is shown by a letter of his, but he did believe
in the bill itself. " Tip " Wells and " Hatch " Williams *et als.*
were living witnesses of the necessity of some control at the
polls in the South. In his conduct of the election cases he
had become acquainted with their shotgun policy, he had
learned much about their ways in his sifting of the evidence.
He believed in the necessity of Federal control. His spirit
burned within his heart at what he thought an " ancient tale of
wrong," and the feeling gave fire to his words. His defence
of the bill was eloquent and forcible, and made him the focus
of all eyes. It drew the intense attention of the whole House
and aroused the enthusiasm of the Republicans.

"Mr. GREENHALGE. Whenever, Mr. Speaker, I am in doubt
as to the wisdom or expediency of any proposed legislation in
this House, I have a certain rule which enables me to at once
resolve any such doubt. If I find that opposition to a pending
measure is coupled with a virulent attack upon Massachusetts
or upon some of her distinguished thinkers or scholars, like my

colleague in this house [Mr. Lodge], whose ability, integrity, and high purposes are a glory to Massachusetts, I know that the measure thus opposed is one in the interest of progress, of order, of liberty, and of equality.

" It is natural, Mr. Speaker, that these attacks upon Massachusetts should be made. As her flashing ideas march out like battalions from the citadel of her peerless intellect, it is only natural, it is only to be expected, that the forces of vice and corruption, the guerillas of political society, should hang upon the flanks of her forces and attempt to impede and interrupt their onward march. This is as natural as that vice should hate virtue. When Iago, speaking of the man whose honesty he hated, said, ' There is a daily beauty in his life which makes mine ugly,' he only repeated the sentiment which finds voice whenever the ideas of Massachusetts come to the front. Why, it is true that all the ideas that have come from that noble Commonwealth are not perfect.

" It must be remembered that from the alembic of her glowing thought thousands of new opinions and new theories are brought before the eyes of the world. Some are transmuted into gold and abide forever; some are discovered to be dross and are thrown away. But what we complain of, and what we have a right to complain of, Mr. Speaker, is that we find men and communities to-day using as their daily standard diet, relishing as the tid-bits and delicacies of their table, the garbage which was flung from her kitchen a hundred years ago ! This is the fault which we have to find with some people, with some individuals, and with some communities and sections to-day.

" It is enough, Mr. Speaker, to be assured that a measure is right, to find coupled to the opposition this feeling in regard to the old Commonwealth.

" Now, Mr. Speaker, I have listened with a good deal of interest to the objections made upon the floor of this House to the pending measure. Those objections are not without a certain interest. They are worthy of consideration. When Rip Van Winkle, awaking from his sleep of twenty years, came down the mountain side, old and gray, and with flowing locks, to mingle again with busy men, his ideas were interesting, although not particularly original or instructive. [Laughter.] Now, some gentlemen upon the other side resemble Rip Van Winkle in one particular, — they have slept twenty years; but, unlike Rip Van Winkle, they have not yet awaked, nor do they show signs of waking. [Laughter.] I was pleased, Mr. Speaker, to hear my venerable friend from Pennsylvania yesterday [Mr. Vaux]. I have now dropped the subject of Rip Van Winkle. [Laughter.] Comparisons are odious. [Laughter.] I welcomed him as what is called by some *laudator temporis acti*, a glowing and genuine eulogist of the days that are no more.

"I like to hear that expression of regard for what we shall probably see no more in this country, or upon earth. I like to hear my friend's interpretation of the clause of the Constitution now under consideration. There was a freshness and *naïveté* about his interpretation of the words to 'make or alter' [laughter] in this clause. I thought perhaps the interpretation was characteristic. I am not very familiar with the subject by which he endeavored to illustrate his construction of this clause, but as he and some other gentlemen seemed to speak with considerable feeling upon the subject, I may be permitted to hope there was no sad personal experience which led them to take that somewhat gloomy view. [Great laughter.]

"I only know this, Mr. Speaker, that when the interpretation of the Constitution is given into the hands of a strict constructionist, — and I gather that most of the gentlemen who have spoken on the other side are strict constructionists of the straitest sect, — somehow or other, by fair means or foul, by logic or lack of logic, their interpretation results in the emasculation of the Constitution. [Laughter.] Now, I say, Mr. Speaker, that the Constitution gives in clear and unmistakable terms authority to this Congress to enact the legislation proposed in this bill. I say that the exigency requiring that legislation exists in the lawlessness, in the illegal proceedings at numerous election precincts, which is matter, I believe, of common knowledge and common shame, and, I hope, common regret. This is not so much denied, as it is justified under the circumstances.

"Now, when I speak of the Constitution, and in its praise and support, I shall not use 'vain repetitions as the heathen do.' I shall not do it mouth honor, and then, by my conduct, prove that I believe it to be an instrument which ought to be 'more honored in the breach than in the observance.' I say that the terms of the Constitution upon this particular matter are susceptible of only one explanation, and no other explanation of them ever was given until this afternoon by the gentleman who has just sat down [Mr. Buckalew]. 'Make or alter,' he says, means only that Congress may intervene where the States have failed to make regulations. How, then, does he dispose of the word 'alter'?

"Certainly not in so felicitous a manner as his colleague from Pennsylvania [Mr. Vaux]. If it means only to supply a defect, — to do something for the State which has not been done, — how can anybody, even the Congress of the United States, 'alter' what does not exist and what never existed?

"They tell us upon the other side that the proposed measure is revolutionary. I should say, Mr. Speaker, that when you consider the causes, the events which brought into existence this republic, the noblest of all commonwealths, ancient or modern, the application of the term 'revolutionary' is, to say the least, unfortunate. It must have been devised by some consummate master of infelicitous expression upon that side (and I know there are many there), because it is a matter of common knowledge that the people of this country are accustomed to associate with the term 'revolution' the idea of independence, of political equality, of civil liberty.

"If this measure is revolutionary, it is in the high sense in which the Declaration of Independence is revolutionary, in the same sense in which the Virginia Bill of Rights is revolutionary, in the same sense in which the Constitution itself is revolutionary. Why, to call this bill revolutionary is a contradiction in terms, if what is meant is that in its relation to the Constitution and the laws it is revolutionary. Its whole purpose, aim, and scope, — leaving out of account any question of imperfection, of detail, of this or that feature upon which honest men may differ as to its being expedient or objectionable, — its whole aim and purpose is to conserve, to defend, to save the Constitution, and to give equal political rights to every one of the people of the United States. [Applause on the Republican side.]

"Mr. Speaker, when we consider this bill in these aspects, from this standpoint, I think we have a right to repel the accusations and insinuations that have been made that this is a bill in the interest of partisan aggrandizement. I say here, upon my honor as a representative, if I believed that, I would not vote for this bill, nor for any section, clause, or line contained in it. I want simply fair and free elections, and if the gentleman from Pennsylvania, who last took his seat [Mr. Buckalew], would reason for one moment, he would be slow to hurl at the Committee on Elections of this House these charges of unfairness and partisanship.

"Why, sir, after the most careful scrutiny, after a delay which I should think would convince any fair-minded man that this matter does not proceed with undue heat or partisan haste, we have not seated half the contestants who have come before that committee; and the fact that members have been left in their seats because upon our conscientious view of the evidence in their cases we were unable to come to a different conclusion, when, if we acted from partisan feeling, if all we required was a partisan majority, it would have been just as easy to seat A as to seat B, the whole seventeen contestants as five or six, — that fact, I think, entitles me to resent these insinuations upon the honor and the conscience of this most responsible and honorable committee. Such wild and reckless charges savor more of blind partisan frenzy than any act of that committee. Mr. Speaker, I look at this question in a widely different manner from that of a partisan. I think there is a deeper and broader and more pregnant meaning than that; and I reason in this way: The theory of this government vests all sovereignty in the people. The only way in which the people can exercise that sovereignty is by means of the ballot. The ballot is the very breath of life of the body politic.

"Stifle the ballot and you strangle the body politic, you strangle the people. And if a political wrong is done in one State of this Union, that wrong causes a thrill, a vibration, a shock through every State in the whole Union. So perfect, Mr. Speaker, is this Union to-day, thank God, — the Union of this vast republic, across which 'deep calleth unto deep,' the Atlantic to the Pacific, the Gulf to Superior, — so close, so sensitive, yet so strong is this fabric, extending over this vast area, that a wrong done to the meanest citizen in the remotest corner of this Union is felt as a personal wrong to every citizen in the most distant part of our land. And it is necessary that this feeling should exist, that it should be cultivated.

"Why, sir, a crime against the ballot is a crime not only against the man, the individual, it is a crime against the majesty of the State; it is a crime against the majesty of the United States throned here, — here, in this noble Capitol. And if you permit a wrong to be done to the humblest citizen, white or black, — a political wrong, 'the danger-light upon your charter,' — that wrong will come home to you in whatever section of the country you may live.

"They tell us, Mr. Speaker, that involved in the question before the House is a mighty and stupendous problem; that there is in effect here a race issue; that we are attempting by this bill to establish an empire of ignorance over knowledge, of barbarism over civilization, of an inferior race over a superior. God forbid! I would be no party to any movement or measure of that sort. But I am surprised that this cry of distress comes from that strong race which has trod the earth for a thousand years a conqueror.

"Now, I do not believe that under any law, in any system of society, the brute force of Caliban can ever overcome the magic power of Prospero's intellect. Only in one case, Mr. Speaker, can that result ever follow; that case is when the master intellect stoops to use the base and brutish methods of the slavish monster at his feet. It is only then that any community is in danger from what are called its lowest and its worst classes. The kingly power of one man's intellect will sway by the arts of justice and truth scores and hundreds and thousands of inferior beings; and the same rule is true where one race has been accustomed to hold a subordinate position, and the other race has always held the position of the superior.

"I am surprised to hear some of the objections made to the constitutionality of this measure. Why, sir, this question is discussed in a well-reasoned article in the Federalist, No. 59, referring to this very clause, that 'the times, places, and manner of holding elections for senators and representatives shall be prescribed in each State by the legislature thereof; but the Congress may at any time by law make or alter such regulations, except as to the places of choosing senators.' After stating the objections which were made, — not at the time when the provision was adopted, but after it was adopted, — it is said : —

"'In answer to all such reasoning, it was urged that there was not a single article in the whole system more completely defensible. Its propriety rested upon this plain proposition, that every government ought to contain in itself the means of its own preservation.' . . .

"'A discretionary power over elections must be vested somewhere. There seemed but three ways in which it could be reasonably organized: It might be lodged either wholly in the national legislature, or wholly in the State legislatures; or primarily in the latter, and ultimately in the former. The last was the mode adopted by the convention. The regulation of elections is submitted, in the first instance, to the local governments which, in ordinary cases, and when no improper views prevail,' — and the question is, whether the views prevailing now in some sections are proper or improper, — 'may both conveniently and satisfactorily be by them exercised. But in extraordinary circumstances the power is reserved to the national government, so that it may not be abused, and thus hazard the safety and permanence of the Union. . . .

"'Nothing can be more evident than that an exclusive power in the State legislatures to regulate elections for the national government would leave the existence of the Union entirely at their mercy.'

"These sentiments are quoted and approved in the great work of Mr. Justice Story upon the Constitution of the United States, chap. xi. sec. 814. And Mr. Rawle, a constitutional lawyer from the State of Pennsylvania, in his learned work upon the Constitution, takes precisely the same view, and approves the principles here laid down. I say, then, Mr. Speaker, that we have clearly, unmistakably, the right to enact this legislation.

"I have noticed with some care the various objections made to the particular plan suggested in this bill. No bill is entirely perfect. There are some provisions here which even now, from my standpoint, might be amended and ameliorated. But the chief objections which seem to come to these features of the bill from the other side relate to extravagance or economy, and to expediency.

"The proposition of the gentleman from North Carolina [Mr. Ewart] would seem to be that if he is well off in his district, if I am well off in my district, or another gentleman in his, our view should extend not one rod beyond the limits of our districts; that if our neighbor's house is in flames, or if robbers and murderers are assaulting him, we should shut our doors and go quietly to bed, to 'sleep the sleep of the just.'

"Now, I admire the chivalrous, noble, public-spirited position of the gentleman from Maryland; and I believe it is more impregnated and more inspired by the fire of a true American citizenship than that of the gentleman from North Carolina. We do not live unto ourselves alone. We want justice and peace to prevail from one end of the Union to the other.

"Mr. Speaker, my time is short, and I am not permitted to go into the various special features of this bill as I should be pleased to do. But I say to my friends on the other side of the House, I am not inclined to take any view savoring of levity; I am not inclined to speak lightly or unfeelingly of the troubled situation of affairs, — of the disturbed condition of political society in their section of the republic. No; I say that grave and appalling problem is one that will tax all the genius and all the strength and courage of this invincible people to solve.

"But I take this ground, that Lincoln, giving gifts to men, and he gave many, gave liberty to the Afro-American. When the shackles are once broken, when they are once removed from the body of a man, — and all history and law concur to establish this principle, — when they have once been stricken off, no power on earth, no power in hell, can put those shackles upon that man again! The Afro-American is enfranchised. He has been clothed with citizenship. You cannot extirpate, you cannot destroy, you cannot exile him. All that is left for us to do, then, is to humanize, to civilize, to educate, to elevate him. That is the only path of safety. The freedman has now become a citizen, a unit of sovereignty, an integral part of the great people of this republic.

"The old maxim tells us to do justice though the heavens fall. The heavens never fall when justice is done. It is when injustice is done that the heavens fall, — in thunderbolts, in fire, in ashes, in 'plague, pestilence, and famine, in battle, murder, and sudden death.' The duty of our people towards the republic in every State, in every congressional district, is clear. There is only one path which can be travelled with safety. Let justice and equity prevail, let the laws be obeyed, give to every citizen his full political rights, and I believe that this line of political demarcation between the races will be obliterated; I believe that every great obstacle, keeping one race from living in amity with the other, will be removed.

"I remember in the evidence in the Alabama case of Threet *versus* Clarke one striking and vital statement was made in the simple, grand language of one of the colored witnesses. Speaking of the gentleman from Alabama [Mr. Clarke] he said: 'When he held the office of county attorney, he did not know black from white. He treated all men alike.' He did justice; and if you judge the cause of the poor and needy, then it will be well with you. Then there will be amity, — not necessarily social equality; that is a matter of individual liberty and choice; but you will have, I think, taken the right course to cut the Gordian knot now entangling the vitals of the republic. [Applause.] You will have done something towards making this country a land —

'Where the common sense of most shall hold a fretful realm in awe,
And the kindly earth shall slumber lapped in universal law.'

[Prolonged applause on the Republican side.] "

The ideas of Greenhalge upon the tariff were firm and just. He suffered somewhat in his own district because he felt obliged to consider the question as a whole, as for the interest of the entire country. Many of his constituents wanted free wool. He believed it necessary to yield something to gain the support of the country; the interests of no section were paramount. To ask for free wool, and at the same time for a high tariff on textiles, seemed unwise. The West also should benefit by the bill.

His re-election was said to be endangered by his action, but he was moved by no personal consideration. As to the principle of free trade, he thought it to be Utopian, a creed of the schools. It is needless to discuss the question; in this he stood with his party, with his city, with his neighbors. Free trade, even if just, would be intolerable, destructive to the interests of his own people. He spoke in the debates upon the Tariff Bill, May 16, in part, as follows:—

" And, therefore, I say that while this bill may in this particular or that particular bear unfavorably upon the interests of Massachusetts and New England, yet, speaking in that spirit of compromise to all sections, and in the spirit of mutual concession, I believe that the most important duty of this committee and of the House is to stand by the provisions of the bill with such amendments as I understand are to be offered by the Committee on Ways and Means. . . .

" But after all the discussion, after all the parade of the statistics of the schoolmen, after all the declamations about trusts and strikes and mortgages, one great fact remains unalterable, undeniable, unmistakable. The net result of a day's labor in the United States is greater than in any other country upon which the sun shines; and this is the great fact,— this is the very foundation and bed rock upon which this republic is established. Prosperity may shine in palaces, in temples, in the market, in the factory, in forest and field, but is a delusive and evanescent light, a will-o'-the-wisp, unless it shines first of all and brightest of all in the humble dwellings of the land, occupied by the self-respecting citizens of America, — the millions who earn their bread by the sweat of their brow. The happiness of a country is measured, not by the condition of a few favored by chance, by birth, by genius, but by the condition of the great army of workingmen and workingwomen. "

Greenhalge was devoted to the ideas of Civil Service Reform. He was one of the first reformers. His broad statesmanship made it to him a fundamental question; it seemed strange to

15

him that it should need defence, that there could be two ideas
about it.   He believed the Republicans to be pledged to support the principle.   To attack it indirectly through the appro-
priations seemed to him hypocritical.   The principle had been
written upon the statutes of the United States.   He believed
it to be a poor policy to skulk and to stab the law, as it were,
in the dark.   The dignity of Congress demanded that it should
be supported.   He said during the debates in the House : —

" I stand here as a civil-service reformer, if I am only one
of a dozen in this House.   I did not expect to be called upon
to defend this principle, in which I believe there is life and
energy and immortality.   I did not expect to be called upon
by my Republican associates on this floor to defend what I supposed had been written into the political law of the Republican
party.   I did not expect to hear these attacks from the other
side when I remembered that the same political principle had
been written into their platform.   Why, Mr. Chairman, are
we to stand here as mere hypocrites and humbugs?   Are
we to listen quietly to these statements, that when we write a
declaration into a party platform we do not mean it, but that
we consider it is put in for ' buncombe,' and as the most mean-
ingless sentimental declamation?   Mr. Chairman, in my
assignment to the Committee on Elections, I have been placed
in a position, fortunately or unfortunately, which has required
my action in this House to be such as could not fail to awaken
violent political feeling upon one side and the other, and
necessarily so; but, speaking in the spirit of some of the noble
and high-minded declarations made by the gentleman from
South Carolina [Mr. Cothran] yesterday — and I wish to God
we had more such judicial and honest expressions of opinions
in this House upon both sides — speaking in that spirit, I say,
I do not believe that when the Democratic party wrote that
principle into their platform they were hypocrites and liars,
or wrote it simply to deceive the American people. "

After the close of the first session of Congress Greenhalge
returned to his home in Lowell.   In the ensuing campaign he
was almost immediately engaged in an unremitting series of
political duties.   There was to be no rest for him; his career

in Congress had made him famous; his name was spread far and wide. He had done his work well, and it was admitted by friend and foe alike that he had displayed eminent abilities as a debater and achieved a success almost unparalleled for a new member. He could not but have thought that he had paved the way for further success, and that his future course in politics would in a measure be easy and uninterrupted. He came home crowned with success, and looked forward to a triumphant vindication at the polls, both for himself and the great party he served so well. But while this great Congress was engrossed in the performance of the duties which devolved upon it, while the men that formed it were busily engaged in the service of their country, devoting themselves with self-sacrificing ardor to what seemed to them the great tasks of patriotism and duty, — while they were so active in behalf of what seemed to them the best interests of the nation, calumny and misrepresentation had also been busy. The power of a shibboleth had made proselytes in every State. The political pendulum had oscillated to the opposite extreme; the country had deserted them. The knowledge of this change in public opinion was slow in coming to Greenhalge and to his peers in Congress; they could not reasonably foresee it, nor understand it when it came; they looked to receive their reward, and they found only contempt. They had fought one of the hardest fights ever fought in Congress, as they thought, for the good of the country, and returned from it to find the country ranged upon the opposite side; they returned home crowned with laurel to find themselves discredited and discarded. It was a sudden turn of Fortune's wheel.

It must have come with peculiar bitterness to Greenhalge, who had achieved so much in so brief a time, who was so thoroughly convinced of the greatness and true intent of the Fifty-first Congress, who so firmly believed in the Republican party, who had neglected his own interests during the campaign, speaking only once in his own district while devoting his whole time to the party and addressing audiences in every part of the State, leaving his own election entirely to the good-will of his friends and to the justice of his cause. His services were unremitting during this campaign. He spoke in most of the cities of the Commonwealth; he gave himself, heart and soul, to the conflict, and awaited the invisible event with confidence. Everywhere his speeches were received with popular applause; it seemed as if the Republican party must triumph, and it met overwhelming defeat. Perhaps active politicians are the less likely to foresee the defeat of their party, because the same enthusiasm prevails at their rallies on the eve of disaster as of victory. During campaigns their orbit is one of ovations and triumphs. The old guard is always around them, but they see nothing of the hosts, it may be, of deserters.

In this political crisis the Mugwumps played a conspicuous part, — if they were not as important as they seemed to be. Greenhalge did not look upon this party, or shred of a party, with much bitterness. He had, of course, respect for principle of any kind, and he got much apparent amusement out of the Mugwumps. He had much to say about them in his speeches, and received some hard blows from their political organs.

Greenhalge was perfectly fearless and independent. He himself had revolted from the Republican party. He preferred to see a good Democrat in office to a base Republican. Yet he differed entirely in his views from those held by the Independents, so called, at this time; he could not see the justice of their course of action. He believed the Democratic party to be more corrupt and incompetent than the Republican party, yet he could sympathize with a good and stanch Democrat. He could not sympathize with the Mugwumps because, though he may have thought them sincere patriots, he believed them to be unjust, prejudiced, and partial. He saw, too, the humorous side of the situation in any apparent league between men like Eliot and Everett and politicians like Hill, — between Harvard and Tammany.

The Mugwumps were undoubtedly sincere and patriotic. There always have been Mugwumps; they represent a very old party indeed, old as the political contests in the ancient Greek cities. The chief fault in their position is that it is an impractical one, — like the Roman patriots who, to escape the evils of the senatorial system and the domination of Pompey, threw themselves into the arms of Cæsar; they gained nothing, in the eyes of Greenhalge at least, by their desertion of the institutions of their fathers. The intentions of the Independents were strictly honorable, but honest wedlock with either party was not their desire; they were not tired of unchartered liberties. They put too much faith in the promises of Cæsar. Such was the idea, as a Republican, of Greenhalge.

Soon after his return to Lowell he was selected as chairman of the Republican State Convention, which was held that year in Tremont Temple, Boston. His speech before the convention, September 17, increased his reputation as an orator. From the Republican standpoint it was a masterly effort. It reviewed the history of the party's legislation in Congress, and touched upon the points of the coming election. His appearance on the platform was the signal for great enthusiasm on the part of the vast audience, and his reception showed how much he had raised himself in the estimation of the Republican party in Massachusetts by his career in Congress. He had become one of its chief representatives in the State, and the convention applauded him to the echo. In a passage of his speech, he said: " I never say harsh things of my Independent friends; more in sorrow than in anger, I note their inconsistencies. They are eloquent in denouncing Quay and Dudley, but how much more eloquent is their silence as to Hill and Gorman and Higgins and Brice and Croker and Mayor Grant ! " In closing, he spoke in elegant and eloquent language of the Republican party, and of the fair prospects which he thought lay before it: " Gentlemen, the Republican party is at the helm; the ship of State moves gallantly on; everywhere we see ' beauty and life and motions as of joy. ' We see new hope and strength in the civil service of the country, now daily improving in efficiency under the vigorous management of the present commission; there is new life in the army and navy, — in every department of the government. Under the influence of this vitality the gavel of Reed becomes as the hammer of Thor, and its every stroke is a victory for the people, for business, for human rights, for law. Watch the operations of the new vital force as manifested in foreign affairs ! See how it sparkles on the rocks of Samoa, as if American diplomacy were inspired by the glory won there by

American seamanship! See how it touches and warms the chilly waters of Bering Sea! . . . It is well with the nation and well with the State; greater prosperity shines before us."

With such hopes for the future and congratulations for the past, Greenhalge and the Republican party entered upon the campaign. There were omens and signs of coming disaster, but they were not visible to the active participants in the struggle. October 1, 1890, Greenhalge was unanimously renominated for Congress. The delegates received him with the same enthusiasm as did the convention, and his speech of acceptance was strong and hopeful, like his oration before the State delegates.

As usual, Greenhalge did not pursue his own personal advantage in this campaign; his own election he disregarded, and made no personal effort to obtain it. He exerted himself energetically for the party, and delivered speeches all over the State; but only once did he speak in Lowell,—on the eve of the election he addressed a large audience in Huntington Hall. Signs were not wanting that all was not going prosperously in his district, but he had been absent and far too busy to observe them. He evidently thought his election assured. He must have felt that he had earned it.

The author well remembers the last night of the campaign. Greenhalge was fatigued by his arduous labors, yet he spoke with his usual vim. He referred to the tone which had prevailed during the campaign; with some feeling he said, " These contests are contests between friends and neighbors, and never in any political, professional, or other combat have I struck a man a foul blow." When he retired to rest that night, it was probably with confidence in the event of the morrow; the morning, however, revealed a disaster. His own defeat he bore, as usual, with equanimity if not nonchalance; he could be witty as usual at his own expense. There was a salve in the very extent of the defeat; it could not be taken in a personal sense.

The vote for Congress in his own district resulted in a plurality of 563 for his opponent. The ballots cast for Greenhalge were 11,205 in number; as it was, he ran ahead of his party.

Referring to his defeat, he said, " I expected to carry my own district by a small plurality. If I had thought differently I would have given it more attention. I do not think it was anything personal against me that caused my defeat, for I ran ahead of my ticket in Lowell and in many of the towns. And you will observe," and there was a twinkle in his eye, " that I carried Dunstable. "

This was a period of deep gloom in the Republican party. Greenhalge returned to Washington and found the party leaders very much downcast and disheartened. His own standpoint was brighter, and he still looked forward with confidence.

The following letter expresses his own feelings and those of his friends : —

December 11, 1890.

Mr. Andrew and other Democrats here think the Republican party has gone forever. Cogswell is bluer than blazes, and Lodge, after listening to Andrew and Cogswell, was bluer than Cogswell. I do not agree with these prophets. I think the Republican party has much to change and much to do, but it still lives. I find satisfaction in thinking I am out of the press at such a time as this. Some people will begin to realize what the recent elections have accomplished. I was disappointed in the city election. But let the disaster be as complete as possible to stir the people to action.

The regrets for Greenhalge's own defeat were widespread. His speech before the Convention of Massachusetts Republicans had been received with congratulations by people of the highest standing in the party, and by men noted for intellectual power. The letter following was written after his return to Washington from the convention. It refers to some of the praise his speech called forth.

" Curtin has been in, fresh from Cambridge. He says ' One of the great ones ' — who, he won't say — ' declares that for the first time the true type of the Sophist or Rhetor has entered into American politics. '

" This, Curtin says, is the grandest compliment that could be paid me; and he says that I have now a standing in the

Republican party and the country which would make anything possible; all of which is simply an emphatic national way of declaring that the speech was a success. "

After his return to Washington Greenhalge addressed the House only twice. The first time, January 16, he made a memorable reply, already noted in these pages, to Congressman Stone of Missouri, after his speech attacking Massachusetts. His second speech was in relation to the Civil Service Bill of that year. There was again a disposition on the part of Congress to withhold the appropriation necessary for the clerical expenses of the commission. Greenhalge, together with Lodge, succeeded in their effort in behalf of the commission. Greenhalge said: " It would be unreasonable to expect that the annual appropriation should go through without the annual attack [by the enemies of the bill]; but our party and the party on the other side have declared in favor of the principle, and I believe in standing to a resolution whether it wins or loses. I respect even the utterances of ex-President Cleveland; they show courage, whether those utterances are in favor of free trade, in favor of Civil Service Reform, or against free coinage. For God's sake let us have some men in this republic who have the courage of their convictions. If it be true that a majority of this House — a majority of the Republican side, or a majority of the Democratic side — desire to wipe this law from the statute-book, let it be done in a manly fashion, and let those who do it take the responsibility. Do not let them rise to some mere parliamentary punctilio. The people care nothing about that. We are here as to things of substance, not after matters of form. "

Greenhalge's congressional term was now drawing to a close. His short and brilliant career ended in the midst of a general calamity to his party. The results were so tremendous to the Republicans that the defeat of any single person was scarcely remarked. Had Greenhalge been defeated in quiet times, the event would have evoked extraordinary attention through the country; for his success had been singular, — scarcely to be paralleled by the career of any new and untried member. As to the impression he created upon the Congress, we are fortunate in having the testimony of his peers, the witnesses of his triumphs; friends and foes alike were impressed.

Senator Lodge shared with him in all the conflicts and labors of Congress. There could be no better judge of the effect of his oratory upon the House. I have included in these pages, therefore, the following passage from his eulogy delivered in Mechanics' Hall, Boston : —

" The Fifty-first Congress was not a peaceful one. It was the second Republican Congress since the days of Grant, and the party majority hung by a slender thread. There was a great work to be done, — nothing less than the reform of the rules, and the restoration to the majority of its rights and responsibilities.

" The opening days of the session were marked by great turbulence, and all the known tactics of obstructive parliamentary warfare were resorted to by a resolute and defiant opposition. It was a time which demanded the best resources of trained and experienced leadership, and there seemed to be but a slight opening for new and untried men. When the House organized and the committees were announced, Mr. Greenhalge found himself placed on the committees on Elections, Revision of the Laws, and Reform in the Civil Service. To the first of these committees was intrusted the important function of hearing and deciding contests for seats, of which there was an unusually large number in this Congress, most of them coming from Southern States.

" Party feeling ran high, and the debates which followed the various reports on election cases provoked great partisan bitterness. To the work of this committee Mr. Greenhalge devoted himself with his accustomed energy and ability.

" The first case to be called up was the one of Smith *versus* Jackson, from West Virginia. During this debate Mr. Greenhalge made his maiden speech. The occasion could not have been more happily selected. The House was crowded and the interest was intense. His analysis of the legal points involved was lucid and convincing, and the whole speech was tinged with a delicious satire which caught the House at once. At the close he was accorded hearty and enthusiastic applause.

The House recognized at once that he was a sound lawyer, a brilliant speaker, and a strong debater; and the opinion of the House on those points is of the best, and is not easily won. It was a triumph for a first speech. Henceforth his place was secure, and he became at once one of the leaders of the House. His reputation thus made, he found himself beset by every contestant for assistance. These appeals he found it difficult to resist, and he did much effective work in placing these election controversies before the House. The amount of labor involved in sifting evidence in each case was immense, but the reward came in the form of an established legal and forensic reputation."

Greenhalge left Washington at the end of his term and returned to his quiet home at Lowell without personal regrets. It is probable that he considered that his public service was over, for some years at least, and that (under the circumstances) "the post of honor was a private station."

He had achieved much in a very short time. Besides the speeches in Congress, he had made many brilliant addresses before lesser audiences. The fame he had acquired brought him many invitations to speak at public meetings. Upon one notable occasion especially he spoke very finely. May 21, 1890, together with Hon. N. C. P. Breckinridge, of Kentucky, he delivered an address before the Humane Society from the pulpit of All Souls' Church, Washington. Speaking of this noble charity, he said: "It rises among other charities like the Parthenon among other temples. Nay, more. You have seen, in pictures or reality, the grandest cathedrals in the world, splendid with their airy pinnacles, their groined arches, and their storied windows, or you have read Ruskin's description of them, more splendid still. These are the temples of the living God. But when you take a child and begin your labors upon his body and soul, you are at work upon a grander structure still, — the living temple of the living God."

Greenhalge came to be considered by many Democrats as an extreme partisan. His speeches excited the wrath of that party. It was reported that Congressman O'Ferrall, of Virginia, had written a letter to a prominent Democrat in Greenhalge's district, telling him that national and Democratic necessity demanded the defeat of Greenhalge. " He is by far the most dangerous man on the Republican side. "

Greenhalge had never before been regarded as a blind partisan even by the Democrats; it was not true that he had become such. The patronage of his office was not desired as a personal attribute by him, and was not used by him in a merely partisan spirit; he re-appointed a Democrat as postmaster at Concord, Massachusetts; the appointment of Mr. Burbank as postmaster at Lowell justified itself; even before his appointment, Greenhalge had tried to induce the Republican City Committee to select a candidate for that office, but they had refused his request. In his choice of Mr. Burbank, he ran contrary to the wishes of many in his own party, and his independence was plainly manifest. His career in Congress was not viewed by all the Democrats in that body as a purely partisan one. On the contrary, it called forth the praise of some of them for its fairness. Hon. J. H. O'Neil, who was one of his Democratic associates in the House, has spoken of his independent course on the Committee of Elections.

As to the accusation of partisanship in Congress brought against him by some, Judge Lawton says: —

" To those who never thoroughly knew Greenhalge it seemed as if his temperament changed at that time, as if it had been melted in a furnace-blast and had been transformed and hardened. It was not so. He was the same Greenhalge who had been a non-partisan mayor, — almost a non-partisan member of the General Court of Massachusetts.

" There had been a clean-cut division between the two great parties of the country. There had been a canvass of votes on a great question of national commercial policy. Both parties wanted the best, but they differed as to what was best. He was there as an instructed representative of one side of a principle of trade and revenue for which he must fight. The vote had fairly been taken before he and his colleagues had been sent to Washington. On such an issue he would no more desert his party than he would desert his client in court, no more than he would desert his colors on a field of battle. There never had been so heated a contest in any Congress over the seats of members as in this one. Greenhalge was a member of the committee of the House to whose consideration were referred all these contested seats. He had always been fair and judicial in his treatment of his political opponents, and he was at this time. It is not necessary to make the claim in these pages that he was right in all the cases of these contested seats, and that the opposition in that House was always wrong. There would be an impropriety in a claim that he was always right when he differed from his own party associates on that committee. One fact will be enough. Of all his party in that committee, on that question he was the most conservative; of them all, he conceded the most seats to the opposition. He respected the opinions of his party friends and believed them to be conscientious. When their report was made up, modified, and restricted by his influence, he felt that it was reasonably fair, and felt bound to give it his support. So much had the conclusions of the committee been modified by his efforts, his fellow-members placed upon him a great part of the work of maintaining them before the House. In a succession of speeches and debates, he presented his cases with wonderful eloquence and great logical power. Thus, although in his first term, he sprang into eminence at once. If he was fortunate in the Congress to which he had been sent, fortunate in the crisis, and in the white heat at which party conflict glowed, he was doubly fortunate in that he had gone there endowed and equipped to meet every emergency that arose."

As soon as the defeat of Greenhalge became known, many of the Republican papers while commenting upon it took the occasion to put his name forward with flattering praise as a candidate for Governor of Massachusetts in the next election. The desire for his candidature continued to find expression in the papers and among the people, until in 1891 he was one of those most prominently mentioned for that high office. He himself, however, appeared to have no desire to become again a candidate for any office. He refused afterwards to run again for Congress, and seemed to consider his political career as over, at least for the present. He looked forward to the enjoyment of a more restful life, and to the practice of his profession, long interrupted by his political duties. There is no doubt but that he felt his defeat severely, the more because it was unexpected, and came after so brilliant a term in Congress. He never despaired of his party, however, and to its service continued to give his untiring support during the campaign in 1891 upon the stump, and won golden opinions for his unselfish devotion to the Republican cause.

In the spring of 1891, in an interview he said, referring to the prominence of his name as a candidate for governor: " I have stated frequently, and with some formality and emphasis, my position as to the nomination for governor. More than three months ago the question was asked me whether I would accept the nomination if tendered me. I replied that however good the possibility of such a thing, my circumstances would prevent my being a candidate. I reiterated my position at Melrose at a public banquet, March 12, and on various other occasions. I have every confidence that the Republican party will be successful in the coming contest, and I believe that any one of the persons whose names have been suggested would be elected. I am devoting myself at present to my private business and private interests, which have been much neglected and impaired by my public service. I think I have a right to attend to these matters now and for some time to come." This interview and the decided manner of his refusal could not altogether put a stop to the expression of the desire of many people for his candidature, but practically the question was settled, and it became evident that another candidate must be found. He was selected for chairman of the Committee on Rules in the Republican Convention, and his acceptance of that office was still further evidence of his position as to the governorship.

The party platform which he wrote for the convention was a highly finished paper, and called forth numerous complimentary comments. The convention finally nominated a fellow-townsman of Greenhalge, Mr. Charles H. Allen, as the Republican candidate for governor. There was not an ounce of jealousy in Greenhalge's nature, and he gave his earnest support to the party and its candidate. It was not a disappointment to him; he was out of the race, and by his own desire.

It was fortunate, in view of his political career, that he was not a candidate. The Republican reaction had not yet set in; the popularity of Governor Russell was very great; and the election of any one to the office of governor by the Republicans would have been doubtful in the extreme. "There is a tide in the affairs of men that taken at the flood leads on to fortune."

Two years later Greenhalge found his great opportunity. At this time, however, he was not a candidate for any political office; he had no ulterior views in his refusal to become a candidate; he desired rest from his political labors, and to give his attention to his private business and the practice of his profession. The campaign resulted in the re-election of Governor Russell; but, as before, the Republicans, disappointed by the defeat of the head of the ticket, were successful in the election of other State officials, and in carrying the House of Representatives and the Senate. The State was still Republican, with a Democratic governor. The year preceding his own election by the people to the governor's chair was singularly eventful: in the business world a year of unexampled depression; it was a time of trial to the American people, and the uneasy spirit of the nation bore it with growing impatience and distrust of the Democratic party.

At this time, however, the Republican party was defeated and discredited, and in his hours of leisure Greenhalge wrote numerous editorials for the press, which appeared in various papers, sharply criticising the Democratic policy. They attracted considerable attention, and were notable contributions to the political controversy. They were admirable instruments of attack. Their sarcasm was biting and their invective powerful. They were partisan efforts, and directed with great effect at the weak spots in the Democratic régime. Being written by him, they have not suffered like his speeches from bad reports.

As they are interesting from their incisive style, and as the productions of such a man, I have included one of the best of them in these pages. It appeared in the "New York Recorder," Jan. 10, 1892. It was written to serve a party purpose. It is necessarily thoroughly partisan and aggressive in its tone.

THE DEMOCRATIC SITUATION.

At the opening of the year 1892, we may note many unmistakable indications that a critical period has been reached in the political affairs of the United States. A glance at recent political events may be useful in an examination of the present situation.

The Democratic party achieved a great victory in 1890. But the victory was more apparent than real. It would seem that there was dissatisfaction with the Republican party, but it is not at all clear that this feeling led to satisfaction with the Democratic party. The Fifty-first Congress undertook a series of herculean labors, any one or two of which would have been sufficient pabulum for a political campaign in an off year following hard upon the inauguration of an administration compelled either by duty or pressure to make many appointments to office and necessarily a great many more disappointments. But this Congress performed gigantic feats. It passed the Silver Bill, a measure of colossal proportions, which, while holding back the strong tide of free-silver sentiment, maintained the true standard of value in money. The Pension Bill was an act of justice and gratitude worthy of a great nation anxious to keep its plighted faith with its defenders, and preferring to give more than justice required rather than less. The Tariff Bill was another great stroke of legislation, of which we may say that few or none of the evils prophesied in regard to it have come to pass, while many benefits unforetold have followed in its wake. The act for the Relief of the Supreme Court, the Anti-Lottery Bill, the Anti-Trust Bill, the Administrative Custom Bill, the Direct Tax Bill, the French Spoliation Claims, and a dozen other acts of equal importance are among the works of this indefatigable body. In addition to all these acts of legislation, the great ruling of Speaker Reed made a new era in the parliamentary history of the United States.

Now, the people are not specially gifted with receptivity, — not even the people of this country. Their power of assimilation is limited. The vigor, the push, the onward movement of the Fifty-first Congress within so many legislative fields, coupled with the bold iconoclasm displayed in the destruction of a parliamentary precedent at least a century old, took the people off their feet. The banquet was too rich, the food too strong. There may be too much even of a good thing. The Fifty-first came nearer to fulfilling its pledges to the country than any preceding Congress, and the people were taken aback. They were not used to this sort of thorough and effective work, or to the fulfilment of pledges in such a complete and painstaking way.

It was out of the vacillation and surprise of the people, then, that in 1890 an ostensible Democratic triumph arose and the Fifty-second Congress came into existence, —

" Monstrum horrendum, informe, ingens, cui lumen ademptum."

While there have been noticeable signs of reaction in almost every election held in 1891 throughout the country, signs of more significance may be observed in the victorious Democracy itself. The original or simple elements of the recent Democratic party — as it may be termed, in contradistinction to the compact, homogeneous body which marshalled itself under the party banner up to 1884 — do not appear to be specially adapted to coalescence. There are the Democratic party of 1880, and the Democratic party of 1884. It was the moving spirit of the party of 1884, the party of Cleveland, the pseudo-Democratic party, in mechanical, not chemical, union with Tammany, with the Farmers' Alliance, with the pro-silver faction and with every vagrant, anarchical element in the country, which achieved the victory of 1890. And the renegade Republican — the Independent, the Mugwump — is the differentiating factor in the party of 1884 in comparison with the party of 1880, or with the genuine Democratic party. Now, when the differentiating factor of the party of 1884, the delicate Democrat, the genuine Bourbon or Tammany Democrat, the pro-silver Democrat, the O'Neil Democrat (for " the rift in the lute " of the New England Democracy is quite noticeable), all come together in Uncle Sam's barn, there is not that complete and intense satisfaction and harmony which would naturally and ordinarily be the concomitant of a " famous victory." The first note struck in the Fifty-second Congress is a discord, and one which will echo through the session and through the party for a long time. The music of the cats this time is not conducive to the increase of the breed; there is a Kilkenny strain about it which must disturb the thoughtful minds of the party. With an immense preponderance, apparently, of the Democratic power in the House, with a phenomenal numerical majority, the representatives of the party have tumbled over each other, have fought, stretched, and pulled hair *inter se* to such an extent that if a Democrat whose eyes have been gouged out by some friendly hand should ask, like the blind Spartan, to be placed with his face to the enemy, the chances are that in the present prevailing confusion he would find that his hostile *vis-à-vis* was a sterling Democrat. Even old Mother Herald recognized the solemnity of the situation, and crazed by the shabby treatment given to her bantlings, declares spitefully and significantly that "the Democratic party can win next year if the breach in it is mended forthwith." And then that loyal Mugwump paper, "Harper's Weekly" exclaims in shrillest tones, "What breach? Is the defeat of Mr. Mills evidence of a breach?" and proceeds to lecture the angry old pedagogue the "Herald," its quondam ally, on the subject of breaches, and finally caps the climax by arraying the names of Quay, Elkins, Dudley, and Platt as representatives of the Republican party against the shining names of Hill, Gorman, Crisp, and the leaders of Tammany Hall as the representatives of the Democracy; which to the Mugwump turned Democrat is the unpardonable sin, coming from a Republican turned Mugwump. Here again, is a breach. Mr. Curtis quarrels with the "Boston Herald." Let us devoutly pray that Mr. Godkin of the "Evening Post" may not attack the "Springfield Republican," as nothing would be left but "the wreck of matter and the crush of worlds." This journalistic "School for Scandal" has been teasing the honest Sir Peter Teazles of political life for a long time; it would be only poetic justice if the old vixens should at last fall foul of each other, and any honest man would be delighted to see fair play.

It is clear, however, that a "line of cleavage" begins to manifest itself in the victorious Democratic party, and it is, perhaps, as apparent among the æsthetic camp-followers of

the party, the delicate and dilettante Democrats, who joined
the party simply to use it as a beast of burden for certain
leading ideas as anywhere else. We see already two opposing
camps of "Independents." As previously intimated, there is
on the one side the Republican turned Mugwump and on the
other the Mugwump turned Democrat, with all that the term
implies. Mr. Curtis is the only survivor known to the public
of the true Mugwump, the genuine, simon-pure type; all others
are spurious. He has not bowed the knee to the Baal of
Tammany, even when Mr. Cleveland stood as an acolyte at the
altar, lighting the devotees to worship. It is possible that he
still cherishes some tenderness for the rights of men, for the
sanctity of the ballot, for honest money, for sound education, for
progress and decent government; and believes that the matter
of raising a revenue or even the triumph of Mr. Cleveland is
not the only burning question before mankind to-day. And
it may be that he is not quite determined yet with which of
the great parties he will cast in his lot, or whether he will
with either. This is a genuine and respectable independence,
not a sham, an imposture, masking Democracy. The spurious
Independent is not an exhilarating subject to anybody, not
even to himself. The importation of slaves was prohibited by
the Constitution after the year 1808, but whether by erasion
of this section of the Constitution or not, the importers certainly have slaves here, and they are found in the ranks of the
Mugwumps turned Democrats. They are now engaged, when
dyspepsia permits, in a chemical analysis of the American
flag, which it seems is simply a "textile fabric of three colors,"
etc. The vivisection of his own grandmother by one of these
gentlemen to ascertain the true springs of natural emotion will
probably follow in due course. The Tammany tiger had no
terrors for him until a stroke of his paw upsets the Cleveland-
Mills "combine," and then the true inwardness of the tiger
was revealed to the aspiring politician of the nursery, who
went about squalling that the beast was a "horrid thing."
This is the farcical feature of the political drama now being
played. There are more serious and portentous developments
in the play. Bad blood has been engendered in the balky
Democratic majority of the House, and it is very doubtful if

even the sagacious Crisp can educe order out of such a tumultuary body.

The simian activity of Mr. Springer will not contribute an iota of influence to establish order, discipline, or harmony. He is a man of ability, but his ability is not of the constructive order; it comes forth only to create or increase confusion. He never was in earnest in his life, and he cannot persuade anybody now that he is to take any part in the House but that of the Lord of Misrule.

Mr. Crisp could not but fail in arranging his committees; he has satisfied nobody, not even himself. No serious dependence can be placed upon Mr. Springer. Mr. McMillen on the Committee on Rules will prove an "envious Casca," and Semmes of the "Alabama" might better have been trusted with the commerce of the country than Mr. Mills.

Meanwhile the banners of Governor Hill are flying triumphant in New York; Messrs. Gorman, Brice, and Fowler are in full control of the Democratic party, and the well-meaning men who could not endure the wickedness of the naughty men in the Republican party now find themselves either cheek by jowl with Democratic rascals ten times blacker, or trampled helpless under the feet of their brutal allies.

Meantime "God reigns and the Government at Washington still lives." President Harrison meets every exigency, within and without, with firmness, wisdom, and dignity. The business of the country flourishes, reciprocity moves on from one victory to another, and the protective principle points the way to greater development and prosperity. A compact, well-disciplined body of eighty-eight Republicans is on the alert for any opportunity dropped by the clumsy, slipshod majority of the House of Representatives. It is a Democratic night, "but the morrow is yet to come."

Greenhalge spoke many times in the campaign of 1891, and always before appreciative audiences.

"He stands, I am assured, upon the threshold of a long and distinguished national career." These were the words in which Senator Hoar introduced him at a Republican rally in Worcester. Had he lived, they would surely have come true.

There was an attempt on the part of Governor Russell to make a State issue in this campaign in the matter of the Governor's Council, which he proposed to abolish altogether. Greenhalge refers to this in a speech at Springfield, October 14. He said : —

" The Executive Council is as old as the Constitution and the Commonwealth. It is, and has ever been, an integral part of the Constitution, and yet when the Constitution was adopted in 1780, the men who made that Constitution had in mind arbitrary power, and the proper limitation and checks upon that power. They had had arbitrary governments before, and they were bound, if human foresight could permit, never to be under the power of arbitrary governors again ; and so while the governor is given certain executive powers which he can exercise without the advice and consent of the Council, there are certain acts and functions which he cannot perform without the limitation of the Council and its powers. I think the Governor is in error in his construction of this clause in the Constitution."

After the election of Russell, Greenhalge was complimented by various Democratic organs on his conduct and gentlemanly bearing during the campaign. The following passage from the " Lowell Sun " contains one flattering notice, noteworthy because it was praise from an enemy : " To the credit of Hon. F. T. Greenhalge it can be truly said that of all the speakers who stumped the State for Allen, he was the only one that did not descend to narrowness or appeals to prejudice. He stood squarely upon the party platform, and used his oratory honestly to convert his hearers to Republicanism."

February 22 the Michigan Republican Club celebrated its seventh anniversary by a banquet in Detroit. It was one of the most notable political gatherings in the history of Michigan. The speakers were men of the most brilliant minds and party leaders of the highest class. The speech of Greenhalge on this occasion was one of the best of those delivered. McKinley, Fassett, and Greenhalge were the guests of General Alger during their stay in Detroit.

It had been the hope of the Republicans of Lowell that Greenhalge would again be their candidate for Congress. He had silently determined against their desire, and, April 4, 1892, wrote to the chairman of the Congressional Committee the following declination, which was made public. It was a decisive refusal, and reluctantly accepted by his party.

LOWELL, MASS., April 4, 1892.

MY DEAR SIR, — In response to frequent inquiries, I think it due to the Republicans of this congressional district to state that I shall not be a candidate for Congress in this approaching election. This conclusion is forced upon me by private business and the circumstances in which I am placed.

I announce my position thus early in order that no misunderstanding may arise, and that the party may have ample opportunity to select a candidate who will assure Republican success beyond a doubt in the coming contest.

At the present time, this important district needs more than ever a Republican representative in Congress for the preservation of its most vital interests.

Permit me to thank your committee and the Republicans of the old Eighth District for the kindness hitherto shown me.

Respectfully and sincerely yours,

FREDERIC T. GREENHALGE.

ALBERT G. THOMPSON, Esq., Chairman Congressional District Committee.

The Republican State convention to elect delegates to the presidential convention at Minneapolis met in Boston, April 20. Greenhalge presented the name of General Cogswell in an eloquent speech. The "Boston Herald" said of the address: "It was very clever. It was delivered with great dramatic effect, and evoked round after round of applause." About this time Greenhalge became prominently mentioned as a strong candidate for United States Senator in succession to Senator Dawes. His popularity was steadily increasing. His disinterested course in politics was now fully appreciated, and his ability everywhere admired. But he did not seek or desire that office, or any other.

July 8, on being asked if he would accept the nomination for governor, he replied with emphasis: "No, sir; I am not a candidate for the office in any sense, and have not the slightest desire for it. I see that Mr. Pillsbury is mentioned; he would make an excellent canvass."

In an interview, August 28, Greenhalge expressed his opinion as to the situation, predicting success for the Republican party. Referring to the election of 1890, he said: "I was not sanguine in 1890. The Fifty-first Congress did such a vast amount of work that the people could not possibly accept, realize, or digest it. The Fifty-first was the Titan of Congresses, and it will require years to gain an adequate and lucid comprehension of its gigantic labors. But every year the forceful and determined character of its legislation, with its vast and multifarious scope, and its intelligent purpose and beneficial result, will become more and more patent to the people. It is — and will in all probability remain — the distinctive Congress of the second century of the republic, giving direction, tone, and spirit to the country, and setting the pace, indeed, for the remainder of the century."

The Republican party, however, were doomed to be disappointed, and Cleveland was elected. In Massachusetts, Russell was chosen governor for the third time.

With the advent of the year 1893, a new era dawned for the Republican party, — a dawn that brightened over the stagnant morass of business depression, and over the wrecks of a thousand commercial failures, and the melancholy figures of deserted and silent mills. In the midst of such distressing scenes the sun of Republicanism was destined to rise again, — brighter for the surrounding gloom.

Saturday, May 27, the "Boston Globe" contained an interview with Greenhalge. In it he gave his consent to the use of his name in the gubernatorial contest. He consented to become a candidate. He said: "A nomination tendered with cordiality, and coming at a time when an exigency may be supposed to exist, is something that must be treated with the utmost respect and most careful deliberation.

"There are circumstances which, barring accidents, might make such a proposition seem almost like a command. Possibly these circumstances will not arise, or some one else may be found who will meet the requirements of the situation."

Asked as to what the requirements were, he replied: —

" I should say in the first place that the needs of the Republican party are consolidation and union, an aggressive stand on all Republican principles and Republican measures, and an organization under the fundamental principles of the party.

" The Republican party, of course, is a national party, but it is also a State party in that it is interested in good politics and good government of counties, cities, and towns, in the maintenance of business prosperity, so far as legislation, whether State, national, or municipal, can conduce to that result. Whoever this year fills the requirements of the Republican party, and is closest in touch with popular sentiment, should be, and, in my opinion, will be, the Republican candidate for governor.

" It would hardly become any of the gentlemen whose names are mentioned in this connection to anticipate the popular will. Thus far I have remained silent, and would not have you understand now that I have come to any positive and permanent decision. Many prominent Republicans and a far greater number of the rank and file have pressed me to be a candidate, but thus far I have chosen to hold my own counsel. I am saying more to you now than I have yet said to my most intimate advisers. All I can say is that I mean to await the trend of events, which will make more manifest the preferences of the Republican party.

" The manufacture of sentiment in this direction has but little weight. I take no stock whatever in that.

" It is my opinion now, as it has been in years past, that a fuller and fairer opportunity should be given to the great body of the party to choose their candidates. If this is done, the responsibility is with the majority, and does not rest upon any wing or section of the party, or any combination within its ranks, whatever the result."

This announcement of his position by Greenhalge was the cause of great rejoicing among his personal and political friends. His canvass from the first made steady progress. July 7 he said in an interview published in the "Boston Globe": "I cannot say what the other candidates are doing, but my friends tell me that affairs look favorable; and, indeed, I am surprised at the spontaneity of the sentiment which comes to me from all sections. I had not thought it possible that I could have so many friends, and while I mention the fact, now mind you, I do not say it boastfully, but rather with thanksgiving and the utmost gratitude of my nature. I noticed it particularly in Newburyport; and the way in which the people came to me there and assured me, all unsolicited, of their support, was very gratifying, you may be sure."

The "Boston Herald," however, looked upon his prospects with anything but a favorable eye; it saw no chance for him. It said: —

"It is a matter of surprise that the friends of Mr. Greenhalge take his candidacy for the nomination of governor as seriously as they seem to. It may be that we are entirely mistaken, but, judging from the straws that have thus far blown within our range of vision, we should say that the Lowell statesman would not be likely to poll at the State convention more than a fifth, or a quarter at most, of the votes cast, if he should continue to keep himself in the running. We should say that Mr. Greenhalge's support would be larger than that of Mr. Hart, but only larger by a small fraction. It may be that we are, as we have said, greatly mistaken in this, and that there is an undercurrent of Republican sentiment which makes a demand that only Mr. Greenhalge's candidacy can satisfy. If this is the case in this part of the country, it is one of those movements so deep and profound in their character as to make no ripple of excitement on the surface."

In another interview Greenhalge spoke at length upon the subject of his candidature. These interviews at the present time are interesting as the voice of one who is dead. They exhibit in a true light the character of the man, and show the serious thought with which he reviewed the responsibility of his position. He said: —

"As to the preliminary contest, I have endeavored to conduct it in a way which would prove to the other gentlemen who are candidates my full appreciation of their excellent qualities and the pleasant relations that have always existed between us. From the beginning I have determined on one thing, and that is, not to be outdone in fairness, courtesy, and magnanimity. How this may be determined is for the public to decide later. I hope there will be nothing in this preliminary campaign that will remain to humble the self-respect of any person engaged in it on the part of any candidate. I sincerely believe this to be the case.

"From all external indications I am led to believe that the sentiment of the Republicans of Massachusetts is favorable to my candidacy. My only object from the beginning has been to get a free, hearty, and sincere expression of their opinion.

"You may remember I stated to you in my first public utterance upon this question, when you asked me whether I was a candidate and would make any canvass whatever for the nomination : 'That depends. A nomination tendered with cordiality, and coming at a time when an exigency is supposed to exist, is something that must be treated with the utmost respect and most careful deliberation.' I also said, you may remember, 'There are circumstances which, barring accidents, might make such a proposition almost like a command.'

"I may say now that the external indications seem to show that the condition of affairs then indicated has been realized. Furthermore, I will say what I never said in terms before, that I am a candidate, and that the nomination tendered under such circumstances cannot but be regarded by any citizen of Massachusetts as the highest honor he could hope to win.

"I feel, of course, the immense responsibility which this state of things imposes upon me, but whatever the final result may be, I shall always be cheered by the exhibition of respect and kindly feeling which Republicans, and even men of other parties, have evinced toward me, from one end of the commonwealth to the other. If any word or act of mine or my friends has savored in the slightest degree of discourtesy or bitterness, it will be the only source of regret which I have. Thus far I have heard nothing of any such manifestations on the part of my supporters.

"I feel a certain repugnance to making any personal statements which may seem to be tainted with egotism, and I hope that in view of the whole situation such a personal aspect may be regarded as perhaps a necessity in the case of a man who is before the public as at this time I am.

"The success of the Republican party is our paramount end and aim, and whatever may be the result of the action of the convention on next Saturday, I shall be found, as in other years, fighting the battles of the Republican party in behalf of any leader chosen by that party."

It gradually became evident that Greenhalge was the popular candidate of the Republican party. The contest narrowed down until it came to be between three candidates, the others being Pillsbury and Hart. Mr. Hart early withdrew, but Mr. Pillsbury seemed to be a strong candidate. A section of the party looked upon Greenhalge as the hustling candidate, — as too much of a politician; his managers were thought to be skilful manœuvrers. The "Boston Herald" and other Mugwump papers were the leaders of this portion of the party and in favor of Pillsbury.

It would be absurd to-day to regard Greenhalge as a hustler and partisan and scheming politician, — him who represented in all things the best elements of the Republican party, its highest ideal of patriotism and statesmanship. It was also absurd then; the people looked upon him with different eyes. The motion and impulse behind him was that of the Republican party, in all its strength and with all its purity of motive; the impression he had made was deep and lasting. The Boston caucuses revealed the strength of his position and led to the withdrawal of Mr. Pillsbury.

Greenhalge spoke again about his candidature as follows: "The general good-feeling toward me in spite of my many defects and faults has been extremely pleasing to me. My friends on the other side dwell a great deal on my tendency to sharp language and sarcasm, but somehow it is difficult to find on either side anybody who seems to have any but the kindest personal feelings."

October 3 Mr. Pillsbury wrote a letter withdrawing from the contest. The letter of Mr. Pillsbury and Greenhalge's reply were as follows: —

BOSTON, Oct. 3.

MY DEAR GREENHALGE, — I am not yet out of court long enough to have learned much of the political situation, but without disputing as to the preferences of the delegates, I am satisfied that you have a sufficient lead to entitle you to the nomination, and that there ought to be no contest over it. Under these circumstances I shall act upon the impulse of the friendship which has always subsisted between us, and do all in my power to promote your nomination with the harmony and unanimity which will go far to secure your election; and as my office and official duties disable me from much active participation in the campaign, it will give me pleasure, if you and your friends desire it, to move your nomination in the convention. I am as ever,

Yours truly,   A. E. Pillsbury.

Lowell, Mass., Oct. 3.

My dear Pillsbury,— Your kind and manly letter entitles you not only to my gratitude, but to that of every good Republican in the State. I have decided that whatever contest there might be should be carried on in an honorable and kindly spirit worthy of the Commonwealth, of the party, and of ourselves. This feeling I know has been shared and acted on by you and by all engaged in the canvass. I accept with pleasure and sincere thanks your kind offer of moving my nomination in the convention. This courteous and graceful act on your part only strengthens the bond of friendship always subsisting between us.

Yours sincerely and cordially,
Frederic T. Greenhalge.

The convention assembled October 8, 1893, amid great enthusiasm. Greenhalge was nominated by Mr. Pillsbury in a kindly and eloquent speech. He said: "He is my friend and I am his. He is a whole-souled and high-minded man. He is one of the best-known and most popular citizens of Massachusetts in any political party. He has had a varied experience in public life and in every office which he has held he has recommended himself to advancement. He served his apprenticeship to legislation in our House of Representatives, and he served there with ability and fidelity. He was elected to the lower House of Congress, and it is not too much to say that there he made an immediate reputation as an equal among the first of that body, and proved himself not only skilled in legislation, but a master of debate. He has demonstrated his capacity for administrative office at the head of the government in the flourishing city in which he lives, and the people in Lowell are with him as one man. He is an orator whose voice has been heard with delight and admiration from the stand and the platform in every part of Massachusetts. He is an earnest, a thorough-going, and an unflinching Republican. He is from heel to crown a loyal and patriotic American. He has every quality of a successful candidate, and every qualification for the great office which it is within the power of the Republican party to bestow upon him. In his nomination the Republican party will distinguish itself, and will make the first step and a long step in a spirited and victorious campaign."

With a tremendous cry of "Aye!" the motion for the nomination of Greenhalge was carried by acclamation. In his speech of acceptance, he said, after being received with enthusiastic applause: —

"MR. PRESIDENT AND GENTLEMEN OF THE CONVENTION, — I accept the nomination. I accept it as the greatest honor of my life, and thank you for it with the deepest gratitude. I accept it also as the greatest responsibility of my life, and I trust I may assume that responsibility in a spirit befitting the confidence you have reposed in me. My deep sense of my defects and shortcomings is increased by the high and honorable character of the able and distinguished men whose names have been before the party as candidates, and whose patriotic action has contributed so much to the harmony of this great convention.

"Gentlemen, the Republican party is indifferent to nothing that concerns the welfare of the Commonwealth, or the welfare of the nation. To keep Massachusetts foremost among her sister States, — peerless among her peers, — none of the great agencies of civilization must be neglected or ignored. Education, justice, economy, temperance, equality must still lead us on to better government in State, in town, and city.

"The State must be just to all, subservient to none. Hear the words of the fathers in Article VI. of the Declaration of

Rights of our Constitution: 'No man, nor corporation, nor association of men, have any other title to obtain advantages, or particular and exclusive privileges, distinct from those of the community, than what arises from the consideration of services rendered to the public.' In the spirit of these words public interests will ever be preferred to private interests.

"The condition of national affairs must excite our keenest solicitude. An indignant country asks the Democratic party, 'Where is the prosperity of 1892? Give us back that prosperity, with its business, its dividends, its wages.' The reply is not satisfactory. While the Republican banner floated over the Capitol, while Republican laws were administered by Republican hands and brains, we had prosperity. Now we are awaiting its return. The prospect of vicious legislation scared away that prosperity. But the Sherman Act, they say, is the root of all this evil. Every intelligent man in this country knows how and why that act was passed. But the Sherman Act is charged to the Republican party. That party erected a dike to check the flood of free silver. The Democracy cry out because the flood here and there breaks through the dike. But who prepared the flood except the Democratic party? As well might a Tory censure old Putnam because the rail fence at Bunker Hill was not of more scientific construction.

"Now we are all in favor of repeal. The Democratic party is in power. We Republicans are not such partisans that we cannot as patriots thank the President of the United States for his patriotic service in behalf of sound money; and if his own party fail him, the Republican party will be found — a legion of salvation — standing at his back in this patriotic work. We say to him, 'Hold the fort, for we are coming.' [Great applause.] So we say, 'Repeal!' They say, 'We cannot yet.' And their majority in the Senate stands helpless before a corporal's guard of garrulous silverites. Let them go, then, to the armory of parliamentary weapons, and if their hearts fail them not, let them draw from thence the flashing blade with which Thomas B. Reed dealt such valiant blows for the true welfare of the country. And they may depend upon it they will have as allies the Sage of Worcester, the wisdom and strength of our senior Senator, and the youthful vigor and dauntless intellect of the delegate from Nahant, Henry Cabot Lodge.

"If the Democratic party fails of repeal, then we charge them with the worst of political crimes,— imbecility and impotence.

"We say another word of advice to the Democratic party: The election laws help to secure free and honest elections. You have already made elections in some sections a mockery. Do not seek to extend your malignant influences to darken the free North as you have darkened the South.

"Again, we would help you to restore prosperity to the country. To that end, we say, tamper as little as possible with the great revenue system established by the Fifty-first Congress, and tell us at once how little evil you intend to work. If you do this, every industry will blaze with new light from Atlanta to Lewiston.

"Gentlemen, I believe, and you believe, that the Commonwealth of the Pilgrim Fathers, founded on their broad and lofty principles — on their righteous and equal laws — is safer with the Republican party than with any other. What thoughtful man will say that Massachusetts is any better — in industry or charity, in character or influence, in substance or promise — for the three years of Democratic supremacy now closing, not soon to be renewed? Let us, then, in this solemn hour, lift high the banner of our party before the face of the Lord! Every good patriot, every business man, every loyal soldier, every bread-winner (and we mean to have no bread-*loser* under *our* policy) will look to that banner as the symbol of rescue, of safety, of hope. Let the redemption of Massachusetts begin to-day! Gentlemen, I thank you from my heart."

The scenes at the reception of Greenhalge, in Huntington Hall, at Lowell, Saturday night, on his return from the convention, were never forgotten by those who gathered to honor the successful candidate. The audience was made up of his friends and neighbors. Democrats and Republicans alike were there to welcome him. Greenhalge arrived in Lowell at half-past seven. The route from the station to the hall was one blaze of colored lights. The candidate's entrance on the platform was the signal for enthusiastic applause. It was genuine feeling that animated the vast throng, — a sincere admiration for Greenhalge, and, on the part of many, a sincere friendship and love.

Such scenes may be thought common in political contests, but there was something on that occasion more than is usual. It was in part, at least, a personal tribute to the man, inspired by true affection and appreciation. Greenhalge was deeply moved himself. His foreign birth had been referred to in the public prints, and his spirit of patriotism was aroused and perhaps a little hurt. The excitement was intense, and people stood on seats to cheer him; he could not make himself heard for some time. He began his speech as follows : —

" Fellow-townsmen, I have only a word to say. It seems but yesterday since I stood in this old hall declaiming as a high-school graduate Curran's immortal speech on ' Universal Emancipation.'

" Lowell is my adopted city, and to her and to Massachusetts I would devote every drop of blood in my body.

" You know my life. It has not been the best one possible. I never claimed that. But I hope that when the One above looks it over, He may never find that I have been unjust to any man, whatever or whoever he may be, whether he be black or white, Englishman or Irishman, Democrat or Republican.

" Lowell is my adopted city. Oh, they are going to make that an issue! Let them dare to do it! Let any man dare to charge me with being an alien to Lowell or the old Bay State! In Lowell are buried the remains of my sainted father and mother. Here lies buried my first-born. Here is the home of my wife and children. I say that God will have some chosen curse to blast the man who dares to take away from me my chosen country.

" You know me. Have I been unfair to any man? Let any man — Irishman, Englishman, black or white — say that I ever wronged him! We want liberality ; we want broadness of feeling.

" Friends of Lowell, I say this : If anything gives me one thrill of pride to-night, it is that it is possible for me to bring

home this honor that I have received to-day. I have not cared
for public office for myself. I have been charged with indifference on this account. But I love this city of Lowell and this
dear old county of Middlesex, and if I can bring to them any
honor I am willing to exert every effort that lies within me to
do so. I do want to show that I am not one of the evils of un-
restricted immigration, and I am going to win and bring home
to Lowell every honor that it is within my power to obtain."

The following account of this remarkable meeting is by an
eye-witness, and well pictures the scene : —

"Just prior to entering the hall, he was told that a Lowell
paper had that day deprecated his nomination because he was
of foreign birth. Being the first speaker, he had practically no
time in which to prepare what he said upon that subject. With
the love which he felt for Massachusetts, the taunt which had
been flung in his face the day of his victory, you can well
understand, aroused him to the greatest earnestness when he
spoke. After a few introductory sentences, the following was
the language used by him : —

"'They are going to make that the issue, are they? Let
them do it if they dare! An alien? Let the man rise up who
dares to charge me with being an alien to this Commonwealth,
to this republic, to this nation. Here are the ashes of my
father and my mother, of my first-born ; here are the hopes of
my wife and children, sons and daughters of the Revolution.
I say God will have some chosen curse to blast the man, the
wretch, who dares to take away from me my country ! You
know me. Have I ever been unfair ? Let any man, Irishman, Englishman, German, African, or Indian, say that I have
wronged him !'

"As he reached the climax, for a moment I could see but
dimly through the tears with which my own emotion partially
blinded me; but in another instant I discovered that I had
nothing to conceal, for every eye within the range of my vision
betrayed the emotion of strong and stalwart men, — men in
broadcloth and men in overalls; and in an instant, that audience as one man rose to their feet, standing on chairs and set-
tees, with hands aloft, tears coursing down their faces, and with

one long and mighty huzza, which might have reached the arch of high heaven, indorsed his sentiments."

The following letter of Mr. Reed explains itself. It was written during the campaign, and bears witness to his high appreciation of Greenhalge, and of the talents of the latter displayed in his congressional career. It was a compliment richly deserved, and attracted wide attention. Greenhalge's known admiration for the character of Reed made it doubly pleasing to him : —

I say to you that Frederic T. Greenhalge is a man worthy to be Governor of Massachusetts ; and I say it knowing well the splendid list of famous men to which his name will be added next November. Frank, generous, high-minded, intelligent, and capable, he deserves your utmost support.

With a single exception or two, I know of no one who has so commanded the undivided attention of that most jealous audience in the world, — the members of the House of Representatives. A man who can hold his own there, can hold it in a great many places in this world.

THOMAS B. REED.

The political speeches delivered by Greenhalge in this personal campaign for the governorship of Massachusetts may be considered as his greatest achievements upon the platform, — they were an admirable series of addresses. His personal efforts were immense and incessant. As a leader he was indefatigable. He seemed incapable of fatigue. He traversed the State from end to end, speaking nearly every night, and often twice or thrice on the same evening in different towns and cities. Never since the days of Robinson was such a campaign. As time went on, the people everywhere became interested in the splendid display of vigor by the Republican candidate. He was sharply criticised by the Democratic orators concerning trivial matters. Their sharpest attacks produced little effect. His success on the platform was indisputable ; his energy and fire carried the people with him ; his speeches rose to the highest standards of political oratory ; he was the people's candidate, and they elected him Governor of Massa-

17

chusetts by thirty-five thousand majority over Hon. John E.
Russell, the Democratic candidate.

The victory was not confined to Massachusetts. The Republicans were victorious all along the line. It was a time of
public rejoicing and renewed hope. On the morning of the
election Greenhalge wrote in his diary: —

"*Tuesday, Nov.* 7, 1893. — A bright, clear day, — God's day,
and, I hope, mine. Election day. I have finished a hard
campaign, and have done fairly well. I am going to vote
soon. My dear ones are well. I am well. May all things
go well."

Later he writes: "On Wednesday, November 29, I was
elected governor by 35,677 plurality, — the total vote being, for
me, 192,613. I ran third on the ticket; and I am a little surprised that, after a contest for the nomination and a hard fight
in the campaign, with the objection of foreign birth and former
contests, I was so well sustained. I am feeling well bodily,
ready for work, and doing much every day. I want now a
conference of New England Republican governors. I thank
God for his mercies."

The following is a good example of the character of the
speeches delivered by Greenhalge in the course of this campaign. It was delivered at Taunton: —

"Mr. Chairman, Ladies and Gentlemen, Friends and
Fellow-Citizens of Bristol County, — I knew that I had
some friends in Taunton, but I did not know that I had quite
so many. I thank you for your attendance here to-night to
listen to the discussion of the great subjects which ought to
come home to the heart and mind of every thinking man and
every thinking woman in the Commonwealth.

"What are the great political and business topics which are
of the most paramount importance to-day? They are what
have interested men for many years — for many centuries.
They are, as ever, the question of the currency; secondly, of
taxation; and thirdly and generally, of business. These matters concern every man, no matter to what political party he
belongs. He must take an interest in those matters. And I
shall try to speak to-night in such a spirit that it will be less

a partisan appeal than an appeal to the reason, the judgment, the intelligence of every man of every shade of political creed. We talk about taxation. Let us consider that subject for a moment as it is connected with the administration of the Federal government. It takes a great deal of money, my friends, to carry out this great government. It takes a great deal of money to insure to you the comforts, the advantages, the privileges which the United States of America gives to every man, woman, and child under the folds of the Stars and Stripes; and there is not a man in this audience, there is not a man in Taunton, who objects to paying a dollar of just and equal taxation if he gets the dollar's worth of good government back for it. We then start with the great general and fundamental principle that the best party is that party which gives to every man an honest dollar's worth of good government for every honest dollar that is taken from his pocket. How, my friends, is this matter of Federal taxation regulated and carried out? Let me tell you briefly and simply. It costs to carry on the great general government of the United States somewhere between $350,000,000 and $400,000,000 annually; and let me also tell you one pleasant thing at the outset,— that while the Democratic party and the Republican party have been fighting each other for thirty years and more, they have been forced, in practical administration, to this important conclusion, that to carry on the government a certain amount, and they are not wide apart as to the amount, for annual expenditure is necessary.

"I am going to be entirely fair and candid in this matter. We have heard much said about a billion-dollar Congress. I remember that in the last campaign we replied, or some of our friends on the Republican side replied, that the Fifty-second Congress had actually appropriated and expended more than the Fifty-first Congress, the so-called billion-dollar Congress. But I took this ground all through the campaign, and I hold it to-day, that I will not throw it in the face of any party if they have spent a little more money than my party has spent, if, upon the whole, they can show that their intentions were good, if they can show that upon the whole the expenditures were wisely made; while I might perhaps show

some grounds of complaint, while I might say here and there
was extravagance on the side of the Fifty-second Congress, I
will say if the two parties can get anywhere near together
upon that important matter let us agree for the moment on
one thing, if we disagree on everything else. So I take the
expenditure of the Forty-ninth Congress, of the Fiftieth, of the
Fifty-first, and the Fifty-second, and compare them, and I say,
without any invidious distinction at this time, we have come
to one great general result, and that is that it costs something
between $350,000,000 and $400,000,000, laying aside what we
may call certain fixed charges, to carry on the government of
this country. Now, then, I say, the people do not object if that
expenditure is wisely and intelligently made. The American
people are not mean, niggardly, or parsimonious. If they find
that any party has done substantially well in appropriating
and expending money, they do not go about cavilling, except in
some cases where politicians of a partisan character are compelled to make some little partisan capital. But they have a
right to inquire, ' If you have expended so many millions on this
or that score, what have you done with the money?' And if
the Administration replies, ' With that we have irrigated the
arid regions of the West and converted waste places into fertile
regions,' the people will say, ' Well and good, we find no fault
with that. And what have you done with those thirty or
forty millions there?' 'With that amount of money we have
built and improved harbors; we have dug out the channels of
these rivers here and there; we have erected fortifications there
to defend and insure the safety of the country.' And again the
people say, ' Well and good, we find no fault with that. And
what have you done with this large amount here?' 'With
that we have seen to it that no veteran of the war should
suffer from poverty, or should spend his days in any alms-
house, or his children beg their bread.' And again the people
will say, ' Well and good. But what have you done with that
amount there?' ' With that we set a great fleet upon the sea
ready to maintain and preserve the dignity of the United
States in every sea, and protect every citizen, white or black,
native or adopted, in any part of the globe.' And again the
people will say, ' Well and good, we find no fault with that.'

"Now then, my friends, how shall this annual amount be raised?

"About $150,000,000 of this is raised from internal revenue, — taxes on tobacco, spirits, oleomargarine, opium, etc.; articles either of luxury or whose consumption need not be encouraged. The balance, about $200,000,000, comes from what we call customs revenue, — that is, from duties levied on imports; and there is where the two parties differ in a very important degree. They say, 'You must levy your impost duties in such a way that certain articles may take the whole or the large burden of the tax.' They say, 'Here is our list of articles upon which you shall impose what is called the tariff.' Then we, the Republican party, say, on the other hand, 'No, we do not agree with you upon your list of articles.' Remember, my friends, that all this time we agree upon one thing, that this amount of money must be raised, that it costs this amount; and I have been able to find no case of extravagance in the administration of the Republican party which merits your condemnation. Therefore we say, 'Now take our list of articles;' and our list of articles is different from theirs. What is theirs? Such articles as tea, coffee, sugar, molasses, in fact everything in which labor does not enter as a factor of production. We say, 'Wait a moment. We know that that is an ancient system; it has been tried in certain countries; but cannot we do better than that?' So we put up our list and we say, 'Whatever we put on that list shall come under certain heads. First, that list shall contain articles of luxury which are not matters of necessity; and, secondly, — and here is the great and important distinction, — it shall cover all articles into which the labor of the American working man and woman comes as a factor. There is a difference between the two parties. And observe that our friends on the other side do not propose to free you, my friends, from the burden of taxation. They tell you that they will when they come here before you on your platform, but as near as we can find out to-day, all the change they propose to make is to take the tariff off the list into which your labor enters and put it upon the list of articles into which your labor does not enter. And so the proposition would be to take from woollen goods, cotton goods and steel and machinery and products of iron,—to take the duty off those and put it back upon sugar, upon molasses, and upon articles of a kindred nature. When I talk on this matter of tariff, I sometimes leave out the word 'protection,' and I will tell you why. I say it is a question of equalizing taxation, of adjusting equal and just taxation, rather than a matter of protection. Let me illustrate what I mean, as I have had occasion to do previously, by a case of goods of some sort made here in Taunton and a case of goods over from Mullhouse or some European manufacturing city or town. Observe, when this case of goods is put into the market,—the one into which your labor has entered,—it represents every dollar that employer and workingman and workingwoman has. It represents their capital, their profit, their wages. In that case of goods is their fortune, the happiness and prosperity of their families, of their wives and children. Out of that case of goods has come the money to build your cottages, to deposit in your savings-banks, to build your roads and bridges, to erect your libraries, your city halls, your hospitals, and everything that goes to make the civilization of the United States the highest and most advanced in the world. All that is represented in your case of goods. Have not our people paid their just share of the expense of government in that case of goods? Have not we all borne our fair and equal proportion? Has not the workingman who has put his labor in paid something to the carrying on of the great government, something to the support of the city of Taunton, of the county of Bristol, of the Commonwealth of Massachusetts, as well as to the United States of America? He has paid his full share. His wife has helped. His wife and children have helped in an indirect way, because they have been consumers and helpers in that way. So I say, my friends, your case of goods has done its full duty, its just and proper share. But here comes in the other case of goods from across the water somewhere. What has it paid? Now, the question between the Democratic party and the Republican party is how much it ought to pay to earn its footing, to come into the market and compete with the products of your labor. Why, it is not an unfair estimate to say that the value of that case of goods has contributed thirty, forty, and in some cases fifty per cent *ad valorem* of its value to the country here. It costs something to maintain this great market-house of the United States. It cost something to win it originally. It took labor, energy, treasure; it took blood; it took human life. It takes something now to maintain and carry on that mighty market-house stretching from the Atlantic to the Pacific. All we say is that your labor, that your capital, that your interests and fortunes shall at least stand on an equal footing with that of the new-comer on this side. So we say, is there anything unreasonable in saying that before the case of goods shall come in, and, freed from the burdens which you have borne to maintain this market-house, paying the rent of the store, keeping it clean, protecting it from fire, protecting it from danger of every kind, and doing all that out of your own pockets and out of your own labor, — is it fair that this case of goods, coming in on the other side, should push out and out the domestic product made here in Taunton? We say, equalize the taxation; and so, before that product shall come in here it shall at least pay an equal amount with the case which has paid its way, and which has contributed to the support and comfort and success of the country. That is simply a question of equalization of taxes. I have not gone into the question of protection for protection's sake. It is not necessary to go into the fine distinction of the books about diversifying industries, about promoting labor. I put it to-night on the simple ground of justice and fair play to the workingmen and the workingwomen of the United States, and say there is nothing unfair in that view of the case. Consider, then, my friends, if this is anything more than the simplest justice dictates and requires.

"My friends, it is always important, even after you have adjusted your revenue laws, — and those come under the subject which I have mentioned as taxation, — that the great basis of value which we call money (currency) shall be safe, steady, as little changeable in value as possible. Money, the dollar that you put into your pockets after you have earned it, is the measure and the representative of your labor. It is, therefore, of the highest importance that that representative and symbol and actual embodiment of value shall be all it is represented to be, — that it shall be indeed 100 cents, and not 80 or 75 or 70. That matter is of as much importance, I may say it is even of paramount importance to any other. If after you have done your work, if after you have put in your plant and run your business, you take something which is fleeting, changeable in value, you might just as well stop working one time as another. Therefore it is of the highest importance that the money question shall be handled with judgment, with discretion, and, above all, with integrity, sterling as the gold itself.

"Now, then, let me see about the aspect of things to-day. Money is important, not merely to the capitalist, it is more important to the workingman and the workingwoman. The capitalist can always protect himself in some way or other. It is the other people who are prevented from protecting themselves against the incursions of false standards. So that I do not want you to think that this question of currency is one in which you are not deeply interested. What, I say, then, is the aspect of this question of monetary value to-day? It is not in a satisfactory condition; and I want to ask my friends on the other side, and any of them may reply to it at their pleasure, whether in 1892 a Democratic majority was obtained in the Senate of the United States? I understood, and very clearly understood, from the manifestations made to make it clear to me, that in 1892 our friends on the other side had made a clean sweep, and had obtained possession of the Executive, of the House of Representatives, and of the Senate of the United States, so that those three branches of government were in their control and possession. If it is not true to-day, when did the change come? I therefore say that if there is a Democratic majority in the Senate of the United States to-day, they cannot, as my friend Thomas has said, escape the responsibility of the delay which is now injuring the financial confidence in this country. Why, if they have a Democratic majority, what prevents them from passing, by concurrent action, the bill to repeal the purchasing clauses of the Silver Act which has been passed by the House?

"Well, they tell us that their majority is too small, that they have no such rules as those which governed the House of Representatives. Thus they pay a splendid tribute to the genius of Reed, who made the rules for the House of Representatives, which were approved and indorsed by the members of that House, — rules which enabled him, with a majority, to carry out the legislation of the people at that time. So we say, if you have the majority, if you have the disposition to pass this bill, do not find fault because there is a garrulous senator talking against time here and there, but send out your Committee on Rules to bring in a rule fixing a given day, and that as early as possible, to pass the bill, and to bring all the confidence that can be brought by that measure. I say, if they fail to do that, they fail to execute the will of the people, and the failure is directly chargeable to them. Now, my friends, this is a matter of the weightiest importance. It is a matter which deserves the thought and care of every intelligent man; it deserves the thought and care of every Senator of the United States.

"And do you think there is the slightest question as to where the noble senators from Massachusetts would stand if any measure were brought forward to hasten the decision of this momentous issue? Do you think there is any question where George Frisbie Hoar would stand if a rule were brought in to hasten the day of voting upon this question of repeal? Do you think there is any question of where Henry Cabot Lodge would stand upon this matter? I say, then, as my friend has said, the Republican party stands ready, willing to support this policy at this time, eager to forget in their duty as patriots any duty that a partisan spirit might suggest, and to say to the President of the United States, 'We stand at your back whether you are a Democrat or not.' There they stand, as they stood in the Fifty-first and as they stood in the Fifty-second Congress, making no partisan appeals, making no effort at obstruction in any measure which concerned the welfare of the country. My friends, the position in this country has gone beyond the mere partisan narrow limits.

"It has come to be a question, as I said, which comes home to every home in the land. It comes home to every man and woman in Taunton. It is the business of any party to assist in helping its own people in providing them with every advantage that legislation can give; and legislation cannot do a great deal even at the most. But at the same time your interests, the interests of the laboring classes, lie at the foundation of all good government. It is not the success of this or that wealthy man that makes the greatness of a country: it is the success of the fifteen, of the twenty millions of the bone and sinew of the United States which makes the happiness and glory of the United States. And so we may say that this question of finance is of the utmost importance. The question of revenue policy is also of vast importance. Why, my friends, if by the imposition of a duty in the raising of necessary revenue you can do two good acts at once, is it not wise to do that?

"If you put a duty upon coffee or sugar, it benefits no living man in America; but if you put a duty to raise the necessary revenue upon woollen goods, upon manufactured cotton goods, upon manufactures of iron and steel, then you not only lift the burden of taxation and make it easier, but you confer a boon upon the American laborer, upon the American workingman. This country, I may say, is peculiarly circumstanced in one respect. You have here the highest standard of living which can be found anywhere in the world That circumstance makes it important that every advantage which can be derived from a fair and equal system of taxation shall be given to this people and not to some other people.

"The American workingman is a citizen charged with important duties. He has more political obligations and more political power than any citizen or subject of any country in the world. He needs more to maintain that higher standard of living than any other person in any other country similarly placed. He is a governor; he is a ruler. It is important for the safety, for the prosperity, of the country that he should be intelligent, and in order to be intelligent and prosperous he must be well fed and well clothed and well sheltered. He needs certain things for his comfort which people in other places do not have and do not seem to demand. He must have his daily newspaper; he must have leisure to attend political meetings, and I do not care of what party he may be; he must have means to send his children to school; he must have means to contribute to these expenses of government of which

I have spoken. And therefore we say that these are exceptional circumstances. And while it is true, as has been stated in the books, that it is always best to buy in the cheapest market and to sell in the dearest, the question comes to the thoughtful man, 'After all, which is the best? Which is the cheapest and which is the dearest?' Under the system of Alexander Hamilton, under the system of Henry Clay, of Blaine, and McKinley, there has been an increase in manufacturing products.

"We are following the standard which will lead us to the very van in the manufacturing countries of the world; we are making rapid progress in improvements; we are getting to be more scientific, more successful, every day. We have this theory: It is not by beating down wages that you get the best results. That is a slight factor. And reductions of wages do not result always in the net reduction of expenses. The true policy which the Republican party believes in is, raise and improve the standard of your laborer, contribute all you can to make him healthy, strong, intelligent. Let him make his way with the best advantages you can give him, and our notion is that the skilled artisan of Taunton will, under that policy, turn out more products than the artisan of any other country in the world; and if we can keep on with this policy we shall not have any question about opening up our ports to the products of any country.

"Now, my friends, it is of the utmost importance that this policy should be maintained. It has been the policy of the country for more than thirty years; it has been the policy recommended by wise and thoughtful statesmen. At least in 1892 we had a year of prosperity. My friend on the other side has said that 1892 was not a prosperous year, that there was an outflow of gold, and that business was diminishing; and yet in the statements of the Annual Statistics of Manufacturers of Massachusetts the record is entirely the reverse.

"In the year 1892 the increase in the value of the product of the nine leading industries of Massachusetts was $33,180,865 over the total value of the product of the preceding year.

"The rate of gain ranged from 2.68 per cent on cotton goods to 10.94 per cent on leather. The average gain was 5.37 per cent, the largest in recent years, the 'normal' rate of increase being 3 per cent.

"In the 4,473 establishments considered in these nine industries, there was an increase of 13,515 hands, or 4.53 per cent in one year. In January there were 303,910 persons employed. In the vacation season in August there were 309,308 employed, and in October 317,007, which dropped to 313,606 in December."

The return of the Governor-elect to his home in Lowell, at half-past twelve on the night of the election, was perhaps the most remarkable political event in the annals of the city.

A vast crowd waited for him at the station; it was a cheerful and happy assembly of excited men. The time was long before the train arrived.

It was as noisy as the Fourth of July. There were Roman candles and rockets. The crowd sang "Marching through Georgia" and other popular airs. At last the train arrived, and the enthusiasm of the people vented itself in a royal welcome. Sober citizens, heads of families, grandfathers as well as young men, carried away by the excitement of the moment, united in dragging the open barouche, in which sat the hero of the hour, to Huntington Hall, accompanied by the wildly cheering crowd. Bursting open the doors, the throng flowed like a sea wave into the hall and up to the platform. It was one o'clock in the morning, and a strange, inspiring scene, when, mid the greatest enthusiasm, Mayor Pickman introduced the Governor-elect : —

"Fellow-citizens, the race is ended; the battle is won. Lowell has been loyal to her foremost son, and Frederic T. Greenhalge has been elected Governor of the Commonwealth of Massachusetts. Party lines have been forgotten. There is but one name in Massachusetts, that of our honored statesman. Such a scene as this to-night is almost unprecedented in the history of Lowell. But you did not come here to listen to me, and I am proud, then, to introduce the next Governor of Massachusetts."

After his introduction Greenhalge spoke as follows : —

"My friends, it is not late Tuesday, because it is Wednesday already. I have only a single word to say. What can I say after such a demonstration as you have given me? The last thing I said when I left the city this morning was, 'Give me the vote of Lowell, and I will sacrifice five thousand votes in other parts of the State.' I am told that I have the vote of my own people, and I have not sacrificed a single vote in the remainder of the State.

"What does it mean if it does not mean good to every mother's son of you? — for I see there are no daughters here. I am not here as a partisan, in spite of what many of the newspapers have said. I have never meant to be a narrow partisan. I have tried to be a friend to every man that needed friendship. I have not been an illiberal man. I have tried to crush out party animosities. I have tried to bring the different elements here into one brotherhood.

"Of course we differ. It would be a dull world if it were not so. I should hate to have to live with any one who always agreed with me. Even my beautiful wife and my son and daughter do not always think as I do. Still, we are one family. I want fair, broad, honorable treatment on all sides. In this campaign, terminated to-night, I have struck no blow below the belt. I want to stand by the men who work for their living, — not because I want their votes; I never ask a man to vote for me. Give me an election that comes from the hearts of the people, and it is the grandest glory that comes to a man."

At these last words cries of "Aye! aye!" were heard from all parts of the hall.

The day after election Greenhalge said in an interview: —

"I do not regard the result in any sense a personal triumph. While I may have had enthusiastic friends who had my personal interest at heart, I still believe that these friends were actuated by motives of principle and a desire for the public welfare.

"If they regarded me in any friendly way, it was chiefly because they regarded me as an instrument calculated to perform the task which they desired, or which they intended.

"As for an explanation of either the preliminary campaign

or the election, I think the duty of explanation belongs to the other party. I do not want you to leave out the word 'other.'

"Some explanation seems to be due from some of the political prophets. We simply point to the campaign and to its results. It is not a time for any partisan jubilation; it is a time for the serious consideration of the present condition of affairs and the remedies applicable thereto.

"How much the voice of Massachusetts, and the voice of other States speaking in the same tones, will aid against the bigots of theory, is the question to be solved.

"For my part, I shall endeavor that the voice of Massachusetts shall have its full and salutary effect upon the national council. I feel the utmost kindness toward the Democratic candidate for governor, on account of the fair and rational method in which he discussed party issues, which was in delightful contrast with the discouraging exhibitions made by partisan politicians and partisan newspapers on the Democratic side.

"It is desirable to raise the standard of party journalism to a point at least of respectability.

"I deprecate any demonstration of partisan exultation in the presence of the grave crisis in the affairs of the country."

Greenhalge had now reached the summit of his career. He was elected Governor of Massachusetts, the grand old Commonwealth, whose chief magistrates have always been men of distinction and character, — whose great traditions he reverenced, whose citizens he regarded as the most intelligent in the world; he, who was only an adopted son of Massachusetts, had been held worthy of the highest office in the gift of her people. His heart was full of gratitude, and with the deepest feeling he looked forward to the honors and responsibilities of his high position. His whole being afterwards became absorbed in its duties. He gave himself without reserve to his great task. Conscience prescribed his course, and he never swerved from the appointed path.

I will here again avail myself of the opportunity Judge Lawton has afforded me of illustrating Governor Greenhalge's character and aims by the just and discriminating words of one who knew him intimately and well. He writes of him as follows, referring at first to the period of his defeat in re-election to Congress : —

"He returned to the practice of the law with a sharpened appetite. He had not lost his interest in the great popular contests over public policies. He was willing, even eager, to lead in those contests. He wanted to be a 'free lance for a while,' he said. He did not 'wish to be voted for any more.' He loved the public platform, and by no means intended to abandon it. Hereafter the law was to be his vocation, and everything else subordinate to that.

"His plan was not that of the people of Massachusetts. The party to which he belonged, in the person of its candidate for governor, had been three times in succession defeated in the same State which had before been its stronghold. The last defeat of this kind had been in the presidential year of 1892. This frightened the leaders of the party in the Commonwealth. After much discussion the conclusion was reached that the very best must be nominated, or another defeat would follow. It was plain that many Republicans did not think that the tariff was involved in State elections. There was no State issue upon which the political parties were fairly divided. The personality of the candidate had come to count for more than ever. The youthful and talented Russell, after a treble election to the chief magistracy, had created a personal party which seemed to dominate in Massachusetts. A candidate had been indicated to succeed him who, by his experience, his learning on all public questions, and by his forensic abilities, seemed hardly inferior as a getter of votes. There was no lack of substantial and sound men in the Commonwealth who might be chosen to oppose him. It was felt that something more was needed. A man was wanted who was this, and besides should have that brilliancy of personality, that magnetic attractiveness, that should fairly overmatch and outshine any favorite that could be pitched upon as a Democratic candidate. The selection of such a man was left to the rank and file of the Republican party. After a few weeks of suggestion and discussion, the response came from the people with

no uncertain sound. Wherever he had appeared upon the
platform Greenhalge had fixed the admiration and won the
hearts of all who had heard him. Before the convention for
nomination had assembled, the dispute as to his pre-eminence
had practically ceased. He who alone seemed to be able to
divide that convention, with grace and magnanimity advocated
the nomination and the loyal, unanimous support of Greenhalge. In the canvass that followed it soon became apparent
that his election was sure.

"He was three times elected governor by majorities which
exceeded the hopes of his most ardent supporters. He performed all the duties of that office, not only with the grace
which had been anticipated, but with a courage and wisdom
that brought back the best days of the best governors of the
old Commonwealth. There was no power behind the throne.
There was only one governor while he occupied the chair.
Honest and public-spirited men sometimes disagreed with
him. Mere politicians and mere place-hunters seldom agreed
with him. He considered well every responsibility placed upon
him. He patiently and without prejudice heard both sides
and all sides. When he reached what he believed to be the
right conclusion, no friend, no man, no influence could swerve
him from it. No son of Massachusetts, though born on her
soil, ever reverenced more her great history and her great
influence in America. Her democracy of two millions and a
half of people was to him the advance guard of the civilization
of the world. Every act, every utterance of Massachusetts,
through its legislature or its governor, was sacred. He had
been advised at his third nomination to conciliate a powerful
faction in the convention which all his timid friends feared
might defeat his re-election. An election had never been an
important matter to him. It was no more so then than ever
before. But the principle of opposition to him was of great
importance. He did not hesitate to discuss that principle in
his address of acceptance. To some it would have been a duty
to truckle — to concede something. This he never did on an
'essential.' He calmly reviewed what he had done and what
he had said that had given offence ; he stated his own position

with patience, with toleration, and adhered to it with firmness. John A. Andrew was the 'war governor' of Massachusetts. No one will ever crowd him from the pedestal on which he stands. But Massachusetts was a unit behind him from the very beginning to the end of his great achievement. He led Massachusetts to the field as really as if he commanded her soldiers in the fire of battle. Greenhalge came to the governorship of Massachusetts at a time when the wavering and fickle popular majority had demoralized even those who were at once good citizens and earnest partisans. They began to think that a party, to get into power and keep it, must deal timidly with questions that divide the people. Those who were politicians and nothing else thought the party's power and the candidate's popularity depended on the cunning evasion of all burning and disturbing questions. They thought it a candidate's duty to his party to conceal any opinion he might have which might appear unpopular. In the days of Andrew one great question swallowed all others, and the governor could afford to be independent and candid. But the politicians thought the times had changed.

"Governor Greenhalge, however, seemed never to realize that his party was made of glass. Very early in his first term he developed a candor and an independence that some timid souls felt had destroyed every chance of his re-election. He was re-elected, however, and pursued the same course all through his second term, and to the amazement of many, he was triumphantly elected for the third term. Said one of his friends at that time, 'I have always said that the Governor was no politician. I have said it over and over again; I thought it was true, but it is n't. There is only one politician in the whole world, and his name is — Greenhalge.' This was intended as a sort of a 'Scotty Briggs' tribute to the Governor. In the best sense it was a tribute to him. It was an unconscious tribute to the people of Massachusetts. It contained the lesson of lessons of Greenhalge's life and of his public service. As long as a democracy worth having shall stand, he is the best politician who deals with the people on the highest plane. The time had come when the Governor

18

of Massachusetts seemed to depend entirely for popular favor
on his personal attractiveness and on the confidence of the
people in his personal fitness. They found out that they had
elected a man to be governor who, while he occupied the
chair, would be governor alone, — in whose courage, justice,
and wisdom they could confide ; and they kept on electing him
until he died.

CHAPTER VIII.

THE inauguration of Governor Greenhalge occurred January 4, at the State Capitol, in Boston, with the customary interesting ceremonies and that republican simplicity which is the honorable characteristic of American institutions. Governor Greenhalge succeeded the late Governor Russell, who, like him, was re-elected three successive years to office, and who, like him, came nearer, perhaps, to the hearts of the people than almost any of their immediate predecessors. They differed widely in political beliefs; but the power which they exercised over other minds had something in kind, and in their deaths they were to be, alas! nearly united. The honorable ambitions of any man might well have been satisfied to have attained the position Greenhalge now occupied. The Republican party of Massachusetts had honored him with the highest office in their gift, and he began his first administration with the good wishes of even his political opponents.

The inaugural address of a new governor is always looked forward to with interest by all parties, and is naturally a subject for criticism by those of opposite political beliefs. The speech of Governor Greenhalge was well received, and few of its suggestions called forth adverse remarks. It was an admirable state paper, and satisfied the people of the State that they had, as their chief magistrate, a man of practical ability, and one well fitted to occupy so eminent a position. During his terms of office it was his fortunate destiny to continue to grow and develop in popularity and character, with ever-increasing appreciation and admiration by the people of the State, who came to know him well, and to give him

full credit for the qualities he possessed. In his inaugural
address Governor Greenhalge made some suggestions which
were indorsed by Democrats and Republicans alike. He en-
joined upon the Legislature the necessity of economy in view
of the general condition of business. He spoke of the too
common evil of stock watering, and advised that laws should
be enacted to prevent it as much as possible. He commented
favorably upon woman suffrage, and hoped to see a better
understanding between employers and employees as a necessity
of business life. A portion of his address touched on the
following subjects, and I insert the passages in which he
speaks of them : —

EDUCATION.

Public education is one of the primal factors in the development and advancement of the people. The education of all
by all, for all, is the corner-stone of the Commonwealth.
There is no room in this system of public education for narrowness, for intolerance, for prejudice. In its construction, the
great object aimed at was to ascertain, not on how many points
the people differed, but on how many points they agreed ; so
that this common ground of agreement having been found,
many diverse elements could be brought together, and thus the
spirit of unity which should animate every citizen could be
cultivated and developed. Upon this broad and enduring
foundation the fabric of the Commonwealth is reared. Here,
upon the ductile and plastic mind of childhood, are indelibly
impressed the lessons of equal rights, equal duties, and equal
opportunities before the law, and the great duty of patriotic
devotion and service to the Commonwealth. Other institutions
of learning may devote themselves each to its special object,
but I firmly believe that the daily association of the diverse
elements of the population in the period of youth, their daily
common occupation in the same tasks and the same sports,
bring together the children of the Commonwealth, and unify
them as no other agency can do.

In 1891 there were 657,137 foreign-born persons in Massachusetts ; and persons having one or both parents of foreign
birth numbered 1,259,943. The total population of Massachusetts for the same year was 2,307,374. These figures are

substantially the same now, and bear substantially the same relative proportions as in the year 1891. The work of unification and assimilation has been for many years going on quietly, thoroughly, and successfully, and Massachusetts has not lost the high reputation for the personal character of her citizens which has so greatly distinguished her from the very beginning. This vast and wonderful work has been largely helped by the system of public education. It has been said that Waterloo was won on the playgrounds of Eton; with equal truth it may be said that many a well-fought field from Baltimore to Appomattox was won on the playgrounds of the grammar-schools of Massachusetts, and the spirit of fraternity and patriotism cultivated in the studies and sports of boyhood blazed into clearer and warmer glow at the bloody angle of Gettysburg or before the defences of Port Hudson.

I am aware that there are alleged to be defects in this system as regards both principle and method. Some of these defects I may be pardoned for mentioning, because Massachusetts should have not only the best schools in the country, but the best in the world; and every defect or alleged defect should be inquired into, and if discovered should be promptly corrected. Among other complaints, it is alleged that there is a lack of co-ordination between our common schools and the higher institutions of learning. It ought to be possible for the humblest child in Massachusetts, in any part of the State, to obtain in the public schools the preparatory instruction necessary for admission to the best university or college in the country. It is for you to determine whether and how the State shall assume the responsibility of providing or requiring equal facilities in elementary or secondary schools in all parts of the Commonwealth. Again, has sufficient provision been made for manual training throughout the Commonwealth? I may say, further, that there is complaint in some quarters that there are not normal schools enough to furnish properly trained teachers, especially for giving instruction in the arts of manual training. Our public schools should, in principles, methods, teachers, and equipment, be brought to the highest possible standard of efficiency.

There were 376,986 pupils in the public schools in 1891,

when the latest enumeration now available was made. It is safe to say, with a reasonable degree of precision, that more than eighty-five per cent of the children of the Commonwealth of school age are to be found in these schools.

TEMPERANCE.

The subject of temperance and the legislation designed to remove or to control the evils resulting from the manufacture and sale of intoxicating liquors have always and properly commanded the earnest consideration of the people of Massachusetts. Intemperance and the temptations which lead to it should be guarded against in every possible way. The cause of temperance can best be advanced by practical legislation, founded upon and supported by public opinion. Public opinion is not often created by law; law is usually created by public opinion.

I am aware that many objections are urged against the existing system of law relating to the manufacture and sale of intoxicating liquors. Undoubtedly, some of these objections are well founded. It is claimed that the limitation of the number of licenses in proportion to the population has worked injury rather than good to the body politic.

I desire to point out, however, that much has been effected under the present system, faulty as it may be. During the year 1893 twelve cities and two hundred and sixty-two towns voted " no license." In view of these results, it would seem as if the friends of temperance might, with strong hopes and encouraging prospects of success, direct their labors to the several communities of the State so as to develop and strengthen public opinion in the desired direction.

The most momentous questions affecting public interests are subordinated to the inordinate and reckless desire to obtain licenses, and city and town affairs are thrown into confusion by the struggle between applicants. It is also urged that the work of distributing licenses would be much more honestly and judiciously performed by license boards appointed by the mayor and aldermen of cities, or by the judges of local courts. The farther removed the officials intrusted with the distribution of licenses are from political, corrupt, or pernicious influences of any sort, the better for the accomplishment of what must be at best a difficult and troublesome task. There is no influence which is so liable to disturb our moral and political welfare as that of the groggery and the saloon.

Public sentiment is naturally opposed to the glaring moral evils which arise from the selfish and indiscriminate sale of liquor; and political purity will be impossible so long as the influence of the sale and use of liquor plays so large a part in the discussion and solution of political questions.

CORPORATIONS.

I deem it important that suitable legislation be enacted to prevent the watering of the stock of quasi-public corporations, either through the instrumentality of construction companies or otherwise, and also to prevent the issue of bonds as a bonus to parties who subscribe for stock; to confine the expenditures of these corporations as strictly as possible to the purposes for which they are organized, and to insure honesty in dealing, both with the stockholders and with the public. And, further, all contracts for the lease, sale, or purchase of railroads or street railways should be subject to the approval of the Railroad Commissioners.

There seems to be no good reason why all quasi-public corporations should not come under a similar rule.

The evils attending the inflation of securities of corporations which receive from the public great privileges not granted private corporations, are so prejudicial to the welfare of the people that judicious measures for the prevention of such inflation are imperatively demanded.

FAST DAY.

I heartily concur in the recommendation made by my immediate predecessor for the abolition of Fast Day, and as a substitute therefor the observance by solemn and patriotic ceremonies of the 19th of April. It is vain to attempt to maintain a custom which has become "more honored in the breach than in the observance."

If the public opinion which has hitherto sustained it has ceased to exist, the outward observance of such a day becomes a mere ceremony, which does not stimulate the reverence or devotion of the people.

The substitution for Fast Day of the 19th of April may well commend itself not only to the patriotic but to the religious sentiment of the people. The earliest memories of this historic day are forever associated with the maintenance of religious and civil liberty, represented by all that is sacred and valuable in the life and institutions of the Massachusetts of 1775. The day derives additional sanctity and significance as commemorating the patriotic spirit and devotion of 1861. Religion and patriotism may, therefore, unite in consecrating this day to the great memories of 1775 and 1861 by appropriate observances, which will exalt the devotion and stimulate the patriotism of every good citizen of the Commonwealth.

SUFFRAGE.

The expediency and justice of extending to women the right of municipal suffrage has been brought to the attention of previous legislatures. The tendency of modern thought and modern civilization points strongly in the direction of this extension.

The services of women in various public departments are now acknowledged to be of the greatest benefit and efficiency. Upon school-boards and in the administration of our public charities there can be no doubt that a higher development and a rapid advance in methods of management and treatment have been accomplished; and, furthermore, the participation of woman in the sterner business of life in almost every line of occupation and work has been constantly increasing. Her performance of labors which tradition and convention have assigned to men would seem to indicate her capacity for sharing in the most important business of the individual and of the community, namely, the conduct of public affairs ; and also to demonstrate the benefits derivable from such participation, and might seem to justify the further step of granting to her the right of municipal suffrage.

I, therefore, commend this subject to your most serious consideration.

PERORATION.

Gentlemen, among the commonwealths of the earth we believe that Massachusetts is *facile princeps.* What was said of the masterpiece of Grecian architecture two thousand years ago may well be applied to Massachusetts now. To her belongs "the grandeur of antiquity and the grace of novelty." Her achievements in science, literature, and art, her intellectual development and the grace and completeness of her culture, have made her the Attica of the New World. In schools, in courts of law, in works of charity, in factories and in workshops, in peace and in war, on land and on sea, her energy, example, and leadership have been everywhere felt and everywhere respected.

Almost three centuries of marvellous vicissitudes have robed her in the purple of heroic achievement and heroic endurance, and her brow is radiant with the newest thought of humanity. No accumulation of wealth could compensate for the loss of individual or national character. But Massachusetts has attained extraordinary material gains without losing the nobility and simplicity which marked the character of her early inhabitants. As I have before suggested, the unification of the diverse elements of her population has been proceeding with a wonderful rapidity and completeness. The oneness of the spirit of her people will manifest itself in the faith, energy, and courage with which she will meet and surmount every obstacle in her pathway to peace, prosperity, and glory.

Upon one thing we must insist. The people of the newer Massachusetts must be taught to revere and emulate the people of the elder Massachusetts in their fidelity to the principles of constitutional liberty, in their public spirit, and fervid devotion to the common weal. In this way only can you be assured of the efficacy of the prayer, *Sicut patribus sit Deus nobis.*

At a banquet of the Grand Army of the Republic in Music Hall, February 8, the new Governor was a guest. His speech on this occasion was one of those patriotic addresses which he loved, perhaps, best to deliver, and which were always eloquent and earnest: —

" I rejoice that I am permitted to be with you for even a few brief moments. There is inspiration, there is patriotic fervor, in standing before a gathering of thousands of men like you. I like to hear the hoarse call of the bos'n, though I do not quite understand it. I like to hear the old songs that the veterans sing to remind them of the beautiful and graceful moments snatched from the severe toil of war and of battle, of prison and, as it were, of suffering. I see before me the army and the navy of the good old Commonwealth, — ' The Army and Navy forever! Three cheers for the Red, White, and Blue.' I am glad to meet these distinguished strangers. I like to sit next to this gallant veteran, Walker, of Indiana, — the State of that other gallant veteran and soldier (we leave all politics out to-day), — that other gallant soldier Benjamin Harrison. It is not without a feeling of local pride that I see Department Commander Hall sit where he does, — an old Lowell boy, who is just as old as they ever get to be. Do you think it gives me pain to see Jack Adams sit where he does in the highest office of the order? It is another wreath in the crown: some of us want to wear crowns, — the crowns of colonels, if nothing else.

" I rejoice to be with you, the most magnificent organization the world ever knew, in war and in peace. The world never knew before of an army of a million of men, who at the tap of the drum at Appomattox blended so quickly and easily into the ranks of the people, and with not one sign of disorder or lack of peace and harmony, became adherents of law, of peace, and of harmony. When we read in history of the returning veterans of yore, we read of times of lawlessness of every sort; but this army of citizen-soldiers of the United States became in a moment, as by magic, citizens again, — just as when the call came in '61 the citizen sprang from the farm, from the factory, and from the office to defend the life of the nation. So when the war was over, the flag of the country again floating over the whole land with not a star or stripe erased, then they said the work is done, we are again citizens of Massachusetts. It is not often, my friends, that such an event has been seen in the history of the world. I say that it has never been paralleled; and if, my friends, there should come trouble, or the appearance of trouble, from without or within, I know that the Grand Army of the Republic, to the last survivor, while there was a single bugle to blow, would be arrayed on the side of law and order, on the side of the Commonwealth of Massachusetts, of the United States.

"Why, then, should not the Commonwealth bring her warmest tribute of gratitude and respect to men like these? It was in her hours of discouragement, it was in the hours of dismay throughout all loyal America, that the messages of good cheer came from your rifles, from your muskets and cannon; it was the sound of your measured tread that brought to Massachusetts and to the whole country courage and good cheer and good tidings."

In less than two months after his inauguration the course of events brought to Governor Greenhalge an opportunity of distinguishing himself and gaining the confidence of the people of the Commonwealth, the like of which is not often given to the Governors of our quiet States. It is needless to say now that he availed himself of it with energy and determination. He proved himself to be emphatically the man for the hour, and from that moment he possessed the real confidence of the people. He showed that he possessed the qualities which they most admire, — resolution and readiness in an emergency, and the command of men. The people of the State were suffering at the time from the prevailing business depression; a large number of men were out of employment, and the consequent poverty pressed hard upon them. Things were not at so extreme a pass in Massachusetts as elsewhere in the country, but they were bad enough. It was the day of Coxey's army, when the singular scene was witnessed of great bodies of men, discontented and out of work, marching from remote parts of the country to the Capitol at Washington, their ranks continually reinforced from the cities and towns on their way, — a motley and incongruous crowd, carrying banners inscribed with socialistic mottoes. A similar spirit was roused in all parts of the nation, and the strange pilgrimage was imitated in various States. Hard trials were indeed upon the people, and the socialist leaders with their doctrines found an opportunity of which they greedily availed themselves. Discontent and poverty are the only levers by which these agitators can move the people. In Massachusetts the accents and doctrines of socialism sounded strange, and failed to influence many; yet there were a number of men who held such ideas, and more who, for mere excitement, were ready to follow them on any wild errand. The leaders of these malcontents in Boston were Morrison I. Swift and Herbert N. Casson, both young men. Headed by them, the first mass-meeting of the unemployed was held on the Common January 31. Mayor Matthews and the Relief Committee were denounced, and resolutions were adopted. The following is an account of the memorable meeting which took place subsequently on the Common on Tuesday, February 20 : —

About the middle of February Governor Greenhalge received a note from Morrison I. Swift, intimating that the unemployed of the city would like to call upon his Excellency and receive from him advice and assistance. The Governor consented to receive the unemployed, and the time appointed was February 20, at half-past two o'clock.

On that day, long before the appointed hour, a crowd to the number of over one thousand or more gathered on the Common. A motley crowd it was. The clothes, countenances, and language of the majority proclaimed their recent arrival in this country. After listening to addresses from Swift, Casson, and other Socialist-Anarchists, as they styled themselves, they proceeded to the State House, where Swift and Casson were made delegates to wait upon the Governor with a petition.

Governor Greenhalge received them courteously and read carefully their petition, which was as follows : —

To the Governor of Massachusetts :

We have decided to confer with you in a body, because we are anxious to hear from your own lips what effort you will put forth in our behalf. In periods of special emergency strong men in office have grappled with trying problems in a great manner, and have conferred lasting services by their discernment and vigor. The present is such an opportunity for you. Will you earn the approbation of your fellow-citizens by putting the deeply significant nature of this crisis of workingmen's want before them, so far as you can, to cope with it earnestly and in no slighting or temporary spirit?

We give you with this a transcript of our petition to the Legislature, the articles of which we would have you support with your influence. The plan of State farms and factories is, we believe, the most direct, efficient, and enduring way to deal with the problem now.

The proposition for the establishment of a permanent commission on the unemployed is one that we would particularly urge upon your attention for the following reasons : —

1st. It is held by the intelligent members of the working-class, who should and do know most about the question, that the unemployed are no new phenomenon, but that each year many industrious persons are obliged to suffer deprivation through enforced idleness. If this is so, temporary relief would be ineffectual.

2d. The number of unemployed is always growing, because machines are discharging many annually who thereafter find no continuous work.

3rd. It is further believed, with the sanction of present experience, that through this disruption of industry there will be an unprecedented number out of employment for a long time.

4th. Want of preparation for the emergency, want of knowledge how to face it, the absence of all scientific means for ascertaining correctly and quickly the number of unemployed and their condition, have had for results feeble and restricted relief efforts, bold denials of facts by those who wished to shirk responsibility, and at length the almost complete indifference, exhaustion, and paralysis of public endeavor to provide for the unemployed toward the end of the winter, when the distress has reached its highest.

Considering these facts, we believe that a commission on the unemployed is indispensable.

Adopted by the unemployed on Boston Common, Feb. 20, 1894.

When he had finished his perusal of the document, the Governor said to Swift: " You would scarcely expect a reply off-hand to your propositions, would you?"

"Well," replied Swift, "we have made a strong point on State farms and factories. You might do something on those things now."

"You must remember," said the Governor, "that State farms cannot be lightly disposed of."

SWIFT. We have made certain propositions. Something must be done. The case is urgent; we cannot go on starving.

GOV. GREENHALGE. Of course you yourself are one of the unemployed? The necessity of which you speak is yours?

SWIFT. Oh, yes.

GOV. GREENHALGE. Now you say that we must formulate plans for you, — that we must do something. Why should that labor devolve on us; or why should not those affected, those deepest interested in the solution of the problem, do the work? These general demands for help are insufficient. These people who are in distress ought to know what they desire.

SWIFT. They want work, — you will have to do something; they will no longer be put off with words. If there is a desire to do this, we want to know it, so we may know how to go ahead.

The Governor replied simply by defining what a State is and what it means. He explained how the majority of the people by thrift or inheritance are able to subsist without complaint; that there are others who want work, — know how to get it, and do not on the least pretence cry out to the State. "Now you propose," he said, "that that large majority bear your burden. Do you think they are bound to give to the unemployed work or public employment if the work is not necessary or beneficial to the community?"

Swift unhesitatingly replied in the affirmative.

"We have come," said Casson, "for assistance to the place where laws are made."

"You have come," quickly replied the Governor, "to the Executive, who is as much a servant as any. I simply suggest to you," he continued, "the difficulties that are in my way. Were I a despot, I might remedy the situation at once. But I am not. This matter is rather one for the Legislature to deal with. I readily admit the gravity of the situation; it demands the earnest thought and sympathy of every intelligent citizen. I want to do everything that can be done under the Constitution, careful not to transgress the rules and regulations of our government."

Swift replied loudly, " Change them ! "

CASSON. There is an intensifying force that may turn out destructive to the State. We feel that something might happen. While we are sitting on the safety-valve, the Huns and Goths may break forth and —

GOV. GREENHALGE. There are no Huns and Goths out there in the multitude, are there ?

CASSON. There is the making of Huns and Goths in them.

" Let me tell you," replied the Governor, with determination, looking Swift in the face, " the covert threat never appeals to me." With a few words more the interview ended. The delegates returned to their followers; while the Governor, having willingly consented to address the crowd, who were waiting in front of the State House, passed down through Doric Hall, and, alone, went out to meet the excited crowd. He delivered his speech from the steps of the Capitol.

" I do not know how many there are of you," he said, " but I presume that every man here to-day is a loyal citizen of Masssachusetts. Is that so or not ? [The crowd applauded faintly.] Now you have presented to me a memorial containing some important propositions and questions. I shall treat that memorial with consideration and respect. You are also to present a memorial of similar character to the Legislature of the Commonwealth, and I think that, knowing that body, I can assure you that it will receive respectful and careful consideration.

" My friends, you ask, as I understand it, for employment. Consider, first, what the function and powers of the Governor are. Consider, again, what the functions and powers of the Legislature are. This is a government of laws and not of men. The Governor has not despotic power, he is bound by the Constitution and the laws; and so is the Legislature; and these laws and that Constitution have been framed by the people for the Commonwealth of Massachusetts. If there is anything wrong about either, it is the fault of the people of Massachusetts.

"Now, my friends, you say you want public works to be started, and you want the State to furnish you with employment. Let me suggest some of the difficulties which stand in the way. What is the State? The State is the tax-payer, the working men and women of Massachusetts. No public work can be undertaken in this Commonwealth unless, first, it is necessary; second, unless it is beneficial; third, unless there is enough money in the treasury to pay for it."

Here were sounds of dissent in the crowd, feeble shouts of disapproval being heard.

"Is not that reasonable and sensible?" continued the Governor.

Shouts of "Yes" and "No" arose, — the latter predominating.

"Consider the limitations of our position. In the history of Massachusetts her laws have been treated with full respect. No official of this Commonwealth can be intimidated. We want to treat our brothers and sisters in a true, fraternal spirit. Everything that can properly be done under the Constitution and laws, either by public or private means, to relieve distress should be done. If industry can legitimately be started, my best endeavors shall be given to that end."

While the Governor was speaking, he was joined by Adjutant-General Dalton and Mr. Thomas; and when he had finished, they returned together to the State House. Morrison Swift was raised to the shoulders of one of his followers, and from that position shouted out his orders to the crowd, telling them that all were to enter the State House, where a petition would be presented to the Legislature.

The crowd thereupon thronging into Doric Hall, Swift mounted to the balcony over the entrance to the Adjutant-General's office, from which position he could speak to the crowd below. He advised them all to go up into the corridors surrounding the hall of the House. "We are going," he said, "to present our petition to the House; and if the suggestions contained in the Governor's speech are not carried out, we'll clean out every man in the Legislature! We will clean out the State House if we don't get what we want." This incendiary utterance stirred the blood of every man (who was not one of Swift's followers) that heard it. Mr. Thomas, the

Governor's private secretary, who stood near Swift, hastened to the Executive Chamber, where the Governor was pacing back and forth alone. "They are threatening to clear out the State House, Governor," he said. Governor Greenhalge, without a word, stepped into the corridor, and, going directly to Swift, said very quietly, but with great determination: "You promised me that if I would receive you and address the gathering outside, you would use your influence to preserve the peace. Did you just now state that you would clean out the State House?"

Swift cowered. "I did," he answered; then half muttered, "But I stated that we would do it with the ballot."

This statement was entirely false.

"You wish to make that qualification?" asked the Governor.

"Yes," replied Swift.

"Very well," said the Governor, "I accept your explanation; but remember that all the civil and military forces of the State will be used, if necessary, to preserve the good order of the Commonwealth, and you, sir, will be held personally accountable for any incendiary act that may occur."

The Governor then returned to the Executive Chamber; while Swift, slipping out of sight, mingled with the crowd which, on the arrival of the police, soon melted away, down the broad steps, out into Beacon Street, gradually making its way back to the Common, where they were again harangued by Swift and others. A few days later Swift, through Mr. Rufus Wade, Chief of Police, asked if he, with his followers, would be allowed to come to the State House. To which the Governor replied that he would see Swift himself upon the matter. Mr. Swift accordingly came himself, with the request that he and his followers be allowed to march to and enter the State House in a body.

This permission the Governor refused to grant, saying that the unemployed could send a delegation like any other organization or organized body.

To Swift's inquiry if they would be permitted to have their gatherings on the Common, the Governor replied he had no control over that; personally, he had no objection to addresses on the Common provided they were not inflammatory or belligerent. He then explained to Swift the steps that had been taken in behalf of the unemployed, adding that if the people of the Commonwealth were satisfied the intentions of the movement were peaceful, matters would be facilitated and harmonized, otherwise not much progress would be made.

Swift thanked the Governor for his candid statements, and asserted that he desired and intended to keep within the law.

So ended the most dramatic episode of Greenhalge's political career, and one of the most exciting in the annals of the State since the war. Throughout the State the majesty of Massachusetts and of the law was thought to have been insulted, and a feeling of indignation was everywhere expressed. Massachusetts, proud of her traditions of order and of her fair fame, felt the insolence of these men deeply, and stood behind her Governor with immense enthusiasm. The Press echoed the sentiments of the people unanimously and gave voice to their feelings. Praise of the Governor's action was heard everywhere. His actions, his bearing, his words, on this exciting occasion commended themselves to all, and rose to the height of the event which called them forth.

They were right and noble; and how characteristic they were, rightly understood, of the man himself! What a sharp thrust was that when the Governor, replying to Swift, who had spoken of the want and poverty of his followers, asked him abruptly, " The condition of which you speak is yours ? " How sarcastic it was! He evidently was extremely doubtful about the sufferings of Swift. Such gentry often make considerable profit out of the suffering people, drawing frequently a salary for their disinterested services. How indignant too was his utterance later to the same Swift, after his incendiary speech to the mob in the State House rotunda! All who knew Greenhalge well knew him to be capable of anger at every form of insolence. The Governor's words and action were overwhelming to the cowardly leader, who seemed little to expect that he would be taken to task so vigorously for his bravado and effrontery. The insolence of Swift on this occasion was indeed beyond endurance. His threat to clean out the State House was enough to call down on him even more than the

sharp words and reproof of Governor Greenhalge; it was full
of unbounded arrogance, as was Casson's reference to the
Huns and Goths. How cringing also was Swift's palliating
effort to make his meaning out quite different from what it ob-
viously was! "By the ballot," — did he have this excuse ready
from the beginning, to evade the anger his expression roused
in the minds of the Governor and of the people? Such double
meanings suit with double dealings. The speech of the Governor to the crowd on the Common was just and reasonable.
He hardly at the time realized the nature of the assemblage;
it was not such as he had been accustomed to address. The
men who formed it were not of the type of Americans who
uphold the policies of the Republican party and frequent its
political meetings. It merited the term of rabble, and consisted of men of no political party. They were incapable
of appreciating the Governor's speech. Patriotism and respect
for the law were not terms that appealed to them. It is no
wonder that they greeted his speech with faint applause or
hisses.

It should have appealed to them with all the force of the
Governor's meaning. It was not likely to occur to them that
many of their claims were absurd, that the Governor had not
the power to relieve their distress. Swift was, so to speak, an
educated man; he had studied in Germany, — a quite distinctive fact; he was inoculated with German socialism. He had
also studied in an American college, — a fact not so distinctive;
socialistic tendencies are not developed, happily, in American
universities. Of small interest now are Swift and Casson,
and their beliefs and actions; they have passed into the limbo
of forgotten things, or have left only the memory of their
insolence and cringing in the face of the Governor's rebuke.
Swift was well aware of his insolence at the time probably,
— perhaps he hoped to escape its inevitable results, — but he
found that the Governor of the State of Massachusetts was
master of the situation. It was well it proved to be so.

Much as the American people admire eloquence and the gifts
and graces of political life, they, like all people, respect more
the display of firmness and resolution by their leaders and
rulers; and from this time they never doubted the possession

of these qualities by the man who held the position of their Chief Magistrate.

The evening of the riot Governor Greenhalge spoke at the annual dinner of the Underwriters' Association. All were eager to hear what he would say concerning the event which engrossed the thoughts of all; what he did say called forth the greatest applause. He was strongly moved, and spoke with suppressed feeling. The experiences of the day had tried him severely, — alas! there was something prophetic in what he said referring to the risks to which his life was exposed. The danger to which he referred was not the risk to be most feared, however; that was concealed in the darkness of the future and of fate. His speech was as follows : —

" I think I need all your good wishes in the present exigency, I doubt whether any life-insurance company at this day would consider me an ordinary risk. [Laughter and cries, ' Try it! '] That is the most encouraging answer that I have received. I am very glad to receive assurances from societies, organizations, which really mean business, carried on with an equal step, according to the life and the vicissitudes of life to which man is subject.

" Do you know, Mr. President, that your line of business runs closer to the career of mankind than any other which can be suggested? A man may insure a building, he may take his chances upon a speculation. You and your companies take your chances on your speculations upon human life, and that brings about the grandest inquiry and investigation that can be instituted by men. You say you are willing to take the chances on my life. It depends, after all, upon the scientific information and calculation of your actuary; it depends upon long study and calculation, and the result of experience. Anybody can calculate the chances of the life of a building. Has it anything of the delicate vicissitudes of a human being? I think not. You tell me you have been carrying on this business successfully. I think the proof of that statement is in the presence of these gentlemen here to-night. There appears to be at least no question about their success in business. They have done their work; they have made their computations nicely, accurately, and exactly.

" Yet, my friends, the finest point that occurs to me is that point of the president's remarks which referred to the part taken by Massachusetts in the work of life insurance, — first of all States to bring this whole subject into order, into beauty, into symmetry and law. Is not Massachusetts always the first of all States to bring everything into order and law and symmetry and beauty ?

" I come from strange and disorderly scenes, I stand here to ask the support of the men of orderly mind in Massachusetts.

" Massachusetts means business, not merely in life insurance; and I hope it means business in that line so far as I am concerned. It means equal rights and equal opportunity, the best advantages for any child of man that lives; and it makes my blood boil when I find men complaining that Massachusetts and her laws are unjust, unfriendly, and unequal. I say it is for conservative institutions like yours to say how much it costs to insure the lives of your citizens; and that is the whole business of commonwealths when we trace their action to the last analysis. I want, and so do you, to give equal rights, equal opportunity, fair play, and justice to every citizen, to every inhabitant of Massachusetts; and when I see disorderly people crowding through the streets, I say, Is not this a question which Massachusetts must answer?

" Yes, she has answered every question of that sort in times gone by, and she will always answer those questions and be true to her ideas, her principles of equal right and liberty and justice.

" Therefore, Mr. President and gentlemen, I say that we have no reason for discouragement. We simply want the loyal men of Massachusetts, the business men, the men who insure lives and property, to stand by the Commonwealth of Massachusetts, and we shall pass through all these dangers as the sunbeam passes through the mist.

" I respect the man on the right [referring to Major Merrill] because he has been in the right. What we want in your insurance companies, or in any insurance company that does business within the limits of the Commonwealth, is honesty, faith, solidity. Although this man [referring to Major Merrill] made his war against a company in which I myself held a policy, what could I say ? We want men of a calibre infrequent in these days, who will stand up against all corrupt influences or mean advantages of any sort.

" I am delighted, my friends, to be here for one brief moment. You may notice that I am not entirely devoid of appearances of fatigue. I admit that for once in my life I do feel inclined to sleep; yet whenever the exigencies of the Commonwealth call upon me, I think as long as there is any life left in me, I shall ask for insurance at your hands, and shall endeavor to be true to every interest of the Commonwealth of Massachusetts. "

The Governor, true to his word, a few days after the riot, sent to the Legislature the following message : —

GENTLEMEN, — I beg to transmit herewith a petition presented to me on the 20th inst., and I suggest that it be considered by you in connection with a memorial of a similar tenor which I am informed was presented to you on the same day. While many of the propositions contained in the communications transmitted may appear to be beyond the scope of your powers under existing laws, yet the Commonwealth never turns a deaf ear to the just complaint or claim of any of her citizens; and, moreover, an inquiry into the conditions and circumstances therein set forth may be productive of great benefit in serving to make clear such conditions and circumstances, as well as the duties and powers, under the law of State, city, and town, and, further, to stimulate private effort and private benevolence to suggest or furnish a remedy for the difficulties confronting our community. With this purpose in view, I transmit to you the accompanying petition.

Very respectfully,

FREDERIC T. GREENHALGE.

A petition similar to that given to the Governor had already been presented to the Legislature on the day of the riot by Representative Mellen, of Worcester, who disclaimed any sympathy with disorderly proceeding of any kind in relation to the labor movement or to the present petition. These petitions resulted in the appointment of a commission by the

Governor to consider the present condition of distress and the means that might be taken to relieve it.

This practically ended the movement begun with such scenes of disorder on the 20th of February. The business of the country was doomed to suffer from depression for further years of trial; but the idle and discontented classes ceased to proclaim their distress by the means taken during this year or violent proceedings of any kind. They seemed to give up their idea of forcing the State to take measures for their relief, and to await with more patience a revival in general business conditions.

Governor Greenhalge, soon after his election, determined to call a conference of the Governors of the New England States, to consider the business situation of the country. The party leaders, however, were averse to the idea, and the Governor finally relinquished it. Dec. 1, 1893, the "Boston Journal" made the following announcement of his intentions:—

"Governor Greenhalge has decided that as soon as possible after the assembling of the Fifty-third Congress, he will call together a Conference of the Republican Governors of New England, including Governor Cleaves of Maine, Governor Fuller of Vermont, Governor Smith of New Hampshire, Governor Brown of Rhode Island, and himself, to consider the present condition of the country, and determine what steps, if any, should be taken to conserve and advance the interests of the New England States.

"The conference originated with Governor Greenhalge, and is in keeping with the statements he made during the campaign, — that he would do all in his power to protect the business interests of the people."

The Governor explains his intention in an article in the "North American Review," which will be found in the Appendix at the close of this book.

The recommendation contained in Governor Greenhalge's first inaugural to abolish Fast Day and to make the nineteenth day of April a public holiday was carried into effect by the Legislature, and the first public celebration at Concord of Patriots' Day, as it was called by Governor Greenhalge, occurred

the nineteenth day of April in that year, 1894. The name of
Patriots' Day was merely suggested by Governor Greenhalge
as good and satisfactory, and was welcomed in many editorials
as being an admirable idea. Governor Greenhalge delivered
an oration in Concord at the celebration. Like all his
patriotic speeches, it was a stirring address.

The Governor had previously issued the following proclamation : —

"By an act of the Legislature duly approved, the 19th of
April has been made a legal holiday.

"This is a day rich with historical and significant events
which are precious in the eyes of patriots. It may well be
called Patriots' Day. On this day, in 1775, at Lexington and
Concord, was begun the great war of the Revolution; on this
day, in 1783, just eight years afterwards, the cessation of war
and the triumph of independence were formally proclaimed;
and on this day, in 1861, the first blood was shed in the war
for the Union.

"Thus the day is grand with the memories of the mighty
struggles which in one instance brought liberty and in the
other union to the country. It is fitting, therefore, that the
day should be celebrated as the anniversary of the birth of
liberty and union. Let this day be dedicated to solemn, religious, and patriotic services, which may adequately express
our deep sense of the trials and tribulations of the patriots of
the earlier and of the latter days, and also especially our
gratitude to Almighty God, who crowned the heroic struggles
of the founders and preservers of our country with victory and
peace. "

The following is the address of the Governor in Concord at
the first celebration of Patriots' Day : —

"MR. CHAIRMAN, LADIES AND GENTLEMEN, — I bring to you
the message of Lexington, full not only of fervor, but of fraternal love, of deepest sympathy. If there is one beautiful feature of this consecrated day, it is the exalted and magnanimous
spirit of your reverend fellow-townsman, who belongs not only
to Concord but to the State and to the country. It is in this
spirit of fraternal love that true patriotism expresses itself in

the noblest and highest way. What does it matter who has the honor and who does the work so long as it belongs to the nation, and has resulted in the benefaction of the whole civilized world? These sentiments will grow stronger, and warm and exalt the hearts of our children. I count it a privilege to be here to-day, and to hear the grand address just delivered. It is instructing and elevating to listen to this grand scholar. These exercises have an elevating and ennobling effect.

"What is it that gives this event its importance, its significance, its grandeur? An event is not so much that which has happened as something that causes something else to happen. The crucifixion darkened the face of heaven, but its results have illumined all mankind. The battle at the old North Bridge had little military significance, but it resulted in the foundation of this great republic. We come here as we may trace the windings of a noble river, from a mountain rill to a mighty stream, which bears upon its bosom the navies of the world. Here we find the beginnings of constitutional liberty.

"It is unnecessary to go over again the details of this story, — you know it by heart, the world knows it by heart. When that shot was fired, the standard of royalty went down forever upon this continent, and the first true republic of this earth arose before the astonished eyes of men. The consequences of that little skirmish were greater than those of the skirmish on Chalgrove Field, where John Hampden poured out his life. The memories of April 19 are greater than those of any other date on the calendar. They are not limited to any one war or any one year. They tell of liberty in '75 and union in '61. Boston, Worcester, and Lowell alike step in and claim their share in Patriots' Day.

"I would not limit it by calling it Massachusetts Day, because it is not limited to Massachusetts, but will be taken up by every State and Territory in the Union.

"It would be difficult to find any place in the world carrying a greater significance to men than ancient Concord. Here Liberty and Literature walked hand in hand. Law and Order dwell here. Poesy has put her finest wreath in the crown of patriotism in the hymn you have just sung. If the silent and inflexible figure of the Minute Man must always appear to stand guard at one end of the old North Bridge, surely the great spirit of Emerson stands sentinel at the other.

"Think of the line which may be drawn from the lantern tower of the old North Church to the old North Bridge! You can imagine a triumphant arch of freedom through which every bondman oppressed may pass to find liberty. What kind of a fabric has been reared by the people whose sires laid down their lives at Concord? What is this republic? Is it only a prison, imperfect, defective, out of repair? Is it a fact that the children of men do not find protection within it, that it is not a true home? The test of a good government is whether wrongs can be righted and improvements made. Does any one declare that the fabric of this republic does not fulfil that test? Tell me if any law is unjust and unequal, if there is any wrong to be redressed and improvement to be made, any flaw in the Constitution to be remedied. An examination of the history of the Constitution and statutes will show that from the beginning equality, justice, and liberty — the three inseparable qualities — have been written in every law and in every line of the Constitution.

"The uprising in 1775 was no wild rebellion, no lawless proceeding. It was well ordered by keen, law-abiding freemen. When, therefore, men not in sympathy with our institutions come demanding some violent and radical change, we must remember what the men of Concord were and what they represented.

"What is the duty of patriotism to-day? It is not, thank Heaven, to march with gun and sword. It is to defend the spirit of the law and the Constitution, to keep sacred the Commonwealth of Massachusetts in all its parts, in all its relations. You may not hear again the wild gallop of Paul Revere, but Wisdom hangs out her lantern from every church, every college, every school, and Conscience, like Paul Revere, drives on and on, through the night and through the day, to summon every sleeping force that patriotism can command against the midnight march of corrupt influences, against the attacks of disloyal traitors against the institutions and the Constitution which we love.

"This day was consecrated one hundred and nineteen years ago by the blood of those who sleep here. I am glad that industrial success has left Concord in her idyllic condition. It seems providential. Let Concord and Lexington be regarded as the Campo Santo of constitutional liberty to which the world may turn for instruction and inspiration.

"My friends, in behalf of the Commonwealth, I hail this day. I bid you Godspeed, and wish you many anniversaries, and I hope that every son and daughter will remain true to the principles for which their forefathers died."

One pleasant event of the Governor's first year of administration was a reception given by him to the working-people of Lowell. "I have been given so many banquets and receptions," he said, "I should like to give one myself to my own townspeople." The reception was given under the auspices of the People's Club, of which the Governor was president, and took place May 28. Mrs. Greenhalge, with members of the Staff, assisted the Governor in receiving his guests, of whom there were over two thousand men, women, and children; and for each one the Governor had a pleasant word.

Nothing in Governor Greenhalge's years of service as Chief Magistrate of the State brought him more praise and encouragement than the vetoes that he sent to the Legislature. They stamped him as a truly fearless and independent statesman. The people recognized that fact at once and upheld him in his action. Considered as the moves of a politician, some of them assuredly would not have been called clever in the inner circles of Tammany Hall. They were adverse to some of the strongest supports of the politician, — to some of those large corporate interests and aggregations of capital which sometimes supply the sinews of war to carry on the contests of political wire-pullers, and the power of which is often felt in the politics of the country. It requires unusual courage, an independence of character rare in any party, to stand fearless in opposition to such powerful adversaries.

Such moral courage as the Governor displayed in some of his vetoes is admired by the people, and they stood behind him with their support. They gave him their confidence; were it not so, the punishment feared by the politician might have overtaken him. The powers behind the throne, the strength of moneyed interests, and the prejudices of party might have brought disaster upon him politically.

But it was not so. His actions turned out to be good political moves, though they were the result of the unselfish determinations of a disinterested statesman. The good sense of the people can be trusted and calculated on in all political combinations. The mere wire-puller may not esteem it a factor of much account, but it is apt to make itself evident to his ultimate consciousness and the confusion of his ideas.

The vetoes of Governor Greenhalge form the keynote of his administration. They display his character before the people. He was that *rara avis,* — a perfectly fearless and honest politician. He never sought to advance his own selfish interests; he never feared to injure his political chances. His course was straight onward; he had a political conscience, and he listened to its voice.

After his veto of the Bell Telephone Bill many of his friends said, " I knew that the Governor would veto the bill. " In this case the unexpected did not happen. His friends knew beforehand how he would decide; yet it required unusual courage. The Bell Telephone Company is a powerful corporation, and the Legislature was strongly in favor of the bill. The veto of the Veterans' Preference Bill, which he sent to the Legislature in his second year, was another strong proof of his truly independent character. The soldier vote is an important factor in the political party he represented; his action might have offended a large section of that party. There were, however, many veterans of the war who thought as he did, and he received a great number of letters from patriotic old soldiers, in which the writers expressed their satisfaction at his course, and their esteem for him and the motives that influenced him. No man in the country had a higher admiration than he for the veterans of the most patriotic war in history. Many of the veterans knew this, and most of them, I believe, admired him for his independence. These two vetoes were the most important of those which he sent to the Legislature, and he gained

in popularity by them. The vetoes were convincing in themselves,— admirably composed, thoughtful, and logical. His
reasons are fully set forth, and the defects of the bill plainly
discovered.

On the 23d of April the Governor sent in his first veto.
The bill provides that " Trout artificially reared in private
ponds and streams in this Commonwealth may be used for food
during February and March under such restrictions as the Commissioners on Inland Fisheries and Game may prescribe, except
in the counties of Hampden, Hampshire, and Berkshire."
The veto was as follows : —

To the Honorable Senate and House of Representatives :

I return herewith without my approval Senate Bill No. 66,
entitled " An Act to permit, during February and March, the
sale for food of trout artificially reared in the Commonwealth,"
assigning for such action the following reasons :

1st. The words in the Act " artificially reared " are not pre-
cise and definite, and are liable to various interpretations ;
meaning, on the one hand, trout reared in hatcheries of elaborate construction, and, on the other hand, trout reared in a
greater or less degree on food artificially supplied in ponds and
streams, or in enclosures of rude construction.

2d. The difficulty of readily distinguishing artificially
reared trout from wild trout must make the administration
of the proposed law practically ineffective.

3d. The opening of the closed season in the manner proposed, even with restrictions prescribed by the Commissioners,
would in effect tend to bring in all kinds of trout, wild or artificially reared, and to annul or impair the policy of preserving
and protecting fish and game which has become the established
policy of the Commonwealth.

4th. The discrimination in regard to the counties of Berkshire, Hampden, and Hampshire does not appear to be based
on constitutional principles or on good and sufficient grounds.

The veto of the Trout Bill was followed, May 14, by
the following veto of a bill removing restrictions on shad
fishing : —

To the Honorable Senate and House of Representatives:

I return without approval Senate Bill No. 73, entitled " An Act to remove the restrictions upon shad and alewife fishing in the Merrimac River," for the following reasons: —

The removal of the restrictions as contemplated by this bill must tend to undermine the whole body of the law now in force in this Commonwealth looking to the preservation and protection of fish and game, and is likely to work injury which it would be difficult and perhaps impossible to remedy. Furthermore, the policy now established in the Commonwealth relative to the fisheries on the Merrimac River is interwoven in a measure with the policy of our sister State, New Hampshire, and of the New England States; and a change of legislation such as is contemplated by this bill should not be made if it tend to impair the mutual understanding hitherto existing.

Both of these vetoes were sustained by the Legislature.

On May 31 the Governor sent to the Legislature a message vetoing a bill relating to the sealing and attestation of deeds, giving as his objection to the bill, that " portions of it are, if *not harmless* in their provisions, unnecessary, in declaring a deed not under the seal of a corporation, but under the seal of one or more other parties, to be in effect the deed of such corporation. It aims to provide for the case of a corporation which has adopted no particular form of seal; but if a corporation affixes a seal to a bond or deed, that seal becomes the seal of the corporation, and the present law would appear to be sufficient. The transfer of real property should be governed by clear, simple, and well-defined rules, — a requisite which the proposed Act, in my judgment, fails in several respects to meet. "

This veto also was sustained by the Legislature. Of this veto the " Boston Herald " said : " Governor Greenhalge's latest veto is a merited rebuke to the legislators for the loose and ambiguous manner in which bills are drawn up and incorporated into our statute books. This bill appears to be a mass of ambiguities and contradictions, and the Governor does not hesitate to say so. The form and phraseology of our public statutes need more careful attention, and this veto ought to furnish the necessary inspiration to this end."

Upon the 26th of June the Governor sent to the clerk of the House — the Legislature not being in session that day — a veto of the American Bell Telephone bill. This bill authorized the company to increase its capital stock in the manner provided by law at such times and in such amount as it might from time to time determine, provided that the whole amount of the capital stock should not exceed fifty million dollars.

To the Honorable Senate and House of Representatives:

I return House Bill No. 620, entitled "An Act to authorize the American Bell Telephone Company to increase its capital stock," without approval, for the following reasons:—

While there may be no objection to any reasonable increase in the capital stock of the American Bell Telephone Company, it is material and important to inquire why, and under what terms and conditions, such increase as is now asked for should be allowed.

The general principle governing such cases is as follows: No increase of capital stock should be granted to any corporation, whether public, quasi-public, or private, unless good reason is shown for such increase, and unless the public interests are secured by suitable and ample guaranties.

The general policy of the Commonwealth is to impose proper and salutary restrictions upon any increase of capital stock in quasi-public corporations, guarding against stock-watering and against any measures tending to the public detriment. The proposed Act provides that the American Bell Telephone Company may increase its capital stock in manner provided by law.

The company was incorporated by the Statutes of 1880, Chapter 117, and by that Act was made subject to the provisions of Chapter 224 of the Acts of 1870; by Statutes of 1889, Chapter 385, it was authorized to increase its capital stock (which, by the original chapter, was limited to $10,000,000) up to $20,000,000, the increase to be made "in the manner provided by law." The Statutes of 1870, Chapter 224, by which the charter of the Telephone Company was expressed to be governed, were incorporated into the Public Statutes in Chapter 106. The material section of Chapter 206 is Section 37, which provides substantially that when any corporation, subject to this chapter, increases its capital stock, each stockholder may take his proportion of new shares by paying therefor the par value.

Unless, therefore, other legislation has provided differently, the bill for the present increase authorizes the corporation to issue its new stock to its present shareholders.

The Legislature has, however, enacted a law this year (Statute 1894, Chapter 472) providing that corporations named therein can only issue their new stock upon payment by the shareholders at the market value of the shares at the time of the increase, to be determined by the State Board under whose jurisdiction the several corporations enumerated are, including the following : " A corporation established for and engaged in the business of transmitting intelligence by electricity." Is the American Bell Telephone Company such a corporation?

The charter of the company (Statutes of 1880, Chapter 117, Section 1) incorporated it for the purpose of " using, and licensing others to use, electric speaking telephones and other apparatus and appliances pertaining to the transmission of intelligence by electricity; and for that purpose constructing and maintaining public and private lines."

The American Bell Telephone Company, therefore, is a corporation " established for " the business of transmitting intelligence by electricity.

I understand, however, that it is claimed that it is not engaged in that business for the reason that it only manufactures telephone apparatus to be sold or loaned to other companies; and it is quite possible that it may claim, as indeed I am informed that it is liable to claim, as not being engaged in the transmission of intelligence by electricity, that it is not within the provision of the Statute of 1894, Chapter 472.

It is an ambiguity which might easily be remedied by a proper section. As the legislation now stands, apparently it may increase its capital stock under the provision of the proposed bill by issuing its shares to its subscribers upon the ground that it is not now engaged in the business of transmitting intelligence, etc., and, having obtained its increase, proceed to engage in the business.

Unless I am mistaken, the law is drawn with this very possibility in view.

Nor does it appear that this large amount of increased capital is at present needed; but a more important question arises: Is this a quasi-public corporation?

Legally and potentially it is. Its charter, as I have before stated, gives the company the right of using and licensing others to use electric speaking telephones and other apparatus and appliances pertaining to the transmission of intelligence by electricity, and for that purpose in constructing and maintaining public and private lines. The company has, therefore, the legal power to maintain and operate telephone lines; and this mere fact that its business is done with the public in a less open and direct manner than by other companies ought not to exempt it from the ordinary and regular legal restriction and safeguards established by the present policy of the Commonwealth.

In the Legislature the motion to pass the bill over his veto was rejected by a vote of 49 yeas to 115 nays.

Requested about this time, by a Boston journal, to write for publication a letter giving his idea as to what an ideal vacation should be, Governor Greenhalge sent the following brief exposition of his views. The letter was published with others on the same subject written by various distinguished men.

"My ideal vacation is to be free from office-seekers, in a place where I am not obliged to give opinions on matters which are not before me, or to consider speculative ideas; an opportunity to take rational physical exercise, and to pursue the study of literature, political justice, and poetry, in the society of family and friends.

"I care nothing about hunting, fishing, or sports. These may be means to an end; but it must always be remembered that life is too short to indulge in sporting fads.

"A true rest is not idleness, but the opportunity to reflect, and to pursue the studies that a man loved in his youth, and still loves to follow when he can.

" A mere stopping of mental work is stagnation, and helps neither mind nor body; neither can a man, nor ought he, to get out of touch with the work of the world. "

One of the last Acts of the Legislature of 1894 was the passage of the Rapid Transit Bill, — or Meigs Bill, as it was commonly called, — a bill to incorporate the Boston Elevated Railway Company. This bill was strongly opposed in the House, but was finally sent to the Senate, where the opposition was continued with the understood assistance of the Governor, who allowed it to be known that without material changes and the insertion of the referendum clause the bill would not receive his signature. With many of the objectionable features changed, with the referendum included, and by the aid of the Subway Bill attachment, the bill passed the Senate, and on the 3d of July received the Governor's signature.

August 16 Governor Greenhalge delivered a lecture at the Old South Meeting House, Boston, the subject of which was John Winthrop, Governor of Massachusetts. The following report of the lecture is fragmentary, and inadequately represents his literary style : —

"MY FRIENDS, LADIES AND GENTLEMEN, — I approach the subject assigned to me with a good deal of diffidence and reverence. I wish that more ample histories or biographies had given an adequate conception of the remarkable man whose life and character I am to briefly sketch and comment upon.

" I know of no more dramatic period in English or American history than the time of John Winthrop. And yet I think, after the scholarly efforts of Fiske, of Robert C. Winthrop, the illustrious descendant of an illustrious ancestry, after the very striking and dramatic work of Mr. Twichell, we still must admit, as I think they themselves would admit, that this great period of history has not been treated, either in biography or in history or romance or dramatic art, as the mighty lives of its partakers truly deserve.

" I remember one impressive story written, I think, by a

descendant of the Connecticut branch of Winthrop, — that wonderful novel, 'Edwin Brothertoft,' by Theodore Winthrop, — one of the best historical stories, by the way, I remember to have read, and I commend it to the attention of these students and searchers after historical knowledge, with its gay and striking portraiture of Major André, of Howe and Clinton, and many of the leaders in the time of the Revolution.

"We all remember the striking and gloomy stories of Hawthorne, in which some of the early Governors appear. Yet the great, splendid, stern, strong, and merciful man whom we are to speak about briefly to-day, I find almost unsung though never to be forgotten. And therefore it is with a good deal of hesitation, a good deal of trepidation, that I approach a topic so momentous and with which this awakening spirit of love for true historical proportions will find an adequate and proportionate grandeur in the history of the world.

"In the annals of the English-speaking people everywhere, and also in the evolution of civil liberty among all nations, the year 1629 was a memorable and significant period. For many years a struggle between king and people, parliament and prerogative, had been going on in England. This struggle was imbittered and inflamed by the deeper antagonisms developing between the Church and the increasing body of independent and advanced thinkers, between ecclesiastical arrogance and Puritan dissent. The Puritan exodus had already in 1620 been heralded and foreshadowed by the daring band of godly pioneers who had reared the standard of the Lord and of liberty at Plymouth.

"And several other brave little garrisons of advanced religious and political thought were 'holding the fort' at various points in New England. In March of this eventful year, 1629, two great events occurred. Parliament was angrily dissolved by Charles I., and at the same time was signed a great charter which held the destiny of Massachusetts and the principles of civil liberty. And it came into the hand of John Winthrop, which never relinquished it. So that, as the fated house of Stuart hurried to its doom, as monarchical principles tottered to their fall, as the cloud of smoke of civil war settled down on the old country, a band of intelligent men, with full sense of responsibility and glowing with solemn and lofty purposes, crossed the sea, and with the inspiration of their efforts a new England, brighter and fairer than the old, arose in the Atlantic main to cheer the sons of freedom all over the world.

"Let us look at the dominant figure, standing stately, grave, and gracious, in the portals of New England, — John Winthrop. He was a remarkable man, specially equipped for a remarkable work. He was a Puritan such as Macaulay loved to paint, and a Puritan in action upon a field as great as that on which Cromwell spent his 'dearest action' — for Winthrop, too, 'had a kingdom for a stage, princes to act, and monarchs to behold the swelling scene,' — but the kingdom was a commonwealth, the princes were the captains of freedom, and the monarchs who beheld the scene were freemen everywhere.

"Winthrop's life and career were not entirely marked by felicity and success. He had many trials. He was a 'man of sorrows and acquainted with grief.' Sickness, death of wife, children, and friends, poverty in advancing age, all these he had to bear. He had sharp conflicts with Deputy-Governor Dudley, he differed frequently from Endicott, he had a controversy with Governor Bradford of Plymouth, he was pestered and annoyed by Bellingham, he was impeached by Peter Hobart of Hingham, he was opposed by Governor Vane and a majority of the Church in the Antinomian dissension, and several times he was superseded by men of mediocre ability for no reasons whatever except such as mediocre men always assign on such occasions to justify their own preferment. But his infinite, almost divine, patience supported him under all these trials. The great charter was safe, the Commonwealth was safe, the supreme law — namely, the safety of the state — had not been violated, and therefore all was well. He was the guardian, defender, and preserver of the Charter. He guarded, defended, and preserved it against all enemies, against assailants from within and from without, against Roger Williams, against Charles, and against Cromwell. The events of Governor Winthrop's life were some of them extraordinary. He was born in 1588, — a period marked by trouble and change, — the execution of Mary Stuart had just occurred, the invincible Armada of Spain was about to sail. Winthrop entered college before he was fourteen; he was married very early, at the age of seventeen years three months four days,— and this is one of the early marriages which turned out well. His eldest son was John Winthrop, Jr., the future Governor of Connecticut,— a man whose career illuminated the history of that noble Commonwealth with living light, just as Winthrop's own career illuminated the history of Massachusetts. He had many noble children besides. Winthrop, the father, was Lord of the Manor of Groton in the county of Suffolk; he became a lawyer, and had an excellent practice; he was the friend of Hampden, Cromwell, Sir John Eliot, and all the great freemen of that age which saw the monarchy of England become the Commonwealth of England.

"Winthrop was a model in all the domestic relations, as husband, father, neighbor, and friend. At the age of forty-one years he was made Governor of the Company of Massachusetts Bay, at a General Court held in London, Oct. 20, 1629, superseding Endicott at Salem upon his arrival after a voyage of eighty-four days. Endicott himself had just superseded Roger Conant. Winthrop's life in the New World exhibits the growth and establishment of a great State.

"As has been said, Winthrop's journal is one of the most remarkable compositions ever written or read, because it tells the real history of New England, just as Bradford's record gives the history of the earliest colony of Massachusetts. But Winthrop, with all his greatness, with all his success (and after all his trials and struggles, he was undoubtedly a man whom the world would crown with the laurels of success), was as human a man as ever stood upon the shores of Massachusetts. His journal, his letters, his every utterance, show how true and tender, how careful of everybody's feelings, he always was, and yet he accomplished the mightiest results of any one man in his day and generation, and perhaps through a long period. I say he was a very human man, a man whom you could know and sit down with and talk to, and in finding out the hidden springs of his action you could always find the principle of benevolence, of truth, of justice, the love of Christianity, and the fear of the Almighty. From birth and sta-

tion and training, he was naturally and inevitably inclined
to aristocracy; yet liberal, just, and full of humility, and always ready to acknowledge his transgressions, — to himself,
to the people, to his Maker. Beneath his placid, cold, and
dignified exterior, his wonderful journal and his letters tell
us what warm passions burned, what strange emotions disturbed. Full of tact and courteous consideration, he never
trimmed or compromised where principle was concerned. He
was eager to be forgiven, often when there was nothing to
forgive. He was more eager to forgive often when he might
well have condemned. In fact, he was charged by his stern
associates with a crime, — the crime of leniency. Notably in
the case of Roger Williams he was guilty, and practically
confessed his crime; but he did not amend his conduct in
this respect, and died with this sin of mercy and tenderness
upon his soul, — his greatest, if not his only, sin in public
office. He was conscious of his own faults, sometimes mor-
bidly so; and his journal is full of consideration for sins of
which there was no external evidence made known either to
private or to public judgment. In fact, the Governor was the
Governor's severest critic. And the stern Pilgrims of Plymouth
and of Massachusetts Bay loved him; and when reverses came
upon him, for he was not exempt from adversities, Endicott
protested his regard for Winthrop with symptoms of deep emotion. The towns, the Church, forced money upon him, and
even wild Tom Morton — the Wildrake of New England history, — who calls him 'King' Winthrop at one time and com-
plains that when he, Morton, wanted to speak in his own
defence, interrupting Winthrop, there was a deep roar of 'Hear
the Governor, hear the Governor!' — can find as the harshest
thing he can say of him only the name of 'Joshua Temperwell.'
He was as stout a soldier of the Cross as ever buckled on armor, yet he was pre-eminently a peacemaker. Upon the tomb
of his ancestors, in the Old World, are inscribed (now faintly
seen) the words 'Beati pacificati," — a new force and light from
Winthrop's life has brought out that half-effaced inscription.
With those stern, strong, resolute Puritans, he knew when to
recede and when to insist, when to be gentle and when to be
inflexible; he was a practical, reasonable man, with the light

of genius and the light of Christianity to guide and support him.

"He found in his old age that he had been stripped of most of his property, and about the same time a claim was made from the Deputies that he should present a strict account to the Colony, or to the magistrates, of his expenditures and receipts. There is something pathetic in his dignified statement that, so far from having made anything out of them, he had expended twelve hundred pounds from his own estate for public purposes which he had never asked to have repaid.

"And so these critical people discovered the kind of man he was, and when misfortune and sickness came upon him they hastened to make such amends as they could. Endicott sent messages of singular tenderness for that inflexible and icy nature.

"There was a great contest going on in this evolution of civil and constitutional liberty; and it is true that Winthrop sided, as I say, naturally and inevitably, with the magistracy, — with the constituted authorities, because they had been put in power by the people and by the voice of the people, and for a certain term, at least, they were almost as absolute as any emperor or king, — and this position of his had awakened a good deal of ire among these stern and independent souls who had never brooked the king, or a leader, or anybody who was better than themselves. In fact, they illustrated their idea very fully with philosophical statements, which were sometimes paradoxical, — like one of the sons of Hibernia, who said that one man was as good as another and a good deal better too; and they fully believed that this principle meant that each man had a full and equal right, and that when any question came between him and any constituted authority, he was as likely to be right as any authority. And so when this question came between the magistracy and what we may call the commonalty, they tried John Winthrop, and impeached him on the question of the appointment of the captain of a train-band in Hingham; and I think the Governor speaks of Hingham as the 'mutinous Hingham,' though they have long since got rid of any such title as that.

"After the inquisition was over, and Winthrop, who not as Governor but as Deputy had until then stood within the bar, the greatest among the assembly, yet giving the court its full right and power and authority, claiming nothing for himself by virtue of the previous office which he had held, — was acquitted and had resumed his seat upon the bench, the court being about to rise, he desired leave for a little speech. That 'little speech' is a lesson in constitutional history and in constitutional government, — it should be in all the reading-books. And then may I say that the Governor was a good deal more than a statue.

"He wrote the finest love letters that I have read in the English language. He had the grace of Sidney, with less of his stiffness and clumsiness. He wrote in terms full of poetic fire, full of eloquence, and every sentence marked by scholarly diction. He writes from the vessel, as he was waiting for favorable winds to cross an unknown sea, this farewell letter to his wife, Margaret, —

"'And now, my sweet soul, I must once again take my last farewell of thee in Old England. It goeth very near to my heart to leave thee; but I know to whom I have committed thee, even to Him, who loves thee much better than any husband can; who hath taken account of the hairs of thy head, and puts all thy tears in his bottle; who can, and (if it be for his glory) will, bring us together again with peace and comfort. Oh, how it refresheth my heart to think, that I shall yet again see thy sweet face in the land of the living ! — that lovely countenance that I have so much delighted in, and beheld with so great content! I have hitherto been so taken up with business, as I could seldom look back to my former happiness; but now when I shall be at some leisure, I shall not avoid the remembrance of thee, nor the grief for thy absence. Thou hast thy share with me, but I hope the course we have agreed upon will be some ease to us both. Mondays and Fridays, at five of the clock at night, we shall meet in spirit till we meet in person. Yet if all these hopes should fail, blessed be our God, that we are assured we shall meet one day, if not as husband and wife, yet in a better condition. Let that stay and comfort thine heart. Neither can the sea drown thy husband, nor enemies destroy, nor any adversity deprive thee of thy husband or children. Therefore I will only take thee now and my sweet children in mine arms, and kiss and embrace you all, and so leave you with God. Farewell, farewell. I bless you all in the name of the Lord Jesus.'

"And it seems to me that even the great souls who wrote or translated the Bible of King James — not even Milton himself — wrote any finer or more exquisite language, or gave vent to higher, more beautiful, or more touching thoughts, than we find here.

"And the whole collection of that devoted and illustrious man, Robert C. Winthrop, in his 'Life and Letters' of the Governor, furnish so much rich and beautiful, abiding and ample thought, that I would recommend the reading of those letters and of that journal by every true and earnest student of American history.

" It is a remarkable fact that both the early Governors of the early Colony were historians. Bradford was an historian of the highest merit, and of the most complete authority; and so in the case of Winthrop. He, too, was an historian and also an orator, — not merely a thinker and a statesman, but a man who knew how to put his case in the very best way, — and he was always confident, and had a right to be confident, that his case was a just one.

"Is it necessary to point out that in the case of both Bradford and Winthrop this was a Cæsarian quality? Julius Cæsar, the one man who could have accomplished the Gallic War, was the one man who could have written of the Gallic War as Cæsar did. And so we find the type of these men of action to be also the type of men of action and thought, and the historian is frequently the greatest actor in the things of which he writes.

"They gave Winthrop an island in the harbor, and it was called the Governor's Garden. It is now occupied by a frowning fortress. We may say to-day that all New England is the Governor's garden. . . . The sermon preached after his death spoke of that monument which should always remain to him, — *Novanglorum mœnia*, 'the walls of New England.' Yes; but the walls of New England in a changed, expanded form, — rising, enlarging, and embracing millions, where a little community lived before. And these walls of New England, however high they may rise, and whatever glory may be cast upon them by the rising and by the setting sun, will always be a monument to the self-sacrificing spirit, to the earnest Christian purpose, and to the inflexible resolution of that soldier of constitutional liberty, the great guardian and preserver of the charter, — John Winthrop, Governor of Massachusetts."

The appointments to office made by Governor Greenhalge during his three terms met in some instances with criticism, and it would have been strange if there had been no case in which they were not unanimously approved; but the character of the men singled out by him left little to criticise, and as a whole his appointments gave general satisfaction to the people of the State. It was a somewhat singular fact that his predecessor, Governor Russell, should have had many more vacancies to fill in the Judiciary than Governor Greenhalge.

On January 25 the Governor sent to the Council his first list of appointments.

The first in importance was that of Henry D. Sheldon to be Justice of the Superior Court, to succeed Judge Thompson. This appointment was a surprise, as Mr. Sheldon, though a profound student of law, had never taken any active part in politics. He was a classmate of Governor Greenhalge, who, besides the strong personal affection which he bore him, had the highest appreciation of his judicial ability. Indeed, when the opportunity came to him to make this appointment to the bench, his first thought was, "Sheldon is the man;" from this opinion he never wavered.

On April 26 the Governor appointed as Police Commissioner, in place of Mr. Lee, whose term had expired, Gen. A. P. Martin, and also designated him as Chairman of the Commission, which caused much surprise and comment.

He also nominated, as members of the new Commission of the Unemployed, M. D. K. Dewey, of Boston, an instructor at the Institute of Technology; D. F. Moreland, of Woburn, and J. F. Carey, of Haverhill. The appointment of the latter, who was a socialist, met with much disapproval; and the Council refused to confirm it. The Governor afterward appointed in his place

Mr. Perham, of Lowell. Governor Greenhalge never felt, however, that his first appointment was a mistake. With a board of which one member was a scholar and trained statistician, and two representative (one conservative and the other radical) of the labor elements, he thought that some thoughtful and practical solution of the problem might be reached.

On that same day he appointed to the new position of Associate Justice of the Municipal Court of Boston, Mr. J. B. Lord, of Boston. This nomination he afterwards withdrew on the Advisory Committee reporting against its confirmation; later he nominated to the position John F. Brown, Clerk of the Municipal Court of Boston.

At the next meeting of the Council the Governor sent in the names of Colonel Borden, Mr. Stanton, and Dr. Aldrich as members of the Police Commission of Fall River. The latter name he afterwards withdrew, and appointed Mr. Joseph Healey.

August 16 the Governor nominated, as members of the Metropolitan District Commission on Greater Boston, Mr. B. Rice, of Quincy, Osborn Howes, of Brookline, and Charles P. Curtis, Jr., of Boston, all of which nominations were confirmed.

September 13 he sent in the name of George Field Lawton, of Lowell, to be Associate Justice of the Probate Court, which nomination was confirmed.

The State Republican Convention of 1894 was held in Music Hall Saturday, October 6. It was the shortest Republican convention ever held in Massachusetts; and the platform, of which Senator Hoar was the author, was the briefest in the history of the party. The entire ticket of the year before was renominated.

Gen. William Cogswell had been elected chairman of the convention, but was too ill to be present; and Hon. Samuel E. Winslow was elected in his place, Mr. Curtis Guild, Jr., reading the address which the General had prepared.

The name of Governor Greenhalge was presented for nomination by Senator Lodge, who, in his eloquent speech, said: "It has always been the custom of the Republicans of Massachusetts to recognize and reward the faithful services of those whom they have placed in the high offices of State and nation.

. . . In accordance, then, with the good traditions of New England, of Massachusetts, and of Massachusetts Republicans, I have risen to ask you to show your appreciation of high character and distinguished service by nominating the second time the present Governor of the State. He led you to a brilliant victory last year. He has given you the best fruits of victory in an honorable and successful administration of his office. . . . He has met all his responsibilities face to face. All bills sent to him have met either his approval or his veto. He has shown himself cool, brave, and effective in the moment of sudden emergency, diligent and painstaking in the performance of daily duty, always and everywhere the fit representative of the honor, the intelligence, the free spirit, and the ordered liberty of Massachusetts. His eloquent speech, his scholarship, and his ability have reflected honor upon his State, upon his party, and upon himself. We can all be proud of him, and we know that he has deserved well of the republic. . . . Therefore I ask you to renominate Governor Greenhalge. I ask you to do it with the enthusiasm and the determination which this year of all years demands. 'Do it with a spirit that shall start the earth along.' Nominate him as you were wont to nominate Andrew in the days of storm and strife. The time is again ripe for such action and such spirit. Then an armed South struck at the nation's life. Now an unarmed South strikes at the nation's prosperity. Massachusetts did not falter then; she will not fail us now. I move you, sir, that Frederic T. Greenhalge, of Lowell, be declared by acclamation the nominee of this convention for the office of Governor of the Commonwealth."

The name of the Governor was greeted with great enthusiasm, and the motion to nominate him by acclamation was carried with a tremendous burst of cheers. There was not a single dissenting voice.

The name of the Lieutenant-Governor, Wolcott, was offered for nomination by Hon. Frederic H. Gillette, of Springfield; he also was renominated by acclamation, as were all the other nominees.

In his address of acceptance, which was received with much enthusiasm, the Governor spoke as follows : —

" MR. PRESIDENT, AND GENTLEMEN OF THE CONVENTION, —
I thank you, Republicans of Massachusetts, for the expression
of continued confidence conveyed in this renomination. The
year has not been altogether free from trials and perplexities.
I thank the Legislature, the State officials, and the Executive
Council, never more serviceable and helpful than now, for most
efficient co-operation in enabling me to meet these trials and
perplexities with whatever measure of success may have been
attained.

" Nor can I refuse to pay my tribute to our delegation in the
Fifty-third Congress who have served the State so well, — with
such fidelity, courage, and wisdom. I rejoice in the presence
of our honored Senators and Representatives, and I join with
all my heart in sending a message of good cheer to Gen.
William Cogswell, of Salem, — ' Good at need !'

" Gentlemen, I believe that the best service to the party can
only be rendered by the best service to the Commonwealth.
Good administration is good Republican doctrine and good
Republican work. It is true that affairs of state are not the
only matters coming before the people for judgment at this
time. The affairs of that larger Commonwealth, the whole
country, must claim our earnest consideration now. We are
soon to meet our ancient enemy. In what guise does he
come ? He comes in worse guise than ever before since he
came as the ally of rebellion and treason. He comes branded
with the misgovernment of eighteen months, arrayed in the
shreds and patches of ruined industries, and heralded by the
execrations of an indignant people.

" The work of the Democratic party cannot be satisfactory
to the country; it is not satisfactory to the Democratic party.
That work is based upon no principle; it does not even represent Democratic principles. And we have the unparalleled
spectacle of a great party leader — a Democratic President —
sounding the knell of his own party, and with blistering words
stigmatizing the *magnum opus* of a Democratic Congress as
the consummation of 'party perfidy and party dishonor.'

" We are treated to the strange spectacle of a President
without a party, and a party without a principle. Our opponents promised to reduce the burden of taxation. They fulfilled

their promise by placing a burden of $45,000,000 on sugar, and by imposing an income tax, the nice features of which I leave to the 'inner consciousness' of our Democratic friends. They promised to stimulate our foreign commerce, and they destroy reciprocity, which had already carried the flag of our commerce to new realms, brought profit to American industry and glory to the country. Every dollar from the Republican system of revenue brought life to our enterprise ; every dollar from the Democratic system is a deadly blow to our industries. They have lifted the burden from the foreign manufacturer and placed it on the domestic manufacturer. They have cringed and fawned before the throne of a barbaric and dissolute sovereign, and turned their backs upon liberty standing at the gate.

"They who claim to be Democratic leaders have 'crooked the pregnant hinges of the knee' to monopolies, and have vied with each other in servility to trusts. Tariff reform ? What crimes are committed in thy name ! How different the record of the Republican party ! How its principles shine and glow in the letters of living light coming from the heart and brain of our honored Senator ! You have placed the great standard of the party in my hands. I accept it reverently. Let the word ring along the Republican lines : Forward to the rescue of the country and its best and dearest interests ! Victory awaits you, I firmly believe. And when I return this standard to you, may every one of the principles blazing upon its folds shine out untarnished, clear, and bright as in the golden days of Lincoln and Andrew."

The fall campaign of 1894 was spirited and full of enthusiasm on the part of the Republicans. The series of addresses made by Governor Greenhalge equalled the remarkable efforts of his first campaign. The feeling of revolt against the Democratic régime had increased during the year, and a larger Republican vote was confidently expected. The result was even more agreeable to the Republicans than they had hoped for, and afforded a grand proof that the people were greatly roused, and desired to ratify the principles and policies of the Republican party by a tremendous vote.

Twelve Republican Congressmen, out of a total of thirteen,

were elected, and the city of Boston was almost lost to the Democracy. The vote for Governor was: Russell, 123,769; Greenhalge, 187,435, Governor Greenhalge's plurality being 63,666. The vote revealed the fact that the Governor had lost no prestige during his year of office, and that the people of the State were more than satisfied with his administration, — that they were enthusiastic, indeed, and resolute in their determination to support him.

Hon. John E. Russell was for the second time the Democratic candidate for Governor. After the election Governor Greenhalge said in an interview: —

" I am perfectly satisfied with the result. The apparent majority, in spite of unfavorable weather and the danger of extravagant confidence, is something surprising, and indicates the profound feeling of Massachusetts on the great issue of the hour. . . .

" The results in the congressional districts are, of course, of chief importance, the State ticket being a secondary issue, because it is, as it were, not a disputed issue. If I could give of my plurality to help out in the congressional districts in this State or elsewhere, I would cheerfully do it. . . .

" New York is the great pivotal centre. Give the Republican party possession there, and I believe that the cause of good government, of law and order, will be promoted. . . .

" If any discrimination for any reason has been made against my honored friend and associate, the Lieutenant-Governor, it is a grave mistake, which will profit no good cause. He ought to have received every vote which was given to me. A truer servant of the people in the Executive Council or anywhere else I have never found. Petty jealousy or inordinate desire for political preferment never entered his mind. Through all the trials of a very difficult year I found but one line of action on his part, and that was patriotic, intelligent business service to the Commonwealth. I have made him chairman of every important committee in the Executive Council, and his work has been performed as accurately and as efficiently as could be done by any man. He is a true son of Massachusetts, with a great record of his ancestry before himself which I, even as a stranger, am bound to revere. . . .

" Of course my own congressional district, the Fifth, has been a matter of great concern to me.   Next to that, I have considered the pivotal State of New York.   The defeat of Hill means vastly more than a mere political controversy.   It is a matter of morals and decency in free government; and if the methods of Hill and Tammany were strengthened and continued, there might be danger to constitutional liberty.   But the genius of the American people in finding out the trouble will always be able to save the country. . . .

" I believe that the result of the election in New York means a great contribution to the salvation of free government upon the earth.   The victory all over this State and country brands the Democratic party and policy as unworthy the confidence of the American people. "

As the appointed time came round during his first year of office, Governor Greenhalge, following the established custom of his predecessors, issued his Thanksgiving Proclamation. The spirit of the writer was reverent, and the tone and expression of the proclamation are such as were natural to him at a time of considerable business depression and hardship to the people of Massachusetts.   It is equal to the best of those issued in the past history of the State.

THANKSGIVING PROCLAMATION, 1894.

Commonwealth of Massachusetts,

BY

FREDERIC T. GREENHALGE, *Governor.*

In all the trials and reverses of the past year, the hand of the Lord has uplifted us, and the light of his countenance has always cheered our souls.   Well may the Commonwealth say, ' Praise the Lord, O my soul, and forget not all his benefits, ' and well may the voice of thanksgiving rise from all her altars.

Therefore, by and with the advice and consent of the Council, I appoint Thursday, the 27th day of November current, as a day of solemn thanksgiving to Almighty God, our Heavenly Father.   On that day let the whole Commonwealth become the holy temple of the living God, wherein shall be heard the prayers, praise, and thanksgiving of the people.   And on that day, also, let the noble traditions of the Commonwealth glow with new life and light, let the wandering children gather again in the old homestead, and the comfort and peace of every family shall be for a sign that the Lord has watched over and preserved us.

At the celebration of Forefathers' Day in the City of Brooklyn, New York, Dec. 21, 1894, Governor Greenhalge was present. The speech that he delivered there was short. He said : —

" It is quite appropriate that a celebration of Forefathers' Day should be held here in Brooklyn, the city of churches, and a city strongly marked by New England ideas. New York is cosmopolitan and commercial, and must for a time remain so. New York is not yet New Englandized, if I may have the permission of the ' New York Sun ' to use that word, though a strong gust of Puritan freshness and coolness has just blown through the island from one end to the other, from the Park to the Bowery. And it is well, therefore, to come together in Brooklyn and on Forefathers' Day, 1894, two and three quarter centuries nearly since the Pilgrim Republic was founded, and take an account of the descendants of the Forefathers, and of their works in the land of their fathers. And the question is, Does the line bid fair to perpetuate itself and to continue like a parabola into limitless space ? It is to be noted at the outset that the Forefathers and their children were not mere money-getters, not wholly devoted to commerce and wealth, that their chief products were ideas, their richest wealth was the wealth of the mind and the soul, and their noblest work — their *magnum opus* — was the establishment of great systems and lofty principles inspired by a sublime religious faith and an absolute trust in Almighty God. Not a day passed that they did not eagerly seek the ' light of his countenance,' not a line of their laws was written which was not based upon his Holy Word.

" Mr. Benjamin Kidd, in his great work on ' Social Evolution,' recently published, demonstrates that the chief factor in social evolution among nations is religious belief; that there never has been a rational sanction for the condition of national progress, but that nations march on from strength to strength,

build cities, overcome enemies, establish empires, under conditions and influences which are not accepted by mere human
reason, but which depend upon a super-rational sanction.

"The Sphinx of Egypt lies buried in the sands of centuries;
it is silent; no gospel falls from its stony lips to guide and
bless mankind. Plymouth Rock, too, may be covered by the
tides of ocean or hidden beneath the sands, but the Rock is
not silent. Its message has gone forth; from that Rock,
smitten by the rod of the Forefathers, have poured forth, and
will forever flow, streams of living water to develop and
fertilize the soil and soul of humanity over not one nation
alone, but over all the nations of the earth.

"We come not so much to stand by the graves of the Pilgrim Fathers; we come to glory in the great nation of which
they were the founders; we come to learn again in this practical nineteenth century from the wisdom of Bradford, to hear
again the prayer of Brewster, to see again the lost sword of
Standish flashing from its sheath.

"The character of the New Englander is as massive, as
strong, as unyielding, as lofty to-day as it was in the time of
Bradford and Winthrop. In some respects the New Englander
is quite as English as the English themselves, if not more so;
he has changed less. In other respects he is *sui generis.* He
is passionately attached to law and order, to justice, to liberty
and equality. He is tenacious of his opinion, conservative,
and yet liberal and tolerant to others. He readily adapts
himself to new places and new associates; but the adaptation
is only skin deep. He retains his ideas, his tastes, his peculiarities. How many of the gentlemen here have risen discontented from a banquet like this, from a feast of Lucullus, to
explore the two cities for a boiled dinner? How many are
there here who have felt keenly one defect of an otherwise perfect wife, namely, that, not being a New England woman, she
could not quite give that last touch of grace to that brightest
glory of the morning, — buckwheat cakes? And it must be a
very dull, narrow mind which fails to perceive the intimate
and indissoluble connection between baked beans and fish-balls
upon the one hand and the maintenance of civil and religious
liberty upon the other. He may change his sky, but never

his heart. If he cannot remain in New England, he makes a New England wherever he goes. His institutions, his purposes, his way of life, such as he knew on the hill-farm, in the country-store, and the school-house, he is sure are the best in the world; and he insists upon them, whether in the metropolis of New York, in Atlanta in the South, or in a brand-new city of Colorado. The home, the family, education, religion, — these are his Lares and Penates, the foundation of all good government and all true happiness.

"Plato's 'Republic' was a dream, Sir Thomas More's 'Utopia,' the fancy of a freeman and a scholar writing in the shadow of the scaffold, Bacon's 'Atlantis' never rose from the Atlantic main; but the Forefathers were not merely saints and heroes, they were eminently practical men; and when they built their ten rude houses with oil-paper windows, they laid the foundations of the first true republic of the world. Its majestic pillars rise now from the gulf and lake; they beat back the Atlantic surge on the one hand and glitter with the spray of the Pacific on the other; the vast interior gives forth, not the 'still, sad music of humanity,' but the cheerful chorus of a great people full of heart and hope, and confident that the future holds for them and for their children the highest glories of development and achievement in estate, body, mind, and soul yet vouchsafed to the sons of men.

"Will the power of New England be continued and extended? There was a time when the development of manufacture brought a flood of foreign immigration to her shores, and at the same time the New England family began to shrink in numbers, and the extinction of the great race was foreboded. But the thin line never gave way. It was once said, 'The guard dies, but never surrenders;' the vanguard of the human race never dies and never surrenders."

The first administration of Governor Greenhalge closed with the year. It had encountered few criticisms even by the opposite party. For him it had been a year of incessant activity and labor, well repaid by the confidence and esteem of the people. At its close his reputation stood very high with all classes. He enjoyed their regard, and it was the only recompense he desired.

The following list of his engagements for the year shows unmistakably the immense amount of labor he had undergone. It stands, I should say, unrivalled in this respect. On nearly all these occasions he was expected to speak, and did.

Anniversaries	5
Balls	25
Banquets	111
Board of Trade Meetings	11
Military Camps	5
Commencements	8
Convention and Campaign Speeches	20
Dedication Addresses	5
Exercises — School and Society	22
Fairs, etc.	29
G. A. R. Meetings	20
Lectures	17
Official Meetings, etc.	69
Receptions	12
Reviews	7
Weddings	3
Women's Clubs, etc.	10
Total	379

All these burdens were additional to the responsibilities and duties that properly belong to the executive office.

It is a matter of regret that he should have been compelled to answer so many unnecessary calls, so many demands upon his strength.   Occasions insignificant in themselves became serious in their results, taxing as they did so severely his vital forces in the fulfilment of their demands.   He felt it to be his duty to answer them all, and he did so far as he could.   It was not because he enjoyed public appearances and displays.

CHAPTER IX.

THE inauguration of Governor Greenhalge for his second term occurred Jan. 3, 1895. His first year of office had been very successful, and the second was to prove not less so. The Governor looked forward to it with confidence, unmindful of its fatigues and hazards. The calls upon his time and energy were not lessened, but continued to impose a great burden upon his strength. His second inaugural address, delivered Jan. 3, 1895, was pronounced by the papers of the day " a clear, reasonable, common-sense statement of the public business of the Commonwealth," " a strong, direct plea for comprehensive legislation," " characterized by good judgment and good taste." We give the conclusion of the document: —

"Charity, gracious but inexorable, demands from you the magnanimous response which Massachusetts has never failed to give. Education lays its imperial tax upon the treasury with an autocratic power readily acknowledged and obeyed by the intelligence and conscience of the people. Justice insists that her temples shall be kept pure; that the ermine of our judiciary shall continue to be spotless; that the profession of the law shall be the practice of exalted principles developed by the wisdom of ages; and that juries shall be 'good and true men,' fit to decide honestly and wisely the rights of intelligent freemen.

"Comprehensive legislation, not multiplicity of legislation, is to be sought; the principle *multum non multa* may well be followed in your law-making labors. Special legislation is to be discouraged on all accounts.

"You meet for the first time in this noble and classic hall; and may the great memories and associations which cluster

around the venerable building which you have left be only the
forerunners of the patriotic labors and achievements to be done
and performed here by you and your successors, and which
shall consecrate and endear this grand structure to the hearts
of the people to the latest generation !

"May the true voice of the people always be heard in these
halls ; may the people inspire their representatives, and may
their representatives in turn inspire the people ; may this building, as long as one stone rests upon another, be the temple of
constitutional liberty ; here let the tongue of the demagogue
cleave to the roof of his mouth ; let the right hand of the
anarchist forget its cunning ; let these walls echo only with
the loftiest hopes and the grandest purposes of freemen ; may
here forever be found the clear and incorruptible source of
the wise, just, and equal legislation of an intelligent, liberal-
minded, high-souled people, ever true to the purpose of the
Father, directing all their efforts 'to the end that this may be
a government of laws and not of men' ! "

The most important appointments of Governor Greenhalge's
second year of office were those of Mr. F. A. Gaskill as a
Justice of the Superior Court ; Mr. Charles P. Curtis as a
member of the Police Commission, to succeed Mr. Albert S.
Whiting, whose term had expired ; and to succeed Mr. Curtis
on the Commission of Greater Boston, Mr. William Power
Wilson.   As members of the Water Supply Commission, he
appointed Messrs. H. H. Sprague, of Boston, Wilmot Evans, of
Everett, and Hon. J. J. Whipple, of Brockton.   Mr. Augustus
Hemmenway was appointed to the Metropolitan Park Commis-
sion, in place of Mr. Charles Francis Adams, who had resigned.

All of these appointments were confirmed by the Council,
except that of Hon. J. J. Whipple ; and in his stead the Governor appointed Mr. J. J. Freeman, of Winchester.

January 25 Governor Greenhalge, after much consideration
of the question, finally refused to pardon Sanborn and Bailey,
the Old Colony officials, at that time confined in Plymouth
jail under sentence of the courts.   The circumstances of this
case were such as to give a new proof of the Governor's
courage in his final action upon the question, and his decision

brought him high commendation from many quarters. The sentence of these men was due to the following cause: August 16, 1893, the Abington Street Railway Company attempted to lay their tracks across those of the New York, New Haven, and Hartford Railroad at a street-crossing in Abington. Their right to do so was disputed by the Railroad Company, and some of the officials of the latter — Sanborn and Bailey and others — were present with a large force of men.

It was afterward claimed by the railroad people that their only intention was to use constructive force, and to make a test case for the courts. However, a large crowd of people had assembled; and the result was a disturbance that ended in a riot, and acts were committed that were clearly against the laws of the State. The railroad officials upon whom the responsibility of the riot rested were gentlemen held in high esteem in the community. Captain Sanborn, who had served bravely in the War of the Rebellion, was a friend of the Governor, and much respected by him.

Mr. Robert O. Harris, the district attorney in charge of the case, who highly appreciated the courage Governor Greenhalge displayed in the matter, writes as follows of the course the case took in the courts, and the pardon subsequently granted by the Council, which lacked only the Governor's assent to take effect: —

" On Aug. 16, 1893, the riot took place at North Abington. At the next term of the Superior Court at Plymouth, in October, five of the railroad men were indicted for riot.

" By order of the court, the cases were continued for trial until the next term, in February, 1894. In February they were again continued until the June term, and at that term the defendants pleaded *nolo contendere*, and the cases were continued for sentence to the October term.

" At the October term, on the sixth day of November, the defendants were called for sentence; and Judge Sherman imposed sentences of four months in the House of Correction on two of the five, and two months for each of the other three. The sentences were a surprise, as it was hoped that the court would impose fines only, as the railroad had made good all damages caused during the riot. Judge Sherman, however, thought that fine would not be adequate punishment, and gave the sentences of imprisonment. On the eighth day of November, two days after sentence was imposed, petitions were filed for pardon, and hearings were given by the Committee on Pardons, and pardon was denied.

" In January, 1895, the two months' sentences ran out, and a new petition for pardon of the other two was filed, and a strong effort was made before the committee. In January the Council voted, by a vote of six to three, to recommend the granting of the pardon, thus leaving the matter entirely to the Governor. A very great effort was made to induce him to concur in the recommendation of the Council and grant the pardon, and he was besieged by petitions, letters, and the personal requests of many of his best friends and supporters, to sign it.

" Notwithstanding the pressure brought to bear upon him, he recognized the dangers of such a course, and on January 25 finally refused to concur with the Council, and refused the pardon. This incident in his career is useful as demonstrating his full appreciation of the dignity of his office, his duties to the people, and his splendid courage in acting always in accordance with what he believed to be right, even though personal friendship and self-interest might offer more attractive and easy paths to travel in. "

Mr. Harris concludes by saying " The Governor's refusal to grant a pardon after the Council had by so decided a vote recommended him to do so, showed the man in his full power and vigor. "

Among many favorable and complimentary editorials in other papers, the " Boston Transcript " said : " The refusal of Governor Greenhalge to pardon the Old Colony officials goes far to enforce one wholesome lesson. The act committed by these men was clearly and unmistakably in violation of the laws of the land. It is admitted that they had no personal criminal intent. They knew that what they did was a violation of law, but they considered the employing corporation as responsible. The lesson above spoken of is that this cannot be ; that the order of a corporation does not protect a man in the commission of crime any more than the order of any idle loafer in the street. "

Refusing to sign the pardon of Messrs. Sanborn and Bailey, the Governor said to the Council : —

" I consider the case of Sanborn and Bailey, petitioners for pardon, as one of the most important matters yet submitted to the Governor and Council. The language of the Constitution as to the pardoning power is as follows : ' The power of pardoning offences, except such as persons may be convicted of before the Senate by impeachment of the House, shall be in the Governor, by and with the advice of the Council. '

" The meaning of this provision seems clear, though the language is peculiar. Under this provision a committee on pardons is appointed by the Governor, and after a preliminary examination by him of an application for pardon, to see if there is any reasonable ground for an inquiry, the application is referred to the Committee on Pardons of the Council. The investigation, examination of testimony, the hearing of arguments, are conducted by this committee alone, and it is clear that their conclusions are entitled to great respect and consideration. The application now before us took the usual course. It was referred to the Committee on Pardons, and a long, careful, and patient hearing was given to the case. The committee by a vote of three to two recommended that a pardon be not granted. This recommendation was reversed by a full Council; and by a vote of six to three, it was recommended that pardon be granted.

" A grave responsibility is thus imposed upon the Governor. He must reject the conclusions of the Committee on Pardons, which has been specially deputed by himself to investigate the matter; or he must reject the advice of the majority of the Council. It is incumbent upon him, therefore, to consider carefully the facts and the law of the case, as well as his relations to the Council and his duty to the Commonwealth.

" The persons interested in this application are of no ordinary character. They are all, including those who have just served out their sentence for the same offence, men of high standing in the community, and up to the time of this unfortunate occurrence of unblemished reputation; and the excellent personal qualities of one or more of them have enlisted the warm sympathy of many, and make it very difficult for the executive to refuse them clemency. . . .

"It has been claimed that the sentence of the court was severe, erratic, and sensational; that an agreement between counsel and the district attorney, by which the petitioners were induced to plead *nolo contendere* upon condition that they should be required only to pay a fine without imprisonment, was ignored by the court.

"Another claim is that the petitioners were deprived of a trial through a misunderstanding between their counsel and the district attorney, or by the disregard of this agreement by a judge anxious for the notoriety which comes from *ad captandum* sentences. But frequently opportunity for trial had been offered to the petitioners. Many prisoners may well claim that their cause has suffered by reason of unwise counsel, and to admit such a claim might result in a general jail delivery.

"These petitioners had the opportunity of a trial by jury. If they by themselves or counsel declined that opportunity, they must accept the result. There was no mis-trial, mis-carriage, or failure of justice; there was no such error to be corrected as would be implied to exist by granting a pardon. In fact, the arguments advanced for the pardon of Sanborn and Bailey will apply with even greater force to many unfortunates now confined in the penal institutions in the Commonwealth. Messrs. Sanborn and Bailey represent another and a very different type, but the same and even a greater degree of responsibility must apply to them; and no consideration for clemency or favor should be expected which would not apply, if possible, with greater force to the humblest citizen in the Commonwealth. . . .

"It is argued also that the offence of these petitioners has been fully vindicated, and that furthermore the quality of the offence had been exaggerated, and that all that was contemplated by the railroad was a formal act to make a case for the courts.

"This last plea seems to be one of the chief grounds of defence; but to effect such a purpose as that mentioned, a small party of men would have been sufficient.

" It has been said that it was important for the railroad to prevent the crossing of its tracks, because if the street railway succeeded in its purpose, the rights of the Old Colony would be lost or impaired. I know of no such principle of law as is here intimated. The crossing, or attempt to cross, the steam railroad by the street railway would of itself have presented just such an issue as would have enabled the parties to resort to the courts. But starting for Abington with a considerable number of men, perhaps sixty, and finding a crowd of persons assembled at the crossing at Abington, the Old Colony Railroad officials finally secured a force of more than one hundred and thirty men.

" The street railway had obtained a permit from the selectmen of Abington to cross the Old Colony track at this point. It was, therefore, acting under color of law, and the steam railway was not.

" While the crowd at Abington may not have legally assembled, that fact could not justify the Old Colony Railroad in any proceedings calculated to provoke a breach of peace even in the honest desire to maintain its legal rights. . . .

" The law does not favor the assertion of even an undoubted right by means of violence or the show of violence; even a landlord, in attempting to evict a tenant or to obtain possession of his own real estate, commits a breach of the peace at his peril, and it is safer for him to resort to his complaint for possession, for his writ of entry, to maintain his rights.

" The very assembling of such a force as these petitioners had, and conveying it into the town of Abington, as was done, was a menace to the peace of the Commonwealth; and its very appearance was likely to bring about a collision, as actually happened, and result in a most serious affray and riot. While these petitioners, then, might have had no design to use force, or to make an attack upon any person, their demonstration, their appearance, could not but create disorder, apprehension, and indignation. The massing of a large number of men or women to assert a legal claim by a show of force is very much like a naval ' demonstration ' which comes very near to being an act of war; and such an assembly in a peaceful Commonwealth is fraught with untold evil, and likely to precipitate tumults and affrays.

" It has been argued that the railroad was serving humanity in opposing a grade crossing, but even the humane purposes of railroads must be effected by legal and suitable means. Why local authorities continue to legalize and multiply grade crossing it is hard to say in the light of civilization, but we cannot even abolish grade crossings by force and without due process of law.

" These petitioners were acting under orders, it appears, and it is conceded that, except to direct the taking up of a portion of the street railway track within the limits of their own location, that is, the Old Colony's, they committed no acts of violence. It is said they were loyal to the railroad, to their superiors; and this appears to be true. But in so doing any act of violence, or making any show of violence, they took their own risk. Loyalty to the Commonwealth, to the law, and to the public peace comes before loyalty to their superiors. . . .

" My personal sympathy goes out to these men; I could have wished to find some good grounds upon which a pardon could be granted. Their offence in a moral sense is chargeable to others.

" It has been alleged that Mr. Sanborn, a brave army officer in the War of the Rebellion, has been treated harshly in being forced to work in prison in spite of disability caused by a wound received in the service of his country. If through any peculiar notions of prison discipline in the treatment of prisoners the condition of his health has not been taken into account, that matter can speedily be set right. With the sturdy manliness and honesty which marked the man, he leaves to others the task of making that claim.

" It has been stated that the vote of the Council is a vindication of these petitioners; it may possibly be taken at least as an intimation that a majority of the Council regard this offence as technical, or slight, or as having been sufficiently atoned for. But public considerations of a high character seem to require me to refuse a pardon, even though recommended by my constitutional advisers, for whom I have the greatest respect and esteem.

" Massachusetts prides herself on the maintenance of law

and order. Public opinion will not approve any remission of the punishment, because the act for which punishment was inflicted is felt to be an invasion of public rights and a breach of law and order. As long as we have a just and impartial government, it can never be admitted for a moment that an appeal to force in the assertion of legal rights can be tolerated or condoned, either in the case of corporations or individuals.

" I must, therefore, decline to grant the pardon. "

The vetoes of Greenhalge's second year of office were as notable as those of the first. The first in importance was the Veterans' Preference Bill, already referred to in these pages. The veto of the Holyoke Police Bill, and others similar to it, were generally approved; and the principles of government which induced his action were recognized as just and wise by the people of the State.

On Feb. 13, 1895, the Governor sent to the Legislature the first veto of the year, — a veto of the bill to remove the restrictions upon shad and alewife fishing in the Merrimac River, a bill which he had already vetoed the previous year. This bill was passed over the veto by a four-fifths vote.

March 27 the Governor was called upon to inaugurate the important work of the Boston Subway. Accompanied by Colonel Kenny of his staff, he met at the Public Garden the members of the Transit Commission, the engineer in charge of the work on the subway, and the contractors. It was a few minutes after nine o'clock when the Governor took a shining spade, and, holding it before him, said impressively to Chairman Crocker: " Mr. Crocker, of the Transit Commission of Boston, I hereby tender to you this spade, with which you will begin the work on the subway that has been designed by the city of Boston; and I trust that great relief and comfort will come to the municipality when the plans, as laid out by you and your associates, shall have been fully carried out. "

Chairman Crocker took the spade, and, after a few words in reply to the Governor, lifted the first earth for the excavation of the subway. Thus quietly and simply was inaugurated the great work of the Boston Subway, — a work in which the

Governor took the greatest interest, but the completion of which he was not to live to see.

May 17 the Governor sent in his veto of the Holyoke Police Bill. The object of this bill was to place the city of Holyoke under the control of the Metropolitan or State police.

The necessity of this change the Governor did not recognize; though he sympathized with every movement tending to bring about a better condition in the public government of the cities of the Commonwealth, he thought this general principle of taking the control of the police of municipalities from the citizens to place them under that of the State was in some danger of being carried too far. He therefore vetoed this bill, and others similar, which came before him, when he thought it to be in the interests of sound Republican government.

He was undoubtedly right in his action. The faults that appear in the present method and system of the partisan government of American cities will be eradicated when the citizens can be brought to take a more active part in municipal politics, and not to leave their power unexercised by them to fall into the hands of unprincipled men; or, better still, if they can be induced to unite in the interests of good government irrespective of party. The duty of good citizenship consists in the exercise by the people of all its rights and the fulfilment of all its responsibilities. Whatever conduces to the exercise of those rights by the people, is right in principle; whatever dulls their consciousness of responsibility and power, is wrong. In his message the Governor said : —

" Several hearings have taken place before me in regard to this bill. As a result of those hearings, and from information derived from various sources, the following facts appear to be clearly established : —

" 1st. Up to within a very recent period the condition and conduct of public affairs in the city of Holyoke were marked by disorder and lawlessness.

" 2d. Since the establishment of the present Board of License Commissioners, a decided and substantial improvement has been made.

" 3d. The License Commissioners were appointed by the Mayor of Holyoke, and their administration has been distinguished by integrity, diligence, general efficiency, and success.

" 4th. It appears that the public-spirited citizens of Holyoke, without distinction of party, have united on several occasions, and have been enabled to elect able and honest chief magistrates.

" 5th. That the police of Holyoke appear to have given all necessary assistance to the License Board in its official work, and that the present Mayor has the confidence of the public-spirited citizens of Holyoke.

" While it may be well to give police power to the License Board, as was done in the city of Lowell, the question arises whether the State authorities or the local authorities should have the appointment of the officials charged with these multiform and most responsible duties.

" It is clear that the Governor must always come to this task under disadvantages. He can seldom have personal knowledge of the candidates; he must depend upon others, often partisans or interested parties, for information; his judgment must often be at second hand: but the important principle of local self-government — the autonomy of the city or town — is a material factor in this inquiry.

" Every citizen may claim the right of trial by a jury of the vicinage, and while the guardians of the public peace are agents of the Commonwealth, it has always been deemed best, except in special and extraordinary cases, that they should be selected by the local authorities, who have the best means of knowing their qualifications, and that those who have the best means of observing the manner in which officials discharge their duty should have the power of appointment and removal.

" The case of the city of Holyoke does not seem to be analogous to that of the city of Boston or of the city of Fall River. The former is not only the city of Boston, but may be regarded as in a certain degree the city of Massachusetts, in which many persons not legal citizens thereof have vast property or business interests, and which almost every citizen of Massachusetts visits more or less frequently, and in which all take a peculiar and profound interest.

" In the city of Fall River the friends of law and order

appeared for a time to be unable to make head against selfish and demoralizing influences, and were compelled to ask the aid of the Commonwealth to assist them in a great unusual emergency.

" The city of Holyoke appears to have within itself the vital and recuperative energy requisite to effect its own complete deliverance from all its difficulties. Holyoke is now on its way to pure and economical government; and the result has been achieved by the courage, vigor, and patience of its own citizens. I do not believe that the power of appointment of the Board of Police as contemplated in the proposed Act should be given to the Governor. The principle involved militates against the independence of municipalities, and, while necessary in extraordinary cases, should be diminished instead of extended. I therefore decline to approve the Act."

This veto was followed on the 22d of the same month by that of the Woburn Police Bill. In both these vetoes the Governor was sustained by the Legislature.

June 1st the Governor signed the bill giving a new charter to the city of Boston. It was insisted by the Democratic party that this bill should have a referendum attached to it, and the question be given up to the decision of the citizens of Boston.

The Governor believed in the exercise of all their political rights by the people in every case where practicable, but he also thought the present bill too complicated to be submitted to them. He gave his reasons as follows: —

"As to the propriety of submitting such a measure to the people, I scarcely think this is a case where the approval of the citizens of Boston should be asked. In the first place, it is decidedly complicated, necessarily perhaps; and it is hardly to be expected that all should be so far acquainted with the mechanism of government as to pass on it understandingly.

"Only broad plain propositions, involving a principle and radical departures, should be subjects of referendum. I do not conceive that the bill I have signed involves any such principles. It is mostly concerned with and contemplates matter of detail and changes in method of procedure. For instance, the change from three-headed commissioners to single-headed departments is, after all, but a change in the manner of transacting the business of the city.

"The lengthening of the term of the mayor is probably the most important feature. But of late years the tendency has been continually in the direction of extending the office of the chief executive generally. The sentiment is decidedly in favor of extending the term of office of the Governor of the Commonwealth.

"I anticipate no evil results from the lengthening of the mayor's term; for, after all, the mayor of a city like Boston needs a year to become familiarized with his duties, and for a proper appreciation of the city's affairs.

"Personally I might have drawn a different charter; that makes no difference, however. I did not draw it, and do not place what I might have done against that which has been done. It is only where a measure is in any respect unconstitutional, or where a wrong would be likely to ensue from its operation, that a governor is called upon to use his prerogative and veto it.

"I think that the amendments of the charter of Boston will on the whole give satisfaction to her citizens, and find favor with those interested in and anxious for good government."

Of the Governor's vetoes, there was none that excited more interest or called forth more commendation than that of the Veterans' Preference Bill, — a bill which gave to the veterans of the War of the Rebellion the preference for employment in the public service, and moreover exempted them from the civil-service examinations, requiring only a sworn statement of the applicant that he is qualified to perform the duties of such office as he seeks, accompanied by a certificate, signed by three citizens of good repute, stating their knowledge of the applicant's competency.

On the morning of June 3d the Governor sent to the Legislature the veto message: —

To the Honorable Senate and House of Representatives:

I return without my approval Senate Bill No. 3, "An Act relative to the preference of veterans for in the public service," and assign the following re

22

The language of the proposed Act is somewhat ambiguous, and the provisions do not seem to be harmonious. Section 1 provides for the preference of veterans who have been examined and found qualified, and apparently without regard to the age limit.

Section 2 provides for the absolute preference of veterans to all other applicants except women; it further permits the age limit to be disregarded, and a civil-service rule which may be modified at any time is thus modified or controlled by statute. It would seem as if most, if not all, of the applications would be made under Section 2, where no examination is necessary.

Section 3 apparently is intended to emphasize section 1.

Section 4 provides that within five days the Civil Service Commission shall, after any examination or certification of candidates, cause a list of names of those examined to be prepared, with the standing attained, and said lists shall be opened to public inspection from 10 A. M. to 3 P. M. I am informed that it will be scarcely possible to carry out the provisions of this section in so short a time as five days.

Section 5 provides penalties for violations of the law.

Section 6 provides that the word "application," as used in this Act, shall be construed to mean a petition for employment, containing a sworn statement by the applicant that he is qualified to perform the duties of the position which he seeks, and accompanied by certificates from three citizens of good repute in the community, stating that they know said applicant to be fully competent to perform the duties of the position sought.

It will be observed that the citizens who are to furnish certificates of the applicant's fitness are not required to make oath to their statements, while the applicant himself is. The reason of this distinction does not seem clear, but it is plain that the power of selection and appointment is given to the applicant and "three citizens of good repute," and taken away from the magistrates chosen or appointed to perform this duty.

It is also defines "veteran" as a "person who served of detail and States army or navy during the War of the Rebellion the change honorably discharged therefrom," thus excluding from the benefits of the Act the men who served under Custer or in any Indian warfare, who are included in the Civil Service Act and existing rules. In view of these proposed radical alterations in the existing law, the following considerations are offered as bearing on the question involved: —

In administering the public service, the authorities are by the spirit of the Constitution and the laws bound to obtain the best service possible. Any attempt to so limit and hamper the appointing authority as to prevent the best possible selection for the performance of a public duty is an injury done to the Commonwealth and to the people. It is the duty and should be the aim of every magistrate to secure to the Commonwealth as perfect a public service as can be obtained; and if the administration of the public service is confused by efforts to turn it into a system of bounty or reward, instead of qualification and merit, such a duty is made impossible of performance, and such a laudable aim is defeated. Under existing law the veteran may, without examination, be placed upon the qualified list and have preference over others equally qualified.

With these provisions, preference may now be given to the veteran, while at the same time the principles of good administration of the public service are not violated; and the large number of appointments of veterans will serve to prove that in State, county, town, and in all departments, the authorities have, wherever the public interests permitted, given preference to the veterans.

Since 1885, when the civil-service rules went into effect, nearly twenty-seven per cent of all the appointments and promotions (excluding positions held by women or where the age limit governs) have been of veterans. The gratitude and respect felt towards the veteran seldom fail to manifest themselves wherever opportunity offers.

Massachusetts has gained renown by her system of civil-service reform, that system has been copied by other States, and its rules and regulations obtain wider imitation every day. Massachusetts was the first to apply the system to the day laborer. President Harrison and Secretary Tracy adopted the principle, and applied it to the navy yards of the country. The proposed Act will be a severe blow to this system, and is not in the true interests of the veteran. The principle has been tried and approved; it has benefited the cause of free government much, and will produce greater results in the future.

The veteran will not destroy any system which makes for the good of his country and State, which tends to preserve the safety and to enhance the glory of the republic he preserved.

I earnestly beg you to take this important subject once more into your most serious consideration.

FREDERIC T. GREENHALGE.

On the afternoon of that same day the House of Representatives passed the bill over the Governor's veto by a vote of 172 to 23, which example was later followed by the Senate by a vote of 28 to 7.

Among the many letters of congratulation which the Governor received in regard to this veto, none pleased him more than those from the veterans themselves. Of these he received many, all breathing the same sentiment of gratitude for his attempt to preserve the honor of the old soldier. As it may be interesting to see how this Veterans' Bill was regarded by some of these old soldiers, we quote two of the Governor's many letters : —

MY DEAR GOVERNOR, — Permit me as an old friend, a member of the Grand Army of the Republic, but above all as a citizen of Massachusetts, to thank you for the veto of the "Preference Bill."

Whatever may be the action of our representatives at the State House, I feel very sure that their feelings are in accord with the large majority outside of the legislative halls. Even in the G. A. R. I believe the majority will approve of your action; for it is only the barking minority that have been heard in favor of this bill, and whose influence has carried it through. Thanks again for your courage and sound sense in this action.

Sincerely yours,   C. H. C——.

MY DEAR GOVERNOR, — As a private volunteer ex-soldier who enlisted as soon as Fort Sumter was fired upon, and served until disabled by wounds, I wish to thank you for your courageous attitude in your veto of the Veterans' Exemption

Bill. . . . You have done the cause of good government and
the reform of the civil service a great benefit, and have added a
new obligation to the many which the people of this Commonwealth owe you for your manly independence and distinguished
services. I was born an abolitionist, brought up a free-soiler,
and naturally upon attaining man's estate became a Republican ;
and I continued to be a Republican until driven out of the
party by disgust with some of the demagogues who have held
high positions within its ranks. Nothing that one man has
ever done or said has so inclined me to a return of allegiance
to the party which you so honorably represent in this Commonwealth as your last veto; and if the recording of my vote
for you for any office in the gift of the people to which you are
willing to accept the nomination constitutes me a Republican,
I am one already.

Again thanking you for your endeavor to save the good
name of the veteran soldiers from the political blatherskites
who would drag it in the mud,

I am, etc.   ———

The "Boston Transcript" of June 3d contained the following
editorial in praise of the Governor's action : —

"The veto power has seldom been used with greater judgment either in this State or in the United States than by
Governor Greenhalge to-day, in returning without his signature the Veterans' Preference Bill to the branch in which it
originated.

"Governor Greenhalge has been winning golden opinions
from all classes for the freedom and good judgment with which
he has called upon the Legislature to reconsider its action on
bills having a chiefly local significance. This is the first time
in his political career that he has been summoned to exercise
the authority vested in him by the State Constitution on what
may fairly be called a great political question. He asks the
Legislature to reconsider its recent action, and vote against
a bill which it adopted in order to obtain the soldiers' vote,
and for nothing else. . . .

"The other day Senator Hoar said that Governor Greenhalge
had that degree of inspiration as a public man which stops very

little short of genius. But he has something fully as important in a Governor. He has pluck, undoubted pluck, and
will do his duty as he sees it, with little regard to the opposition his course may arouse. Ever since he has been in the
gubernatorial chair, he has been a growing man. And now
the people of the country will see in him a Governor of
statesmanlike proportions, — a worthy successor of John A.
Andrew."

The vote passing this bill over the Governor's wise and
fearless veto by a majority of 172 to 23 is a truly astonishing
example of the power over the minds of men of a patriotic
principle carried to such an extreme as to obscure totally the
pure vision of justice.

The Republican party seems sometimes a little bewildered
by its memories of the heroic past. Cæsar himself, who planted
his soldiers over all the land of Italy without regarding a
single right of possession and occupancy, might have had some
regard for the efficiency of the public service, — which this bill
put at the mercy of chance.

During this year the Governor vetoed several bills to raise
the salaries of public officials. The first of these was an act to
increase the salary of the Clerk of the Police Commission. In
his veto of this bill the Governor said : —

"While it is true many inequalities are to be found in the
scale of salaries as now established in the various departments
of the Commonwealth which ought at some suitable time to be
adjusted or corrected, I am of the opinion that the present
year does not offer favorable opportunity for securing such a
result.

"The tendency in private enterprises has been towards
rigorous economy, reduction in the number of employees, and
in salaries and wages. The profits of business are small, and
competition is close and severe. In such a condition of affairs
it would seem inconsistent for the Commonwealth to move in
the opposite direction, and to adopt the general policy of increasing rather than diminishing the salaries of public officials,
however plausible might seem the reasons for such a course.

"Without any disparagement to the ability and efficiency of

the official named in this act, and regarding the claim that the city of Boston is chiefly concerned in this increase in salary as not affecting the principle involved, I respectfully decline to approve this Act."

The first of these vetoes, that of the Clerk of the Police Commission, the Legislature refused to sustain, and the bill was passed by a large vote; in most of the others the Governor was sustained.

On June 19, 1895, Governor Greenhalge was present on the occasion of the Masonic celebration at Bunker Hill, in commemoration of Gen. Joseph Warren. The Governor's speech was eloquent and timely,— one of the most brilliant of his many speeches. We give the conclusion:—

"Let the message of Warren to-day strike this dark spirit as a scorching blast of God's lightning. Take these self-seekers at this moment. Let them stand, if they dare, in the presence of this 'sceptred spirit of the past,' this patriot who flung his all into the scale when his country's fate trembled in the balance, — rank, fortune, and future hope and ambition, and life itself; who with the highest commission on the field drew that sword of Bunker Hill as a volunteer and fought as a private soldier where he might have demanded obedience as a leader. So Æschylus fought at Marathon; and of such patriots are everlasting commonwealths composed. 'The greatest gift a hero leaves his race is to have been a hero.'

"What sort of commonwealth did Warren wish to build? He had seen and sighed over the wrongs and follies of ancient governments. He desired a new commonwealth, which should give freedom, hope, repose, and comfort to its people. He desired to build up

> 'A commonwealth whose potent unity and concentric force
> Can draw these scattered joints and parts of men
> Into a whole ideal man once more ;
> Which sucks not from its limbs the life away,
> But sends its flood tide and creates itself
> Over again in every citizen.'

"If there are evils in the Commonwealth, some of the fault is yours ; if there are glories, some portion should be yours.

"Patriotism calls to-day, not for great sacrifices, not for life or fortune. Patriotism calls for patient labor in quiet paths, for endurance of abuse, misrepresentation, association and contact with the selfish and ignorant. Are you not willing to take up the burden, to fight for your country even in obscure places? Do you wish to drive hard bargains with your country, to sell your service at an exorbitant price, to stand Shylock-like upon your bond to exact your pound of flesh from the spot nearest to the heart? Are you eager, not to perform, but to evade your duty as a citizen in the militia, the jury-box, the caucus, the town-meeting, — in the church, in the hospital, in charity or brotherly service? Then the brand of treason is upon you, and the message of Warren will come as a curse and not a blessing.

"A great orator once exclaimed on this hill: 'Is Warren dead? Can we not see him, the rose of heaven on his cheek, the fire of liberty in his eye?'

"Is Warren dead? I repeat. No, he lives to-day. He lives in every star on every flag. He lives in the kindling eye of that old patriot who stood here fifty years ago. He lives in the heart of every boy and girl of Charlestown and of the country. He lives in every noble purpose, in every patriotic impulse. Hear his message; keep his memory green. Imitate his example.

"Here Warren fell, and here he shall be raised. Here he died, and here he shall live forever.

"So mote it be."

One very marked characteristic of Greenhalge was his religious breadth. His great good-nature in responding to all calls upon him naturally led to his appearance before audiences almost antipodal in their foundation principles. So great was his catholicity that he could easily and consistently speak some word of encouragement and cheer to all. The three following speeches well illustrate this fact in his character. His appearance and speech at Archbishop Williams' jubilee excited some animosity toward him in the ranks of the A. P. A. He had never hesitated to voice his liking for the best qualities of the Irish race. He scorned the prejudices of religion or race, and his broad mind allowed him to appear with pleasure at the celebrations of every creed and people. The following is his speech at the Jubilee : —

"I consider it eminently fitting that I should bring the congratulations of the Commonwealth to this day of golden jubilee of your beloved archbishop. It is true that the legal bonds between state and church have been long since severed, but it would be a sad day for the Commonwealth of Massachusetts if at any time every church of Christ, Catholic or Protestant, Methodist or Baptist, were not a citadel of the principles of God's truth and of the ever-living principles at the foundation of this fabric of our government.

"So, my friends, while it is difficult for one man either to tell what the creed of another man is or to understand it when it is declared, we at least know what a man's character is, what his life and what the fruit of the tree. And so, coming here to-night, I can say, with a full and earnest heart, the fifty years of godly, righteous, and sober life which you have met to recognize is something which comes home even to the narrowest bigotry, to the meanest mind. These things in a saintly life may be read of all men and understood by all men. 'Integer vitæ scelerisque purus.' We commemorate just such a character on this occasion.

"It was Sir Thomas Browne who said, speaking at an early age, 'My life is a miracle of thirty years;' but what a larger miracle confronts you here to-night, a miracle of fifty years consecrated to the service of the Lord and to the service of humanity. I know something about this most reverend man. I come here to pay to him my tribute, official and personal, as a man of God and as a man of humanity, as the boy of Boston and as the citizen of Massachusetts. Whether at some time during these fifty years such a magistrate as I happen to be would have been invited to such a festival as this, whether these Protestant bishops and clergymen and citizens would have been sitting upon this platform, I very much doubt.

"But, my friends, we have been growing all together. A spirit of liberalism has brightened every sect, every denomination, every party, every race. Your church has not stood still in these fifty years. I love to hear the words recognizing the virtues of the great governors of the Pilgrim Fathers. More

liberal spirits never drew breath, and they said in the olden
days, 'We won't even write our creed, because God's light may
break upon it and greater truth may shine from it still.'

"And I say that the hand of man cannot write any creed for
man upon which God's sunlight will not fall with increasing
brightness day by day. And we have come together more and
more as we have known each other better. I have found the
great and good archbishop a true citizen of the Commonwealth
in the actual affairs of government. He has given ready aid
to the authorities in difficult matters, and his broad spirit and
liberality have never been found wanting. I want to say here
that I have found him always loyal to the tone, spirit, and
principles of civil liberty, as we understand it under the Constitution of Massachusetts and of the United States.

"I rejoice to meet the eminent representatives of religion
present here to-day. I like to see some of these men of whose
works I know something. I know with what interest they
have given of their strength, of their energy, to the cause
of the whole American Republic. It is not the first time I
have heard the honored name of my distinguished friend, His
Eminence Cardinal Gibbons, and somewhere it seems to me
that I have heard something about Archbishop Ireland. As
to Monseigneur Satolli, I am surprised to find him so gentle
and so quiet. The only rivalry between us is that I understand he claims the title of 'His Excellency;' but, of course,
before he can come into any active competition with the other
'His Excellency,' we shall be careful to examine his naturalization papers.

"My friends, this is truly an occasion worthy to go into the
past and to illumine the future. I remember that the last
time I stood in this historic hall it was on a memorable occasion too. It was on the occasion of the celebration given to
the author of the national hymn 'America.' And as I look
into these eager and earnest faces and contemplate these
crowded galleries; as I look at these decorations; as I see the
old flag with the same red incarnadined by the blood of citizens and patriots, without distinction of sect or race or any
narrow difference; as I see the white representing the stainless purity of all blameless lives, and the blue of that heaven

which protects and defends and invites us all, — I say, why is there not a patriotic occasion here present at this time as well as then, and where's the difference?

"To the most reverend archbishop I give my deepest and best wishes for the future; and as this day floats into the past, freighted with the prayers and blessings of all good and earnest men and women, may the fragrance that comes from it and may the melodious echoes that come from it sweeten and make musical and beautiful the future from generation to generation."

The following is an address on "The Citizen and Thanksgiving," delivered by the Governor in the First Congregational Church, in Lowell, Nov. 28, 1895: —

"MY FRIENDS AND FELLOW-CITIZENS, — You have heard the subject assigned upon which a few words are expected from me. You remember also the subject assigned to the preceding speaker, upon which he has made so forcible and eloquent an address; but I declare that I do not see any practical difference between the two subjects, 'The Christian and Thanksgiving' and 'The Citizen and Thanksgiving.' It seems to me, my friends, that the two topics are identical, or, if they are not, they ought to be; that the Christian ought to be a citizen, and the citizen ought to be a Christian. If we view the practical work of the Christian, we shall find him doing practical and substantial work as a citizen. If we find the citizen doing his full duty to the Commonwealth, not by loud proclamations, but in real active work, we shall find the citizen prominent in the work of the Church. So I say we ought to be thankful to realize the indissoluble bond, the unmistakable identity, between the Christian and the citizen.

"We have a right to be thankful, in the first place, my friends, for this beautiful day. I do not imagine that because one day out of three hundred and sixty-five and one-fourth was set apart by the Pilgrim Fathers that they meant the other three hundred and sixty-four and one-fourth should be given up to repining, to complaining, to fault-finding, and to criticism and censure; and yet it must be remembered, when we find so many who are so eager to criticise throughout the year, that some people are never really happy unless they have an opportunity to find fault with something or other. As the gloomy members of the ancient colony sometimes missed God's smile to catch his frown, so it is that, for a great part of the year, the ninety-five per cent of good is lost sight of and the five per cent of failure and evil is unduly and disproportionately magnified.

"It may be well, therefore, my friends, to come here on this holy day and take an account of stock, and see if the fault-finders are justified, and if it is not true that we who with full hearts return thanks to Almighty God are not justified in our action.

"I say we are bound to return thanks, in the first place, for this God's day, with its sunshine and its beauty. Why, it seems as if Autumn, in all her robes of loveliness, were pausing to deliver a sweet farewell, while Winter, clad in icy mail, like a grim knight, still had courtesy enough to allow her to pause ere she passes away forever, and we get the beauty of autumn with scarcely a suggestion of the winter that is at hand. So I say, even in this outward manifestation of the beauty of the Lord, we are called upon for gratitude.

"And then the Fathers believed in publicly coming together and rendering thanks to the Almighty Father for the mercies which he had given, and for the misfortunes which he had spared them. As Massachusetts kneels to-day in her robes of splendor and majesty, she does it not in the spirit of the Pharisees, thanking God she is not as others are; she kneels there with all the traditional grandeur about her, and with the jewels of Atlanta just won, and yet not in a spirit of vainglory, not in a spirit of pride or boastfulness, but in the spirit of devout thankfulness to the God of the Fathers, who has been with the children as he was with them. Yes, we have a right to be thankful, my friends.

"What makes the glory of a citizen? What makes the glory of a commonwealth? In the age of Pericles it was believed that with the glowing walls of Athens, with the splendor of art and of beauty and science, there was the glory of a commonwealth. To-day only the ruins of this beautiful creation remain; we have the statue that Phidias's mighty genius created; we have a few crumbling stones of the Parthenon. And the greatness of Rome was to be in the invincibility of her legions, in the majestic strength of her structures, — the Appian Way, the Cloaca Maxima, and a thousand other things, of which to-day only the ruins remain.

"Is it not a lesson, my friends, that not in creations of this sort is the permanent and abiding glory of a commonwealth found? Does it not all come down to this, — that the greatest political economist this world has ever seen or ever will see was the Saviour of mankind, and that a nation or commonwealth can find in his teaching only the practical and ever-living safety which makes the bulwarks and foundations of the commonwealth?

"And it is in those applied doctrines, it is not in declaration, it is not in sermon or speech, it is in the life as well as with the lips, that these principles must ever be manifested; and certainly it is all the more necessary in the life of a commonweath. This is a Christian commonwealth, — it has been from the beginning; and yet freedom, civil and religious, has been the very keynote, the very divine music, which has sounded from the beginning, when the Pilgrim Fathers landed upon the desolate seashore, down to this Thanksgiving Day of 1895. And we have a right to thank God to-day, because, other things being equal, the citizen of Massachusetts has more opportunity to follow out his way of everlasting life, to get more out of life, which is a suggestion of immortality, we believe, than the citizens of any other commonwealth in the world. Our institutions are based upon that principle, — the right of education, God given.

"And I take especial pride in assuring those who are doubtful or faint-hearted that the system of public education in Massachusetts is the foundation-stone which has just received its reward. It has received the mark of approbation from the great Exposition of the Southern States; and you can imagine the feeling of pride with which the chief magistrate accepts these grand attestations of the progress, the real work, which the great Commonwealth is doing, and which is watched so eagerly, not only by our sister States here, but by communities all over the world, even from far-off and stricken Armenia.

"I say, while we thank God for our privileges, while we

thank God for the blessings which he has given us, let us remember that we, above almost every other State and community, hold as a sacred trust these institutions which are
of the very life, are of the very soul, of the Commonwealth;
and no light word, no expression of doubt even, is to be
tolerated.

"I believe these institutions will remain as long as this
fabric of the universe remains, and doubt is cowardice. I
have full confidence that neither the gates of hell nor any
other force in the world or beneath it can prevail against these
powers of the soul which make Massachusetts the greatest community on this hemisphere or upon any other. But it entails
upon us all the more work; it, as I say, imposes upon us a
trust in which humanity is the beneficiary, and so let us thank
God even for the work he has imposed upon us.

"The earthly commonwealth can be measured in its glory
only as it resembles the kingdom of heaven, and it is in the
near approach to the likeness of that kingdom that commonwealths lose or find their final destiny.

"So, my friends, these maxims of the Bible, these teachings
of the Saviour, are, I believe, the best guides to political wisdom. When we talk of the problems of labor and capital,
when we talk of monopoly here, of everlasting powers there,
the one solution is when, in the spirit of the Lord, the employers shall meet the employed, and the employed shall respond
to the employer. May not I do what I will with my own
property? Not necessarily. Have we not all learned that
whatever gift, whatever wealth, whatever property, is put into
our hands or into our minds, we are still only stewards for our
fellow-men, for our brothers and sisters? and I say that the
solution of all the problems which are confronting us to-day, —
the establishment of godliness, the establishment of simple
honesty, the establishment of temperance, of righteous living
of every sort, — comes from the doctrines which we find in Holy
Writ; and it is the practical man who is the citizen who has
more opportunity than the ordinary Christian.

"And yet I find the Christian women at work in all practical
lines. It is a glorious development of womanhood. They become acquainted with public questions; they do not degrade

and slander public men; they understand more and more the difficulties of the case.

" It is so easy to sit at one side and comment upon the combatants engaged in hot strife! Why was not this blow struck there? Why was this not done so and so? Yet it must be remembered that the public man is bound in his duty of citizenship by his highest duty as a Christian; he is bound to remember that the whole people of the Commonwealth are, as it were, the objects of his care, and by the manner in which he treats all alike, with equal justice and with equal charity, his work as an official will finally be judged by right-thinking people.

" So I say, my friends, it is the duty of every Christian to be a citizen, and to be actively at work as a citizen. He cannot sit quiet and count his dividends or estimate his profits while a city is going down to the shame and guilt of Sodom and Gomorrah. In New York, at the last election, there were 281,000 registered voters; of that number 40,000 proved themselves recreants and traitors by not lifting a hand or uttering a word in defence of good government. I think, my friends, the condition of our own city is one that calls for earnest work on the part of the citizen, on the part of the Christian, — or, I will say, on the part of the Christian citizen, which is one and the same thing.

" We must no longer commit to our most inferior people the business of managing our dearest interests. It is the man of brains, of power, of business experience, and of business sagacity, who must come to the front. If you do not do it, it is because you are not either Christians or citizens. So, my friends, take the work in hand.

" I think we have a right to thank God to-day, because, however active, however mighty, the forces of evil are in any community, the forces of right are there; and when the Word of God reaches those forces of right and puts them in battle array, the cause of good government will be maintained here, in New York, all over our country. In that hope we all live, and in that sign of the Master we shall conquer, and we shall have again another great reason for uttering our thanksgiving to the Almighty Father."

The third speech in this trinity was delivered before the Salvation Army : —

" LADIES AND GENTLEMEN, — I come here to act as chairman of this meeting for a very brief period. I consider it a duty, as the representative of a Christian Commonwealth, to extend a most hearty welcome to any benign and Christian influences that come to that Commonwealth. And so I think I may simply emphasize the welcome already given by Boston and by the Commonwealth to General Booth here to-night.

" I remember when the Army which he represents was considered of little value; when it did not seem to command the support and approbation of the careful, thinking people of intelligent communities. Yet in the last few years we have seen this work grow, expand, bloom, and flourish until the Salvation Army has become one of the recognized institutions of Christianity.

" That is a mighty gain, a great step forward. We cannot have, in these days of trouble and anxiety and unrest, too much religion. All religion, if it is true, is true religion. The people need, in one way and in another and everywhere, this spirit of religion. I remember the words of the prophet foreshadowing the evil days, and saying that ' the Lord God will send a famine in the land,' — not a famine of bread, nor of thirst for water, but of the Word of the Lord, — ' and they shall wander from sea to sea; they shall go to and fro, and shall not find it. In that day the fair maidens and the young men shall faint for thirst ! ' God grant that that day may be far off ! It is in just such living agencies — instruments of the Lord — as these which we see to-night, that that want will be satisfied, and that evil day be put off or indefinitely postponed, if I may use a legislative term.

" My friends, it is in upliftings of this sort that the whole people are benefited; and when we find men and women professing a religion which has for its cathedral the alley and the lane, the haunts of vice and the home of misery, then we know that religion is at least attempting a task which Christ himself would approve.

" It is in this work for the poor and needy that this Army of Salvation commends itself to the judgment of reasonable

and thinking individuals. It makes for peace! It makes for
comfort! It is benevolent and not malevolent! Consequently,
I may say, on the part of this great Commonwealth, that I
welcome a great power, a great spirit here in Boston, here
in Massachusetts, — the spirit of Christianity, which is not
limited by oceans, by continents, by sections, but which com-
prehends the whole habitable globe.

"A great work has already been done, and I can only say to
the General, coming here, in a manner, in his hour of triumph :
'Deal rightly with this people of Massachusetts!' If by your
coming, sir, through any alley or street or section of Boston
or of the Commonwealth, you can give one breath of life and
comfort that will make the humblest, the meanest, the most
miserable feel that he too is the child of God, entitled to fair
and equal terms, even at the tribunal of Heaven, the blessings
of the people of Massachusetts will go with you. We shall
hold you to strict account, — we shall ask, when you have
passed from these triumphant scenes, 'Has the coming of
General Booth really given encouragement and cheer and the
spirit of betterment to our own people?'

"I know what the answer will be! Already there has
been a manifestation of this singular power; and just as I
would hold to account my Adjutant-General, the Chairman
of the Board of Police, the Chief Justice, or any other great
official or magistrate, so spiritually I have to hold to account
these mighty magistrates of the Lord.

"In this spirit, my friends, and in the full confidence that
doubts will be resolved and that the account will be written
as shining pages on the books of Heaven, I introduce that
Great Bishop of the Established Church of the Poor, — General
William Booth!"

Perhaps the most enjoyable to Governor Greenhalge of the
occasions when he was called upon to address the people in
an official capacity were the agricultural fairs so commonly
held throughout the State during the season of autumn. He
loved the homely manners of the agricultural class, and delighted in meeting the country folk, the sterling nature of
whose character he appreciated. During the season when these

meetings usually occur the country-side is perhaps seen at its
best. The rich tints of the autumn foliage, the coolness and
clearness of the atmosphere, render nature most beautiful and
delightful, and seem to gratify all the senses. Governor Greenhalge did not pretend to know much about practical farming,
but he knew how to interest the farmers, perhaps because he
was interested in them; and some of his agricultural addresses
are among his best. I select one that he delivered at the Plymouth County Fair, Bridgewater, Sept. 6, 1895, as a fair example of his speeches on many such occasions : —

"When I last attended your dinner, which I do not think
keeps up to the old-time fashion of a frugal repast, but goes
considerably beyond that, I remember that it was the time of a
storm, when the rain fell upon the just and the unjust alike,
and interfered materially with the attendance at the fair and
with your general success and prosperity. I congratulate you,
Mr. President and friends, that to-day we have the sunshine
with us, plenty of it, perhaps at times a little too much; but,
with the utilitarian spirit which marks the intelligent citizen,
you will coin that sunshine into dollars and put them into the
treasury of this ancient agricultural society. So I am glad to
be here to rejoice with you in your day of success as I was
pleased to be here to attempt to take my share of any adversity
that might have come to you last year.

"I suppose there is nothing which excites so much the risi-
bilities of the critic, the wit of the humorist, as the attendance
of the governor at what are called cattle shows. If a man
invites me to a gathering of this sort, he asks me to an agricultural fair; but if he finds I am going to some other fellow's
attraction, he speaks of it as a cattle show. The point of view
is quite important in determining the epithet or appellation
which shall be given to an occasion of this sort. And some of
the kindly critics always find a good deal of amusement in the
extent of agricultural knowledge possessed by an official who
is invited to occasions like this.

"Why, my friends, is there no serious, no earnest purpose,
no true significance, in visitations of the executive to gatherings
of the people? Is it not right that the executive should find
out what manner of people he has to deal with? Is it not

right that the people should know the manner of man they
have to deal with in official station ? Is it not right that the
chief magistrate should sit at meat with his people, should
meet them as man to man, should understand something of
them beside the relations which exist between him and them
from the platform, in the chair of office, and in their voting
precincts ? After all, my friends, we are men and women, and
it is the character of the men and women which makes the
character of Massachusetts, which makes the character of the
whole country.

" I might say, if we came here simply as critics, it would be
an easy rôle to perform. The critic does not need to know
anything of the subject he criticises. We see ample evidence
of that in every magazine and every newspaper. But I come,
aside from my official capacity, in a character which I think
entitles a man, in a sort of impersonal way, to respect and consideration, because I come here as a consumer, and the consumer
is of the utmost importance to the producer. The consumer is
the keenest and most intelligent critic of the producer. He
knows something of the product of the farm, can tell good
butter and knows if the milk is half water. We all know so
much about the products of the farm that a man of average
intelligence may be able to learn something from a gathering
like this.

" I learned something at the great fair at Worcester, which I
visited Wednesday, and which had the finest exhibit of live-
stock that has been seen for many years. I learned that they
are now introducing two new breeds of cattle, and I am glad
to say this in the presence of Mr. Seth Bryant, who sits here,
at the age of ninety-five years, and who, I trust, in the providence of the Almighty, may live out the full term of one hundred.

" I know that we have reached an epoch in the history
of the introduction of cattle. Mr. Bryant, as I am informed,
first brought into this Commonwealth the Jersey ; and now it is
proposed to give strength and calibre to that breed by crossing
it with the Simmenthaler and the Normandy, the two new
breeds which were shown here for the first time at the fair at
Worcester. This is of interest to every man, woman, and child
in the Commonwealth, because we all want good, pure milk and

honest butter. We all want the best that can be produced, particularly if it is true, as Sir Thomas Browne has said, that man is simply what he has eaten.

"Now, my friends, here in Plymouth County there is some special interest attaching to a society of this sort. The man who touches the soil of Plymouth County ought to find in it a liberal education, a patriotic inspiration. The Almighty said in that beginning of things on this side of the Atlantic : ' I do not give you broad prairies and wide fields of wheat, but here on this rock of Plymouth I will plant the noblest, the first free commonwealth the world has ever seen, and from that rock shall living waters flow, which shall enrich the soil of every State and territory, and shall gladden the eyes and hearts of all the peoples upon the earth.' That is the story of Plymouth.

"I want to see this society keep its membership full. I am glad to see about me these men advanced in years. It is certain that there have been good living and spiritual righteousness here to give that strength and life and vigor to old age which make it as beautiful as if crowned again with youth. I thank you again for the opportunity of being here."

The illiberal movement in American politics known as the A. P. A. — the American Protective Association, as the sounding and pretentious title runs when taken from the obscurity of capital letters — rose into prominence during the first administration of Governor Greenhalge. From the first, it roused his indignation. To his broad liberal ideas and to his "loving catholic heart," such an organization was most antagonistic; its secret methods were opposed to his singularly open nature, and in his second campaign he desired to assert frankly his opinions in regard to it. But the organization was a secret one ; its members, as far as possible, concealing their membership, it was difficult to estimate its strength ; it made great claims, and indeed in several cities and towns had succeeded in carrying the Republican caucuses. This was a critical year. Before another election the organization would decrease in strength. So thought the party managers, and counselled silence ; and the Governor yielded his judgment to theirs. When, however, the time approached for the holding of the State convention of 1895, the organization, instead of decreasing in influence, appeared to have increased. Many of the Governor's acts had called forth adverse criticism from the members of the order, — he had appointed Catholics to office ; he had attended Commencement at Holy Cross College; worse than all, he had attended the jubilee banquet to Archbishop Williams and shaken hands with Satolli ! The organization ranged itself in opposition ; its strength, however, was not so great as had been feared. But the votes given to Morse in the convention which nominated Greenhalge for the governorship for the third time, were like blows to him. He felt that he had deserved the full support of his party.

The State Republican Convention of 1895 was held in Music Hall upon the 5th of October. Curtis Guild, Jr., was the permanent chairman of the convention; Hon. Frederick H. Gillette was chairman of the Committee on Resolutions. Ex-Governor Long proposed the name of Governor Greenhalge for renomination in these eloquent words : —

"Sometimes our constituency — the great Republican party of Massachusetts — sends us here to make selection for it of a candidate for Governor. At other times it sends us here to announce the selection which it has itself already made.

"That is the case to-day. In tones clear as a bell the Republican party — let me say the Commonwealth herself — has long since proclaimed the name of her chief magistrate for the next ensuing year. If for a moment any have questioned that choice, the result has been only to make more certain to them and to everybody else that it is as foregone and inevitable as to-morrow's sunrise. Fortunate indeed the candidate the discussion of whom confirms the assurance of those who enthusiastically rush to his support, and dissipates the doubts of those who come to it at first with some hesitation, but anon with equal constancy.

"Gentlemen, Massachusetts has come to have faith in the ability, the integrity, and the courage of her present Governor. Not by any winning personality, not by the grace and rare eloquence of speech which are his, not by the aptness with which on many occasions he has represented her within and beyond her borders, but by his unflinching discharge of his duty as he has seen it, and by his fidelity to his own convictions, he has won her approval, and she now bids us say to him, 'Well done, good and faithful servant!'

"On his record he stands, and on that as on a rock. He has shirked no responsibility; he has feared to face no exigency and no man; he has recognized no limitation upon the equal rights of the American citizen, be he of whatever color, race, birth, or religion. So thoroughly has he thus secured the confidence of the great body of the people, — even of those who differ from him in this or that measure or in this or that appointment, — that of his own political party those who at first most questioned his fitness are now among his stanchest supporters; while of the other great political party nothing but the frail and tumbling fences of partisan organization prevent, even if they do altogether prevent, its members from a wholesale lurch and flocking to his standard.

"In the name, therefore, of the grand old party whose delegates we are; in the name of the grand old Commonwealth whose commanding voice we utter to-day; in the name of what is large and liberal and sound in American political principles; and in recognition of honest desert and faithful service, I move the nomination for Governor for the next ensuing year of Frederic T. Greenhalge."

After Governor Long had finished his speech, a ballot was called for. The result was 1,363 votes for Governor Greenhalge, 391 for the Hon. Elijah A. Morse, and 8 scattering.

In accepting the nomination, the Governor said: —

"GENTLEMEN OF THE CONVENTION, — I thank you most heartily for the honor you have just conferred on me; it calls for my most profound gratitude and my most earnest acknowledgment. Your nomination, coming to me at this time and under existing circumstances, is, indeed, an honor of triple magnitude and full of uncommon significance.

"I think it may be said that your action is not limited by the lines of mere routine. Perhaps it is not too much to say that it represents the deliberate judgment of the Republican party upon an administration of two years. During that administration many vital and momentous questions have arisen. In the onward movement of a great commonwealth like Massachusetts there is a necessary friction and disturbance occasioned by the velocity of progress. Upon these questions, involving the interests of property, the fortunes of parties, the triumph or defeat of systems, and the sacred rights of men, it is not to be wondered at that honest and marked differences of opinion have arisen, and a great deal of interest and zeal aroused. While I am uncharitable to no man who differs from me, while I ascribe to sincere opposition no unworthy motive, while I acknowledge my own many errors and shortcomings I must say, as I look back upon the past and note the many instances where perplexities arose, where prompt and decided action was required, that I must still hold fast to the principles by which I have endeavored to guide and regulate my course, and, in humble imitation of the great reformer, say, 'So help me God, I cannot do otherwise!'

"I have always believed, I still believe, that to be a good Republican it is necessary for a man to be a good citizen, true and loyal to his country, with a supreme and single devotion. The principles of the Republican party mean progress and development, the lifting up of the individual and of the State. Those principles favor sober, righteous, and intelligent living; they are at once the lamps of the State, the nation, and the home. Education, free as air and lofty as heaven; temperance in thought, word, and life; justice, blind to artificial distinctions of wealth or station, eagle-eyed to the distinction of right and wrong; loyalty to State and nation, rising to a love that 'passeth understanding,'— these, and every principle that makes for good government, are written in the hearts of all Republicans.

"Again, the Republican party believes in the indivisibility of the country; it desires to stimulate and develop that glowing spirit of American nationality which is already stirring in every heart from the Atlantic to the Pacific. We think that the ship of state will meet the stormy seas quite as successfully as one beautiful integral fabric as in sections or compartments loosely jointed together. The unification of States is a noble object, worthy the highest ambitions and the grandest

efforts of statesmanship; the unification of a people making
all Massachusetts one family bound together by ties of affection
and esteem, inspired by the Almighty with the loftiest ideals of
citizenship, is, I am sure, a step in the direction of that

'far-off, divine event
To which the whole creation moves.'

"Gentlemen, I do not think that our party has lost anything
of power or prestige in the last few years. In State and nation,
here at home and in the country at large, that power and
prestige have grown and strengthened; it is therefore fair to
assume that the administration of affairs here in Massachusetts, to a limited degree, in New York, and elsewhere in the
country, has met with the approval of the people; and it is
the people in whose service we are enlisted, whose good is our
highest aim, and whose commands we, as a party and as individuals, must obey.

"Gentlemen, let us move forward to the coming contest with
all courage and confidence, and, above all, with a profound sense
of the immense responsibility which Massachusetts is once
more about to impose upon the Republican party. Gentlemen,
again I tender you my profound gratitude for what I must
consider the crowning honor of my public life."

"When the Governor appeared" (I quote from the "Springfield Republican"), "the feeling was even too intense for de-
monstrative applause. The platform and speeches had been
with the anti-Greenhalge men; but here was the living personality at whom their attacks had been directed, and he had
been vindicated. The stern set face of the Governor, and the
rigor of the muscles that grew tense as he marched towards the
desk on the platform, seemed more inflexible than ever. It
was not an attitude of triumph, but rather the soberness of
one who had won a serious victory. The Governor's voice,
always harsh as he begins an address, was softened, and seemed
unusually clear and strong. When he reached the climax, and
repeated Luther's immortal words, 'So help me God, I cannot
do otherwise,' the most unsympathetic were thrilled."

Governor Greenhalge had not been desirous of a third term, —

as he said to his friends, " I have had two terms, and am satisfied;" but the leaders of the Republican party believed that if
he refused to be a candidate there might be trouble, because of
the sharp contest apprehended for the governorship through
the new element in the Republican party. Having consented
to assume again the leadership of the party, he entered upon
his third campaign with very different feelings from those that
had influenced him in the two former campaigns. For two
years he had filled the executive chair; he had made his
record, it was before the people for them to consider and pass
judgment upon; he felt that the more dignified position for
him was to await that judgment quietly. He was weary, and
longed for rest; let others speak. But again the party managers thought otherwise. The Governor's re-election was assured, but for the good of the party a large vote was needed,
and he must help to call it forth. As ever, when it was only
his own interest that was in question, he yielded, and gave his
strength to his party. In this campaign, however, he felt that
he could follow his own judgment, and speak out the truth he
held in his heart. While on his way to Holyoke, October 12,
where they were to speak that evening, he said to the Lieutenant-Governor, who was with him: "Roger, I do not know
what you mean to do, but I shall speak frankly to-night
against this narrow bigotry." "I will do the same," was the
reply; and most eloquently and unequivocally did they speak.

In the Governor's speech he said: "I say, for the first and
last time, if any organization means to extend and strengthen
the beautiful and beneficent system of public education in
Massachusetts, if they mean an intelligent and loyal spirit to
the Commonwealth of Massachusetts, I say to every true and
loyal citizen of the Commonwealth, 'God speed.' But if they
mean proscription, ostracism, hostility to any man who is a
true and loyal citizen, and the stirring up of race prejudice,
I would rather be defeated than elected by a hundred thousand votes, if one of those votes was meant to favor ostracism
and proscription."

After an arduous campaign during which Governor Greenhalge spoke with his accustomed vigor in many places, he was

elected for the third time Governor of Massachusetts on November 5. Had the truth been known which was concealed even from himself, there would have been something very pathetic in Governor Greenhalge's third campaign. It presents to the mind the idea of a person overtaken, in the midst of overwhelming labors and duties which cannot be laid aside, by ill health, and consequently unable to accomplish an inexorable task without immense self-sacrifice and personal loss. It is true that Governor Greenhalge did not appreciate the fact that he was seriously ill; at the same time he must have felt a real indisposition, and that the work he had to do grew ever harder. There was, however, no appearance of lack of vigor in his speeches and addresses; he would not suffer the fire of his oratory to diminish, nor allow the least duty to be sacrificed. He had not desired a third nomination, but the election gave him pleasure. He carried the State with an increased majority over that of the previous year. There was greater enthusiasm in his cause than ever, and the success of the Republican party was very dear to his heart. The vote for Governor stood: Greenhalge, 173,250; Williams, 112,938, Greenhalge's plurality, 62,371; Mr. George Fred Williams, of Boston, being the Democratic candidate.

After the election Governor Greenhalge expressed his satisfaction at the results. He said: "Of course, there are two reasons why it was desirable to have a large majority, and very gratifying to me. The first, and the most important, is that it is a commendation of my management of the affairs of the Commonwealth during the time I have been in office. The second is for the sake of the influence which a large majority may have on the national election. For both these reasons this election gives me great satisfaction."

The dedication of a national military park, Sept. 19, 1895, on the battlefields of Chattanooga and Chickamauga called Governor Greenhalge in his official capacity to the South, with the governors of other Northern States. The event was national, and attracted the attention of the country. Governor Greenhalge was accompanied by members of his staff and the official delegation from Massachusetts. The ceremonies comprised the dedication of a Massachusetts monument to her honored heroes.

The Governor's party reached Chattanooga early on the 19th, and at four in the afternoon formally dedicated the monument, which was surmounted by a bank of flowers bearing in immortelles the inscription, "Massachusetts Tribute to Valor." At the base of the monument were a crescent of white roses to the Second Regiment, Eleventh Corps, and a star of red roses to the Thirty-third Regiment, Twelfth Corps.

Governor Greenhalge began his dedicatory speech at once, and closed with enthusiastic applause. It was a masterly effort, and attracted wide attention.

" FELLOW-CITIZENS, BRETHREN OF THE NORTH AND SOUTH EAST AND WEST, — The history of the evolution of constitutional government has almost always been written in the blood of freemen. From the days of Simon De Montfort, slain at Evesham, down to the days of Hampden and Chalgrove, the fields of Naseby and Marston Moor, and thence on to 1688 (a period of constitutional development both in Old England and New England), and later to the days of Bunker Hill and Appomattox, great principles have been established by the arbitrament of war. And with the best advantages for determining questions of law with honest and independent judicatures, servile to no king or party, with the most intelligent legislative thought in the world, the Constitution of the United States, the scope and meaning of governmental principles were settled, not in senates or courts, but on the mountain heights around Chattanooga, and the decrees of that august and terrible tribunal were written in the best blood of the country and proclaimed by the thunder of artillery.

" We are to contemplate to-day a great crisis in a great struggle, and to dedicate to eternal peace and rest under the starry flag this place, where the battle raged so fierce, and where the victor 'sank to rest by all his country's wishes blest,' and the vanquished, in his children, shares in the prizes of victory.

" The rapid advance of Rosecrans, the skilful strategy which compelled Bragg to evacuate Chattanooga, the forward movement of the Union forces later, the repulse at Chickamauga, the holding of Chattanooga until reinforcements arrived to complete the rout of General Bragg and to relieve Burnside at Knox-

ville, — all these facts are well known.   The story of this crisis
and of the great battle of the West, of the services of the Thirty-
third and Second Massachusetts, has been told many times.
In such a crisis of the nation be sure that Massachusetts
was represented.   When did Massachusetts ever fail in the
hour of peril ?   The two gallant regiments she contributed at
this time — the Second and the Thirty-third — were the flower
of the Union forces.   It would be difficult, if not invidious, to
rehearse to you the achievements of these two regiments upon
these and so many other fields, embracing East and West,
North and South, previous to Chattanooga and after, on to
Atlanta and Savannah. . . .

"This is a story of heroes told by heroes.   Thomas and
Hooker and other great captains have told it in the simplicity
and grandeur of official orders.   But the men of the Second and
Thirty-third understood well the principles they were fighting
for ; so, too, did their great leaders.   They came hither bearing
colors blistered and torn, indeed, in the fierce breath of many
a battle, and yet in every ragged fold emblazoned with victory.
The stern eye of Joseph Hooker gleamed with pride and joy,
when, as a soldier and as a son of Massachusetts, he watched
these Pilgrims of the Old Colony, these Ironsides of the old
Commonwealth, march by.   If crisis of peril to the country
were near, Massachusetts, with her best blood and her best
brain, was at hand to hold up the arms of the republic.
Webster, the mightiest statesman of the North and of the
South, had pleaded for 'Liberty and union, now and forever,
one and inseparable ;' and probably every man in these two
Massachusetts regiments knew the great words of the constitutional expounder by heart, and as they marched up
the rugged sides of Lookout, these words rang in their ears
above the roar of battle.   Sherman, hurling his flaming lines
upon the foe, knew they were going to bring back liberty and
union on their bayonets.   Thomas, the rock of Chickamauga,
immovable and steadfast, while the billows of Confederate
valor hissed and seethed around him, saw the vision of liberty
and union.   Hooker, the boy of Massachusetts, the plumed
Bayard of our armies, planting the victorious flag of his country above the clouds of Lookout, knew that liberty and union

were safe ; and it is well to remember that the 'Cracker line' of Hooker furnished the very bread of life to the republic in its hour of direst need and suffering.

"Burnside, beleaguered in Knoxville, heard the hurrying feet of the Thirty-third Massachusetts among the foremost rushing to the rescue, and, cheered by their far-off cheers, hurled off, by a supreme effort, his desperate and heroic foe; and Grant, the master mind of all, controlling and inspiring all, the incomparable and invincible captain, amid the shouts of victory, was calmly projecting new battles and new triumph for the cause of liberty and union.

"Cogswell, with his famous regiment, holding with bull-dog grip the line of railroad from Tallahoma, probably repeated to himself the magic words of Webster, which he heard so often declaimed in the public schools of old Essex; and the watch-words of Underwood, charging into the very lines of the enemy, were 'Liberty and union.' . . .

"The victors of Chickamauga were fighting for their homes and firesides. So, too, were these children of Massachusetts. In the broad spirit of our principles, there is not a foot nor an inch of foreign soil, from Puget's Sound to Tampa Bay, from Boston to Galveston. State lines, sectional divisions, in that glowing spirit of nationality which makes every citizen a brother and every sovereign state an integral and indissoluble part of our country, were obliterated by the flashing wisdom of statesmen like Webster, and by the hearts' blood of freemen like those who sleep beneath this sod. The men of Massachusetts fought for the homes of Massachusetts, and they fought, too, for the homes of Tennessee, of California and the Carolinas. It is true that those who loved them might have yearned to have their precious ashes laid in some shaded New England sepulchre, where their eternal sleep might be lulled by the patter of their childrens' feet and the turf above them brightened by spring flowers, bedewed with the tears of their comrades. But we commit them to the care of Tennessee, knowing they are at home. . . .

"There is not opportunity to describe the vicissitudes of the grand series of conflicts which raged along these mountain heights. The armies on each side were marked by dauntless valor, the commanders were renowned captains; the brave and sagacious Braxton Bragg and the indomitable and unconquerable Longstreet were foremost among the Confederate leaders, while the names of Sherman and Sheridan, Thomas, Howard, Rosecrans, and Hooker, were watchwords in the Union army, and their mighty forces were inspired and directed by the inflexible and irresistible genius of Grant.

"Listen to Chickamauga speak to Chattanooga, — deep unto deep, — and the dead of Chickamauga stand in line with the dead of Chattanooga. You may hear a voice from heaven saying above these Confederate graves, 'You fought for no lost cause, your cause was won at Chattanooga. Though vanquished, you were victorious, sharing in the fruits of victory. Liberty and union are henceforth the heritage of your children. The flag is yours, and the bright particular star of your State must only increase your love and devotion to the glory of the whole constellation, Peace and love, union and prosperity, be with your country forevermore.'

"So speaks this voice over the graves of Chickamauga and Chattanooga to-day. And Massachusetts, as she bends over her sons sleeping their last sleep here, under the skies of Tennessee, her grief chastened by just pride in their deep loyalty and precious sacrifices, claims from her sister State, and from every sister State and from every citizen of the republic, the tender yet mighty sympathy which America yields to men who pour forth their life blood to save and to strengthen our common country.

"Forever shall be remembered, as illustrated on the field of Chickamauga with unwonted splendor, and on many a battle-field, the desperate valor, the chivalric spirit, the fervid devotion, which leads brave men to fight and to die for a cause and a principle in which they believe to the last. That valor, that spirit, that devotion, shall gleam and flash in the pages of history, over shattered armies, over bloody defeats, over carnage and ruin, over causes lost and shrivelled up in the flame of battle, and principle trampled in blood and mire. The glory of the Union soldier depends for its very life and quality upon the glory which crowns his heroic opponent. Under the banners of North and South we have 'one equal temper of heroic hearts.' . . .

"Well, we have talked over the old days, of the 'old, unhappy, far-off things, and battles long ago,' but we have come together now. We are brethren. The snows and flowers of more than thirty years have come and gone. A new day has dawned. Commerce, trade, manufacture are coming, and they care nothing for sectional lines. Chattanooga has got a firm grip on civilization. The steady, indomitable energy of Massachusetts and Maine are blended with the dash and *élan* of Tennessee and Georgia.

"Northern capital shakes hands with Southern and Western resources, and, with water power, coal fields, iron mines, stone quarries, giving employment and wages alike to every portion of the country, we realize the utilitarian and practical value of the sentiment, 'E Pluribus Unum.' These grand old mottoes take on new meanings in the light of this new day. Union and Confederate stand together to-day. The blaze of artillery lights the mountain peaks no more. The tender sunlight wraps them in soft radiance. The great flag of the republic, streaming over the blue and the gray, over the living and the dead, over the North and South, East and West, proclaims to us and to the world that we are one people, animated by one purpose, as splendid as ever glowed in the soul of man, with one destiny, so grand and high that it fills the future with a glory such as the sons of men never looked on before, and standing here, under that banner all together, close together, we hear the mighty music of the Union. Rising from every lip and every heart, comes the great anthem of the free, 'My country, 'tis of thee,' swelling into a diapason sweeter in the ears of the Almighty and of all mankind than any ever heard since 'the morning stars sang together and the sons of God shouted for joy.'

"The patriotic dead who died for Massachusetts and for the whole country we shall all hold in everlasting remembrance and gratitude for the mighty work they did to secure to us all liberty and union in a country which shall remain one and inseparable, now and forever. This nation holds the right of the line.

"It leads; it is the vanguard of humanity. In general intellect, development, in social culture, in political improvement, in swiftness of ship or locomotive, in all-roundness of capacity, in adaptability to new conditions, in quick concentration of powers to meet emergencies, the American is 'in the foremost files of time.'"

During the fall and winter of 1895 the Cotton States and International Exposition was held in Atlanta, Georgia. In the Massachusetts exhibit at the Exposition, Governor Greenhalge had taken great interest, and had done much to insure its success. The 15th of November was made Massachusetts Day, and the Colonial Committee of Massachusetts was invited to select the orator of the occasion. This committee was composed of ladies appointed in part by the Colonial Committee of Atlanta and in part by the Governor of Massachusetts. It was their duty to collect and care for the Colonial and Revolutionary relics, an exhibit of which each of the thirteen original States had been solicited to contribute to the Exposition. It was intimated to this committee that should their choice fall upon ex-Governor Russell, who was a great favorite in Atlanta, it would be pleasing to the people of that city. The ladies of the Massachusetts committee, however, feeling that the presence of the Governor of the State would give dignity and brilliancy to the day, and that the honor of the Commonwealth could with safety be intrusted to him, invited Governor Greenhalge to deliver the oration. Though shrinking from the extra labor and the fatigue of the long journey, coming, as it must, just after the exhausting work of the campaign, the Governor accepted the duty, and in his fulfilment of it brought new honor to his beloved Commonwealth. During the stress of the campaign, however, the Governor had found no time to prepare his address, and it was written in the train as it sped on its way to Atlanta. For the Massachusetts exhibit the State had erected a beautiful building, — a reproduction of the old Craigie or Longfellow house in Cambridge. From the steps of this building the Governor on Massachusetts Day delivered his oration.

"Your cordial greeting, my friends, is a most inspiring prelude of the performance of a delightful duty.

"I come here charged with a message as lofty and loving,

as full of affection and respect, as the ancient Commonwealth of Massachusetts can send or the imperial State of Georgia can receive. And if the voice of Massachusetts fails, if we, the representatives of Massachusetts, fail adequately and sufficiently to express to you all the love and good-fellowship, all the sisterly affection, she bears to her sister State of Georgia, we know that our deficiencies, our weak utterances, will be hidden, lost, or made good in the great, undying, ever-increasing song of the angelic choir proclaiming 'Peace on earth, good-will to men,' first heard on the plains of Bethlehem when Christ the Lord was born, and which has filled the world with divine music ever since.

"I bring this message of Massachusetts to Georgia, and it is delivered in a most appropriate place. This mansion of Massachusetts speaks for Massachusetts more clearly than any lips, than any mortal voice. This structure is the counterfeit presentment, the verisimilitude, the true image of perhaps the noblest mansion of Massachusetts, which, though silent, proclaims her history, her life, her thought, her purpose.

"This house stands in Cambridge by the placid Charles. We may not catch here to-day except in fancy the murmur of the river sweeping by the poet's study ; we may not see

> 'the lights of the village
> Gleam through the rain and the mist,'

but we may hear the old clock on the stairs ticking, —

> 'Forever — never —
> Never — forever.'

The sweetness of the 'Children's Hour' has soothed many a mother's and father's heart here in Georgia, and the trumpet blast of the 'Psalm of Life' has stirred every young man's heart from Boston to Atlanta.

"We know, then, that the soul of Longfellow is with us here to-day. And the other great tenant of the Craigie House, the grandest, standing alone, supreme, — Washington, — his spirit is present here. Under the old elm of Cambridge he drew that sword which flashed freedom from Massachusetts to Georgia.

"And be sure that as we gather here to-day a brighter ray of sunlight than common plays around the summit of the gray shaft on Bunker Hill, and the old war-echoes which haunt the peaceful vales of Concord and Lexington come to us softened into murmurs of peace and love.

"We come, then, to encourage, to aid you in a slight degree in your great undertaking. We earnestly hope that you may win solid success and derive substantial profit from your earnest and untiring labors. May they bring you material wealth, and, better still, may they bring you the riches of the mind, the broadening and uplifting of soul more precious than jewels of silver and jewels of gold, and the strengthening of the spirit of fraternity, of patriotic love, which shall warm the great heart of America, giving to seventy millions one flag, one purpose, one destiny, one glory.

"Already upon your State seal you have written, 'Agriculture and Commerce.' To-day you may proudly add ' Manufactures;' and the progress of a community in art and skill and handiwork in the industrial arts means a step in the direction of the highest civilization.

"We see here the dawn of a grand future. The funeral drums of the past are dying away in the distance. This grand exposition; the sympathy and cheer of your sister States from every quarter; the grand message delivered in Boston by that chivalric and high-souled son of Georgia, John B. Gordon, which is even now ringing in our ears; the increasing trade ; the closer business relations, social and political ties; the clearer understanding of the community of interests; the similarity of conditions, — all point to a grander and higher development, a wider and nobler future, not only for Georgia, but for the Union.

"As for Massachusetts, she fears no rivalry; she invites each and all to a generous and friendly emulation. We do not repine because you have captured some of our cotton mills, — be careful that some of the owners do not capture you. If some of the blood of Massachusetts is injected into the veins and arteries of Georgia, it will not be found cold or sluggish; it will give strength of heart and clearness of brain, sound judgment and high courage.

"Massachusetts cannot boast of treasures of the earth, of

vast territory, of coal or cotton, iron or lumber. The best product of Massachusetts is Massachusetts; the best work of her
people is her people. As they wring from the barrenness of
Plymouth Rock the everlasting riches of civil and religious
liberty and well-ordered government, so from every adverse
condition, from every grim obstacle, they wrest the jewel of
success. They see in your glory and prosperity no menace
to their own, but a help and a stimulus.

"If you catch up with us in one line of industry, we must
try to increase our pace. If we cannot do that, we will strike
out in another line. If you must manufacture cotton cloth,
we will dye and print it, and decorate it. If you make our
product more cheaply than we, we will diversify, — invent more
delicate textures, more artistic designs. If we cannot do this,
we will make the machinery for you to do the work. 'One
star differeth from another star in glory,' and the glory of this
star of the South adds to the glory of our star of the East.

"'The heavens declare the glory of God.' Yes! and what
brighter vision of heaven can mortal eyes ever see, what heaven
better declares the glory of God, than that heaven in which the
constellation of the union shines with increasing splendor, every
star lending lustre and beauty to every other?

"In bringing our message we do not hide a single page of
history. In 1799 you wrote upon your State seal, 'The Constitution, Wisdom, Justice, Moderation.' These still you have.
There is the whole story. In the new Georgia, the new Atlanta,
there is so much of promise and hope that we need not dwell on

> 'Old, unhappy, far-off things
> And battles long ago.'

"And upon the most urgent problems of our day, a word of
power and light has been spoken by one of those most interested, Professor Booker T. Washington. It is words of wisdom
like his which give life to nations.

"If we must go back, let us go back to the inspiring recollections of the very origin and foundation of freedom. Let us
remember how, as Pallas sprang, fully armed with spear and
shield, from the glowing intellect of Omnipotence, so the
genius of constitutional freedom sprang in perfect panoply

from the glowing thought of the Revolution,—the mightiest revolution in the recorded history of mankind, whose great waves are even now beating against every throne of oppression in the world. No later shock or disturbance can impair or destroy the grand results of that divine movement of humanity. No subsequent convulsion can dissolve the eternal ties then formed among the thirteen colonies.

" Representing, then, the Sons and Daughters of the American Revolution in Massachusetts, I greet with warmest welcome the Sons and Daughters of the American Revolution in Georgia and throughout the broad land. Keep forever burning the pure fire of patriotic love and patriotic purpose here in Georgia, in Massachusetts, and elsewhere."

The address was received with great enthusiasm. The warm-hearted Southerners expressed with fervor their delight and admiration. Among the guests of Massachusetts was Governor Bradley, of Kentucky, whose State day followed that of Massachusetts. He earnestly solicited Governor Greenhalge to be present at their celebration, and speak to his brethren of Kentucky. To this request the Massachusetts Governor willingly assented. Again he was, as a prominent Kentuckian expressed it, "the star of the occasion." His address was as follows:—

" Massachusetts and Kentucky and Georgia are not divided. They should not be looked upon as States distantly separated, but as Americans closely related. One touch of nature has made the whole world kin. We are brothers and sisters, and we have a common cause and a common destiny. There is no dividing line. That was done away with many years ago, and we have been brought closer and closer together as the years have rolled by.

" We have a way in Massachusetts, as was demonstrated yesterday, of claiming everything. We just come along and take what there is in sight. Yesterday we talked about colonels. But colonels have got to be just a common every-day affair; and unless the inpour of governors is stopped, governors will be as common as colonels. Now, there is Governor Bradley; he will soon be just as common as we are to-day, for now he is one of the elect. He talks about Clay. Why, does not Clay belong to Massachusetts just as much as he does to Kentucky? And what does he say about Lincoln? My friends, do not you know that there are more pictures of Abe Lincoln in Massachusetts than in the whole State of Kentucky? Those great men belong to the Union, for which they devoted the best portion of their lives.

"The history of the State of Kentucky is different in some respects from the others. She stands upon the dark and bloody ground. It is an easy matter for the North to stand guard and fight back the foreign foe. It is an easy matter for California to protect the Western coast; but Kentucky stands between, and keeps peace among her children and brothers. Well do I remember when the question of the late war was brought up in Congress, Kentucky was the peacemaker. She understood the situation, and she said to the North, 'Go slow,' and to the South, 'Hold back; you are all brothers, and do not be the first to take up arms against your own blood.' Kentucky has never yet in the hour of peril hesitated to cast in her lot and destiny with that of the other States of the Union, and she never will. Kentucky is the grand link that binds the North and the South, and she will ever be the one State that will be the first to lift the flag of the Union to the top of the pole.

"Now, I do not care to have politics altogether. I would be just as proud to welcome the Democrats as I am the Republicans, provided I could find them. We are all working for one end and one cause. We are marching side by side. In every earnest endeavor you will find the hearty support of every Massachusetts man. Let us remember the glorious stars and stripes. Out of the forty-four stars, the star of Massachusetts is the brightest, and is the one particular star in the great constellation. We love the white in the flag, because it is the emblem of that which is noble in man; and we love the blue, which, like a type of heaven, floats above us and bids us godspeed in our great work and blesses us.

"If my coming to the Commonwealth of Georgia has been of any good result, I count myself more than repaid. I am first for the good of the country, and I have several thousand people in my glorious State who are of the same opinion."

After three days, full of social and official duties, the Governor, accompanied by his staff and the members of the Executive Council, returned home. Governor Greenhalge, by his cordial genial manner and genuine interest in their affairs, had roused a kindly feeling in all who met him; and with the fond recollections which the people of Atlanta cherish of Governor Russell, who came to them bringing his eloquent tribute to lay upon the grave of their beloved dead, will doubtless mingle pleasant memories of that other Massachusetts Governor who came to bring his message of peace and good-will.

One of the Governor's staff tells us how on their homeward way, as they sat Sunday eve talking in the car, the Governor came to join them, saying, "Let us sing some good old-fashioned hymns." And for two hours they sang, the Governor calling for hymn after hymn; "and if we hesitated over any verse he prompted us, finally closing by singing 'Abide with me.'

"At the request of one of the party for the words of the last verse, the Governor repeated in an impressive, tender way,—

> 'Swift to its close ebbs out life's little day;
> Earth's joys grow dim, its glories fade away;
> Change and decay in all around I see.
> O thou who changest not, abide with me.'"

The Governor reached Boston on the 20th, and two days after we find him again at his work for humanity, speaking in behalf of the Armenians in Faneuil Hall.

The second Thanksgiving Proclamation of Governor Greenhalge was given to the people on November 5. Like the first, it is such as would naturally come from its author,—reverent in tone and finished in expression. It was as follows:—

THANKSGIVING PROCLAMATION.

Commonwealth of Massachusetts.

BY

FREDERIC T. GREENHALGE, *Governor.*

It is fitting that the people of the Commonwealth should remember and acknowledge the manifold mercies shown them by Almighty God during the year now drawing to a close. No signal or overwhelming calamity has visited them; and such troubles or misfortunes as have come to them they have been enabled to meet with patience and courage, brightened by faith and hope.

The family and home are the strong foundations of the Commonwealth, and the light of our political structure is the Word of the Lord. In the family and the home, therefore, as well as in the house of God, the voice of Massachusetts should be heard in praise and thanksgiving for the blessings and mercies of the year. "Blessed is the nation whose God is the Lord; and the people whom he hath chosen for his own inheritance."

I therefore, by and with the advice and consent of the Council, appoint the 28th day of November current as a day of solemn thanksgiving and praise to the Lord, whose loving kindness has been so constantly shown to us in the past, and whose strength and tender care will protect his people from one generation to another.

FREDERIC T. GREENHALGE, *Governor.*

The second administration of Governor Greenhalge ended, like the first, with general approbation. The list of his engagements was as long as that of his first year of office. His duties were not lessened. The wear and tear upon his strength had been enormous, and he plainly showed its effects. I, who heard him deliver the last speech of the fall campaign in Lowell, could not help noticing his extreme fatigue. I had never noticed the least irritation on his part, but that night he was extremely worn and sensitive. His speech was full of fire as usual, but the effort he made was plainly visible.

CHAPTER X.

GREENHALGE'S third inauguration as Governor of the Commonwealth of Massachusetts took place Jan. 2, 1896. He began his third year of office with the congratulations of the people and the good wishes of all. It must have been a great satisfaction to him to know that his administration had given such general satisfaction, and that he had secured so high a place in the estimation of his fellow-citizens. He no doubt looked forward to a successful year of activity and usefulness. Alas! how soon he was called away from his sphere of duty. His last inaugural was as high in tone and as comprehensive as were those which preceded it. The following quotations are taken from it, and show its general character, — practical at once and patriotic. The passage on Legislation reaches a very high level of thought and expression; it is worthy to stand as the last counsel of Governor Greenhalge.

RAPID TRANSIT IN BOSTON.

In conformity with the recommendation which I made a year ago, the Legislature of 1895 passed certain amendments to the laws relating to the construction of subways in the city of Boston. Among other things, the powers of the commission in building the subway under the Boylston Street and Tremont Street malls were enlarged and more fully defined.

As a result of this legislation, alterations in the plans were made, furnishing improved and more ample accommodations for the public. The work of construction is already well advanced, and I am glad to be able to state that there is good reason to hope that before the end of the year the subway will be ready for operation from the entrance in the Public Garden to Park Street, and that the present most burdensome congestion on Tremont and Boylston Streets will be materially relieved by the transferring from the surface of the street to the subway of those Boylston Street cars which now reverse at the Granary burial-ground.

Again I ask the Legislature to give consideration to such amendments, if any, of the acts relating to subways as the commission may recommend for the purpose of facilitating the construction or increasing the utility of this novel and much-needed public improvement.

I am confirmed in the opinion that the subway, when completed, will add greatly to the convenience of the public, and will be found to be in every way a profitable and progressive enterprise. The greatest care must, however, be taken to prevent its being the object of selfish speculation, and to insure that conservative management of it which will regard the public interests as the prime purpose to be attained; and I am confident that satisfactory arrangements can be made to this end. . . .

CORPORATIONS.

I ask you to consider whether it would not be for the public interest to secure some legislation which shall require the terms of consolidation of gas or electric light companies to be approved by the board of gas and electric light commissioners, substantially in harmony with Chapter 506 of the Acts of 1894, applicable to railroad companies.

Section 4 of Chapter 346 of the Acts of 1886 forbids a gas company to transfer its franchise, lease its works, or contract with any other person for carrying them on, and there seems to be no general law authorizing the consolidation of any of these companies; but if this power exists, or should be granted, it should be exercised subject to the restrictions of said Section 4.

Chapter 506, however, seems to apply to special railway consolidation acts, similar to those which may be passed applying to gas or electric companies.

A strict supervision of the operations of corporations, both public and quasi-public, would seem to be demanded for the protection of the public, whether as to increase of capital, extension of functions, leases, or consolidations. And the granting of special charters should be regulated and carefully guarded. The granting of charters to be used only as menaces to legitimate enterprises, or to be sold for speculative purposes, must ultimately work injury to the public.

The recent legislation directed against stock watering has proved effective and beneficial. It would be well, further, to require all corporations chartered elsewhere than in the Commonwealth to come under all the conditions and restrictions applicable to domestic corporations, especially in regard to paying in of capital.

So much complaint is made of the harsh and questionable methods of so-called mutual benefit insurance societies or companies that it is incumbent upon you to consider the expediency of exercising more ample State supervision over them.

Let me call your attention to what seems to me a growing evil. Last year more than $50,000 was expended by the various commissions and boards for counsel fees and legal expenses. This amount will increase rather than diminish, if the present system continues. I recommend your consideration of the following suggestions: Reorganize and enlarge the law department of the Commonwealth. Let the attorney-general have compensation sufficient to command his whole time; furnish the department with all the assistants or deputies necessary to perform substantially all the law business of the Commonwealth in the way of advising the several administrative departments or furnishing other legal assistance. In this way more unity of system and of legal and consistent policy will be obtained than by committing this responsible labor to a dozen or a score of attorneys, acting without reference to any general plan or purpose. . . .

GOOD CITIZENSHIP.

But education, material and intellectual progress, the heaping up of riches, the improvement of our institutions of correction and charity, the strengthening of police and militia, the purification of political methods, the exaltation of justice and its administration, will avail us nothing, if out of all this improvement, development, and progress we do not secure a high standard of citizenship, which is not only the foundation, but the end and aim of all good government.

There are various suggestions as to the mode of improving the quality of citizenship, among them the following: —

1. Greater care should be exercised in the administration of naturalization laws, so far as our State courts are concerned.

2. A probationary period of residence after naturalization might be prescribed by constitutional amendment. The twenty-third amendment was such a constitutional provision; this was repealed as unnecessary and oppressive; but existing circumstances may seem to justify at least a shorter term of probation.

3. While there may be a division of opinion as to disfranchising for felony, as is done in some States, it seems clear that persons undergoing sentence in penal institutions should not be permitted to vote.

The decisive vote on woman suffrage at the recent State election would seem to show that public opinion will not for some time be prepared to accept any radical change in the established system of suffrage; on the contrary, the public mind appears to be growing more and more in favor of biennial elections, and there is no good reason why the question should not be submitted to the people. . . .

LEGISLATION.

The purity and character of a legislature rest largely with the legislature itself, and ultimately — or, rather, primarily — with the people. All laws based upon a reckless assumption of the inherent baseness of legislatures are as likely to aggravate as to remedy real evils, which are, I trust, at present small rather than great. The character of the legislator of Massachusetts should be as high as the character of Massachusetts; it is, in fact, the character of Massachusetts. Yet every safeguard, every precaution, every danger signal, must be used to warn, to admonish, to deter the weakest — or the meanest — mind which could possibly entertain the thought of prostituting the high public trust reposed in a legislator to selfish or sordid ends. Stringent legislation, calculated to emphasize to the legislator the necessity of being above suspicion, and to warn the lobbyist of the peril he runs in even approaching the legislator with corrupt proposals, will serve to prevent those vague rumors which from time to time disturb the public mind without crystallizing into specific cases. Such legislation would prevent rather than recognize the alleged abuses of the lobby. . . .

CONCLUSION.

The growth and improvement of the Commonwealth as here set forth are not limited by material or physical lines. Charity is learning to be business-like without being sordid; correction is becoming gentle without becoming weak; education is bountiful in her gifts, but not extravagant. We must not, however, fall into any such self-complacency as to reject or discourage improvement and further progress. We must not be unwilling to learn from others. Only by maintaining this earnest, open, emulous spirit can we hold and maintain the "glorious gains" of the past and reach out to the future for equal or greater achievements.

Gentlemen, I have thus rapidly sketched for you the present condition of the Commonwealth. Massachusetts now commits her affairs to you. You take upon yourselves a great trust. May you be inspired in the performance of your duty by a spirit of genuine patriotic love and pride. In all confidence, the people commit to your care the future of the Commonwealth.

The last public utterance of Governor Greenhalge was a speech delivered at the Twentieth Annual Meeting of the Boston Druggists' Association, at the Parker House, Tuesday, Jan. 28, 1896.

During Governor Greenhalge's third year of office the citizens of Lowell inaugurated a movement to have made a bust of him, to be paid for by public subscription, and presented to the State in their name. The bust was executed in marble by Samuel Kitson; and the date for its formal presentation to the State at the Capitol in Boston, arranged before his illness, was fixed for February 28. While he lay upon his death-bed, the presentation was made by Mayor Courtney, of Lowell. The occasion was made very impressive by the sad circumstance of his illness, and the people's fear for its result. Lieutenant-Governor Wolcott received the bust on the part of the State.

Ill as he was, Governor Greenhalge still showed interest in the proceedings, and desired to hear about them from the writer, who was present. Courage at any time never failed him.

It is interesting to note that the first act of the Governor's official life was to write a letter of condolence to the wife of ex-Governor Gaston upon the death of her honored husband, as his last was to write a similar note of sympathy to the wife of ex-Governor Robinson. How little it was foreseen that the death of the writer was so soon to follow that of the latter honored citizen !

On the evening of Friday, February 7, a new armory in Springfield was dedicated by a grand ball, — "Governor's Ball," as it was called, — and, though wearied and far from well, the Governor felt that he must be present. It was the last time he was to meet the people of the Commonwealth, — his people, as he liked to think of them.

The day following he returned to his home in Lowell, never again to resume his official duties, — duties so dear to him.

In spite of the trials and anxieties which must come to every conscientious man in positions of public trust and responsibility, the years of his governorship were happy years to him. During his illness, when his wife spoke regretfully of the great tax that had been put upon his strength, how earnestly and with what emphasis he replied, " But I loved it, I love to work." " I am so interested in all these things," he said another time. In all the vast machinery which is necessary in the government of a great State, there was no part so small that he did not make its interests his own. It gladdened his heart to feel he was in touch with the people, that they trusted and loved him.

" Yes," he said, half sadly, a few days before he died, as he listened to an editorial from a paper that had formerly been one of his harshest critics, which spoke of him as " our dearly loved Governor," in words of sympathy and commendation, — " yes, I

think they are beginning to understand me." Happy it was
that the understanding came while he was with us, for no man
appreciated more affection and just commendation, or felt more
keenly misjudgment and misrepresentation.

It was hoped that, wearied and worn out with his many
duties, with rest and change to a warmer climate, health and
strength might return ; and preparations were made for a
journey south, but on the eve of departure the stroke fell
that told to his dear ones that hope was vain. For a few
days he lingered, days full of beautiful memories to those
who were with him. With his mind as clear as ever, and
his wit as keen, many were the smiles his fun called forth
from those about him. Every little incident was greeted
with an apt remark or quotation. True to his love of poetry,
the last book he asked to hear read was the Iliad.

He met death, as he had ever met all troubles, bravely ;
however great his sufferings he uttered no word of complaint,
words only of cheer and thought for those about him. "I have
never known finer courage, or more beautiful cheerfulness, or
more tender consideration for others." Such was the testimony
of that kind physician who, coming to him a stranger, "learned
to love him." "It is wonderful, wonderful. I never saw anything like it," said his own faithful physician and friend of
many years.

At midnight, March 5, while the fierce tempest raged without, the summons came, "Enter thou into the joy of thy
Lord ;" and out from the turmoil and unrest of this life he
passed into that peace for which he had longed, that "peace
that passeth understanding."

So ended a life of singular beneficence and power. Greenhalge possesed a combination of qualities which made him a
unique figure in the Commonwealth. An absolutely pure politician, he was perfectly fearless in word and action. In "the
scorn of consequence," he followed the convictions of an honest
and upright man. In spite of his unbending integrity, he
succeeded in political life. Indeed, it was because of his high-
mindedness and uprightness that he did succeed to a degree
well-nigh unprecedented in his State. He sowed good seed,
and reaped precious fruit in the respect of the community,

the highest interests of which it was ever the object of his labors to raise and multiply. He loved Massachusetts. The State was to him an almost ideal community, — as it were, the conscience of the country.

Though an orator of power, and distinguished by a never-failing faculty of eloquence, the basis of his character was calm and stable. He was just and reasonable; one could rely always on his judgment.

The significance of such a career is wide-reaching. It is typical of the strength of honest purpose. It shows the power of high-mindedness. It teaches to the young aspirant for public honor that there is nothing so successful in the end as personal probity and unselfish devotion to the best interests of the people, — that they can be made the means of advancement to the chief stations of trust and authority.

The public expressions of grief and sorrow called forth by Governor Greenhalge's unlooked-for death were well-nigh unparalleled in their intensity and earnestness by aught in the past history of Massachusetts. Not for seventy years had the death of any of her governors occurred while in office. But it was more than the loss of their chief executive officer which the people mourned. His death had something tragic in it which appealed to all men. Mourning draperies were everywhere seen upon the public buildings. That was public usage, and to be expected. What was moving and human was that the people seemed to feel his death like a personal grief. Many instances have been recalled which revealed in unexpected ways, in all classes, how deeply the people felt his loss. A desire for public and military obsequies, and that his body should lie in state at the Capitol, was widely manifested; but the wishes of the family were respected, and his funeral was that of a private citizen. Yet it was most impressive. Nearly all who were most distinguished in the State were gathered there to do honor to the dead. The funeral cortege passed through streets lined with people, who seemed moved by a common sentiment and were hushed in silent respect. On Saturday, April 18, the State of Massachusetts paid her final honors to her dead Governor. The public ceremonies in Mechanics' Hall in Boston were simple, yet they expressed a grand sentiment, — the loyalty of Massachusetts and her appreciation of all that is best in the character of those whom she exalts.

It is almost with reluctance that the writer brings to a conclusion this record of the life of Governor Greenhalge, lest the full measure of justice be not done, and the portrait remain incomplete in some essential. The attempt might well fail to paint the character of the man. To be gifted with great talents is but an accident; but character grows with the growing spirit of man in the contentions and struggles of life. It comes not without effort, without self-conquest and sacrifice upon the altar of some high purpose.

He possessed an instinct for truth, — an instinct inseparable from any great or permanent work whatever, yet not too common in a world where shams masquerade on all sides, where prejudice and partisanship sometimes appear as patriotism, political manœuvring as statesmanship, and mere words and formulas come disguised as if clothed with divine right.

His nature rested on great fundamental realities. There was no duplicity about him. He did not believe too much in the dupability of men, and knew that truth would make itself known among them. His belief in men gave him courage, so that here was a man who could dare and do. He had the simplicity of nature which endears itself, so that no political leader in Massachusetts possessed a more numerous and enthusiastic personal following. Through them his influence will long be felt in the politics of the State for good; for in the circle in which he moved a liberal tolerance and breadth of view were sure to be taught by contact with him.

More and more as time goes on the people of Massachusetts will demand a high order of leaders, — more liberality, a broader nature, real intellectual pre-eminence, — for things have changed. Life and its interests are more complex; the people themselves are growing into something greater. The mere figure-head should disappear from American politics, and the real chief be found. Wealth alone should be no recommendation, nor mere political wire-pulling and skill.

Few men could have dealings with Governor Greenhalge without owning to themselves that here was a man,—a man of real intellect and power,—needing no notary parchment, no installation, to give him precedence. Time will show what his influence is to be. I believe that his career and that of Governor Russell will raise the level of party nominations; that the people of both parties have learned by them to know that success will follow the lead of men who have real character and power,—even with no adventitious circumstance to help them, and needing none. By the character of its rulers this republic is to rise or fall.

25

POEMS.

PREFACE.

THE best of the verses written by Greenhalge during his busy life have already been presented to the reader in the preceding biography. All of them were written without an idea that they would ever be collected and published.

They are not put forward now as being in all cases worthy of him, nor wholly because of their intrinsic merit; but it is thought that they will have an interest and attraction to many who knew the author as distinguished in a very different field. Some are school and college productions, written in early youth.

The writer feels bound to make these few remarks because it may be that the author of the verses would not have permitted their publication as a whole, though there are among them many beautiful and characteristic poems.

J. E. NESMITH.

POEMS.

THE YOUNG MAMMA TO HER MOTHER
IN ITALY.

BOAST not of soft Italian skies,
  Of moon-lit lake and calm blue sea,
My baby-boy's clear laughing eyes
  Are softer, lovelier far, to me.

I know how well Murillo paints;
  His angels surely could have flown!
But I can see *all* those young saints
  By turns in my sweet boy alone.

And Raphael's cherubim are sweet, —
  On that point we can have no strife, —
A thousand graces in them meet;
  But where's the royal grace of life?

Here's life and motion, smile and tear, —
  The freak, the pet, the sweet amaze,
The baby rashness and the baby fear,
  And beauty shines through every phase.

I love the bards that filled the land
  With strains of melody divine;
Round Petrarch's, Dante's brow my hand
  The votive wreath would gladly twine.

But there's a music sweeter still
  That fills my quiet home with joy,
And, sad or merry, soft or shrill,
  Give *me* the prattling of my boy!

IN A DIARY.

1871.

As naiads bathing in a crystal rill
    To the clear water lend a clearer glory,
So, love, this snowy page make whiter still
    With all the sweetness of thy pure life's story.

As rose-bud June breathes fragrance through the year,
    And cheers a little grim December's gloom,
Thy life shines rose-like in Time's pathway drear,
    And gladdens troubled hearts with its soft bloom.

From one sweet fault, dear girl, thou art not free, —
    Love for a sinner is that single taint;
The precious love that cheers my life makes thee
    A truer woman — and so less a saint.

TO MY WIFE.

To-DAY a strain of melody is heard
    Within the storm-beat mansion of my life;
It hails with all the glee of some wild bird
    The morn that gemmed the world with thee, sweet wife.

See what a light shines in kind Memory's eyes,
    As, smiling, she brings forth her treasures rare;
Mark too the crown that decks her queenly guise;
    Our wedlock years the brightest jewels there.

And yet the past holds grief as well as joy;
    'T is not more blest in quiet than in toil;
And we have learned that life is not a toy, —
    Its strength and hope are gathered from turmoil.

But, like a sunbeam on a dreary morn,
    A diamond sparkling in the dust of life,
A smile, a blessing, in a world forlorn,
    Have *you* been ever unto me, my wife!

TO HARRIET R. NESMITH.

Duchess and Queen are names not worthy *you*, —
  The light world flings them where they least are due;
And Truth, not shrinking from her painful task,
  Shows vice and folly hid behind the mask.
Seen in the radiance of your daily life,
  That starlike shines o'er gladness, woe, or strife,
What are these diadems, these coronets,
  But baubles dark with crimes or wild regrets?
Your noble deeds, true woman, are your throne;
  Your crown — the love God gives his own.

A BIRTHDAY.

Fair as the Day art thou! though ancient earth
Not oft has seen a day as fair as this
Lift its sweet forehead to the sun's warm kiss, —
Fair as the Day, that whispers of *thy* birth!
Behold! by some love-philter joy and mirth
Have charmed old Time! he lies in drowsy bliss,
Nor dreams that Love — and *you* — Love's love, I wis —
This day, at least, will rule the happy earth!
What royal music fills the spacious sky,
With what fond hope all nature seems to thrill!
Like circling gems, the hours all glittering lie
Around your neck, so restless yet so still!
Must such a day blend with the common past?
In my true heart its reign shall ever last.

YOUR BIRTHDAY.

Your birthday? What imports the term?
Time's stealthy flight does it confirm,
Or does it seize the year's wide power,
To rest it in an upstart hour?
Or have those gentle, sweet-eyed days,
That shed such light o'er all your ways,

Been changed, at some dark wizard's word,
Into a Shade, with tears all blurred?
No, no, this day means naught of this —
It shall be sweeter than Love's kiss;
Yes, every joy from out the Past,
Its grace o'er you again shall cast;
And all the Future's promise sweet
Your opening eyes, like morn, shall greet;
And Love, in kingly guise sublime,
Shall haughtily wave back grim Time:
And while this noblest of all wooers
Shall press his fervid lips to yours,
And ever seek with close caress
Your cheek and eyes and loosened tress,
That fair soft cheek shall keep its bloom,
Those eyes love-light shall still illume;
And though the world grow gray and old,
That tress of gold shall still be gold!
Still like the rose, that cheek shall glow,
To hear Devotion praise it so;
Still in those deep, shy, thoughtful eyes,
Be traced sad lovers' destinies;
And floating free that shining hair
To eager hearts still prove a snare.
For here's the charm of noble mind —
Wit keen, audacious, yet refined,
That flashes through the daily life,
Mercutio-like in sport or strife;
High purposes that scorn the earth,
And reach to heav'n, where they had birth;
And tender thoughts that softly go,
Like angels, to the realms of woe;
Courage, that eyes the mid-day sun,
And points to deeds yet to be done;
And Purity, — a sword of flame,
That guards each path from spot or blame.
So, shining with this inner light,
Beauty reigns still in Time's despite;
And, glorious with eternal youth,
Love lives, like Truth, for Love is Truth.

A MEMORY.

AUTUMN, that painter, dark and bold,
Had flecked with crimson hues and gold
The wide picture of the sea,
The shore, the sky's immensity;
The wind breathed like a harper mild,
That seeks to soothe a fretful child;
And soft reply Atlantic's wave
To the pine forest's murmur gave;
Arundel's woods were fresh and cool,
The moss how green, how bright the pool!
'T was early morn, the village bell
In silvery whisper warned the dell,
When through those glades, beneath that sky,
In sweet converse walked you and I.

IN MEMORIAM.

MRS. REBECCA CAVERLY, LOST AT SEA, MAY 7, 1875.

O HOUSE of God, where late she knelt,
  The voice of mourning fills thy walls;
  The dirge is sung, the teardrop falls;
A vague, strange sense of loss is felt.

All burdenless here stands the bier,
  Save for the pressing weight of gloom;
  In vain the flowerets smile and bloom,
To deck a form that is not here.

"Give up thy dead, O stern, cold sea!"
  The billows break with sullen roar
  Upon a bleak and rugged shore, —
The only answer to our plea.

In native earth she may not rest
  Among her household's quiet graves,
  Where, by the soft stream's gleaming waves,
In peaceful sleep repose the blest.

Yet did her pure and graceful life
　　Breathe sweetness on this air of ours,
　　Give lasting joy to fleeting hours,
And bring calm peace to scenes of strife.

And when in sorrowing groups we meet,
　　This thought our tearful grief beguiles:
　　She lives in happy children's smiles,
And in the lives by hers made sweet.

Oh, doubt not, though your grief be wild,
　　That He who walked on Galilee
　　Shone forth on Scilly's raging sea,
And clasped the mother and her child.

J. F. McE———.

REQUIESCAT IN PACE.

WAS it a gleam of the fickle sun,
　　Flashing a moment through mist and cloud,
As the organ's thunder rolled on high,
　　And a thousand heads in prayer were bowed?

Or was it a smile of the pictured saints,
　　As the high-roofed church with music filled?
Or was it that we and the dead we bore,
　　By God's own blessing were strongly thrilled?

Then we thought of the glorious years gone by, —
　　The glorious years of our youth and joy;
When all the sands of the hour-glass ran
　　To sparkling gold without alloy;

And the days like sportive nymphs danced by,
　　Strewing on us their roses and smiles, —
And our boyish hearts, aglow with love,
　　Fell an easy prey to their sweet wiles.

How grandly above the base world's din
  Our joyous roundel and chorus rang!
The star-crowned night would smile and wait,
  And murmur back the songs we sang.

Then highest and clearest and sweetest of all
  Rang the voice now silent to mortal ears —
'T is heard at the gate of heaven to-day
  By Him who wipes away all tears.

IN MEMORY OF JUDGE GARDNER.

GREAT Architect! we are but dust
  Unless thy love smile on us here;
A brother's soul we now intrust
  To thee, O Lord, without a fear.

Whom bring we to the shining door?
  A loyal knight and Mason he —
His virtues he like jewels wore,
  And starred with glory each degree.

For, working in thy temple, Lord,
  With awe he marked its spacious lines;
His heart was but thy trestle-board,
  Whereon were traced thy grand designs.

As in the courts of earth we saw
  His work from youth to life's decline,
We knew he judged so well man's law,
  Because he lived, O Master, thine.

HYMN

WRITTEN FOR THE UNITARIAN CELEBRATION OF THE LAST SUNDAY
OF THE FIRST CENTURY OF THE REPUBLIC.

HAIL to the Sabbath sweet, — the last
  Of all a century's Sabbath days;
Float, blessed day, into the past,
  Rich with a nation's prayer and praise.

Thy power, O God, shines through these years
　　That bound our nation's splendid morn ;
Thy hand each needed bulwark rears,
　　Thy voice 'gainst secret foe doth warn.

Still keep, dear Lord, yon flag unfurled
　　O'er Freedom's chosen citadel, —
Cheering anew the slavish world,
　　And lighting up each captive's cell.

That faith in man teach to mankind
　　That's born of purest faith in thee ;
Then tyrants can no longer bind,
　　And Right will rule from sea to sea.

KENNEBUNKPORT HYMN.

I LIFT mine eyes unto the hills,
　　My strength is thronèd there ;
The rocks, the forests, and the hills
　　To Thee all raise their prayer.

Far up the river's silvery thread,
　　Behold the streaming tide ;
As those bright waves their gladness spread,
　　Thy love is all their guide.

The storm lowers o'er yon restless deep,
　　The seaman holds his breath ;
In safety, Lord, thy children keep,
　　Or be their life in death !

Lo, at thy word Peace rises crowned,
　　And smiles o'er land and sea ;
Thus peace and joy are ever found
　　At last, O Lord, in thee.

HYMN

WRITTEN FOR THE GRANT MEMORIAL SERVICE, LOWELL.

GOD of the free! let thy radiance shine
   O'er the dark tomb where our hero we lay;
Freedom he loved with the furor divine,
   Bless thou his soul whilst a Freeman can pray!
Take to thyself, mighty Lord God of hosts,
   Him who on earth bore thy own flaming sword,
Smiting to death all the traitor's wild boasts,
   Making thy name through all nations adored.

Let him have peace — like the peace that he won
   On the red field where the blood fell like rain;
Grant him thy peace in the name of thy Son, —
   Peace that is earned but by anguish and pain.
Far down the sky hear yon loud trumpet ring,
   "Open God's gates!" peals the archangel's voice,
Cherubs and nations exultingly sing,
   "He is with God! then rejoice, oh, rejoice!"

FALLEN LEAVES.

I KNOW a streamlet, deep and still,
   That through wild woods seeks out a way, —
I saw it when the blasts were chill,
   And o'er it autumn brooding lay.

But soon the wind flung on its wave
   A gorgeous mantle of bright leaves, —
Scarlet and gold and green, they gave
   A glory man's art never weaves.

And as those fallen leaves lent grace
   Unto the streamlet's darkening flow,
And, falling, found as high a place
   As when they bloomed in summer's glow;

So, though *our* labors seem to fail,
    And low our blooming hopes are hurled,
Like fallen leaves they still avail
    To beautify a dreary world.

A MEMORY.

REST, weary heart, in memory's secret glade,
    Far from the vulgar turmoil of to-day.
'T was June; we sat, — so happy, yet afraid, —
    And saw or heard the brooklet glide away.

The brooklet played with every leaf o'erhead;
    It laughed and sang to every stone and fern;
Catching a sunbeam, faster on it sped,
    And brighter, gayer, seemed at every turn.

Do you remember, too, that tender hour?
    Our souls embracing in our meeting eyes, —
Sweet madness! for an instant Love's wild power
    Held sway o'er laws and rules and formal ties.

For hatred, snarling envy, what cared we?
    The columned forest was Love's citadel;
Your eyes were heaven — yes, all of heaven to me!
    Ah, had I dared to yield to their sweet spell!

The moment passed, swift as the currents flow.
    Your way you went, I mine; yet now and then
Rich music floats from out the long ago,
    And brings back all that moment's charm again.

TRUE KINGLINESS.

WHAT is a king without a kingly heart?
The gilded trappings never are a part
Of real majesty; 't is from the soul
Come light and power to dignify the whole.

At noonday, all unseen by mortal eye,
Great Sirius flames in yonder clear blue sky;
The clown has eyes but for the daylight's glare,
Yet that bright presence still is flaming there.

Heroic hearts, faint not if your brave deeds
A sullen world applauds not, — no, nor heeds.
Your work is good; 't will not be more or less
When crowned with that false gewgaw called success.

FONS ARETHUSÆ.

POUR forth, merry hearts, from the music within,
   A glee that shall ring to the sky!
That from forest and hill a rich answer shall win,
   And at last in pure melody die.

A louder strain yet! till the troubles of life
   Are all lost in the depths of your song;
Our souls keener grow for the world's bitter strife,
   And for battle with panoplied Wrong.

The song has been sung — Farewell to the hill,
   To the wood, and the waters dear;
The song has been sung, yet its music will thrill
   Through many a care-checkered year.

We stand by the motionless water that gleams
   Like a gem in its circlet of hills;
The moon in her cold, proud loveliness beams
   Enchanting, although she chills.

The last wheel spurning the frosty road,
   As a far-away echo we hear;
The window is dark in yon lonely abode,
   And silence is queen far and near.

What spirit is hid in the wood or the lake,
   In moonbeam or cloudlet or tree,
That can for worn hearts such a paradise make
   Where they rest all careless and free?

26

No longer the weight of our years we feel,
　The past is illumined with joy,
Whence only melodious memories steal,
　And the gray-beard sings like a boy.

SONG.

Has the Past faded like a flower
　Never to bloom again?
Nor yields it back one trancèd hour
　To art of lips or pen?

Sweet Love that laughed from those sweet eyes
　Has sought less chilly deeps;
And Passion, Love's most beauteous prize,
　Once more, all spellbound, sleeps.

Shall all that shining loveliness
　Be but Love's vacant throne?
Call back the exile, and confess
　The king shall have his own.

VERSES

WRITTEN IN ALFRED DE MUSSET'S POEMS.

A beaker of joy, by the gods!
　A dance of light, color, and bubble —
Drink! hopeless and spiritless clods!
Slaves fearful of prisons and rods —
　Here's a draught that will drown all your trouble!

Your life is but breath, nerve, and blood, —
　It creeps through the days like the snail;
'T is a current with never a flood, —
Withered stalk, without leafage or bud, —
　A voice that is only a wail!

Here's a life that has bloomed into flowers,
  That has sung itself into a song;
That made love to the coy, blushing Hours,
While its heart's blood poured out in rich showers
  Of nectar delicious and strong!

Who sits at the head of this feast,
  With the sweet tender eyes of the dove —
With a smile like the morn-jewelled east,
And a forehead that Time never creased?
  'T is Love! 't is all beautiful Love!

Ah, Time! sly impostor, avaunt!
  Not a scrap from this banquet is thine;
For tribute thou hast but a taunt,
Nor can thy dull scythe ever daunt
  A soul that's already divine!

Then drink — sad or merry heart — drink
  The soul-vintage sweet Love has distilled.
How the wild bubbles beckon and wink!
Ah, Love is life's life, I think —
  And with Love your life may be filled.

SERENADE.

Shine, gentle Queen of Night, oh, shine
    Upon the sparkling wave,
And shed as soft and clear a light
    As thy mild orb e'er gave.
Hushed be all sounds profane, as when
    In love-lit hours gone by,
The night heard but young Romeo's prayer
    And Juliet's answering sigh.

The trancèd lake, the dreaming wood,
    Wait for love's whispers now;
Ah, music hath no charm so deep
    As breathes in lover's vow.

Wake, sleeping flowers, and fragrance lend
   Unto the blissful hour,
Faint odors shed o'er lake and stream,
   O'er forest, hall, and bower.

Now plead, fond youth, thy hopeful cause
   With earnest lips and true,
While kind night hides the sweet girl's blush,
   She'll give the love that's due;
Her heart's dear secret whispered now
   Thy patient faith will bless —
And all the world seems filled with joy
   When sweet lips murmur, " Yes!"

A HOPELESS LOVER.

(AFTER SWINBURNE.)

WHAT is your charm, that thrills like subtle wine
Each glowing drop in this wild heart of mine?
Is it the symmetry of moulded limb,
The grace of form, the waist and ankle slim?
Is it those eyes, whose shy, seductive play
Leaves me uncertain if they're green or gray?
Is it that modest yet audacious mind,
That would be pure, but *will* not be kept blind,
That craves experience of good and ill,
Yet keeps its loyalty to virtue still?
God knows! *I* only know, whate'er it be,
It holds my heart-strings, yet is not for me!
     Whate'er it be,
     'Tis not for me!

Strange impulses I dare not even name —
That turn the tortured heart and brain to flame —
Draw me to you! Powers hellish or divine,
I'll worship if they will but make you mine!
Sweet eyes! lurk bliss or death in their clear deeps,
Downward all reckless my mad spirit leaps;

Yet I must never clasp that supple waist —
I swear 't was only made to be embraced! —
Nor drink in heaven from those dewy lips,
Not even touch with mine those finger-tips!
Ah, no! I feel my fate is but to be
Slave to a charm whose joy is not for me!
Whate'er it be,
'T is not for me!

A LAST FAREWELL.

I SEE the Morning, robed in sunlight, rise;
   Night's pain and sorrow can no longer stay.
The world, half waked, smiles to the smiling skies,
   And bends to catch the blessing of the Day.
Hope, Joy, and Youth are rulers of the hour,
And grand the music which proclaims their power;
But over all forever seems to swell
The endless anguish of a last farewell!
      Farewell! Farewell!

I hear the dashing of the joyful sea
   That sunward gayly flings its laughing waves;
The harbor and the ships resound with glee,
   And all is here that human comfort craves.
Sing, morning stars, and clap your hands, ye floods!
Breathe melody, ye happy flowers and buds!
But, hark! what means that sound, — a slow, deep knell!
The endless anguish of a last farewell.
      Farewell! Farewell!

Farewell! Great God! does tyrant Sadness rule
   The throne where Grace sits smiling to the world?
Is Death lord of sweet Spring and merry Yule,
   And has Christ's banner been in vain unfurled?
I cannot tell. Let others hope and gain;
Their song can never cheer this dull refrain.
Still in my ears there rings a funeral bell, —
The endless echo of a last farewell.
      Farewell! Farewell!

COMPRENEZ-VOUS?

WITHIN a quiet, star-lit bay,
A noble ship at anchor lay.

She seemed upon the wave to rest
Like a lover on his loved one's breast.

No sound save when her timely bell
In silvery tones said, "All is well!"

Beauty is there, on every hand,
Shining on sea and sky and land;

And Peace, with finger on her lip,
Guards tenderly the dreaming ship.

But, see! the Moon ascends her throne —
Among a myriad lights — alone!

And from the great ship's shadowing side
Mark you that shallop swiftly glide?

See you yon wooded shore where gleams
The moonlight over murmuring streams?

Hear you that voice, so sweet and low,
In witching music come and go?

And now the conscious woods confess
They hide a shape of loveliness

So radiant that the sober eye
Might deem it born of ecstasy!

If flesh and blood, give God the praise;
If stone, 't would Phidias' soul amaze!

But onward still the shallop glides;
The voice, the gleaming figure, guides.

And as in dread of starry skies,
Into the forest's shade it flies.

Safe from the moon, from watchful star,
The shallop goes, — who knows how far?

Yet from the lofty ship the bell,
In silvery tones, says, "All is well!"

And all is well! for Love is king
O'er shallop, ship, and everything!

SONG.

As yon soft star of the west
     Is glassed in the wide-rushing stream,
So *your* sweet image doth rest,
     Like light in the depth of my dream!

And it shines, though the wintry blast
     Comes shrieking from Arctic wilds —
And still, though the sky is o'ercast,
     My heart is a sleeping child's.

Then, beloved, withdraw not your light;
     Come near to me, nearer still,
Till, safe in your beauty's might,
     I may nestle and fear no ill!

THE MUSHROOM.

DEAR child of tearful Night, pale as the star
     Chased from yon sky by all-triumphant Morn,
     Who, fired by loftier hates, looks but in scorn
At thee, as on he speeds his glowing car —
Thy hour now comes! When votaries from afar
     Come chanting loud, "The feast is but forlorn
     Which, sprite of savor! thou wilt not adorn;"
While Luxury hails her last-found Avatar!

Woe to the churl who thoughtlessly shall tread
 Thy tender *laminæ* beneath his heel;
For him no bounteous table shall be spread,
 No pungent relish glorify his meal;
But Taste's rare joys make that man half divine
Who bows, imperial Fungus, at thy shrine.

ODE.

Class Supper, H. U., June 25, 1878.

Though youth may be waning and joys taking flight,
The warmth of old friendships will cheer us to-night.
True hearts that we leaned on in life's beaming morn,
  We trust in you still!
  For nothing can chill
The love of youth's fervor and purity born.

With Hope's banners streaming we marched to the fray;
Those banners droop, tattered and war-worn, to-day.
But courage, companions! our swords must not rust —
  Though human endeavor,
  Unaided, fails ever,
Our triumph is sure, for in God is our trust.

Crown Mem'ry with garlands! for, won by her wile,
The Past, robbed of darkness, shines out like a smile;
Roll back, frowning years, all your grief and your care!
  Each soul, now set free,
  Fills night with its glee,
And burns with new courage to do and to dare.

What proofs must we bring this rich welcome to win?
A sword bright with triumph o'er baseness and sin,
A name from whose lustre Shame turns its dark face —
  And *thy* service, Duty,
  Clothe each life with beauty,
And shed o'er our meeting the light of true grace!

MAJOR HENRY LIVERMORE ABBOTT.

Killed in the Battle of the Wilderness, 1864.

So " Little " Abbott 's gone ! — he fell
   With three great wounds upon his breast;
His pure, brave life deserveth well
   The hero's fame, the Christian's rest !
He died as he had wished to die,
   Amid the battle's fiercest glare, —
His faint ear caught the victor's cry,
   His pale lips murmured words of prayer.

He whispered, very near the end :
   " My poor, brave fellows who are slain
Left dear ones, — whom the Lord defend ! —
   All that I leave shall be their gain."
Yes, kind and tender through the past,
   So kind and tender was he still,
When Death's grim shade loomed o'er him vast,
   And strove his generous heart to chill.

In college Henry was our pet,
   The love of all seemed but his due ;
The lines 'twixt this or t' other set
   His loving, catholic heart ne'er knew,
The light of his sweet, happy eyes
   Our silent, dark old rooms made bright ;
His song, his laugh, his quick replies,
   Gladdened us many a frolic night.

Again I see him on the shore
   When Harvard's red-caps lead the race ;
His shout rings high above the roar,
   A smile breaks o'er his stern white face ;
Through every rigid feature gleams
   Heroic purpose, hid till then
By boyish graces, and he seems
   A man to govern warlike men.

Let others tell in lofty strain
  The matchless valor of the dead, —
Pluck honors from the fatal plain,
  And bind them round his sleeping head;
For not so grand he seems to me
  In bloody field or foray wild,
As when he stoops upon his knee,
  And seeks to soothe a crying child.

Bury him by his brother Ned,
  Who fell at luckless Cedar Hill;
Together were the heroes bred,
  Together let them slumber still.
High on the list of Harvard's slain
  Their spotless names shall proudly stand.
Thank God, their blood's not shed in vain;
  That precious blood redeems our land.

POEM

WRITTEN FOR THE SEMI-CENTENNIAL OF THE UNITARIAN SOCIETY
OF LOWELL, 1879.

TELL me, pray, why commemorate this day?
Is it because the swift years speed away?
Why, Man has babbled since he first had speech
Of that dark Angel, whom no prayers can reach,
No tears can stay.   Time, in his dreadful wrath
O'er man and all his works, hath made his path:
Did *he* not drag him from his heavenly place,
The curse, Mortality, stamped on his face?

Yet somehow, after lapse of humdrum years,
Marked but by petty joys or petty fears,
The commonplaces make a total grand,
As some event that saves, or wrecks, a land.
We hear a challenge — like a trumpet's blare —
Ring out a sharp, imperious, "Who goes there?"
And to an unseen sentry we relate
Our humble story up, or down, to date.

Thus we have met to talk about a church
That did not for too high a mission search ;
But, planted mid the sons of daily toil,
Labored to soothe and soften life's turmoil.
And, Truth ! she shrank not from thy form,
Though armed with Death and throned upon the storm.
To purify, to strengthen, and to cheer, —
These were the objects that this church held dear.
No specious arts were used to fill the pews,
No tricks or wiles to cozen or amuse ;
The creed was brief, and all its meanings plain,
Nor did it after ponderous mysteries strain :
With countless tenets Faith it did not flood,
Nor make the Christian thirst for Christian blood.
Good-will to men, and with the will, the deed, —
Trust in a Father's love, — there 's all the creed ;
Not with your lips, but in your lives, you prove
That you are servants of a God of love.
Lessons were failures, if the lessons taught
No gracious influence on the conduct wrought.
Faith leaned, at first, on Reason's mighty strength ;
But that strength failed, and so sweet Faith at length,
When ways grew dark, led her companion on,
And ever through the gloom her bright face shone.

But I must pause, and straight invoke a Muse, —
To seem a poet, I dare not refuse
To use the poet's fashion, and ask aid
Of some kind genius or celestial maid.
Ah, here 's the river ! — none a Muse shall lack
Who dwells along thy shore, sweet Merrimack !
Hunt's Falls — I wish I knew thy Indian name,
For such wild waters ours is very tame —
I mark thy stream, where Dracut's wooded height
Rises, with proud October's glories bright ;
You wooded isles, — I see the waving trees,
And hear their murmurs borne on every breeze.
Oh, bring, bright river, from you snowy hills
The gentle music of thy thousand rills ;

There's poetry in every ripple,—yes,
The stream that turns the factory-wheel may bless
The saddened heart of many a lonely girl,
Her cheerless toil pursuing in the whirl.
Then softly flow, and, rising from thy flood,
Let deep-toned harmonies fill vale and wood,
And, mingling with this graceless song of mine,
Give just a hint of melody divine.

'Tis well, perhaps, that I should something say
About the temple where you meet to pray.
A gray old pile, with ivy overgrown,
An air of by-gone days on every stone;
Rich, pictured windows, where some grim old saint
Scowls at the sunbeam peeping through his paint;
A bran-new Reredos, made to look as though
Some monk had wrought it centuries ago;
Memorial tablets, showing how the rich
May put a scoundrel in a saintly niche, —
Those upright slabs that downright stories tell,
How this man went to heaven, who went — oh, well —
No matter — *Requiescat*, anyway,
But, blest or not, we're blest if we can say.
A bell, that gossip-like will wag its tongue,
When one is married, or another hung;
Groined arches, sounding back the solemn strain
Of *Dies Iræ* wrung from hearts in pain;
Candles, gay altars, altar-cloths of gold,
And all such potent aids to faith grown cold.
For such a church as *this*, go look elsewhere;
Ours is a very modest house of prayer.

Our church is like Mohammed's coffin fixed
Somehow, somewhere, the heavens and earth betwixt,
Or hung like Brunelleschi's dome, in air,
Roofless and baseless — and the walls are bare;
Below, the eager tradesman bows and grins:
Who knows just where the House of God begins?

Ah! though our mansion's in, or near, the skies,
Our title's not so clear to careful eyes;
But rights we have in that brick building there,
And Hosford's bound to keep it in repair.

Shall I tell off the bead-roll of our saints,
Men whose pure lives seemed free from mortal taints?
No! should I call these good men from the tomb,
The world would cry, " Some politician's boom!"
Let their bright names illuminate our hearts,
But spare them from the vulgar's envious darts;
Rascals may buy false praises without stint,
But good men seek not to appear in print.
Let fools and knaves exult in purchased fame,
But why should *we* such doubtful honors claim?

There are too many churches, — where's the sense,
Or piety, in all this vain pretence?
What empty pews, what pastors poorly paid?
Why should the pew-rent be so long delayed?
These tabernacles are but homes of debt,
And bankrupts in their bankrupt churches fret:
God asks no borrowed temples, — how can you
Discourse, good parson, on the maxim true,
"Owe no man anything," when each one knows
The church's creditor will soon foreclose?
My friends, why are these sanctuaries built?
To lead to virtue and to cleanse from guilt?
Oh, no! for see, in this degraded age,
The pulpit's turned into a *vaudeville* stage!
Weak natures madly love, or madly hate;
They know no midway, reasonable state;
Excitement they must have, but when and where
Their pastor, cracked or selfish, must declare.
Of all the knaves that do the world befog,
The vilest is the pulpit demagogue.
Well, let us pause, it takes too long to tell
The story through, and we must say farewell.

Young church! with all thy fifty years, still young, —
Long as pure prayers are said, or sweet hymns sung,
Thy work continue, and the world still bless
With the clear radiance of thy righteousness;
Uplift men's hearts and purify their lives, —
For 't is the only way religion thrives.
And this great truth let all thy history tell:
Who serves Mankind doth serve his Master well.

A POEM

DELIVERED BEFORE THE HIGH SCHOOL ASSOCIATION, 1863.

OFT has the old earth beaten round the sun,
    And into new years borne its human freight,
Since we the world's rough pilgrimage begun,
    And left behind our boyhood's happy state.

How often since, when full of doubt and fear,
    Vexed by the stinging cares that harass men,
We 've paused awhile from our dull labor here,
    And lived in fancy boyhood's life again!

When, to the sounds of Virgil's graceful lyre,
    Our gamesome spirits danced a giddy round,
Or, in the rapture loftier strains inspire,
    We trod in triumph Homer's sacred ground!

How oft have we, stretched dreaming on the grass,
    Sailed with the Ithacan o'er whitening seas,
Struck with the Spartan at the bloody pass,
    And clutched the trophies of Miltiades!

So blessed those days the world to us appeared,
    The bright Atlantis of the sage's dream;
Nor war, nor woe, nor care, we ever feared,
    But Love and Poesy were all supreme.

Strong hands that then our faltering steps did guide
    Have long since mouldered into primal dust;
Brave hearts lie pulseless, — hearts so true and tried —
    On which we leant with perfect childlike trust.

The sweet young hopes that nestled in our hearts,
  Scared by the rude world's din, have ta'en their flight;
Cold Wisdom now her dear-bought lore imparts,
  And sweeps wild Fancy's vision from the sight.

Those burning inspirations of our youth,
  That flashed their splendor on our ardent souls,
The high, chivalric love of Fame and Truth,
  Now with sharp bit stern Selfishness controls.

Fled are the dreams of peace enjoyed of yore,
  The sullen war-drums sound on every hand,
And, spreading on from farthest shore to shore,
  The smoke of battle deepens o'er the land.

Yet, mid the strife that shakes the frighted world,
  Where naught we hear but cannon's deafening play,
And clang of squadron against squadron hurled,
  O'er one spot still doth sweet Peace hold her sway.

And as the praying Hebrew's face doth look
  Still to the city of his fathers' God,
So have our eyes that temple ne'er forsook
  Beneath whose porch our early footsteps trod.

To-night, then, comrades, shall our hearts rejoice,
  Our weary feet no farther now shall roam;
For, with a sweet persuasion in her voice,
  The yearning mother calls her children home.

And now that here, beneath one roof,
  First for long years we've met together,
Let's see how each young fledgeling looks,
  Now that he's blooming in full feather.

  And which one shall we first select,
    And in our chair of state enthrone him?
  Why, him who's called the Ladies' Man,
    Though ne'er a lady cares to own him!
  This is our Lowell Turveydrop,
    Our model of genteel deportment,

And when he walks our city streets,
   Be sure there's something more than sport meant!
Yet though his life may seem serene,
   And though he's blest with health and riches,
He suffers great vicissitudes,
   At least in hats and coats and breeches.
O wind that from old Concord blows,
   Sweet are the tidings thou hast wafted!
Relief thou'st brought to every heart, —
   The city swell at length is drafted!

Then here's our youthful pedagogue,
   The darling of our fond old mother;
She proudly holds him up to sight,
   And, crowing asks you, "Where's the other?"
Yes, here's our Classic Lexicon,
   In size so small — though let none mock it! —
'T is just the sort of handy book
   A man can carry in his pocket!

Here comes our military swell —
   The fair ones say we must bring him in! —
Who's done less harm to Southern foes
   Than to the hearts of Northern women!
With gay-plumed hat and jingling spurs,
   Of admiration what a glutton!
Then o'er his lengthy person mark
   The omnipresent lace and button.
But, maiden! fix your heart elsewhere,
   Or sad will be your young life's story! —
For, as he says, like Swedish Charles,
   His wife is War, his mistress Glory!
And yet, where'er our hero goes,
   The am'rous furor still increases;
A crash of breaking hearts is heard,
   And prudent cries of "Save the pieces!"

Many there are of our old friends
   We cannot pause to even mention,

Yet our prospective parson might
    Claim some small share of our attention.
How sad his life, his mind alway
    Perplexed by Buckle or Colenso;
And still, as each foe flies, he swears
    He 'll ne'er be taken in again so!
Then, too, he 's filled with strange desires —
    For which he 'll scarce get absolution —
To write his sermons with a sword,
    Or teach a cannon elocution.

Nor can we pass without a word
    Our school's most puissant debater;
Compared with Fox or Cicero,
    Why, he 's Hyperion to a Satyr!
Possessed of great command of words,
    His power he sternly exercises, —
Poor thoughts decks out in tinselled words,
    Like fools in masquerade disguises;
And when he 's in his element —
    That 's when the Y. M. I.'s in session —
You 'd think he 'd been to Babel, sure,
    To learn the art of clear expression!

Some that I 've named are dullards, p'r'aps; but know
The brave old school far nobler sons can show.
Go back with me a few short months or more,
Ere victory's blaze had spread from shore to shore,
Ere broken was the haughty Southron's might,
Nor Meade's proud name had leapt into the light.
Look on the land — what doth your dim eyes greet,
But wild confusion, shame, and black defeat?
See where dark Rappahannock's turbid flood
Runs darker with the flow of Northern blood —
And on the sad wind near and nearer comes
The stern defiance of the rebel drums!
Look farther still, and strain the aching eye.
What! naught of comfort do you yet descry?
Oh, yes; for there upon the Southern shore,

27

Through the dun cloud of struggling flame and smoke
That o'er the horrid prospect throws his cloak,
Flashing like meteor through the murky night,
We catch the flutter of a pennon bright,
And borne upon the south wind now we hear,
There comes a faint, far distant shout of cheer.
That thrilling shout bids good men hope anew;
That pennon bears, thank God! the colors true.
Though Treason fell without her walls may prey,
Imperial Orleans owns our Butler's sway!
When sad Mischance on all our steps did wait,
His strong arm still upheld the falling state;
With Hastings' vigor, free from Hastings' crime,
He shone our only hope in that dark time!
And let Detraction howl its vile throat hoarse,
Lean Envy on him waste its puny force,
Indignant Honor shields the hero's form,
And Fame's clear trump rings o'er the petty storm.

Once more look to the pleasant South,
    And mark that mustering host,
The flower of all the Northern land, —
    Your own New England's boast!
Oh, blithe their hearts when sweet and clear
    The morning bugles blew,
When glancing bright in the gladsome light
    Their victor eagles flew!
Hope lit their eyes as then they turned
    Their faces to the foe,
And while their firm tread shook the earth,
    Their song was Southward ho!
The day is spent, their march is done,
    The camp is sunk in sleep,
Save where the wearied sentinels
    Their lonely vigils keep;
And midnight now has thrown o'er earth
    Its blackest funeral pall,
When on the drowsy picket's ear
    Doth a faint, far murmur fall.

'T was not, he knew, the distant sweep
    Of Shenandoah's rill,
Nor the wind's low sigh, through the cedars high,
    That crown the frowning hill:
No! 't was the tread of a mighty host,
    That winds adown the hill;
And a score of quick shots follow fast
    His challenge sharp and shrill.
Then through the sleeping camp ring out
    The alarming bugle-notes,
And hear the answering yell that bursts
    From a myriad rebel throats!
How dauntless is the Northern heart,
    How strong the Northern hand,
Say ye who have seen the Northmen wield
    The deadly battle-brand;
Who 've heard their stern, exultant shout
    When front to foe they stood;
Who 've seen their thirsty bayonets drink
    The traitor's Southern blood;
Who 've seen, too, when, by hot-brained men
    To shameful slaughter led,
How lustre e'en o'er black defeat
    Their desperate valor shed, —
Seen them hurl back the invading foe
    Again and yet again!
Say ye, I pray, what lion hearts
    Are borne by Northern men!
Yet though the Northern arm 's so strong,
    The Northern heart 's so high,
Those arms were weak, those hearts were chilled.
    When pealed that hellish cry,
And down upon them bore the foe,
    Shouting their slogan wild,
Led by that chief whose whispered name
    Will still the Northern child!
Yet one young heart stood firmly then,
    Nor harbored doubts or fears,
And still as higher, higher rose
    Wild shrieks and maddening cheers,

And dreadful clash of meeting steel,
   And cannon's deepening roll
Felt but the rapture music stirs
   Ever in heroic soul!
And where the Southron hardest pressed,
   Upon the bloodiest ground
Caught in the battle's wildest whirl,
   There was our chieftain found.
And when the noise of battle ceased
   Throughout that fatal vale,
And on the wind the Southern drums
   In deepening distance fail;
And when, as, shocked at that sad sight,
   Slow came the shuddering day,
There, foremost in the files of dead,
   The youthful leader lay!
And long as minstrel note shall swell
   With godlike deeds of arms,
Long as the love of native land
   One patriot bosom warms,
So long his story shall be told,
   To thrill the youthful breast,
So long by fervent lips shall be
   The name of *Abbott* blest!

If we look round on those who throng this place,
We miss, alas! full many a well-known face.
Yes! hands that once sweet friendship's grasp but knew,
Now clutch the bayonet moist with bloody dew;
Voices so gentle and benign of yore,
Shout battle-cries above the cannon's roar;
These friends we may not meet to-night, but still
We've sent to them our message of good-will;
And while, dear friends, all gathered here we stand,
Their cheery answer rings across the land, —

   "Comrades! we send you cheer
   From the war-ground black and drear,
Where we lie and watch the camp-fire's dying embers;

And oh, would that we might stand
With our old friends, hand in hand,
For the soldier still his golden youth remembers!

Swift the months have sped along,
Since we marched, a thousand strong,
From the homes where peace and quiet ever slumber.
But how warm would be our thanks,
If from out our death-thinned ranks
We could count a paltry third of that brave number!

"Yet whisper not of rest!
For till Treason stands confessed,
Let the battle-bugle trumpet forth its clearest.
Though the fair-faced earth be stained
With the ruddy life-drops drained
From the manly hearts you cherish as your dearest!

Still let your hearts not faint,
Nor your voices make complaint,
Nor with Treason, though triumphant, ever palter!
But let the guilty fear,
For the righteous blood is dear
To the God whose arm will help us if we falter!

"And although sweet thoughts of home
Ever haunt us as we roam,
Still our hearts are blithe when 'Forward!' is the order;
And to crush the rebel foe,
Still our feet must Southward go,
Till our flag flies o'er the dear land's farthest borders!"

Think not my feeble song has dwelt too long on warlike
    themes;
Nor chide if its rude, loose-strung notes disturb your peaceful
    dreams.
For cold or false that heart must be that feels no joyous glow,
When Pennsylvania's daughters chant deliverance from the
    foe;

When 'neath its glorious burden faints the glad wind from the
    West,
That tells us loyal arms at length have lowered proud Vicks-
    burg's crest!
Yet think not ye who wield the pen, or ye who hold the
    plough,
That Honor's blushing wreath falls but upon the warrior's
    brow.
Your strength's been felt in every blow struck on the bloody
    field;
Your spirit's fired each gallant charge 'neath which the foe
    hath reeled!
'T is you who have those trusty blades beat out from metal
    true.
Yes! if our warriors battle well, their armorers are *you!*
While they have fought, your toil has reaped rich harvest from
    the land,
Your glaring workshops' ceaseless hum been heard on every
    hand!
Your argosies make all our ports gay as a poet's dream,
And every sea upon the globe reflects your pennon's gleam!
You've kept the nation in the van of that grand race that's
    run,
And will be, by mankind through time, till God's whole will
    be done!
And still there's work true arms to nerve, and loyal hearts to
    rouse,
To see no bastard Peace shall e'er write shame upon your
    brows —
We meet, my friends, in stormy times, yet for at least one
    night
Shut out whate'er we see of dark, let in but what is bright;
And ere from out our Mother's sight again we take our
    way,
Our prayers the Father shall besiege to haste that happier
    day,
When war's wild scenes, that fright us now, shall be but
    memories dear,
To stir the patriot's soul to fire, or claim the patriot's tear,

When muskets rest upon the wall, stout warriors guide the
   plough,
And baby hands belabor drums that beat to battle now;
When shot-torn banners that of old streamed in the battle's
   breath
Shall mouldering hang from chapel-roofs in stillness deep as
   death;
When Peace and Honor may at length go smiling hand in
   hand,
And Nature hide with sweet spring flowers the blood-stains on
   the land!

ODE

For the Class of 1860, L. H. S.

WHEN yon sun shall have sunk in the gold-veinèd west,
   Our band will be scattered and fled!
And with sad, solemn thoughts swells the heart in each breast,
   As we think o'er the days that are dead:
Brightest days of our youth! greenest isle in life's stream,
   Where like fairies sweet memories dwell,
And their soft voices, calling, float near when we dream,
   Like the charm of a far-distant bell!

As the days and the months and the years swiftly sped,
   And the hour of our parting drew nigh,
Brighter beams in our hearts friendship's sun richly shed,
   As it shone in the cloud-covered sky;
And still, as old time shall unceasingly run,
   And our future be wed with the past,
May the glories that stream from that ne'er-dying sun
   Burn brighter and clearer at last!

In the bloom of our youth we are gathered to-day,
   And the hopes in our souls are yet green!
While the light of our joy round the future doth play,
   And no shadow throws gloom o'er the scene:

Yet in moments of joy, in our frolicsome glee,
    When unshaken and fresh in our trust,
We shall cherish in memory those we but see
    In the flowers that spring from their dust!

From the reverend walls that have sheltered us long,
    We slowly and mournfully go!
And we hear the old echoes wake forth into song,
    With a melody plaintive and low:
While the magical music floats soft to our ears,
    And a tear-drop bedims every eye,
We will part who 've been banded together for years,
    And repeat a last solemn "Good-by!"

APPENDIX.

APPENDIX.

———◆———

A CONFERENCE OF NEW ENGLAND GOVERNORS.

WRITTEN FOR THE "NORTH AMERICAN REVIEW."

SOME time ago it was intimated by me that an informal, business-like conference of New England governors should be held to consider what steps were expedient or necessary for the preservation and advancement of the interests of all New England. The suggestion thus put forward had not been reduced to shape or proportion, nor were the limits, scope, and purpose of the scheme at all distinctly defined. As neither time nor opportunity has been given for the present realization of this project, it may not be out of place to answer the inquiry as to what purpose and advantage would be subserved by such a proceeding as that suggested.

I shall therefore, as plainly and concisely as possible, state what there was in the proposition as it presented itself in its somewhat crude and undefined form. At the outset I may say that it seems difficult to imagine what possible objection within any sort of reasonable limit could be offered to this suggestion, allowing always for the usual mild alarm which is excited by any novel idea in the minds of the "Forcible Feebles" of newspaper or political circles. To such minds the mere suggestion of such a conference brings up fantastic visions of evil portent. They imagine they see the mysterious John Henry, of Montreal, who during the long embargo attempted to create a feeling of disloyalty in New England towards the Union; the gloomy and sinister figure of Aaron Burr, with his schemes of personal empire, his dark conspiracies, his implacable revenges, rises in all the vast and terrible proportions of Milton's Satan; and inevitably and as a matter of course, the Hartford Convention, the stock *bête noir* of Democratic imagination, again assembles the members of its "infernal court" which, according to ancient Republican nursery tales, was plotting to erect the "Kingdom of New England" with a monarch chosen after the most approved *opera-bouffe* principles.

It may be that comments like those referred to are in the nature of *persiflage* and are not meant to be taken seriously, and it is true that the jests emanating from the class of minds alluded to are so often clothed with solemnity and their serious thoughts so often attired in farcical garb that it becomes difficult to decide what the true intent of the authors is, or whether they have any intent at all. But in answer to all questions and comments which may appear to be worthy of serious consideration, I present the following suggestions relative to the propriety and expediency of a business-like, informal conference of New England governors.

This is the day of organization, of united, collective action, in every line and branch of human industry, effort, action, and thought. The world is learning every day the value and efficiency of union, of consolidation, of the marshalling and massing of forces, for the attainment of any given object, for the preservation of any right or advantage. We have organization, united action, in every direction. Everywhere we find organization in business; of capital, manifested in trusts, syndicates, corporations, pools, combinations, many of them beneficial, and many oppressive and illegal; organizations of labor, forming all kinds of combinations under all sorts of names, — trades-unions, knights, brotherhoods, orders, federations, leagues, lodges, guilds, fraternities. "The butcher, the baker, the candlestick-maker," the doctor, the lawyer, the plumber, the railroad man, the grocer, the soldier, the sailor, — all of them, rich and poor, great and small, appear to have decided to "get together," and to move, not independently and individually, but in masses, by hundreds and thousands, and in very much larger numbers. We have also an infinite variety and number of social and political, as well as business, organizations. City solicitors, bar associations, county commissioners, mayors and ex-mayors, alumni and alumnæ of school, college, and academy, boards of trade of city county, and State, agricultural societies of county, State, New England, and the United States.

The conference and convention are then the ordinary and natural implements employed by the civilization of to-day. It is far more ordinary and natural to employ them than not to employ them. If the mayors of Massachusetts' cities were to hold a conference, in such a time as the present, to discuss methods of relief, of furnishing employment, of dealing with pauperism and crime, of the best system of lighting the streets or of conveying away the sewerage, of meeting pestilence or diminishing taxes, it would probably be admitted that little harm and much good might result. As a conference of mayors might be productive of beneficial results, it would seem as if a conference of governors need not be fraught with peril or evil consequences. As the next larger circle beyond the town or city is the county, and the next beyond that the commonwealth, so by natural and regular gradation or expansion the town or city organization widens into the county organization, and this last becomes in its turn a constituent part of the State organization; and the widest and fullest development of any organization in any of the six New England States is found in New England itself, which has all the elements of oneness contributed by climate, history, and situation, by affinities, habits, pursuits, and interests. And so potent have these factors of unity been that from the beginning the States of New England, both as originally constituted and as existing now, have, in a great majority of cases, acted as a unit, political, industrial, or otherwise.

In the early days of the republic, when interest and sentiment were in an inchoate, if not chaotic, state, the instinct of self-preservation prompted the most jealous watchfulness on the part of one section, or one locality, toward another and every other. The early struggle to maintain and preserve the Union from the time of the adoption of the Constitution to the year 1812 was as heroic as the struggle for Independence or the war for the preservation of the Union. The War of 1812, even though it brought out at times warm sectional feeling, finally cemented and secured the Union. But the men of New England, and particularly of Massachusetts, were constantly on

the alert to detect and resist any hostile combination or any
effort to diminish their influence or prestige in the Union.
Their territory was small, and geographically or politically
more segregated from the bulk of the national territory than
any other portion. For a long period the people had lived, as
Palfrey says, "in remarkable seclusion from other communities."
They were wonderfully homogeneous, and of high and, what is
more, of equal, social grade, and the whole community was
marked by uniformity of character and purpose, which made
New England the great force in the establishment of the United
States and in its subsequent career. The people were accustomed to act together from the first. In 1643 the four
colonies of Massachusetts, Plymouth, Connecticut, and New
Haven formed a league called "The United Colonies of New
England." These little States contained thirty-nine towns and
24,000 people; and the union, rude as it was, proved of great
value in the Indian wars which were soon to follow.

In 1773 Massachusetts, representing New England, came
into close political sympathy with Virginia; and New England and Virginia led the way to the triumph of liberty and
independence in 1783. After the formation of the Union the
"balance of power" was to be preserved. Everything in the
situation had been carefully weighed and measured, before
the Union was consummated: population, territorial area, geo-
graphical situation, wealth, and opportunities for future development. The purchase of Louisiana in 1804 occasioned
much distrust and complaint on the part of New England.
Already the united South had attained an influence in the
national councils fraught with danger to New England. There
were 840,000 slaves in the South, and fifteen votes were given
to that section on account of this part of the population. Even
then the so-called "negro vote" (which was *not* a negro vote)
had been sufficient to secure legislation injurious to New England, and had practically determined the presidential election
of 1801. Massachusetts went so far as to propose an amendment to the Constitution to correct this system of representation, but it was not adopted. In 1808, while the "long embargo"
was still in force, and the "Force Act" was exciting indignation
and resistance throughout New England, a call for a convention

of the New England States was formally issued. It was the firm stand of New England at this time which contributed largely to the passage of the act lifting the embargo, which act was signed by Jefferson March 1, 1809.

The Hartford Convention was held in December, 1814; but as the war soon terminated, and the rights of New England did not suffer in the settlement, the proceedings of that convention proved to be of no lasting importance, except in the minds of strong political partisans, who invest the doings and purposes of that body with a significance and complexion not borne out by evidence or history.

And so from time to time the action and influence of New England have been exerted for the preservation of her rights and interests, and without injury or menace to any other portion of the country. The conference at Altoona in 1862 was a notable instance. To-day New England is practically a unit — political, social, and industrial — but her interests are those of the country at large; she is at the head of the procession, not in the way of it. New York, Pennsylvania, Ohio, New Jersey, and all the industrial States of the Union are in full sympathy with New England to-day upon all the great political and economic questions at issue, and they will welcome her leadership in these matters instead of disputing it.

It is apparent, then, that throughout her history New England has been a powerful factor in national affairs, and in the protection of her rights and interests by acting as a unit; that New England is the natural, convenient, and effective consolidation of the interests and purposes of the several States within her limits; that by reason of her enlightenment, her experience, her devotion to the best interests of the whole country, her success in business, in industry, and in commerce, her educational and charitable institutions, in short by reason of everything which tends to develop, to strengthen, to adorn a State and to promote the happiness and prosperity of the citizen, New England is entitled to the respect and consideration of other States and sections of the country.

But there are dangerous influences and tendencies at work to-day which bode no good to the country. The conservative influences and tendencies of New England should be expressed in every reasonable and intelligent manner. When Caliban rises to threaten the country with crude and reckless theories of business and finance, it is time that the beneficent powers of Prospero should be brought into play. New England has two claims entitling her to be heard: she is most deeply interested in good money and good business; and she has had more experience and presumably has more knowledge in these things than the people of any other equal area in the United States. As regards all the prejudice which may seem to exist against her in some quarters of the country, the depth or sincerity of this prejudice may fairly be suspected because it is contradicted by many honest and genuine tributes of respect which are unmistakably offered to her by imitation of her institutions, her customs, and her methods. As for Massachusetts, she enjoys the loyal respect and love of her sister-States of New England to a most remarkable and gratifying degree. There is a warm sisterly feeling among the States of New England, and not the slightest symptom of envy, jealousy, or uncharitableness, from one to another, so far as my personal observation or information goes.

The questions of raising a revenue or of preserving a correct money standard are not the only questions before the people, though they may be of the first magnitude. There are other important problems which are to be considered and solved. Uniformity in many lines of legislation is important, — uniformity in industrial conditions as affected by legislation, in railroad management, in sanitary regulations, in marriage and divorce, in the laws relating to wills, deeds, etc., in the laws relating to elections, to civil and criminal jurisdiction or administration, and in many other matters.

There happen to be six Republican governors in New England at present. This has not always been the case; and as Maine, New Hampshire, Massachusetts, Rhode Island, and Connecticut have sometimes chosen governors of other political parties, the unanimity of sentiment manifested by the present state of things might serve to promote an important object of the proposed conference, which was to impress the members of the national legislature with the wide-spread opposition to radical legislation in financial or industrial affairs.

In 1890 the population of New England was 4,700,745. The value of its manufactures in 1880 was $1,106,158,303, and the total value of manufactures in the United States was $5,369,579,191, from which it will be seen that New England produced more than one-fifth of the entire value of the product of the whole country. The great State of New York, with a population of 5,981,934 (an excess of 1,281,389 over that of New England) has manufactures to the value of $1,080,696,596, or about $26,000 less than the total value of manufactures in New England. It will be seen, therefore, that New England is as deeply interested in industrial matters or in legislation bearing upon industrial interests as any equal area of territory in the country.

A conference of the chief magistrates of these New England States, a comparison of rules and methods, a discussion of popular and legislative tendencies, of popular and legislative needs or desires, of executive and legislative business and the methods of performing it, might and ought to be as productive of beneficial results as similar conferences of business, political, or social organizations, and it is possible that in critical times the united efforts or influence of the governors of New England might suffice to turn the scale of political or industrial action.

FREDERIC T. GREENHALGE.

PRACTICAL POLITICS.

WRITTEN FOR THE "NORTH AMERICAN REVIEW."

THE practical politician is the necessary outcome of practical politics as we find them to-day. A general understanding of the character of the practical politician is therefore indispensable in the consideration of what practical politics are, and what they ought to be. And we must recognize the fact that the practical politician even now has his uses and his merits as well as his vices and his defects.

He is loyal, diligent, indefatigable in the support of his party and its candidates. The genuine practical politician never bolts the ticket, and he never forgets or forgives the man who does. He is versed in all the learning of political mechanism; he knows just when a caucus is to be held, what States hold elections in any particular year, what majorities were given at this or that election, what "out" there is in any candidate.

If any question of principle arises, he refers glibly to the last party platform; that is his Bible, gospel, and law. In fact, he looks upon principle as a kind of imposture which it may be necessary to employ, — not, however, for the wise and intelligent, but for the ignorant mass which is to be cajoled and taken in.

As I have said, he is loyal in a certain sense and to a certain degree. He is a Dugald Dalgetty enlisted for the campaign; he is, as the lawyers might say, true *ad litem*. He has an inexorable rule by which he can determine whether a public man is politically dead or politically very much alive and at the front, or, as he would say, "on top." He is present at all political gatherings of his own party, and sometimes at those of the other parties. Neither rain, nor heat, nor business, nor family cares, ever prevent him from being on hand

APPENDIX. 435

where any political business is to be transacted. In his moral character he ranks well with the average of mankind. He is, as a rule, neither licentious nor intemperate. His views of principle in ordinary affairs of life do not apply to the business of politics. His justification of questionable transactions brought up to him for discussion by his wife and daughters is that such matters do not fall within the realm of ordinary moral rules; they belong to the mysterious domain of politics.

He comes to think that he makes and unmakes political careers and political reputations; that, after all, he is the main-spring, the force and the regulator of the body politic — to which term he gives a much narrower meaning than the true one. He reverences the machine, because he regards himself as the machine, or as a large part of it; he loves details — he is a detail himself. Principles — great movements of the people — a candidate who has shot into the firmament like a new star, without having been put there, and lighted like a lamp, these things disconcert and irritate him. The " slate " is more important to him than *Magna Charta* or any conceivable constitution. The " slate " must not be imperilled by revolutionary forces. And he says, in the spirit of Louis XIV. : " The Slate, it is I." He relies greatly upon what he calls the " farmer vote," the " soldier vote," the " labor vote," etc., and can tell you exactly and precisely why a candidate will or will not get one or the other of these class votes, which he firmly believes are always cast *en bloc.* He cannot realize the inherent independence and power of reasoning of thousands of soldiers, farmers, or workingmen.

He is a profound believer in thaumaturgy, in *coups d'état*, in surprises. He says : " Wait, wait; this campaign is young yet; something will drop — about — let me see — well, about six — no, five days from now." He always has the air of accurate calculation, of guarded and judicial statement; he is a Delphic oracle, able to prove himself an infallible prophet, whatever happens.

He regards the giving of his vote as a personal favor to be returned by personal favors. A public official who distributes offices among his personal friends and relations, he considers

worthy of all commendation. " Why should n't a man stick
by his friends — why should n't he help his family ? This
method of dealing with the public service is an evidence of a
noble and generous heart. " Family and friends are realities.
The state, the country, the public ? These are mere " platform "
words and are not real entities.

The type of practical politician now under consideration is
a " professional, " living for politics and living out of politics.
He does much political work, but only on the *quid pro quo*
principle. " The laborer is worthy of his hire, " he says with
great gusto, for he loves to defend his position by scriptural
quotations. He must be " recognized, " and he is eager to
point out to the raw recruit also that for everything *he* does,
he must be " recognized. " He loves to go to some young
patriot burning with devotion to his state or his city, who has
swept the corrupt element of a convention like chaff before the
Sirocco-like wind of his scorching invective, and whisper to
him that the reform nominee is bound to give him such and
such a place, " because you made his nomination possible. "

But with all his faults, his follies, his amusing characteristics, it must be remembered that he is a *constant force.* He
never lets anything go by default. He is, indeed, a machine,
tireless, fearless, conscienceless, and remorseless — at least in
his own sphere of action.

He insists upon the unreality of things. A is popular and
always commands applause. To make B " popular, " all that
is necessary is to furnish the applause. C never seeks an office ;
the office seeks him. D can be put in the same class as C ;
a petition of a hundred, a thousand, names can be got at a
very small figure and with very little labor. But the " practical politician " seldom or never deceives the public by these
ingenious but shallow devices. It is easy to distinguish the
true from the false, the diamond from the paste.

Again, our politician places much dependence upon money.
He assumes a cold, practical air. A great idea is mentioned
to him, a plan which will really call a sluggish people to arms ;
but he says coldly and cynically, " Yes, but where 's the
money ? " And many men who have started in politics with
an idea, with a sentiment, with an inspiration, being beaten

down, have become doubly and more the advocates of Mammon. The new doctrine is so practical, they become really ashamed of their ideals; they go to the farthest extreme of the meanest and basest practical politics, and actually seek to hide the early and noble ideals which their young manhood cherished.

The practical politician firmly believes that the sole measure of a man's fitness for an office is the ability to get it. Competency, education, experience, honesty, are merely "platform" words, — strong, but of no real significance. In fact, the less ability the candidate has for a place the more ability he displays in securing it. "He has a right to aspire, — it is an honorable ambition, — and he is n't ashamed to say what he wants and to set his friends to work." This is the language of the so-called practical politician. He admires nothing so much as the brutal frankness of a selfish, sordid creature, whose stupidity makes him proud of his infamy.

Of course there is a very different stripe of "practical politicians." There are men of conscience, intelligence, and patriotic purpose. They have made their influence felt in many ways, — chiefly in local or municipal politics, where, in fact, the widest field is open to their efforts. These are men who believe that the grandest "recognition" their devoted labors can receive is in the strengthening and purifying of the body politic, in honest and economic modes of administration; in extending public benefits to the whole public, and diffusing the blessings of good government, as the Almighty diffuses the sunshine, over each and all alike.

Politics so often deal with ignoble things, — things of the earth, "earthy;" things of the pocket, of the sewer, of the gutter; with disagreeable people, disagreeable places. Patient labor, self-denial, sacrifice are needed. Comfort, pleasure, luxuries, necessities must be given up to insure success. Rebuffs, insults, calumny, ridicule, defeat, and disaster must be met and overcome. This is the environment, these the factors, which confront the earnest patriotic man.

The prospect herein outlined is not encouraging. No wonder that young men of refinement, of ambition, of honesty, of aspiration, glowing with patriotic purpose, eager to serve their fellowmen, shrink from the herculean task confronting them here. But this is the place, and here are the materials, where and with which great souls have labored and have been victorious. Liberty, justice, equality, education, and progress in every direction have been set free from just such elements as these, or worse than these, and have emerged shapes of glory and strength to gladden and comfort mankind. And even now the strong soul can find his loveliest Ideal imprisoned somewhere in this sordid Actual. Thomas Carlyle, in his grim eloquent way, says, in " Sartor Resartus," Book II., Chapter IX. : —

" Yes, here in this poor, miserable, hampered, despicable Actual, wherein thou even now standest, here or nowhere is thy Ideal. Work it out therefrom, and, working, believe, live, be free. Fool! the Ideal is in thyself, the impediment, too, is in thyself; thy Condition is but the stuff thou art to shape that same Ideal out of. What matters whether such stuff be of this sort or that, so the Form thou give it be heroic, be poetic? O thou that pinest in the imprisonment of the Actual, and criest bitterly to the Gods for a Kingdom wherein to rule and create, know this of a truth: the thing thou seekest is already with thee, here or nowhere, couldst thou only see ! "

Truer or more inspiring words than these were never written. Out of the mud, the uncleanness, the dishonors, of the Actual and the practical, it is permitted to the true man, to the patriot and hero of this practical age, to mould the grandest Ideals into realities, living, breathing, working for good. But the heroic, patriotic spirit is indispensable. No *dilettante* devotion, no narrow selfish ambition, will have the power to effect these magic results.

Now, while it is necessary to be right — in order to command success — *it is not enough to be right.* Having determined on what is right, in a given case, you cannot send out your purpose like a stray child to be abused, deceived, and beaten; a strong, well-equipped escort must accompany and guard that purpose, able to deal with friends and foes, to protect in every way the interests of their charge. How to launch a noble purpose at the right time, to provision it, to equip it, so that it may meet the storms which are sure to come, is the true study of the true and honest practical politician. He must be wise as the serpent, and harmless as the dove *to the State.*

Tact in an honest cause is almost as valuable as virtue. Knowledge of men is as necessary to a good man as to a bad one. Too often the reformer imitates the example of Mr. Tupman, who, when Mr. Pickwick broke through the ice, rushed across the fields shouting " Fire," leaving Mr. Pickwick to his fate.

Can a politician be pure and practical ? Yes. Must he be visionary in order to be virtuous ? Emphatically, no. Truth and justice need less management than falsehood and injustice. But intelligent, well-disciplined forces are necessary even to the cause of truth and justice. Prospero must ever be on the alert even if Caliban is his only enemy.

Why does an honest, patriotic man take office? Office seldom enriches the honest patriotic man. A list of the leading American public men to-day will establish this fact. Most of them are lucky if they have a competency, or indeed escape bankruptcy. One of the moving causes, then, must be " that last infirmity of noble minds," ambition, the love of fame, of popular applause, — in short, of glory. But is there not blended with this motive, in many cases, a passionate love of country, an intense longing innate in great souls

> " To scatter blessings o'er a smiling land,
> And read their history in a nation's eyes" ?

The sense of power exercised by a great man for the welfare of his country, of his fellow-men, must make him feel as nearly divine as anything can.

The ordinary practical office-holder is not borne up by any of these visions of glory. The reward of faithful and patient service is the respect and affection of those who come in contact with him, and he consoles himself by reflecting that even if he has only been charged to drive a nail into the timbers or to calk the seams of the ship of state, these simple services are telling their honest story every day that the majestic fabric floats.

Men must make a living, too, and men of wonderful ability can be found in just such subordinate stations who can accomplish great results when directed by others, but who are weak and inefficient when acting for themselves.

The conclusion of the whole matter, then, is that high and noble aims must be supplemented by careful, patient, intelligent labor, — by unselfish courage and fidelity. And the people themselves must regard public service more justly, if not more charitably, than they seem to do at present. The outlook is encouraging; a better, nobler, more patriotic spirit is abroad in the country; men are finding that they must not censure, but act, — that they themselves are largely responsible for what they condemn, — and upon the whole, I believe, we are approaching a new and better era of "practical politics."

FREDERIC T. GREENHALGE.

INDEX.

www.ingramcontent.com/pod-product-compliance
Lightning Source LLC
Chambersburg PA
CBHW031047110726
47900CB00003B/834

* 9 7 8 3 3 3 7 3 9 7 3 7 1 *